SPIDER-MAN
SPIDER-VERSE
SPIDER-HAM

SPIDER-MAN
SPIDER-VERSE
SPIDER-HAM

MARVEL TAILS STARRING PETER PORKER, THE SPECTACULAR SPIDER-HAM #1

WRITER: **TOM DeFALCO**
PENCILER: **MARK ARMSTRONG**
INKER: **JOE ALBELO**
COLORIST: **STEVE MELLOR**
COVER ART: **ROBBI RODRIGUEZ**
LETTERERS: **RICK PARKER & JACK MORELLI**
EDITOR: **LARRY HAMA**

MARVEL TALES #209-210

WRITER: **STEVE MELLOR**
ARTIST: **JOE ALBELO**
COLORIST: **ANDY YANCHUS**
LETTERER: **RICK PARKER**
EDITOR: **JIM SALICRUP**

MARVEL TALES #230 & #233

WRITER: **DANNY FINGEROTH**
PENCILER: **ALAN KUPPERBERG**
INKER: **JOE ALBELO**
COLORISTS: **BOB SHAREN** (#230) &
RENÉE WITTERSTAETER (#233)
LETTERER: **RICK PARKER**
EDITOR: **JIM SALICRIP**

SPIDER-MAN: ENTER THE SPIDER-VERSE #1

WRITER: **RALPH MACCHIO**
ARTIST: **FLAVIANO**
COLORIST: **ERICK ARCINIEGA**
LETTERER: **VC's TRAVIS LANHAM**
COVER ART: **EDUARD PETROVICH**
EDITOR: **MARK BASSO**
EXECUTIVE EDITOR: **NICK LOWE**

SPIDER-MAN ANNUAL #1

"BOARED AGAIN!"
WRITER: **JASON LATOUR**
ARTIST: **DAVID LAFUENTE**
COLORIST: **RICO RENZI**

"A SECRET ROAR RAGES?"
WRITERS: **PHIL LORD, CHRISTOPHER MILLER** & **JASON LATOUR**
ARTIST/COLORIST: **JASON LATOUR**

LETTERER: **VC's JOE CARAMAGNA**
COVER ART: **DAVID LAFUENTE & RICO RENZI**
EDITORS: **DANNY KHAZEM** & **DEVIN LEWIS**
EXECUTIVE EDITOR: **NICK LOWE**

SPIDER-HAM #1

WRITER: **ZEB WELLS**
ARTIST: **WILL ROBSON**
COLORIST: **ERICK ARCINIEGA**
LETTERER: **VC's JOE CARAMAGNA**
COVER ART: **WENDELL DALIT**
PANELS FROM *PETER PORKER, THE SPECTACULAR SPIDER-HAM #15*:
STEVE MELLOR, JOE ALBELO, PIERRE FOURNIER, JANICE CHIANG & **JULIANNA FERRITER**
ASSISTANT EDITOR: **DANNY KHAZEM**
EDITOR: **DEVIN LEWIS**
EXECUTIVE EDITOR: **NICK LOWE**

SPIDER-MAN CREATED BY STAN LEE & STEVE DITKO

COLLECTION EDITOR: **JENNIFER GRÜNWALD** ASSISTANT MANAGING EDITOR: **MAIA LOY**
ASSISTANT MANAGING EDITOR: **LISA MONTALBANO** EDITOR, SPECIAL PROJECTS: **MARK D. BEAZLEY**
EDITOR, SPECIAL PROJECTS: **MARK D. BEAZLEY** VP PRODUCTION & SPECIAL PROJECTS: **JEFF YOUNGQUIST**
RESEARCH: **JESS HAROLD** & **JEPH YORK** PRODUCTION: **COLORTEK, DIGIKORE, JOE FRONTIRRE** & **DAN KIRCHHOFFER**
BOOK DESIGNER: **JAY BOWEN** SVP PRINT, SALES & MARKETING: **DAVID GABRIEL** EDITOR IN CHIEF: **C.B. CEBULSKI**

SPIDER-MAN: SPIDER-VERSE — SPIDER-HAM. Contains material originally published in magazine form as SPIDER-MAN: ENTER THE SPIDER-VERSE (2018) #1; SPIDER-MAN ANNUAL (2019) #1; SPIDER-HAM (2019) #1; MARVEL TAILS STARRING PETER PORKER, THE SPECTACULAR SPIDER-HAM (1983) #1; and MARVEL TALES (1964) #209-210, #230, #233. First printing 2020. ISBN 978-1-302-92521-5. Published by MARVEL WORLDWIDE, INC., a subsidiary of MARVEL ENTERTAINMENT, LLC. OFFICE OF PUBLICATION: 1290 Avenue of the Americas, New York, NY 10104. © 2020 MARVEL No similarity between any of the names, characters, persons, and/or institutions in this magazine with those of any living or dead person or institution is intended, and any such similarity which may exist is purely coincidental. **Printed in Canada.** KEVIN FEIGE, Chief Creative Officer; DAN BUCKLEY, President, Marvel Entertainment; JOHN NEE, Publisher; JOE QUESADA, EVP & Creative Director; TOM BREVOORT, SVP of Publishing; DAVID BOGART, Associate Publisher & SVP of Talent Affairs; Publishing & Partnership; DAVID GABRIEL, VP of Print & Digital Publishing; JEFF YOUNGQUIST, VP of Production & Special Projects; DAN CARR, Executive Director of Publishing Technology; ALEX MORALES, Director of Publishing Operations; DAN EDINGTON, Managing Editor; SUSAN CRESPI, Production Manager; STAN LEE, Chairman Emeritus. For information regarding advertising in Marvel Comics or on Marvel.com, please contact Vit DeBellis, Custom Solutions & Integrated Advertising Manager, at vdebellis@marvel.com. For Marvel subscription inquiries, please call 888-511-5480. **Manufactured between 6/26/2020 and 8/3/2020 by SOLISCO PRINTERS, SCOTT, QC, CANADA.**

10 9 8 7 6 5 4 3 2 1

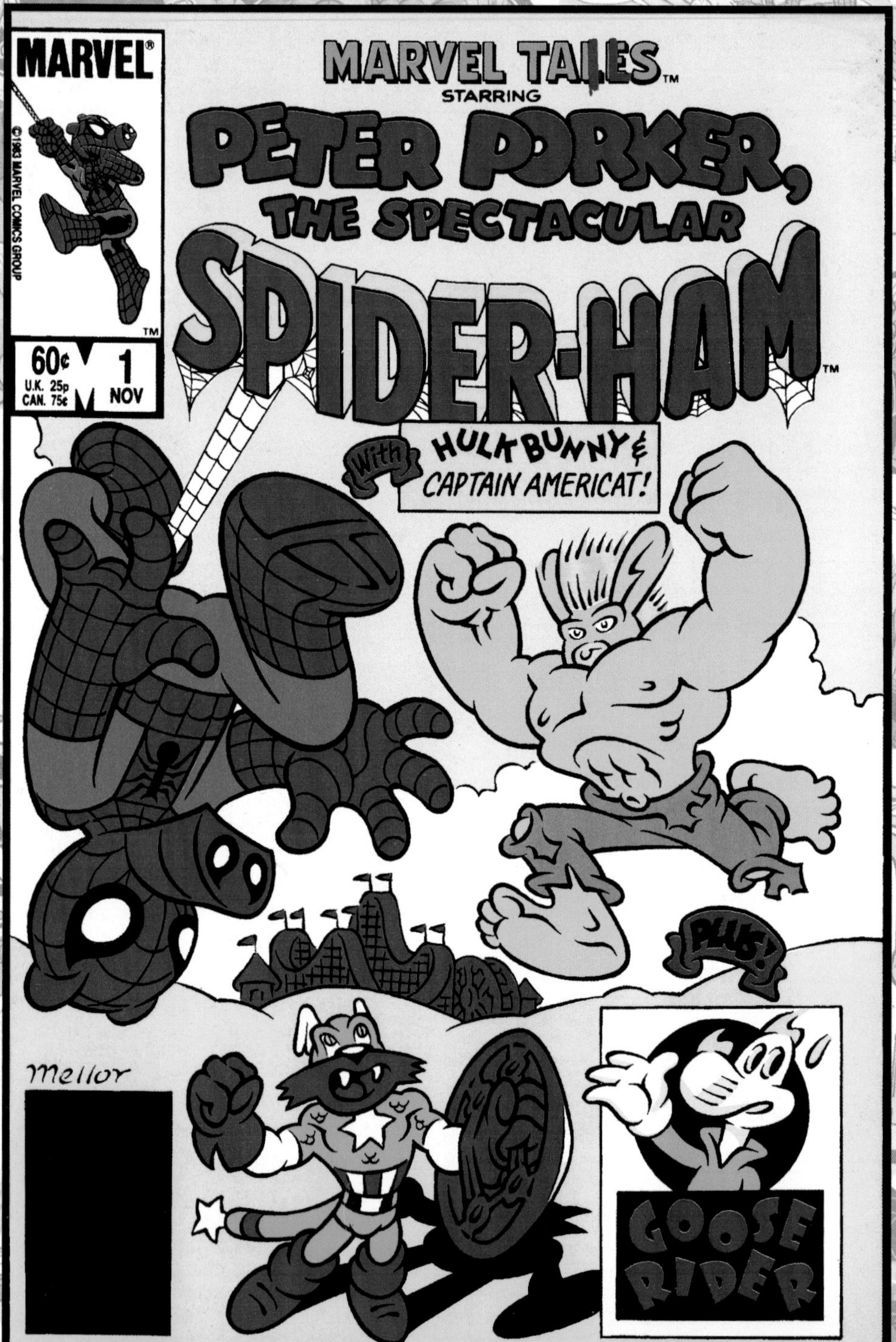
MARVEL®
©1983 MARVEL COMICS GROUP
MARVEL TALES™
STARRING
PETER PORKER,
THE SPECTACULAR
SPIDER-HAM™
60¢ U.K. 25p CAN. 75¢
1 NOV
With HULK BUNNY & CAPTAIN AMERICAT!
PLUS!
GOOSE RIDER
Mellor

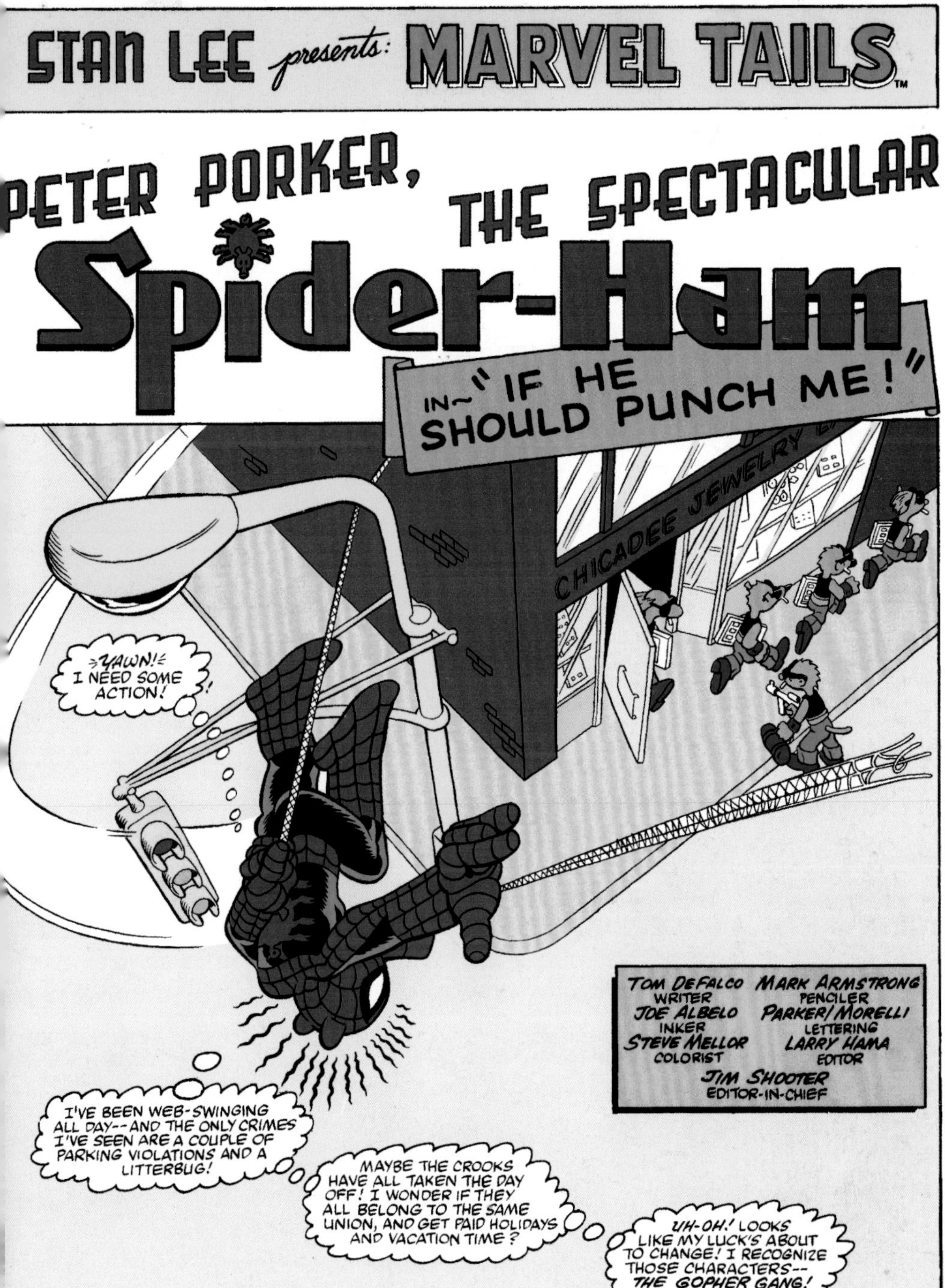
STAN LEE presents: MARVEL TAILS™
PETER PORKER, THE SPECTACULAR SPIDER-HAM
IN~ "IF HE SHOULD PUNCH ME!"
CHICADEE JEWELRY
YAWN! I NEED SOME ACTION!
I'VE BEEN WEB-SWINGING ALL DAY--AND THE ONLY CRIMES I'VE SEEN ARE A COUPLE OF PARKING VIOLATIONS AND A LITTERBUG!
MAYBE THE CROOKS HAVE ALL TAKEN THE DAY OFF! I WONDER IF THEY ALL BELONG TO THE SAME UNION, AND GET PAID HOLIDAYS AND VACATION TIME?
UH-OH! LOOKS LIKE MY LUCK'S ABOUT TO CHANGE! I RECOGNIZE THOSE CHARACTERS-- THE GOPHER GANG!
TOM DEFALCO WRITER
MARK ARMSTRONG PENCILER
JOE ALBELO INKER
PARKER/MORELLI LETTERING
STEVE MELLOR COLORIST
LARRY HAMA EDITOR
JIM SHOOTER EDITOR-IN-CHIEF

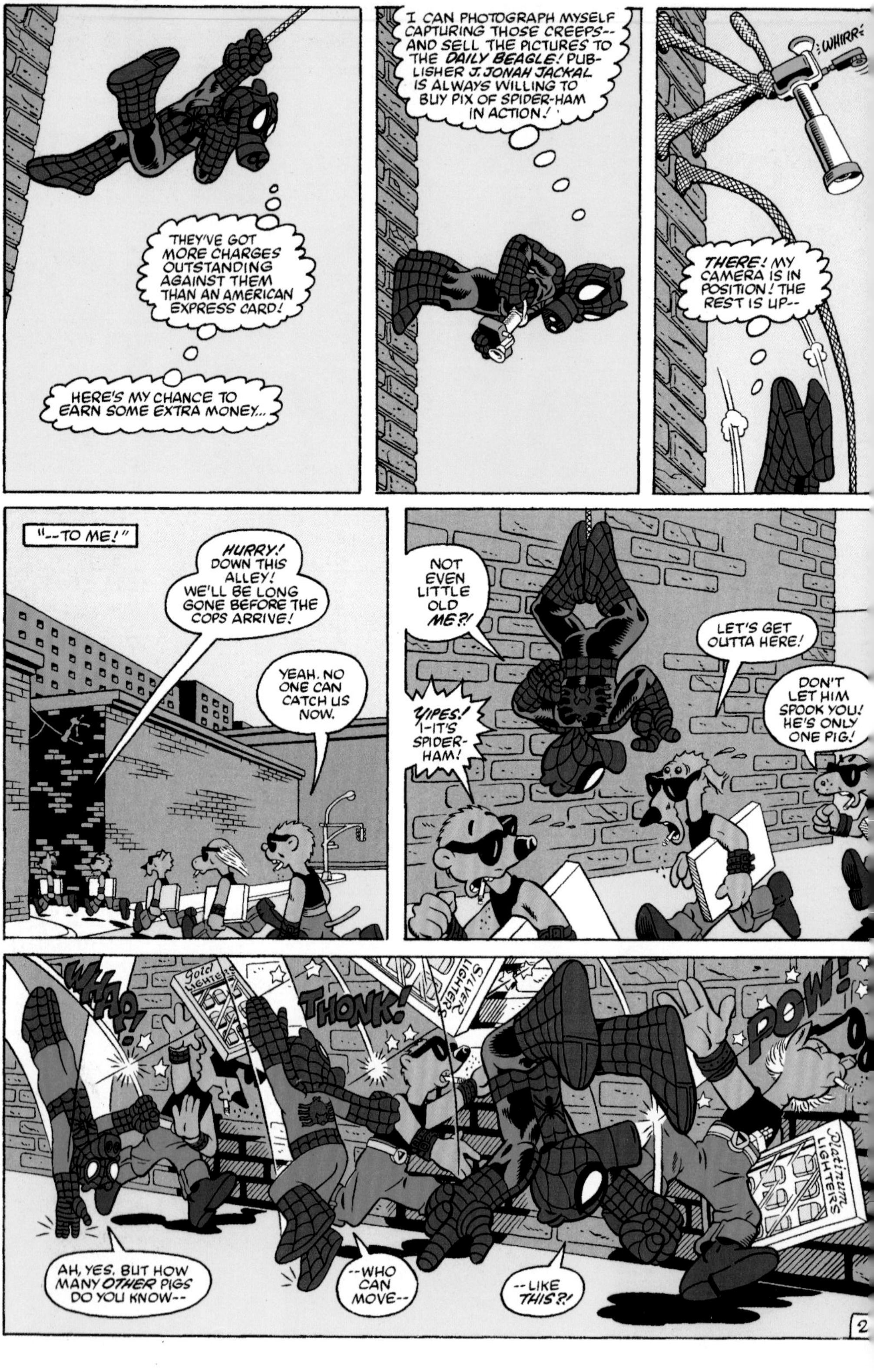

THEY'VE GOT MORE CHARGES OUTSTANDING AGAINST THEM THAN AN AMERICAN EXPRESS CARD!
HERE'S MY CHANCE TO EARN SOME EXTRA MONEY...
I CAN PHOTOGRAPH MYSELF CAPTURING THOSE CREEPS-- AND SELL THE PICTURES TO THE DAILY BEAGLE! PUBLISHER J. JONAH JACKAL IS ALWAYS WILLING TO BUY PIX OF SPIDER-HAM IN ACTION!
WHIRR
THERE! MY CAMERA IS IN POSITION! THE REST IS UP--
"--TO ME!"
HURRY! DOWN THIS ALLEY! WE'LL BE LONG GONE BEFORE THE COPS ARRIVE!
YEAH. NO ONE CAN CATCH US NOW.
NOT EVEN LITTLE OLD ME?!
YIPES! I-IT'S SPIDER-HAM!
LET'S GET OUTTA HERE!
DON'T LET HIM SPOOK YOU! HE'S ONLY ONE PIG!
WHAP!
THONK!
POW!
Gold LIGHTERS
SILVER LIGHTERS
Platinum LIGHTERS
AH, YES. BUT HOW MANY OTHER PIGS DO YOU KNOW--
--WHO CAN MOVE--
--LIKE THIS?!

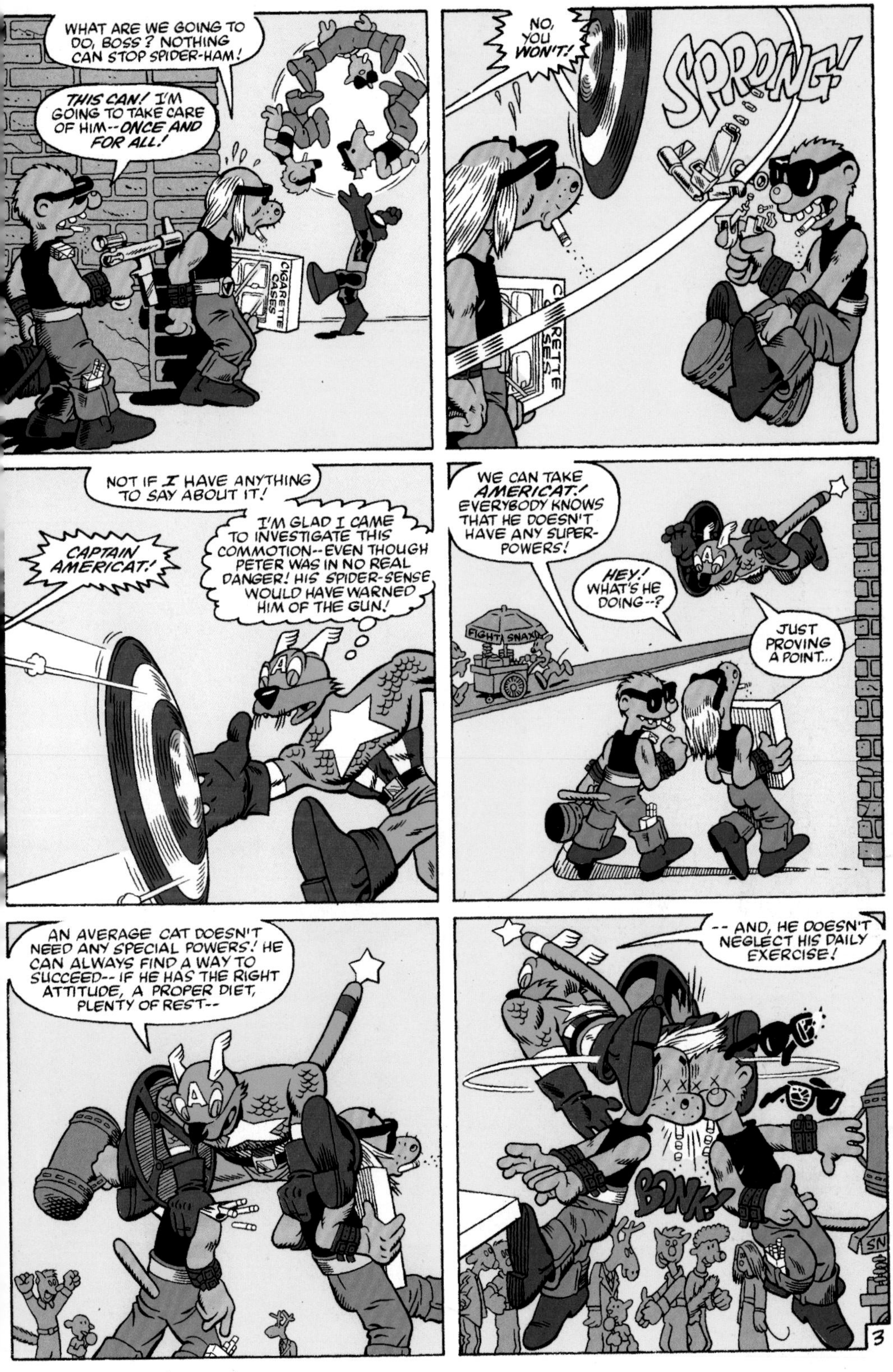
WHAT ARE WE GOING TO DO, BOSS? NOTHING CAN STOP SPIDER-HAM!
THIS CAN! I'M GOING TO TAKE CARE OF HIM--ONCE AND FOR ALL!
CIGARETTE CASES
NO, YOU WON'T!
SPROING!
NOT IF I HAVE ANYTHING TO SAY ABOUT IT!
CAPTAIN AMERICAT!
I'M GLAD I CAME TO INVESTIGATE THIS COMMOTION--EVEN THOUGH PETER WAS IN NO REAL DANGER! HIS SPIDER-SENSE WOULD HAVE WARNED HIM OF THE GUN!
WE CAN TAKE AMERICAT! EVERYBODY KNOWS THAT HE DOESN'T HAVE ANY SUPER-POWERS!
HEY! WHAT'S HE DOING--?
JUST PROVING A POINT...
FIGHT SNAXX
AN AVERAGE CAT DOESN'T NEED ANY SPECIAL POWERS! HE CAN ALWAYS FIND A WAY TO SUCCEED-- IF HE HAS THE RIGHT ATTITUDE, A PROPER DIET, PLENTY OF REST--
-- AND, HE DOESN'T NEGLECT HIS DAILY EXERCISE!
BONK!

HERE'S TWO MORE FOR YOU, SPIDER-HAM!

THE MORE--THE MERRIER! THANKS FOR THE ASSIST, CAP!

THWIP

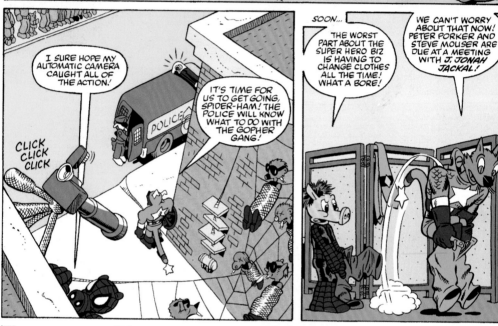

I SURE HOPE MY AUTOMATIC CAMERA CAUGHT ALL OF THE ACTION!

CLICK CLICK CLICK

IT'S TIME FOR US TO GET GOING, SPIDER-HAM! THE POLICE WILL KNOW WHAT TO DO WITH THE GOPHER GANG!

POLICE

SOON...

THE WORST PART ABOUT THE SUPER HERO BIZ IS HAVING TO CHANGE CLOTHES ALL THE TIME! WHAT A BORE!

WE CAN'T WORRY ABOUT THAT NOW! PETER PORKER AND STEVE MOUSER ARE DUE AT A MEETING WITH *J. JONAH JACKAL!*

GOSH, STEVE, IT MUST BE AWFULLY HARD TO CONCEAL YOUR SHIELD-- WHILE YOU'RE IN CIVILIAN IDENTITY.

NOT AT ALL, PETER! I JUST STRAP IT ON BENEATH MY SUIT JACKET.

MY TAILOR IS *VERY* GOOD!

4

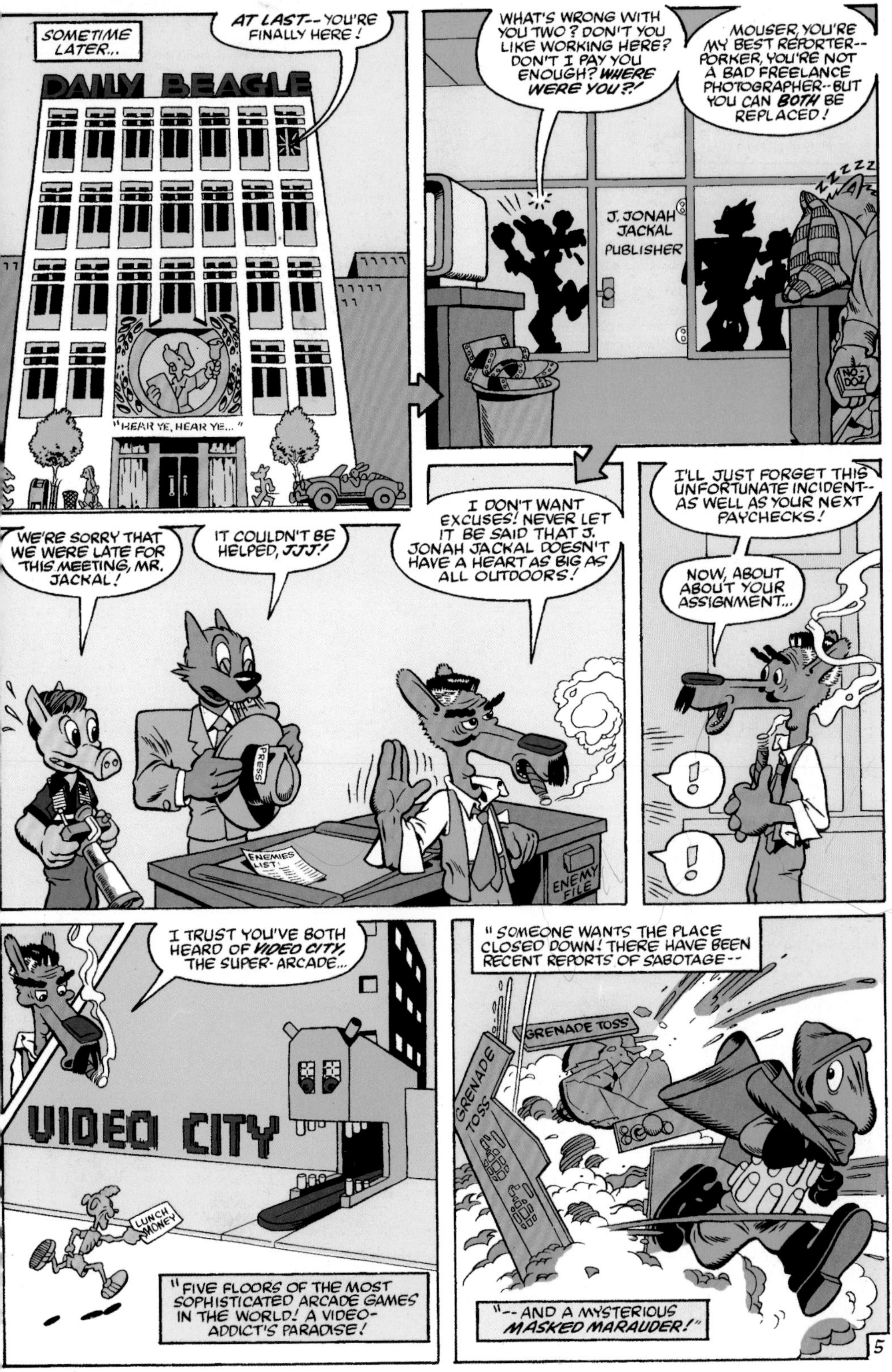
SOMETIME LATER...
AT LAST--YOU'RE FINALLY HERE!
DAILY BEAGLE
"HEAR YE, HEAR YE..."
WHAT'S WRONG WITH YOU TWO? DON'T YOU LIKE WORKING HERE? DON'T I PAY YOU ENOUGH? WHERE WERE YOU?!
MOUSER, YOU'RE MY BEST REPORTER-- PORKER, YOU'RE NOT A BAD FREELANCE PHOTOGRAPHER--BUT YOU CAN BOTH BE REPLACED!
J. JONAH JACKAL PUBLISHER
ZZZZZ
NO-DOZ
WE'RE SORRY THAT WE WERE LATE FOR THIS MEETING, MR. JACKAL!
IT COULDN'T BE HELPED, JJJ!
I DON'T WANT EXCUSES! NEVER LET IT BE SAID THAT J. JONAH JACKAL DOESN'T HAVE A HEART AS BIG AS ALL OUTDOORS!
PRESS
ENEMIES LIST!
ENEMY FILE
I'LL JUST FORGET THIS UNFORTUNATE INCIDENT-- AS WELL AS YOUR NEXT PAYCHECKS!
NOW, ABOUT ABOUT YOUR ASSIGNMENT...
!
!
I TRUST YOU'VE BOTH HEARD OF VIDEO CITY, THE SUPER-ARCADE...
VIDEO CITY
LUNCH MONEY
"FIVE FLOORS OF THE MOST SOPHISTICATED ARCADE GAMES IN THE WORLD! A VIDEO-ADDICT'S PARADISE!
"SOMEONE WANTS THE PLACE CLOSED DOWN! THERE HAVE BEEN RECENT REPORTS OF SABOTAGE--
GRENADE TOSS
GRENADE TOSS
"--AND A MYSTERIOUS MASKED MARAUDER!"

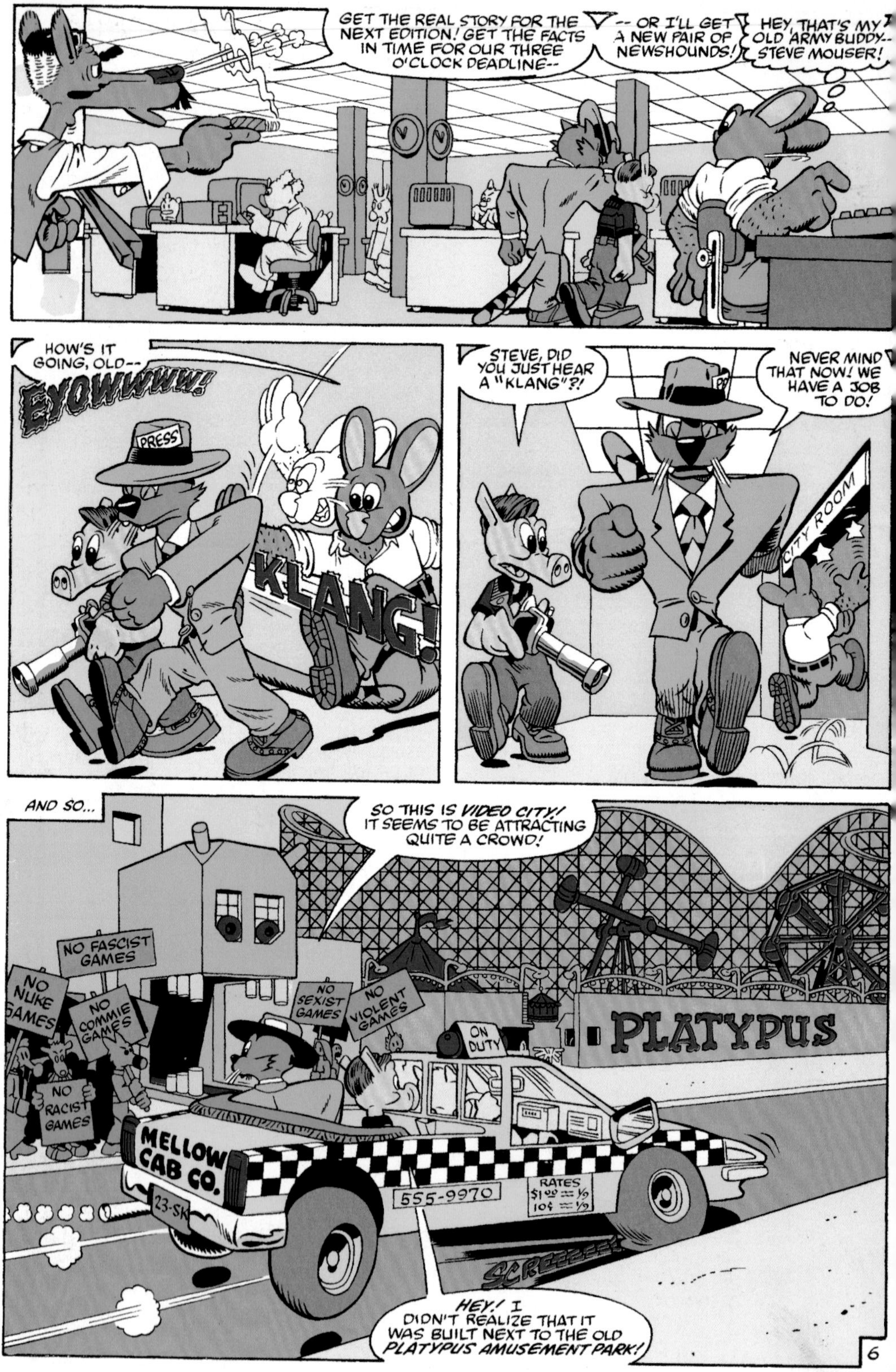
GET THE REAL STORY FOR THE NEXT EDITION! GET THE FACTS IN TIME FOR OUR THREE O'CLOCK DEADLINE--
-- OR I'LL GET A NEW PAIR OF NEWSHOUNDS!
HEY, THAT'S MY OLD ARMY BUDDY-- STEVE MOUSER!
HOW'S IT GOING, OLD--
EYOWWWW!
PRESS
KLANG!
STEVE, DID YOU JUST HEAR A "KLANG"?!
NEVER MIND THAT NOW! WE HAVE A JOB TO DO!
CITY ROOM
AND SO...
SO THIS IS *VIDEO CITY!* IT SEEMS TO BE ATTRACTING QUITE A CROWD!
NO FASCIST GAMES
NO NUKE GAMES
NO COMMIE GAMES
NO RACIST GAMES
NO SEXIST GAMES
NO VIOLENT GAMES
ON DUTY
PLATYPUS
MELLOW CAB CO.
23-SK
555-9970
RATES $1.00 = 1/9 10¢ = 1/9
SCREEEEE
HEY! I DIDN'T REALIZE THAT IT WAS BUILT NEXT TO THE OLD *PLATYPUS AMUSEMENT PARK!*

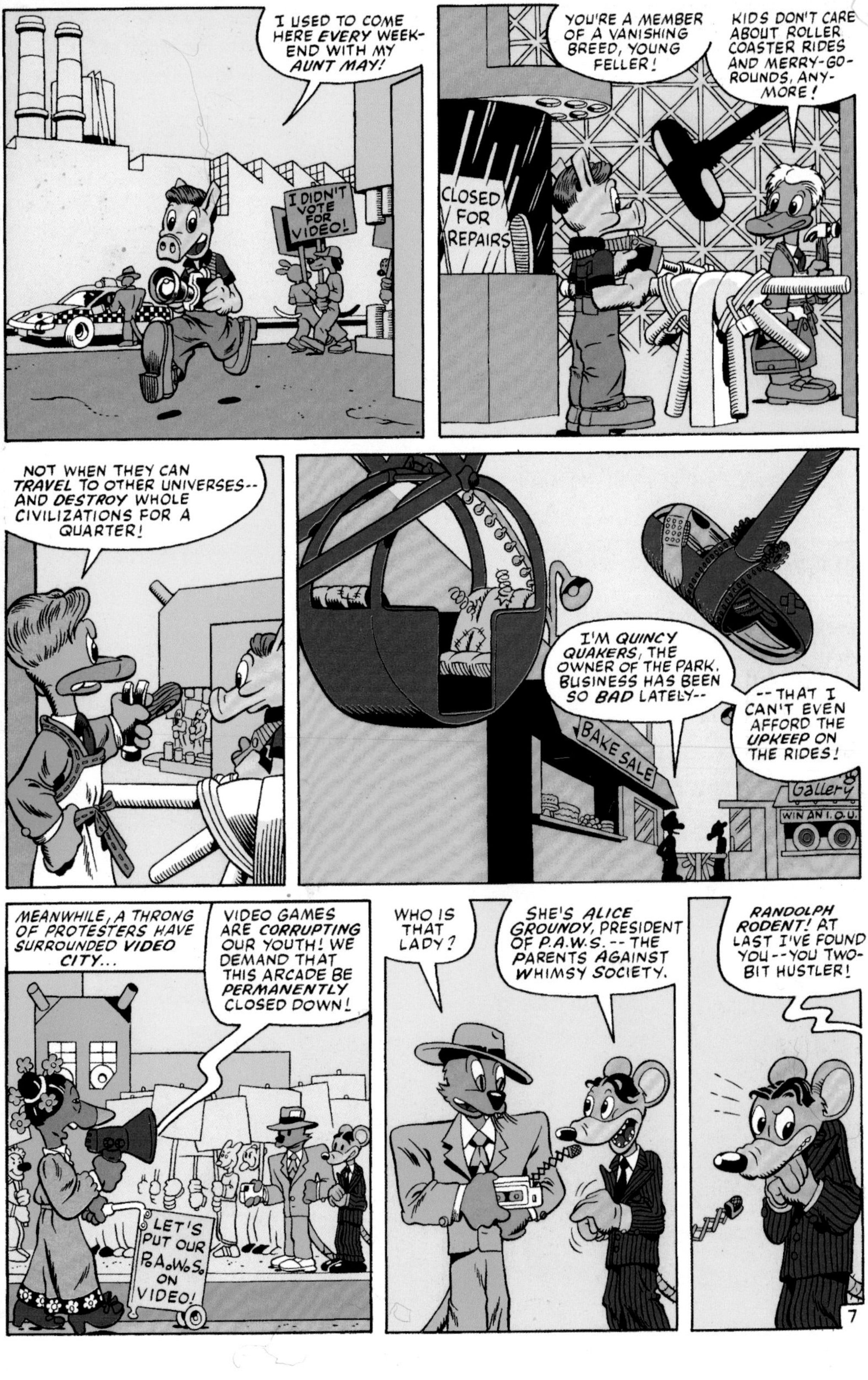
I USED TO COME HERE EVERY WEEK-END WITH MY AUNT MAY!
I DIDN'T VOTE FOR VIDEO!
YOU'RE A MEMBER OF A VANISHING BREED, YOUNG FELLER!
KIDS DON'T CARE ABOUT ROLLER COASTER RIDES AND MERRY-GO-ROUNDS, ANY-MORE!
CLOSED FOR REPAIRS
NOT WHEN THEY CAN TRAVEL TO OTHER UNIVERSES-- AND DESTROY WHOLE CIVILIZATIONS FOR A QUARTER!
I'M QUINCY QUAKERS, THE OWNER OF THE PARK. BUSINESS HAS BEEN SO BAD LATELY--
--THAT I CAN'T EVEN AFFORD THE UPKEEP ON THE RIDES!
BAKE SALE
Gallery
WIN AN I.O.U.
MEANWHILE, A THRONG OF PROTESTERS HAVE SURROUNDED VIDEO CITY...
VIDEO GAMES ARE CORRUPTING OUR YOUTH! WE DEMAND THAT THIS ARCADE BE PERMANENTLY CLOSED DOWN!
LET'S PUT OUR P.A.W.S. ON VIDEO!
WHO IS THAT LADY?
SHE'S ALICE GROUNDY, PRESIDENT OF P.A.W.S.--THE PARENTS AGAINST WHIMSY SOCIETY.
RANDOLPH RODENT! AT LAST I'VE FOUND YOU--YOU TWO-BIT HUSTLER!

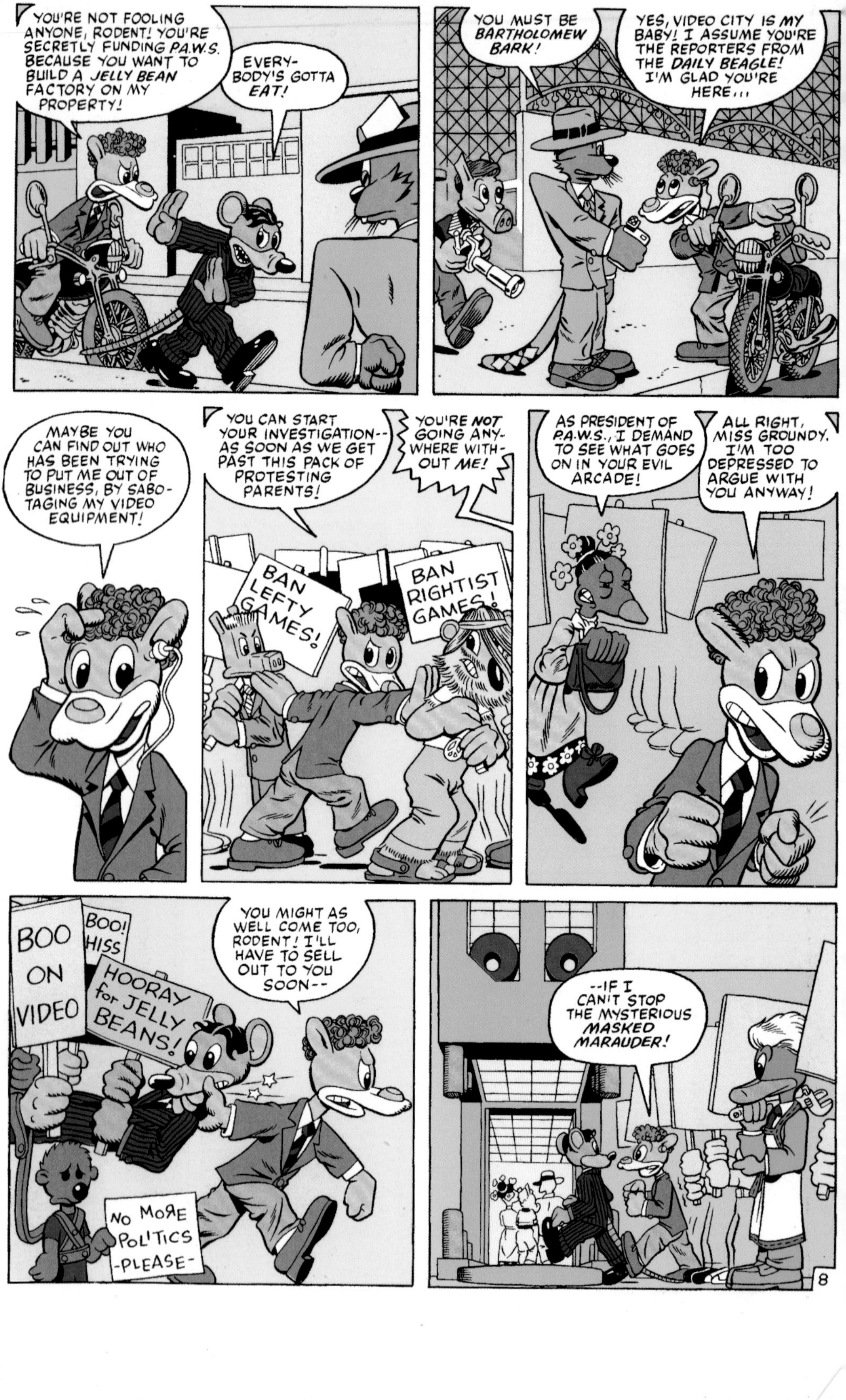

YOU'RE NOT FOOLING ANYONE, RODENT! YOU'RE SECRETLY FUNDING P.A.W.S. BECAUSE YOU WANT TO BUILD A JELLY BEAN FACTORY ON MY PROPERTY!
EVERY-BODY'S GOTTA EAT!
YOU MUST BE BARTHOLOMEW BARK!
YES, VIDEO CITY IS MY BABY! I ASSUME YOU'RE THE REPORTERS FROM THE DAILY BEAGLE! I'M GLAD YOU'RE HERE...
MAYBE YOU CAN FIND OUT WHO HAS BEEN TRYING TO PUT ME OUT OF BUSINESS, BY SABO-TAGING MY VIDEO EQUIPMENT!
YOU CAN START YOUR INVESTIGATION-- AS SOON AS WE GET PAST THIS PACK OF PROTESTING PARENTS!
YOU'RE NOT GOING ANY-WHERE WITH-OUT ME!
BAN LEFTY GAMES!
BAN RIGHTIST GAMES!
AS PRESIDENT OF P.A.W.S., I DEMAND TO SEE WHAT GOES ON IN YOUR EVIL ARCADE!
ALL RIGHT, MISS GROUNDY. I'M TOO DEPRESSED TO ARGUE WITH YOU ANYWAY!
BOO ON VIDEO
BOO! HISS
HOORAY for JELLY BEANS!
YOU MIGHT AS WELL COME TOO, RODENT! I'LL HAVE TO SELL OUT TO YOU SOON--
NO MORE POLITICS -PLEASE-
--IF I CAN'T STOP THE MYSTERIOUS MASKED MARAUDER!

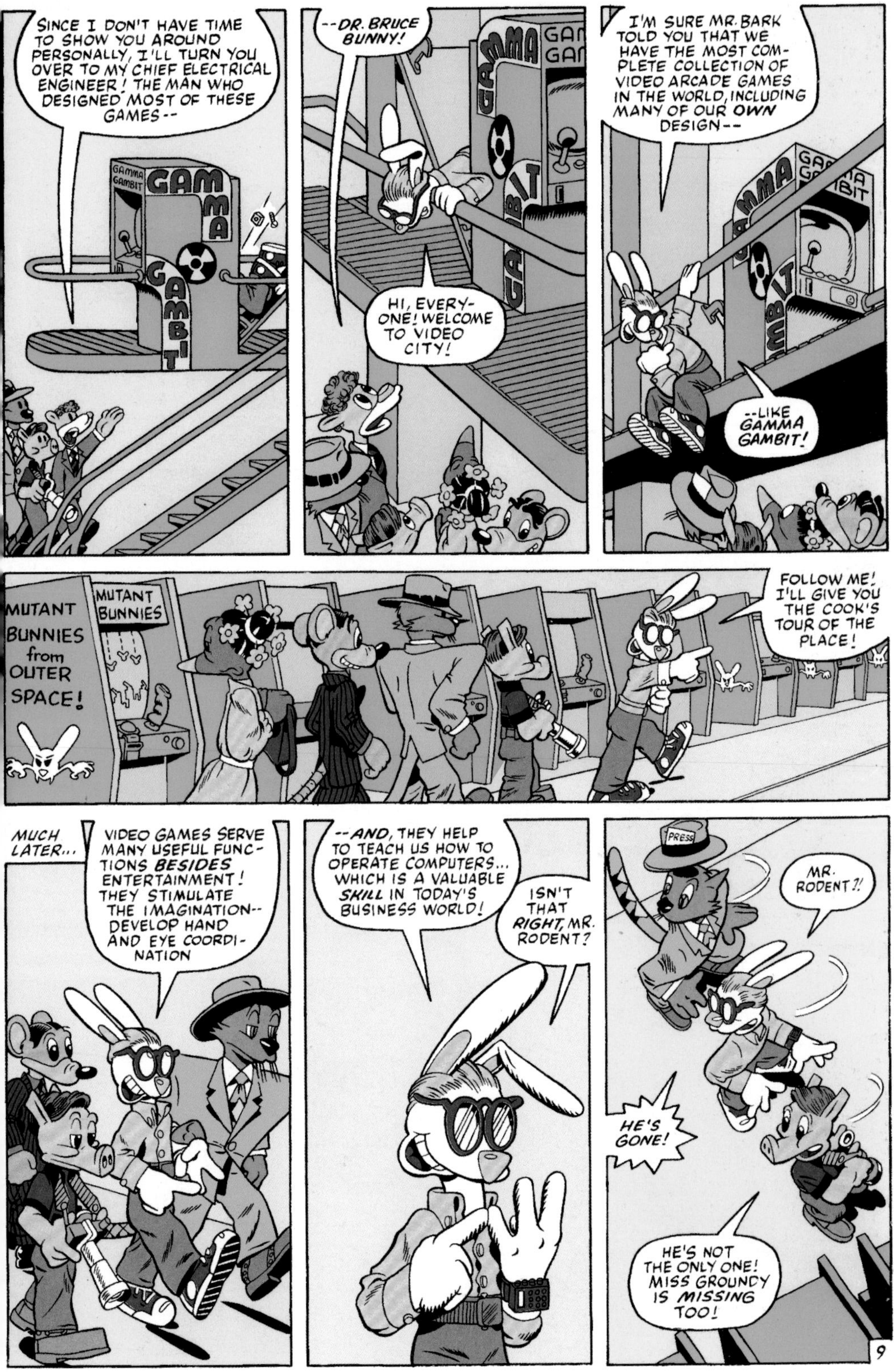
SINCE I DON'T HAVE TIME TO SHOW YOU AROUND PERSONALLY, I'LL TURN YOU OVER TO MY CHIEF ELECTRICAL ENGINEER! THE MAN WHO DESIGNED MOST OF THESE GAMES--
GAMMA GAMBIT
--DR. BRUCE BUNNY!
HI, EVERY-ONE! WELCOME TO VIDEO CITY!
I'M SURE MR. BARK TOLD YOU THAT WE HAVE THE MOST COM-PLETE COLLECTION OF VIDEO ARCADE GAMES IN THE WORLD, INCLUDING MANY OF OUR OWN DESIGN--
--LIKE GAMMA GAMBIT!
MUTANT BUNNIES from OUTER SPACE!
MUTANT BUNNIES
FOLLOW ME! I'LL GIVE YOU THE COOK'S TOUR OF THE PLACE!
MUCH LATER...
VIDEO GAMES SERVE MANY USEFUL FUNC-TIONS BESIDES ENTERTAINMENT! THEY STIMULATE THE IMAGINATION-- DEVELOP HAND AND EYE COORDI-NATION
--AND, THEY HELP TO TEACH US HOW TO OPERATE COMPUTERS... WHICH IS A VALUABLE SKILL IN TODAY'S BUSINESS WORLD!
ISN'T THAT RIGHT, MR. RODENT?
PRESS
MR. RODENT?!
HE'S GONE!
HE'S NOT THE ONLY ONE! MISS GROUNDY IS MISSING TOO!

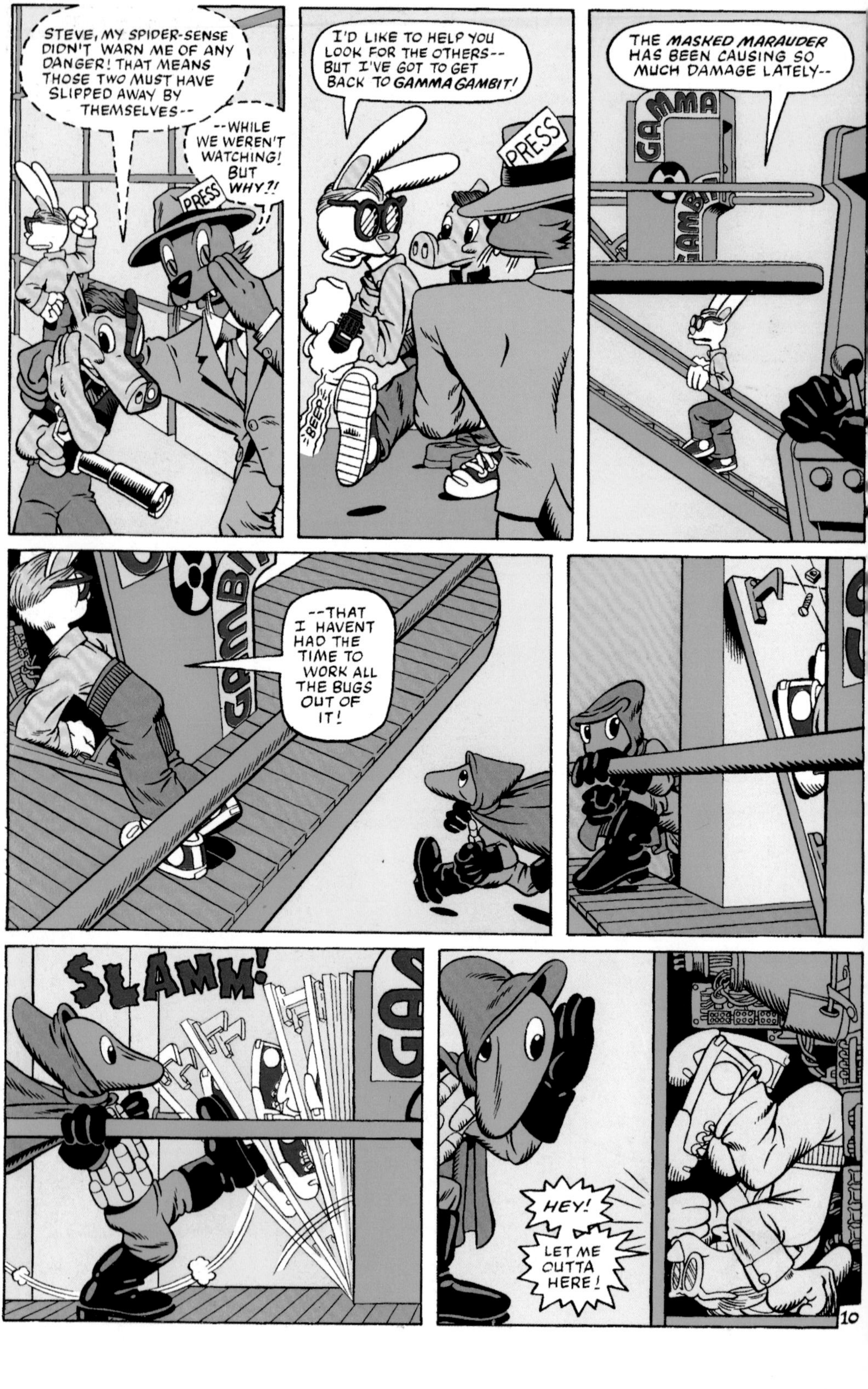
STEVE, MY SPIDER-SENSE DIDN'T WARN ME OF ANY DANGER! THAT MEANS THOSE TWO MUST HAVE SLIPPED AWAY BY THEMSELVES--
--WHILE WE WEREN'T WATCHING! BUT WHY?!
PRESS
I'D LIKE TO HELP YOU LOOK FOR THE OTHERS-- BUT I'VE GOT TO GET BACK TO GAMMA GAMBIT!
PRESS
BEEP
THE MASKED MARAUDER HAS BEEN CAUSING SO MUCH DAMAGE LATELY--
GAMMA GAMBIT
--THAT I HAVENT HAD THE TIME TO WORK ALL THE BUGS OUT OF IT!
SLAMM!
HEY!
LET ME OUTTA HERE!

GOOOBYE, DR. BUNNY!

GAMMA GAMBIT

GAMMA GAMBIT

GLOVED FINGERS ACTIVATE THE GAMMA GAMBIT, FIRING IT TO FULL POWER...

TRAPPED WITHIN THE UNYIELDING MACHINE, DR. BRUCE BUNNY IS BOMBARDED WITH THE FULL FORCE OF MYSTERIOUS VIDEO RAYS...

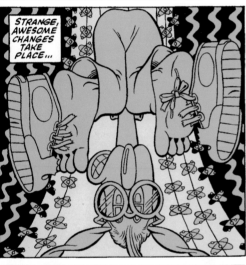

STRANGE, AWESOME CHANGES TAKE PLACE...

CHANGES IN THE VERY ATOMIC STRUCTURE OF HIS BODY....

AND THEN... KA-BOOM!

BRUCE BUNNY IS NO MORE!

GAMMA GAMBIT

IN HIS PLACE STANDS THE MOST DANGEROUS CREATURE OF ALL--

--THE INCREDIBLE HULK-BUNNY!

11

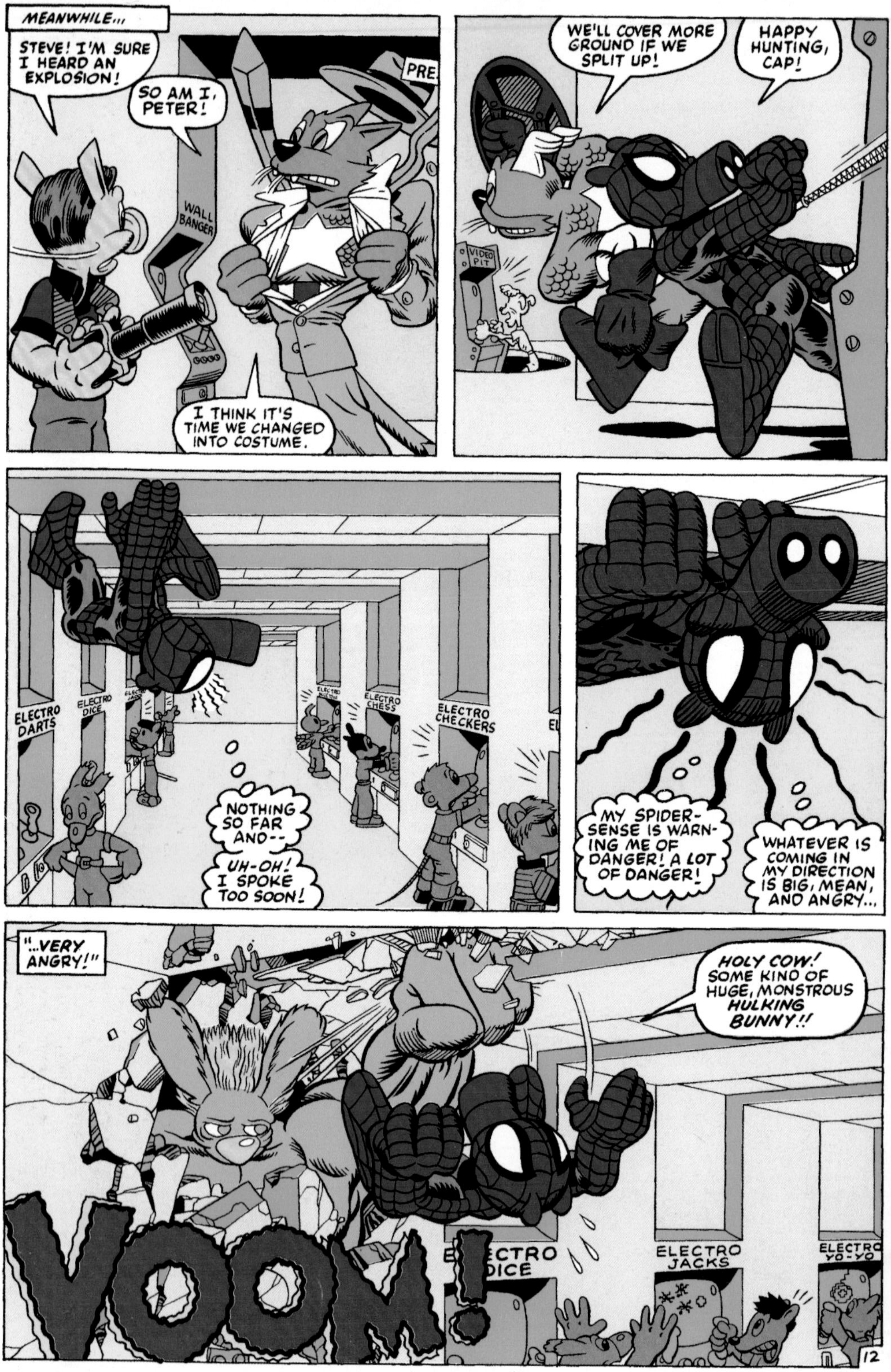
MEANWHILE...
STEVE! I'M SURE I HEARD AN EXPLOSION!
SO AM I, PETER!
PRE
WALL BANGER
I THINK IT'S TIME WE CHANGED INTO COSTUME.
WE'LL COVER MORE GROUND IF WE SPLIT UP!
HAPPY HUNTING, CAP!
VIDEO PIT
ELECTRO DARTS
ELECTRO DICE
ELECTRO CHESS
ELECTRO CHECKERS
NOTHING SO FAR AND--
UH-OH! I SPOKE TOO SOON!
MY SPIDER-SENSE IS WARNING ME OF DANGER! A LOT OF DANGER!
WHATEVER IS COMING IN MY DIRECTION IS BIG, MEAN, AND ANGRY...
"...VERY ANGRY!"
HOLY COW! SOME KIND OF HUGE, MONSTROUS HULKING BUNNY!!
VOOM!
ELECTRO DICE
ELECTRO JACKS
ELECTRO YO-YO

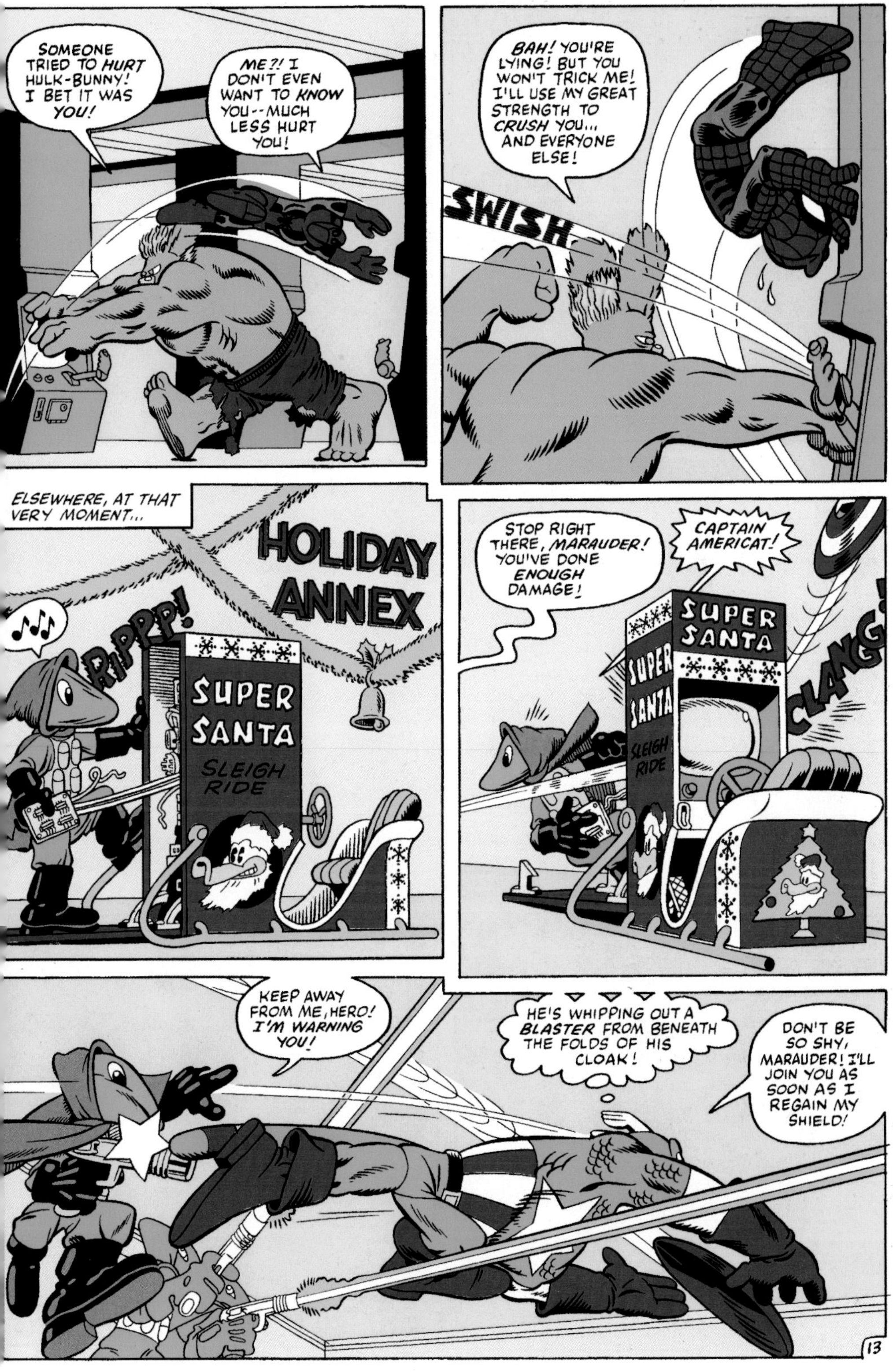
SOMEONE TRIED TO HURT HULK-BUNNY! I BET IT WAS YOU!
ME?! I DON'T EVEN WANT TO KNOW YOU--MUCH LESS HURT YOU!
BAH! YOU'RE LYING! BUT YOU WON'T TRICK ME! I'LL USE MY GREAT STRENGTH TO CRUSH YOU... AND EVERYONE ELSE!
SWISH
ELSEWHERE, AT THAT VERY MOMENT...
HOLIDAY ANNEX
RIPPPP!
SUPER SANTA SLEIGH RIDE
STOP RIGHT THERE, MARAUDER! YOU'VE DONE ENOUGH DAMAGE!
CAPTAIN AMERICAT!
SUPER SANTA
CLANG!
KEEP AWAY FROM ME, HERO! I'M WARNING YOU!
HE'S WHIPPING OUT A BLASTER FROM BENEATH THE FOLDS OF HIS CLOAK!
DON'T BE SO SHY, MARAUDER! I'LL JOIN YOU AS SOON AS I REGAIN MY SHIELD!

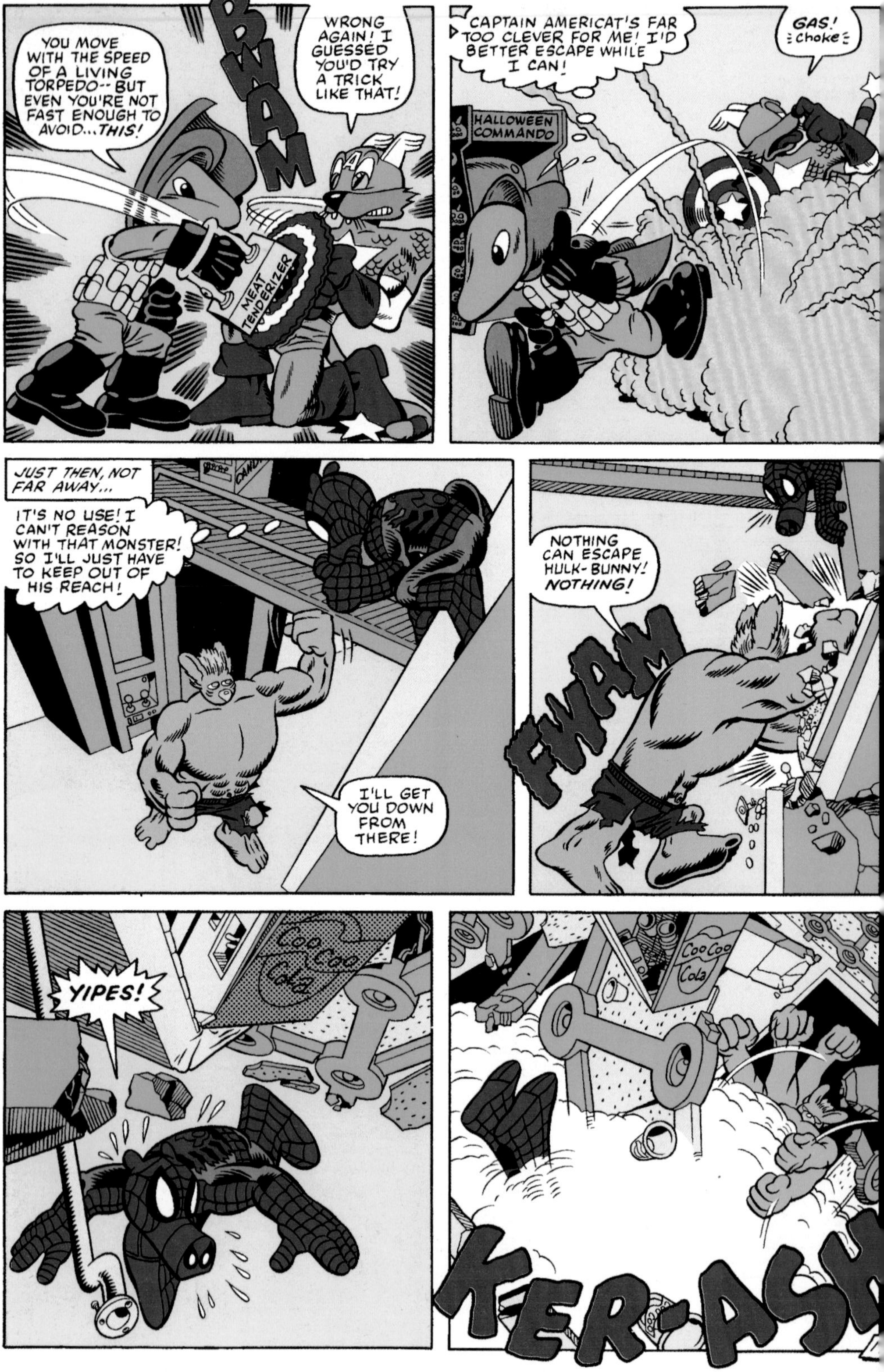
YOU MOVE WITH THE SPEED OF A LIVING TORPEDO-- BUT EVEN YOU'RE NOT FAST ENOUGH TO AVOID...THIS!
BWAM
WRONG AGAIN! I GUESSED YOU'D TRY A TRICK LIKE THAT!
MEAT TENDERIZER
CAPTAIN AMERICAT'S FAR TOO CLEVER FOR ME! I'D BETTER ESCAPE WHILE I CAN!
GAS! Choke
HALLOWEEN COMMANDO
JUST THEN, NOT FAR AWAY...
IT'S NO USE! I CAN'T REASON WITH THAT MONSTER! SO I'LL JUST HAVE TO KEEP OUT OF HIS REACH!
I'LL GET YOU DOWN FROM THERE!
NOTHING CAN ESCAPE HULK-BUNNY! NOTHING!
FWAM
YIPES!
Coo Coo Cola
KER-ASH

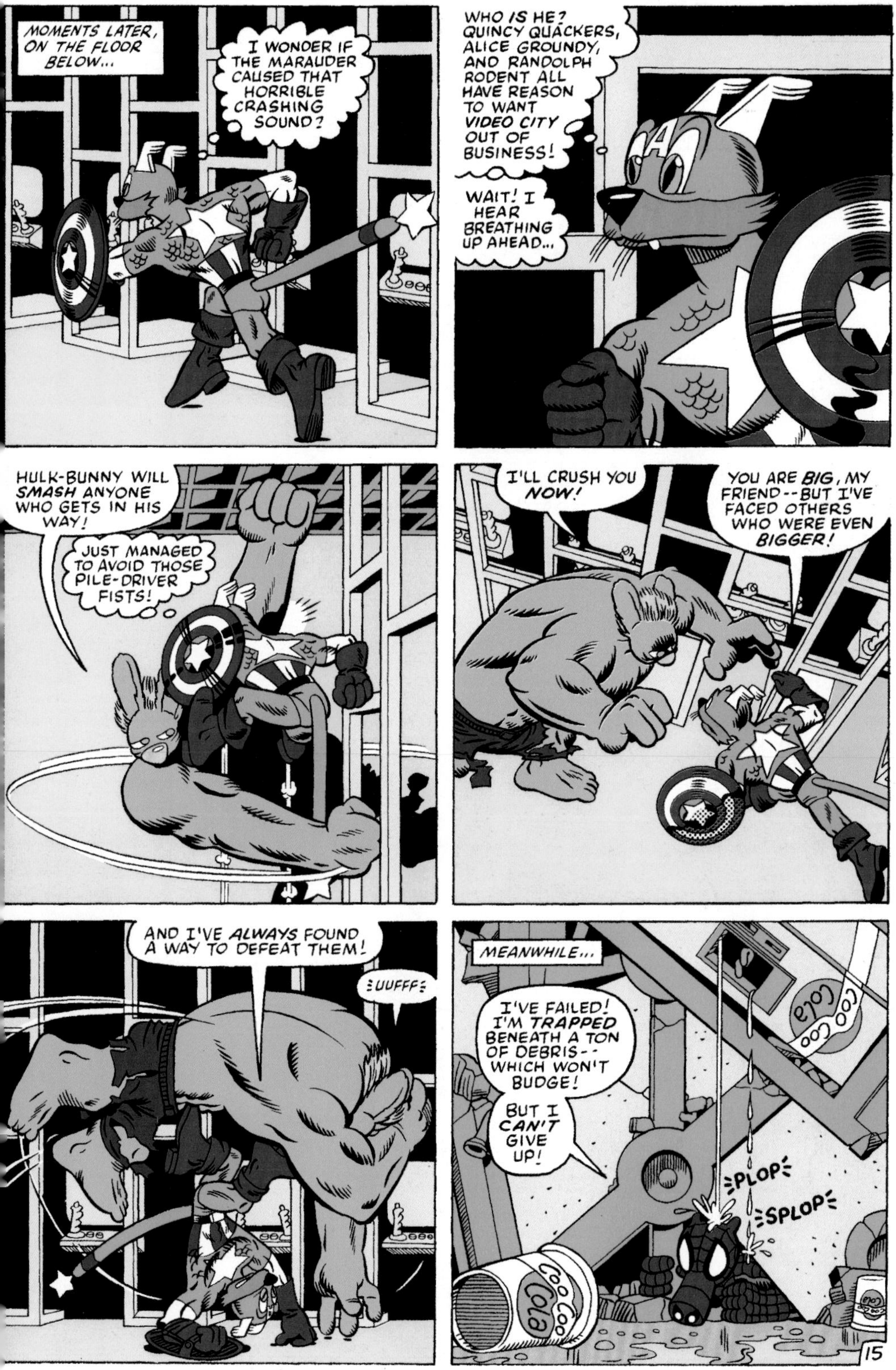
MOMENTS LATER, ON THE FLOOR BELOW...
I WONDER IF THE MARAUDER CAUSED THAT HORRIBLE CRASHING SOUND?
WHO IS HE? QUINCY QUACKERS, ALICE GROUNDY, AND RANDOLPH RODENT ALL HAVE REASON TO WANT VIDEO CITY OUT OF BUSINESS!
WAIT! I HEAR BREATHING UP AHEAD...
HULK-BUNNY WILL SMASH ANYONE WHO GETS IN HIS WAY!
JUST MANAGED TO AVOID THOSE PILE-DRIVER FISTS!
I'LL CRUSH YOU NOW!
YOU ARE BIG, MY FRIEND--BUT I'VE FACED OTHERS WHO WERE EVEN BIGGER!
AND I'VE ALWAYS FOUND A WAY TO DEFEAT THEM!
UUFFF
MEANWHILE...
I'VE FAILED! I'M TRAPPED BENEATH A TON OF DEBRIS--WHICH WON'T BUDGE!
BUT I CAN'T GIVE UP!
PLOP
SPLOP
Coo Coo Cola
Coo Coo Cola

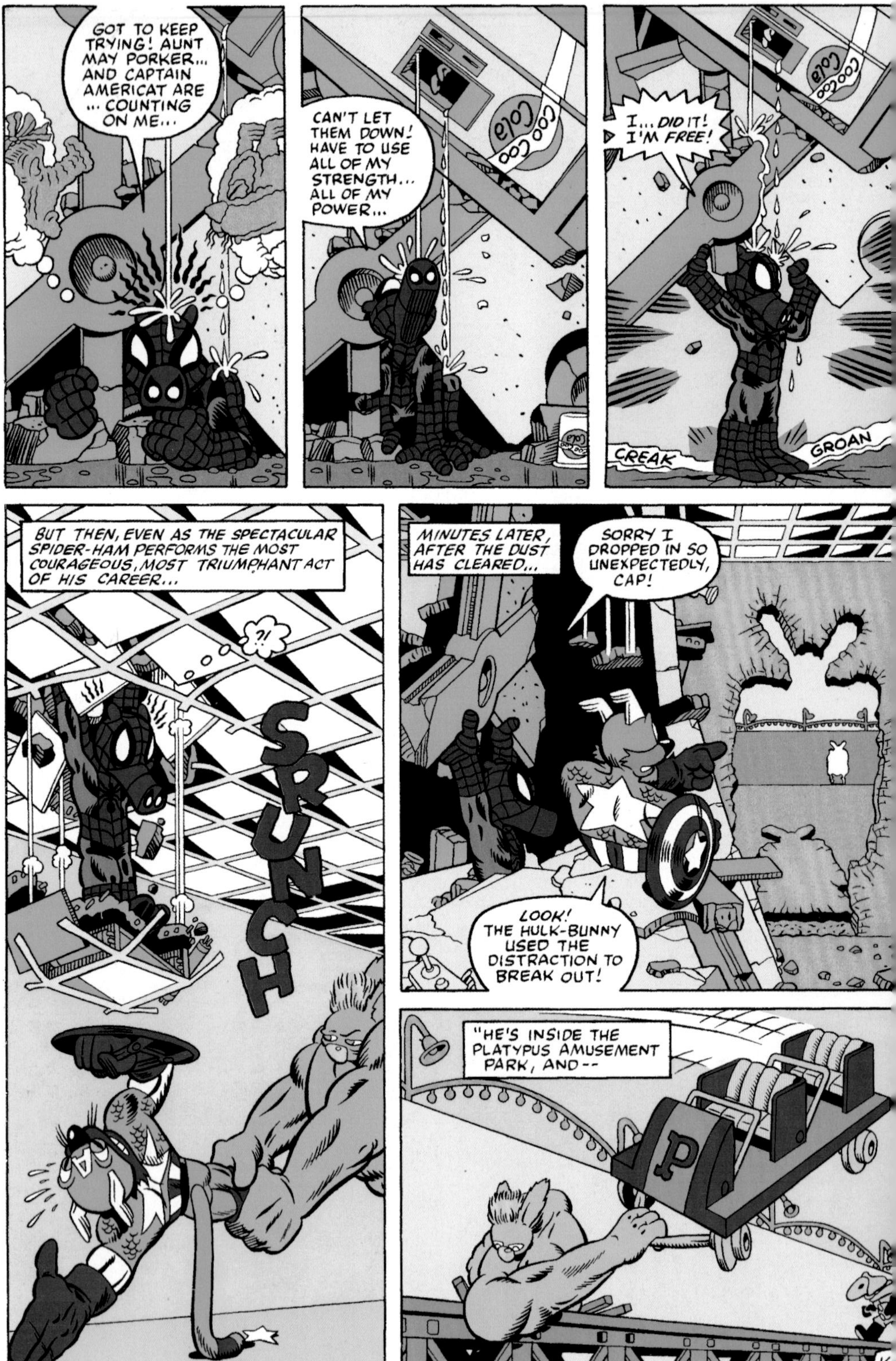
GOT TO KEEP TRYING! AUNT MAY PORKER... AND CAPTAIN AMERICAT ARE ... COUNTING ON ME...
CAN'T LET THEM DOWN! HAVE TO USE ALL OF MY STRENGTH... ALL OF MY POWER...
I... DID IT! I'M FREE!
CREAK
GROAN
BUT THEN, EVEN AS THE SPECTACULAR SPIDER-HAM PERFORMS THE MOST COURAGEOUS, MOST TRIUMPHANT ACT OF HIS CAREER...
?!
SRUNCH
MINUTES LATER, AFTER THE DUST HAS CLEARED...
SORRY I DROPPED IN SO UNEXPECTEDLY, CAP!
LOOK! THE HULK-BUNNY USED THE DISTRACTION TO BREAK OUT!
"HE'S INSIDE THE PLATYPUS AMUSEMENT PARK, AND--
P
16

"--HE'S TEARING THE PLACE *APART!*"

STOP IT! *STOP IT!* YOU'RE RUINING EVERYTHING!

I THINK YOU'D BETTER LEAVE THE HULK-BUNNY TO THE PROFESSIONALS, MARAUDER!

CAPTAIN AMERICAT!?

DON'T BOTHER TRYING TO ESCAPE, FRIEND! YOUR MARAUDING DAYS ARE OVER!

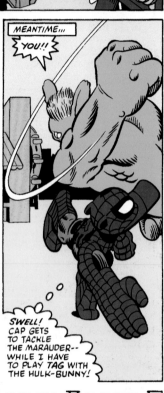

MEANTIME...

YOU!!

SWELL! CAP GETS TO TACKLE THE MARAUDER-- WHILE I HAVE TO PLAY *TAG* WITH THE HULK-BUNNY!

GOT TO KEEP MOVING...

CAN'T STOP...

CAN'T REST... UNTIL I'VE REACHED MY DESTINATION!

YABBA, YABBA!

NYA!

17

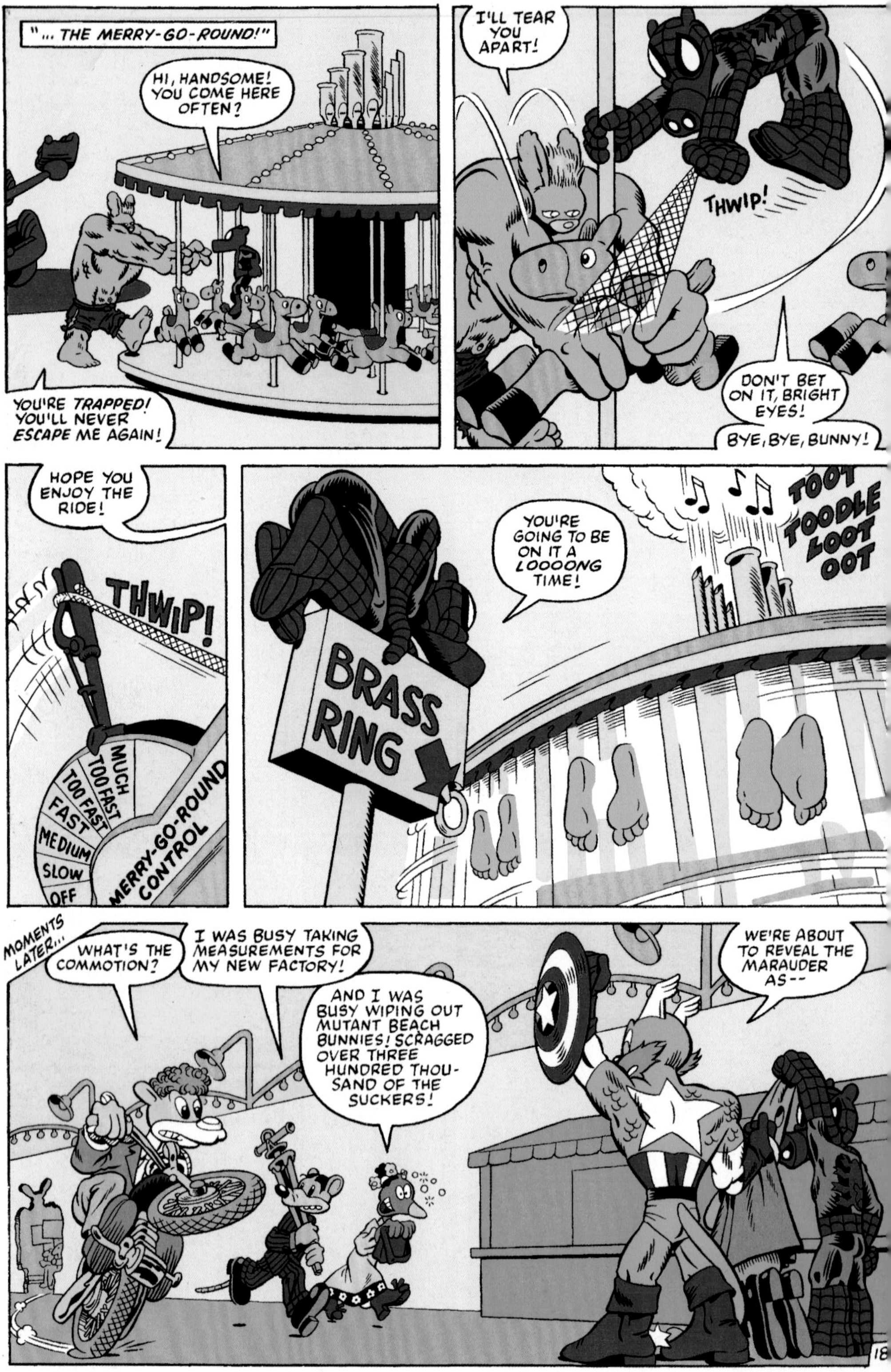
"... THE MERRY-GO-ROUND!"
HI, HANDSOME! YOU COME HERE OFTEN?
YOU'RE TRAPPED! YOU'LL NEVER ESCAPE ME AGAIN!
I'LL TEAR YOU APART!
THWIP!
DON'T BET ON IT, BRIGHT EYES!
BYE, BYE, BUNNY!
HOPE YOU ENJOY THE RIDE!
THWIP!
MUCH TOO FAST
TOO FAST
FAST
MEDIUM
SLOW
OFF
MERRY-GO-ROUND CONTROL
BRASS RING
YOU'RE GOING TO BE ON IT A LOOOONG TIME!
TOOT TOODLE LOOT OOT
MOMENTS LATER...
WHAT'S THE COMMOTION?
I WAS BUSY TAKING MEASUREMENTS FOR MY NEW FACTORY!
AND I WAS BUSY WIPING OUT MUTANT BEACH BUNNIES! SCRAGGED OVER THREE HUNDRED THOU-SAND OF THE SUCKERS!
WE'RE ABOUT TO REVEAL THE MARAUDER AS--

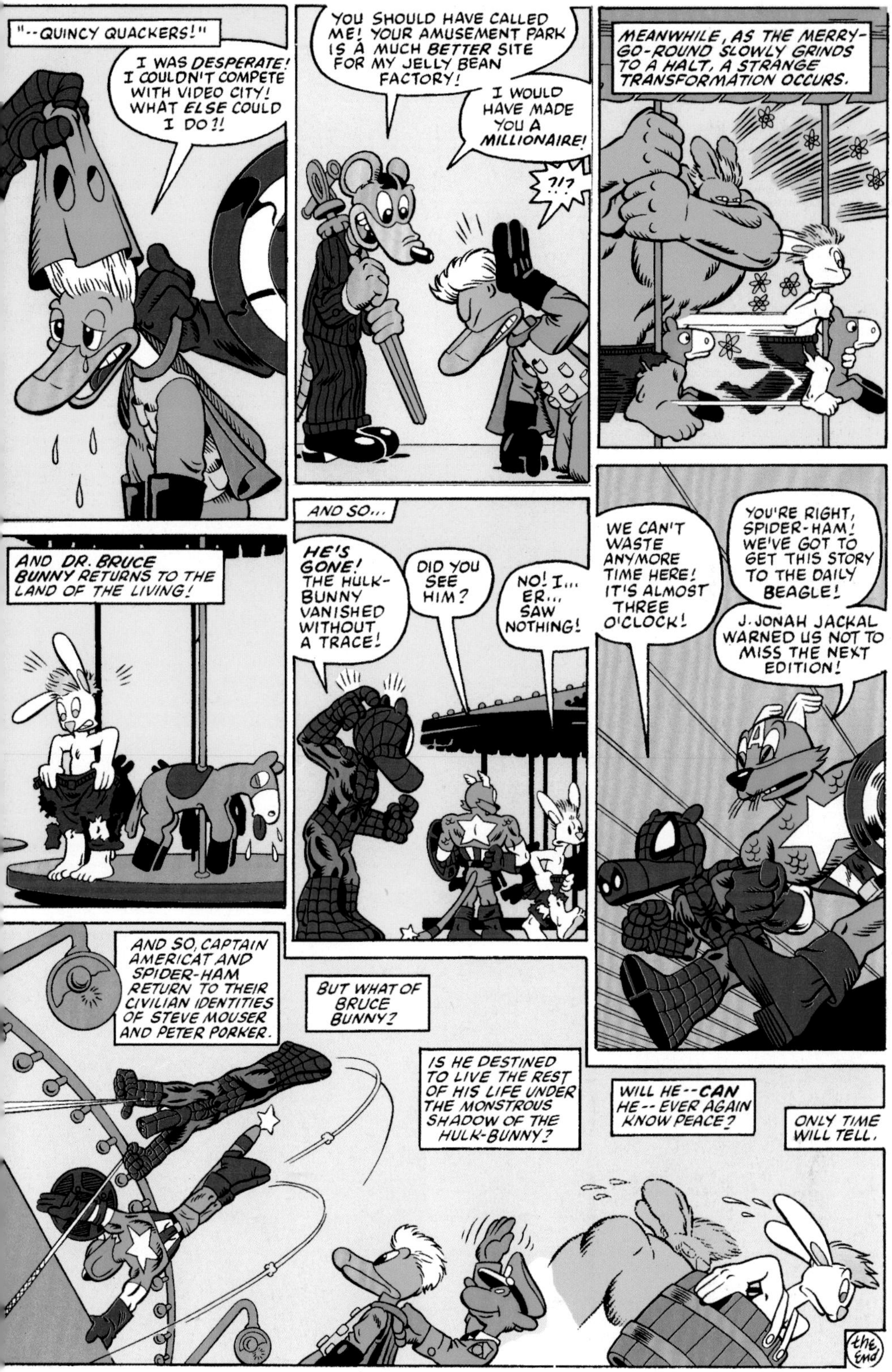
"--QUINCY QUACKERS!"
I WAS DESPERATE! I COULDN'T COMPETE WITH VIDEO CITY! WHAT ELSE COULD I DO?!
YOU SHOULD HAVE CALLED ME! YOUR AMUSEMENT PARK IS A MUCH BETTER SITE FOR MY JELLY BEAN FACTORY!
I WOULD HAVE MADE YOU A MILLIONAIRE!
?!?
MEANWHILE, AS THE MERRY-GO-ROUND SLOWLY GRINDS TO A HALT, A STRANGE TRANSFORMATION OCCURS.
AND DR. BRUCE BUNNY RETURNS TO THE LAND OF THE LIVING!
AND SO...
HE'S GONE! THE HULK-BUNNY VANISHED WITHOUT A TRACE!
DID YOU SEE HIM?
NO! I... ER... SAW NOTHING!
WE CAN'T WASTE ANYMORE TIME HERE! IT'S ALMOST THREE O'CLOCK!
YOU'RE RIGHT, SPIDER-HAM! WE'VE GOT TO GET THIS STORY TO THE DAILY BEAGLE!
J. JONAH JACKAL WARNED US NOT TO MISS THE NEXT EDITION!
AND SO, CAPTAIN AMERICAT AND SPIDER-HAM RETURN TO THEIR CIVILIAN IDENTITIES OF STEVE MOUSER AND PETER PORKER.
BUT WHAT OF BRUCE BUNNY?
IS HE DESTINED TO LIVE THE REST OF HIS LIFE UNDER THE MONSTROUS SHADOW OF THE HULK-BUNNY?
WILL HE--CAN HE--EVER AGAIN KNOW PEACE?
ONLY TIME WILL TELL.
the End

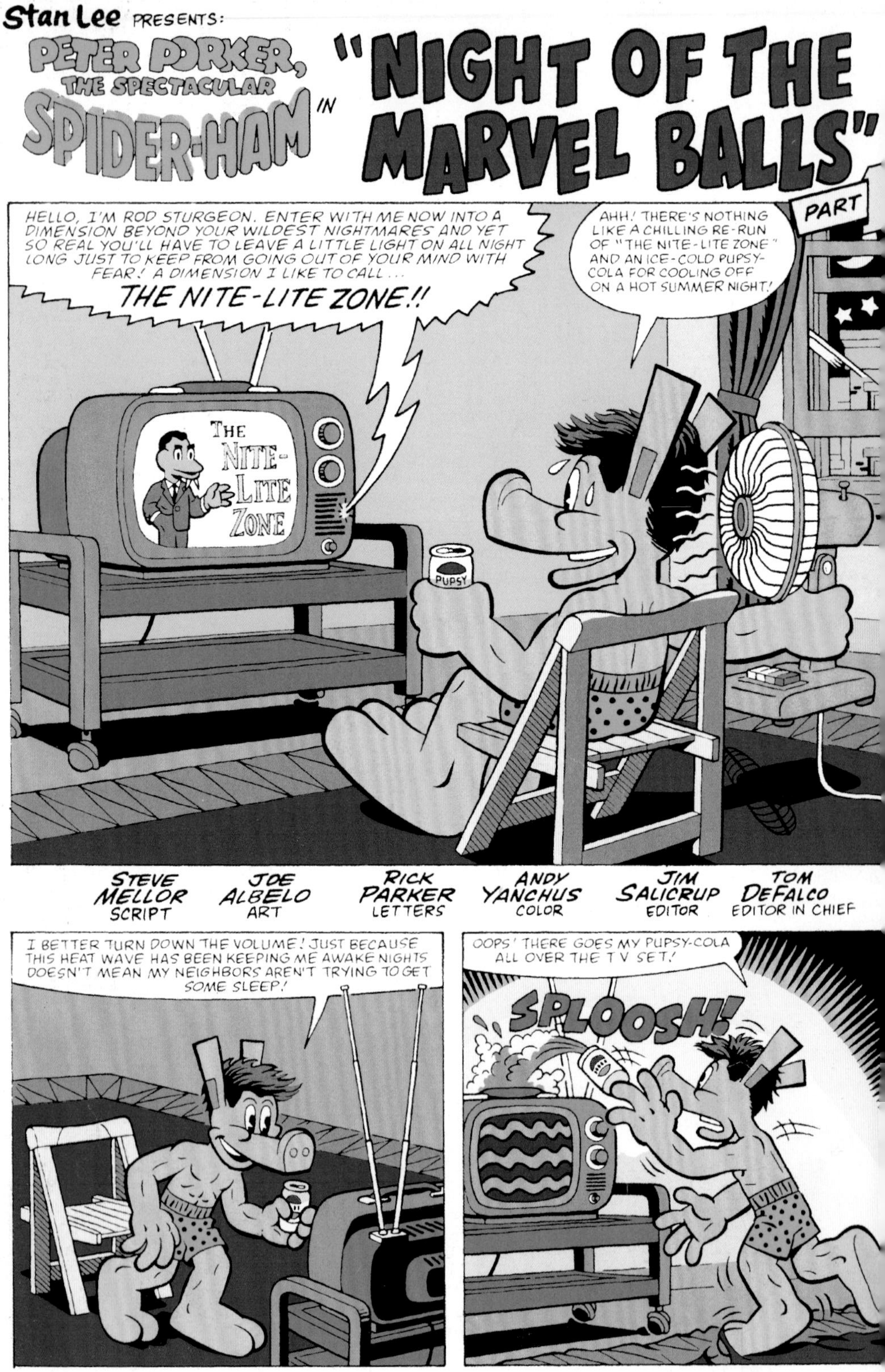
Stan Lee PRESENTS:
PETER PORKER, THE SPECTACULAR SPIDER-HAM IN
"NIGHT OF THE MARVEL BALLS"
PART
HELLO, I'M ROD STURGEON. ENTER WITH ME NOW INTO A DIMENSION BEYOND YOUR WILDEST NIGHTMARES AND YET SO REAL YOU'LL HAVE TO LEAVE A LITTLE LIGHT ON ALL NIGHT LONG JUST TO KEEP FROM GOING OUT OF YOUR MIND WITH FEAR! A DIMENSION I LIKE TO CALL...
THE NITE-LITE ZONE!!
AHH! THERE'S NOTHING LIKE A CHILLING RE-RUN OF "THE NITE-LITE ZONE" AND AN ICE-COLD PUPSY-COLA FOR COOLING OFF ON A HOT SUMMER NIGHT!
THE NITE-LITE ZONE
PUPSY
STEVE MELLOR SCRIPT
JOE ALBELO ART
RICK PARKER LETTERS
ANDY YANCHUS COLOR
JIM SALICRUP EDITOR
TOM DeFALCO EDITOR IN CHIEF
I BETTER TURN DOWN THE VOLUME! JUST BECAUSE THIS HEAT WAVE HAS BEEN KEEPING ME AWAKE NIGHTS DOESN'T MEAN MY NEIGHBORS AREN'T TRYING TO GET SOME SLEEP!
OOPS! THERE GOES MY PUPSY-COLA ALL OVER THE T V SET!
SPLOOSH!

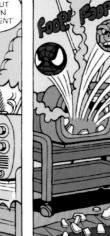

GREAT HOG! I'VE FRIED EVERY TUBE IN THE SET! BUT WHAT'S THAT EERIE SHIMMER AND STRANGE GREEN SMOKE? I'VE NEVER KNOWN A HOME ENTERTAINMENT UNIT TO BEHAVE SO ODDLY!

FOOP! FOOP! FOOP! WHAT IN THE NAME OF...?!

WEIRD LITTLE BALLS WITH DISTURBINGLY FAMILIAR FACES ON THEM! AND THEY'RE WRECKING MY APARTMENT!

HEY, EASE UP, WILLYA?! I JUST FINISHED PAYING FOR THIS STUFF!

FWOOMP!

CRASH!

AS PETER PORKER LIES STUNNED ON THE FLOOR OF HIS SAVAGED ABODE, AN ASTRAL SHAPE ENTERS THE SCENE IN A WAY IMPOSSIBLE FOR ANYONE BUT A MASTER OF THE MYSTIC ARTS...

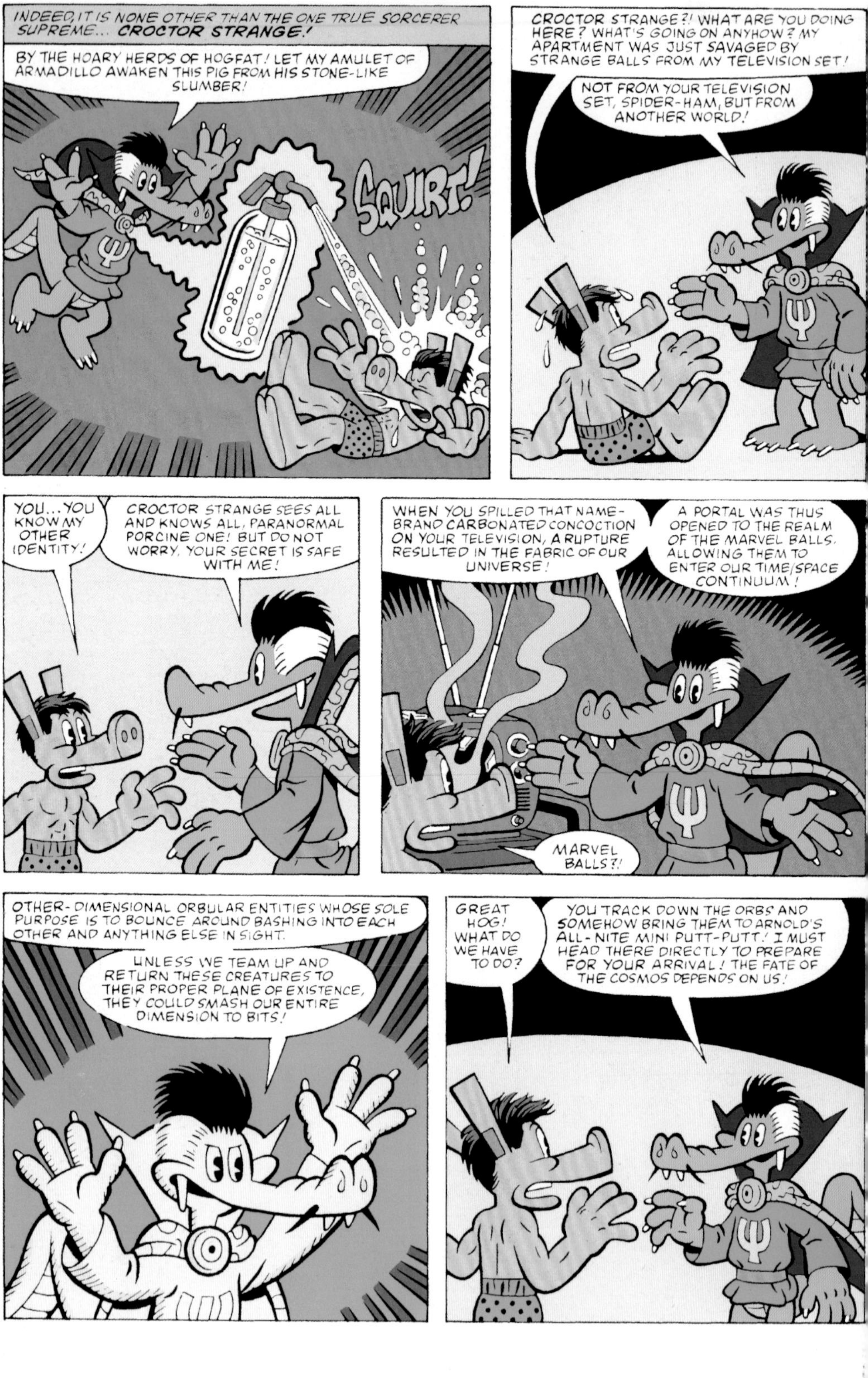
INDEED, IT IS NONE OTHER THAN THE ONE TRUE SORCERER SUPREME... CROCTOR STRANGE!
BY THE HOARY HERDS OF HOGFAT! LET MY AMULET OF ARMADILLO AWAKEN THIS PIG FROM HIS STONE-LIKE SLUMBER!
SQUIRT!
CROCTOR STRANGE?! WHAT ARE YOU DOING HERE? WHAT'S GOING ON ANYHOW? MY APARTMENT WAS JUST SAVAGED BY STRANGE BALLS FROM MY TELEVISION SET!
NOT FROM YOUR TELEVISION SET, SPIDER-HAM, BUT FROM ANOTHER WORLD!
YOU... YOU KNOW MY OTHER IDENTITY!
CROCTOR STRANGE SEES ALL AND KNOWS ALL, PARANORMAL PORCINE ONE! BUT DO NOT WORRY, YOUR SECRET IS SAFE WITH ME!
WHEN YOU SPILLED THAT NAME-BRAND CARBONATED CONCOCTION ON YOUR TELEVISION, A RUPTURE RESULTED IN THE FABRIC OF OUR UNIVERSE!
A PORTAL WAS THUS OPENED TO THE REALM OF THE MARVEL BALLS, ALLOWING THEM TO ENTER OUR TIME/SPACE CONTINUUM!
MARVEL BALLS?!
OTHER-DIMENSIONAL ORBULAR ENTITIES WHOSE SOLE PURPOSE IS TO BOUNCE AROUND BASHING INTO EACH OTHER AND ANYTHING ELSE IN SIGHT.
UNLESS WE TEAM UP AND RETURN THESE CREATURES TO THEIR PROPER PLANE OF EXISTENCE, THEY COULD SMASH OUR ENTIRE DIMENSION TO BITS!
GREAT HOG! WHAT DO WE HAVE TO DO?
YOU TRACK DOWN THE ORBS AND SOMEHOW BRING THEM TO ARNOLD'S ALL-NITE MINI PUTT-PUTT! I MUST HEAD THERE DIRECTLY TO PREPARE FOR YOUR ARRIVAL! THE FATE OF THE COSMOS DEPENDS ON US!

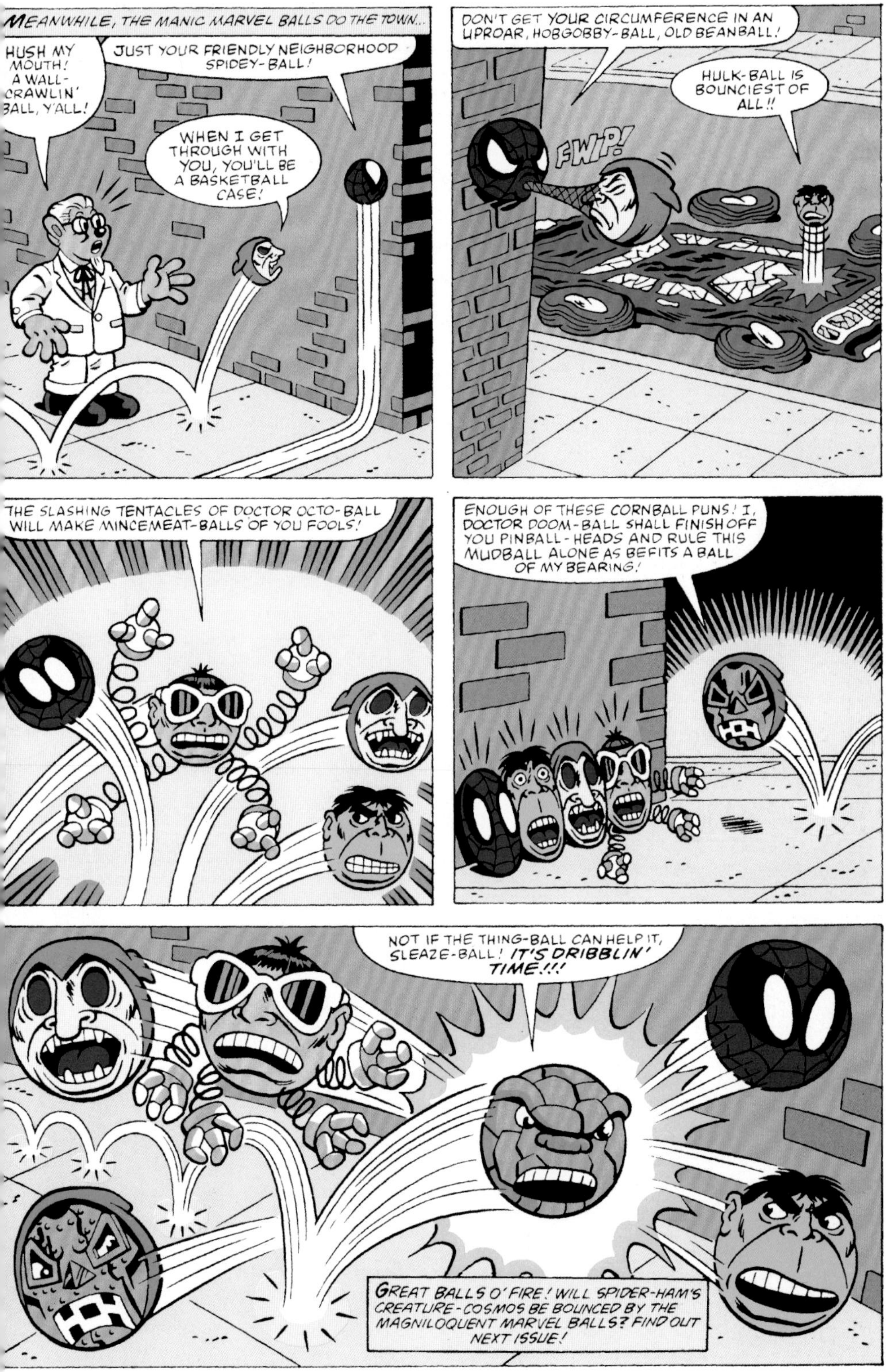

MEANWHILE, THE MANIC MARVEL BALLS DO THE TOWN...
HUSH MY MOUTH! A WALL-CRAWLIN' BALL, Y'ALL!
JUST YOUR FRIENDLY NEIGHBORHOOD SPIDEY-BALL!
WHEN I GET THROUGH WITH YOU, YOU'LL BE A BASKETBALL CASE!
DON'T GET YOUR CIRCUMFERENCE IN AN UPROAR, HOBGOBBY-BALL, OLD BEANBALL!
HULK-BALL IS BOUNCIEST OF ALL!!
FWIP!
THE SLASHING TENTACLES OF DOCTOR OCTO-BALL WILL MAKE MINCEMEAT-BALLS OF YOU FOOLS!
ENOUGH OF THESE CORNBALL PUNS! I, DOCTOR DOOM-BALL SHALL FINISH OFF YOU PINBALL-HEADS AND RULE THIS MUDBALL ALONE AS BEFITS A BALL OF MY BEARING!
NOT IF THE THING-BALL CAN HELP IT, SLEAZE-BALL! IT'S DRIBBLIN' TIME!!!
GREAT BALLS O' FIRE! WILL SPIDER-HAM'S CREATURE-COSMOS BE BOUNCED BY THE MAGNILOQUENT MARVEL BALLS? FIND OUT NEXT ISSUE!

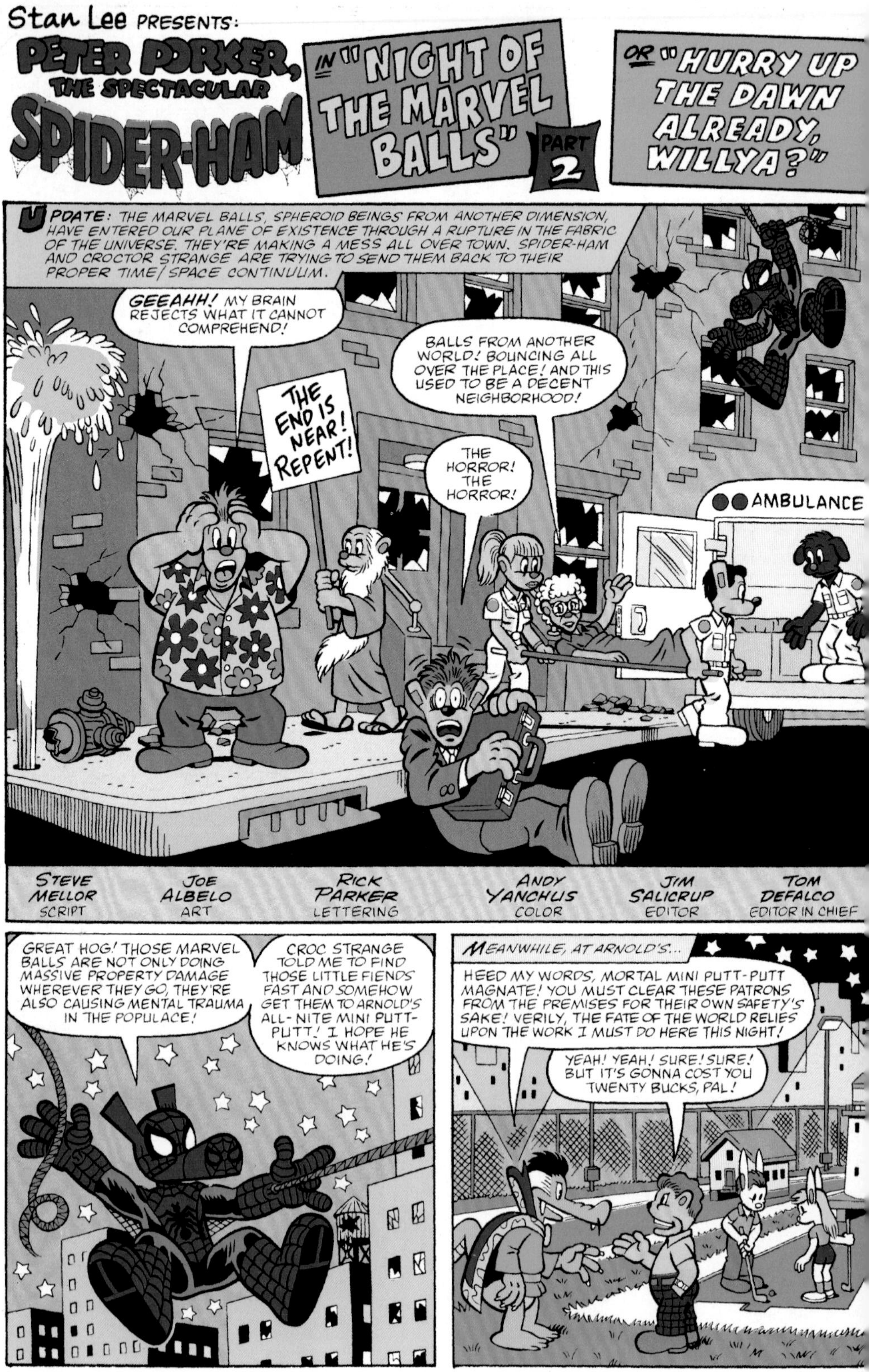
Stan Lee PRESENTS:
PETER PORKER, THE SPECTACULAR SPIDER-HAM
IN "NIGHT OF THE MARVEL BALLS" PART 2
OR "HURRY UP THE DAWN ALREADY, WILLYA?"
UPDATE: THE MARVEL BALLS, SPHEROID BEINGS FROM ANOTHER DIMENSION, HAVE ENTERED OUR PLANE OF EXISTENCE THROUGH A RUPTURE IN THE FABRIC OF THE UNIVERSE. THEY'RE MAKING A MESS ALL OVER TOWN. SPIDER-HAM AND CROCTOR STRANGE ARE TRYING TO SEND THEM BACK TO THEIR PROPER TIME/SPACE CONTINUUM.
GEEAHH! MY BRAIN REJECTS WHAT IT CANNOT COMPREHEND!
THE END IS NEAR! REPENT!
BALLS FROM ANOTHER WORLD! BOUNCING ALL OVER THE PLACE! AND THIS USED TO BE A DECENT NEIGHBORHOOD!
THE HORROR! THE HORROR!
AMBULANCE
STEVE MELLOR SCRIPT
JOE ALBELO ART
RICK PARKER LETTERING
ANDY YANCHUS COLOR
JIM SALICRUP EDITOR
TOM DEFALCO EDITOR IN CHIEF
GREAT HOG! THOSE MARVEL BALLS ARE NOT ONLY DOING MASSIVE PROPERTY DAMAGE WHEREVER THEY GO, THEY'RE ALSO CAUSING MENTAL TRAUMA IN THE POPULACE!
CROC STRANGE TOLD ME TO FIND THOSE LITTLE FIENDS FAST AND SOMEHOW GET THEM TO ARNOLD'S ALL-NITE MINI PUTT-PUTT! I HOPE HE KNOWS WHAT HE'S DOING!
MEANWHILE, AT ARNOLD'S...
HEED MY WORDS, MORTAL MINI PUTT-PUTT MAGNATE! YOU MUST CLEAR THESE PATRONS FROM THE PREMISES FOR THEIR OWN SAFETY'S SAKE! VERILY, THE FATE OF THE WORLD RELIES UPON THE WORK I MUST DO HERE THIS NIGHT!
YEAH! YEAH! SURE! SURE! BUT IT'S GONNA COST YOU TWENTY BUCKS, PAL!

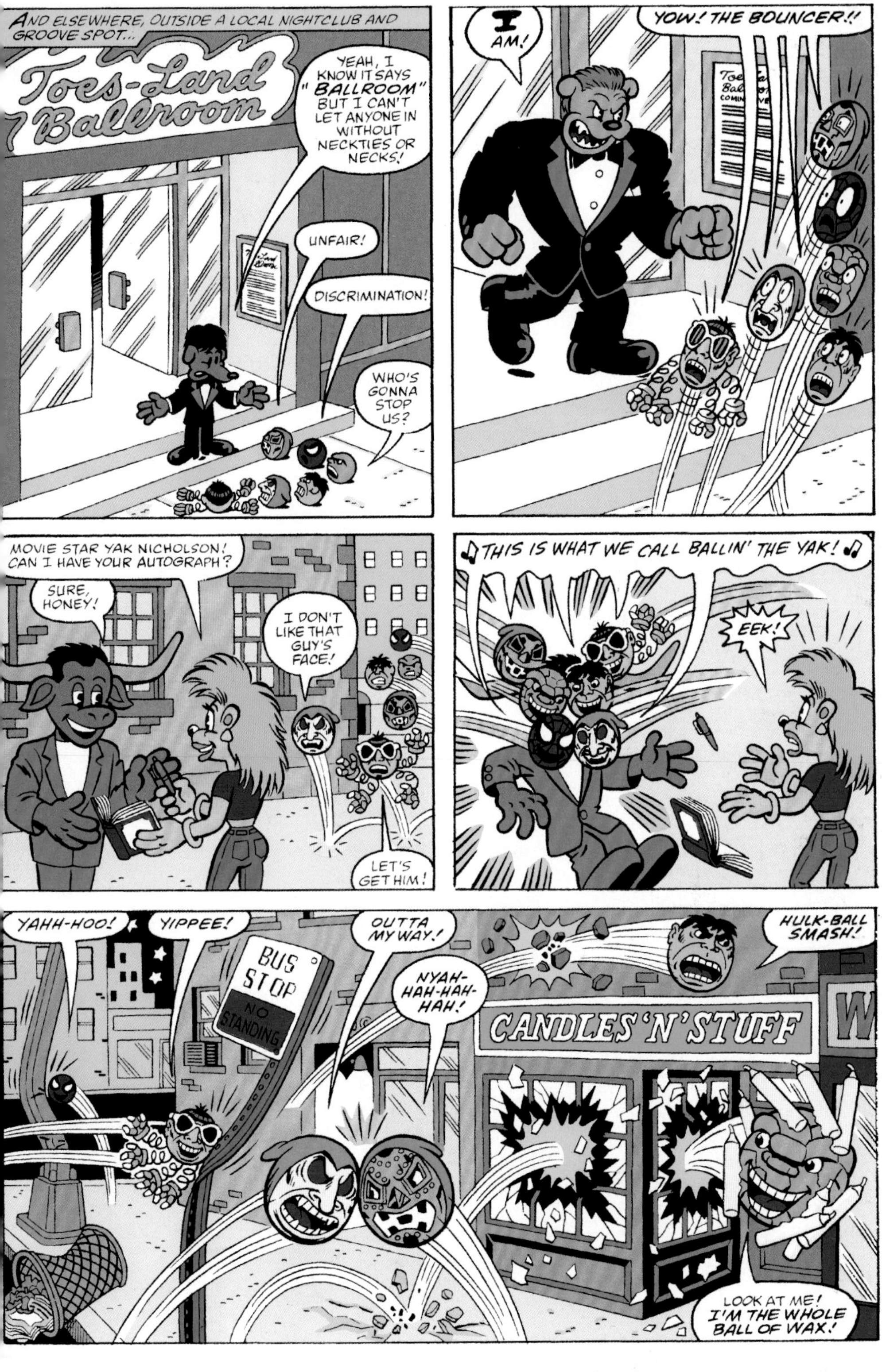
AND ELSEWHERE, OUTSIDE A LOCAL NIGHTCLUB AND GROOVE SPOT...
Toes-Land Ballroom
YEAH, I KNOW IT SAYS "BALLROOM" BUT I CAN'T LET ANYONE IN WITHOUT NECKTIES OR NECKS!
UNFAIR!
DISCRIMINATION!
WHO'S GONNA STOP US?
I AM!
YOW! THE BOUNCER!!
MOVIE STAR YAK NICHOLSON! CAN I HAVE YOUR AUTOGRAPH?
SURE, HONEY!
I DON'T LIKE THAT GUY'S FACE!
LET'S GET HIM!
♫ THIS IS WHAT WE CALL BALLIN' THE YAK! ♫
EEK!
YAHH-HOO!
YIPPEE!
BUS STOP NO STANDING
OUTTA MY WAY!
NYAH-HAH-HAH-HAH!
HULK-BALL SMASH!
CANDLES 'N' STUFF
LOOK AT ME! I'M THE WHOLE BALL OF WAX!

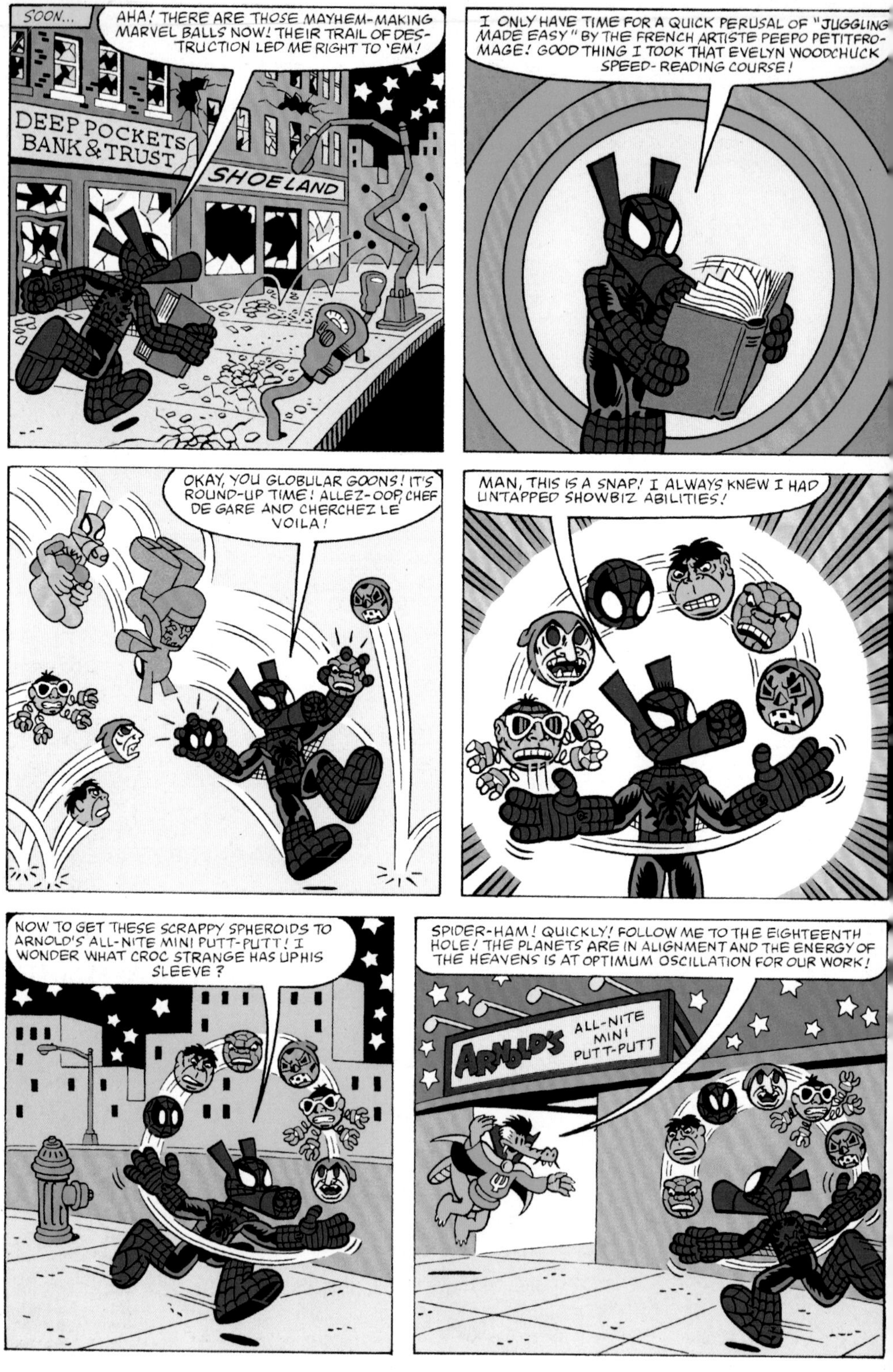
SOON...
AHA! THERE ARE THOSE MAYHEM-MAKING MARVEL BALLS NOW! THEIR TRAIL OF DESTRUCTION LED ME RIGHT TO 'EM!
DEEP POCKETS BANK & TRUST
SHOELAND
I ONLY HAVE TIME FOR A QUICK PERUSAL OF "JUGGLING MADE EASY" BY THE FRENCH ARTISTE PEEPO PETITFROMAGE! GOOD THING I TOOK THAT EVELYN WOODCHUCK SPEED-READING COURSE!
OKAY, YOU GLOBULAR GOONS! IT'S ROUND-UP TIME! ALLEZ-OOP, CHEF DE GARE AND CHERCHEZ LE VOILA!
MAN, THIS IS A SNAP! I ALWAYS KNEW I HAD UNTAPPED SHOWBIZ ABILITIES!
NOW TO GET THESE SCRAPPY SPHEROIDS TO ARNOLD'S ALL-NITE MINI PUTT-PUTT! I WONDER WHAT CROC STRANGE HAS UP HIS SLEEVE?
SPIDER-HAM! QUICKLY! FOLLOW ME TO THE EIGHTEENTH HOLE! THE PLANETS ARE IN ALIGNMENT AND THE ENERGY OF THE HEAVENS IS AT OPTIMUM OSCILLATION FOR OUR WORK!
ARNOLD'S ALL-NITE MINI PUTT-PUTT

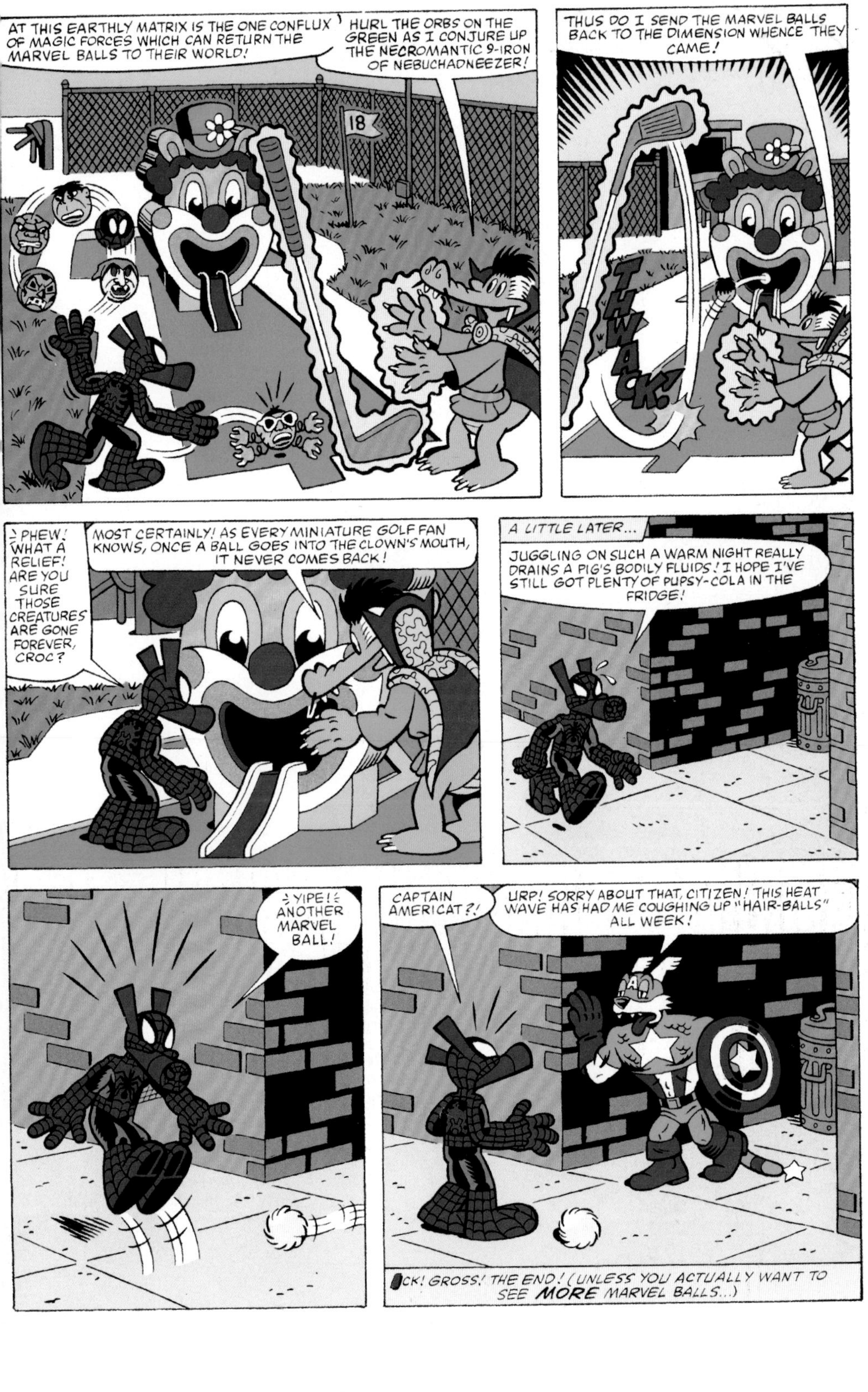
AT THIS EARTHLY MATRIX IS THE ONE CONFLUX OF MAGIC FORCES WHICH CAN RETURN THE MARVEL BALLS TO THEIR WORLD!
HURL THE ORBS ON THE GREEN AS I CONJURE UP THE NECROMANTIC 9-IRON OF NEBUCHADNEEZER!
18
THUS DO I SEND THE MARVEL BALLS BACK TO THE DIMENSION WHENCE THEY CAME!
THWACK!
PHEW! WHAT A RELIEF! ARE YOU SURE THOSE CREATURES ARE GONE FOREVER, CROC?
MOST CERTAINLY! AS EVERY MINIATURE GOLF FAN KNOWS, ONCE A BALL GOES INTO THE CLOWN'S MOUTH, IT NEVER COMES BACK!
A LITTLE LATER...
JUGGLING ON SUCH A WARM NIGHT REALLY DRAINS A PIG'S BODILY FLUIDS! I HOPE I'VE STILL GOT PLENTY OF PUPSY-COLA IN THE FRIDGE!
YIPE! ANOTHER MARVEL BALL!
CAPTAIN AMERICAT?!
URP! SORRY ABOUT THAT, CITIZEN! THIS HEAT WAVE HAS HAD ME COUGHING UP "HAIR-BALLS" ALL WEEK!
ICK! GROSS! THE END! (UNLESS YOU ACTUALLY WANT TO SEE MORE MARVEL BALLS...)

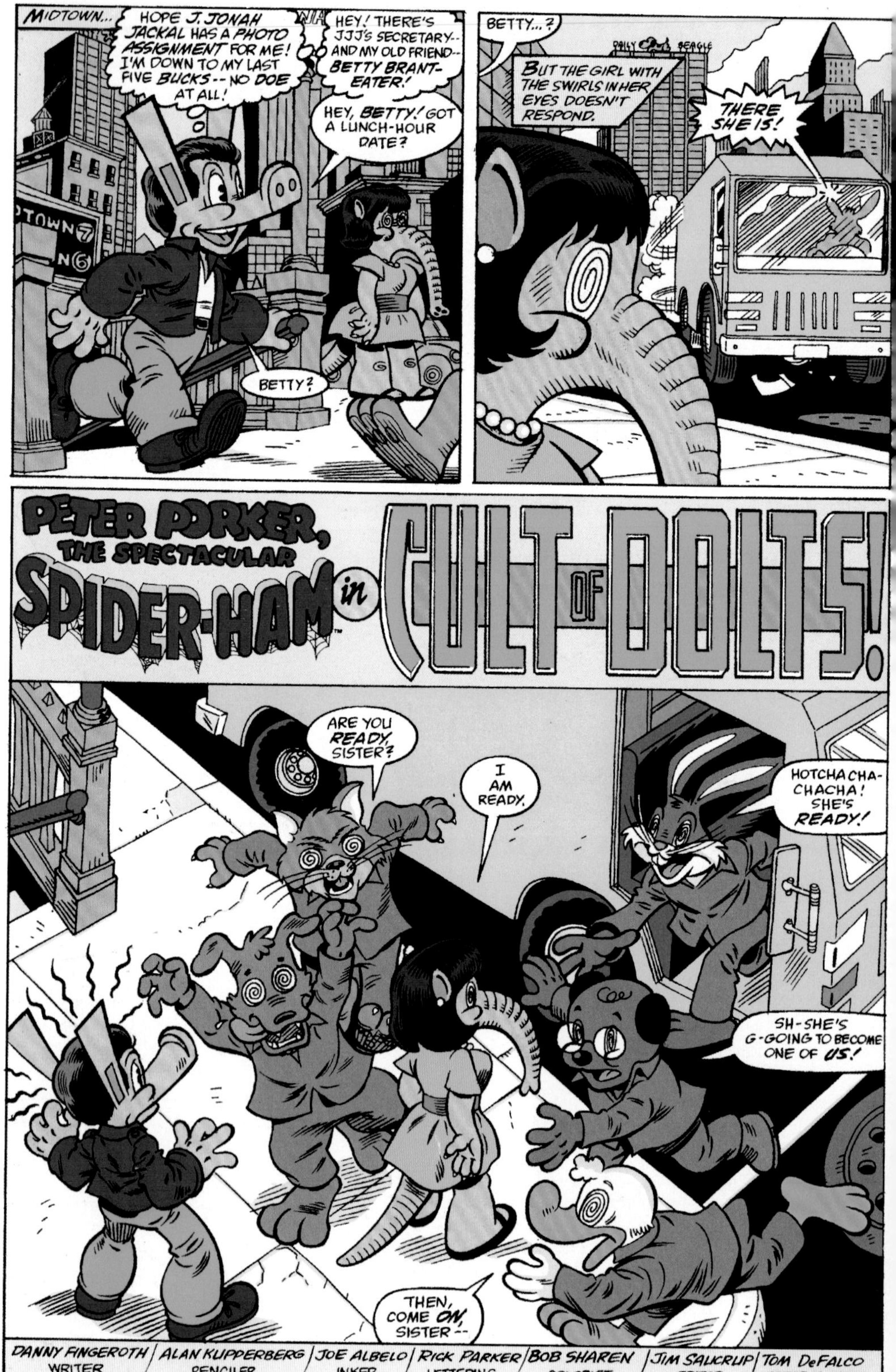
MIDTOWN...
HOPE J. JONAH JACKAL HAS A PHOTO ASSIGNMENT FOR ME! I'M DOWN TO MY LAST FIVE BUCKS--NO DOE AT ALL!
HEY! THERE'S JJJ'S SECRETARY--AND MY OLD FRIEND--BETTY BRANT-EATER!
HEY, BETTY! GOT A LUNCH-HOUR DATE?
BETTY?
BETTY...?
BUT THE GIRL WITH THE SWIRLS IN HER EYES DOESN'T RESPOND.
THERE SHE IS!
PETER PORKER, THE SPECTACULAR SPIDER-HAM™ in CULT OF DOLTS!
ARE YOU READY, SISTER?
I AM READY.
HOTCHA CHA-CHACHA! SHE'S READY!
SH-SHE'S G-GOING TO BECOME ONE OF US!
THEN, COME ON, SISTER--
DANNY FINGEROTH WRITER
ALAN KUPPERBERG PENCILER
JOE ALBELO INKER
RICK PARKER LETTERING
BOB SHAREN COLORIST
JIM SALICRUP EDITOR
TOM DeFALCO EDITOR IN CHIEF

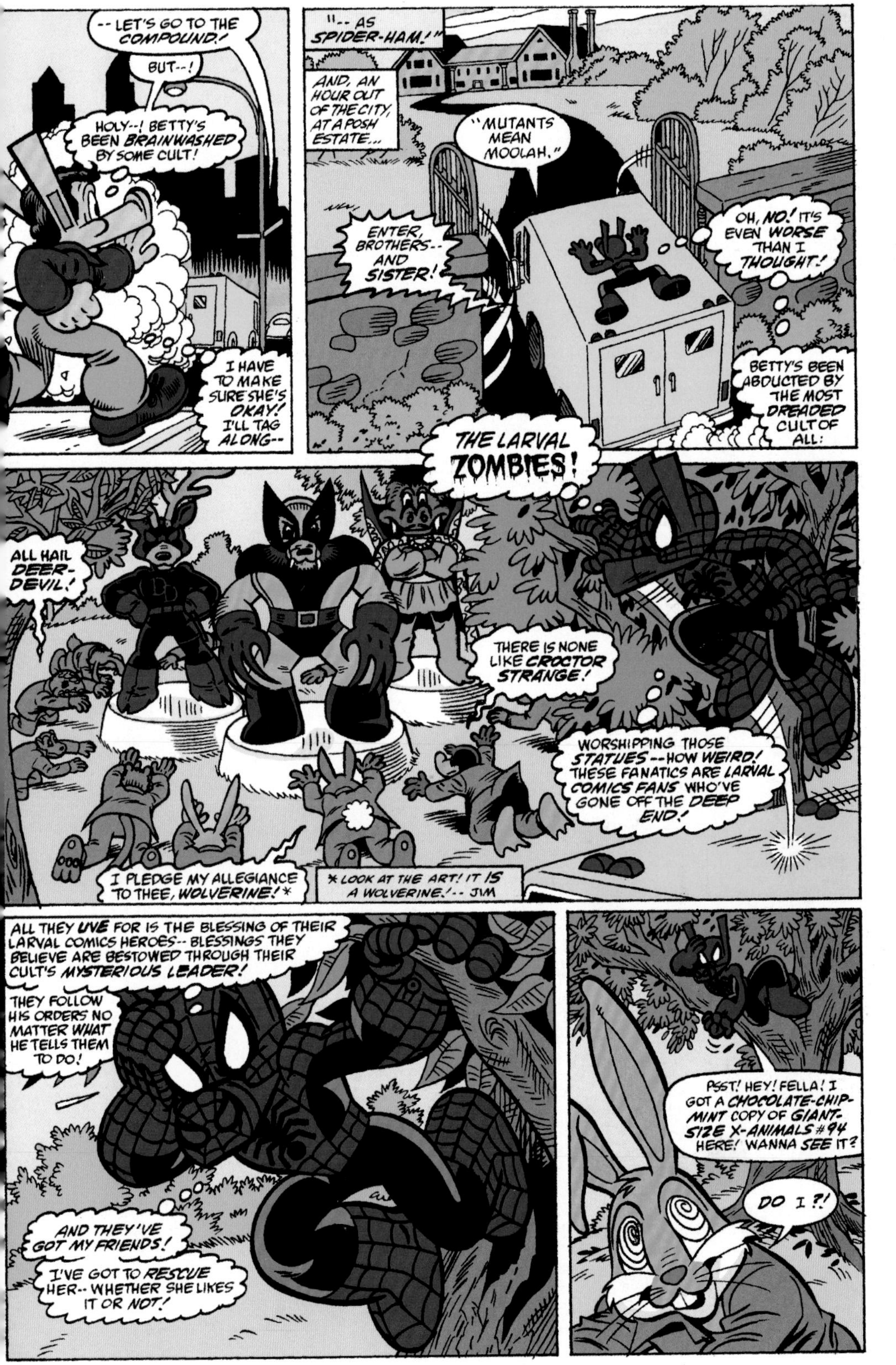
-- LET'S GO TO THE COMPOUND!
BUT--!
HOLY--! BETTY'S BEEN BRAINWASHED BY SOME CULT!
I HAVE TO MAKE SURE SHE'S OKAY! I'LL TAG ALONG--
"-- AS SPIDER-HAM!"
AND, AN HOUR OUT OF THE CITY, AT A POSH ESTATE...
"MUTANTS MEAN MOOLAH."
ENTER, BROTHERS-- AND SISTER!
OH, NO! IT'S EVEN WORSE THAN I THOUGHT!
BETTY'S BEEN ABDUCTED BY THE MOST DREADED CULT OF ALL:
THE LARVAL ZOMBIES!
ALL HAIL DEER-DEVIL!
THERE IS NONE LIKE CROCTOR STRANGE!
WORSHIPPING THOSE STATUES--HOW WEIRD! THESE FANATICS ARE LARVAL COMICS FANS WHO'VE GONE OFF THE DEEP END!
I PLEDGE MY ALLEGIANCE TO THEE, WOLVERINE!*
*LOOK AT THE ART! IT IS A WOLVERINE! -- JIM
ALL THEY LIVE FOR IS THE BLESSING OF THEIR LARVAL COMICS HEROES-- BLESSINGS THEY BELIEVE ARE BESTOWED THROUGH THEIR CULT'S MYSTERIOUS LEADER!
THEY FOLLOW HIS ORDERS NO MATTER WHAT HE TELLS THEM TO DO!
AND THEY'VE GOT MY FRIENDS!
I'VE GOT TO RESCUE HER-- WHETHER SHE LIKES IT OR NOT!
PSST! HEY! FELLA! I GOT A CHOCOLATE-CHIP-MINT COPY OF GIANT-SIZE X-ANIMALS #94 HERE! WANNA SEE IT?
DO I?!

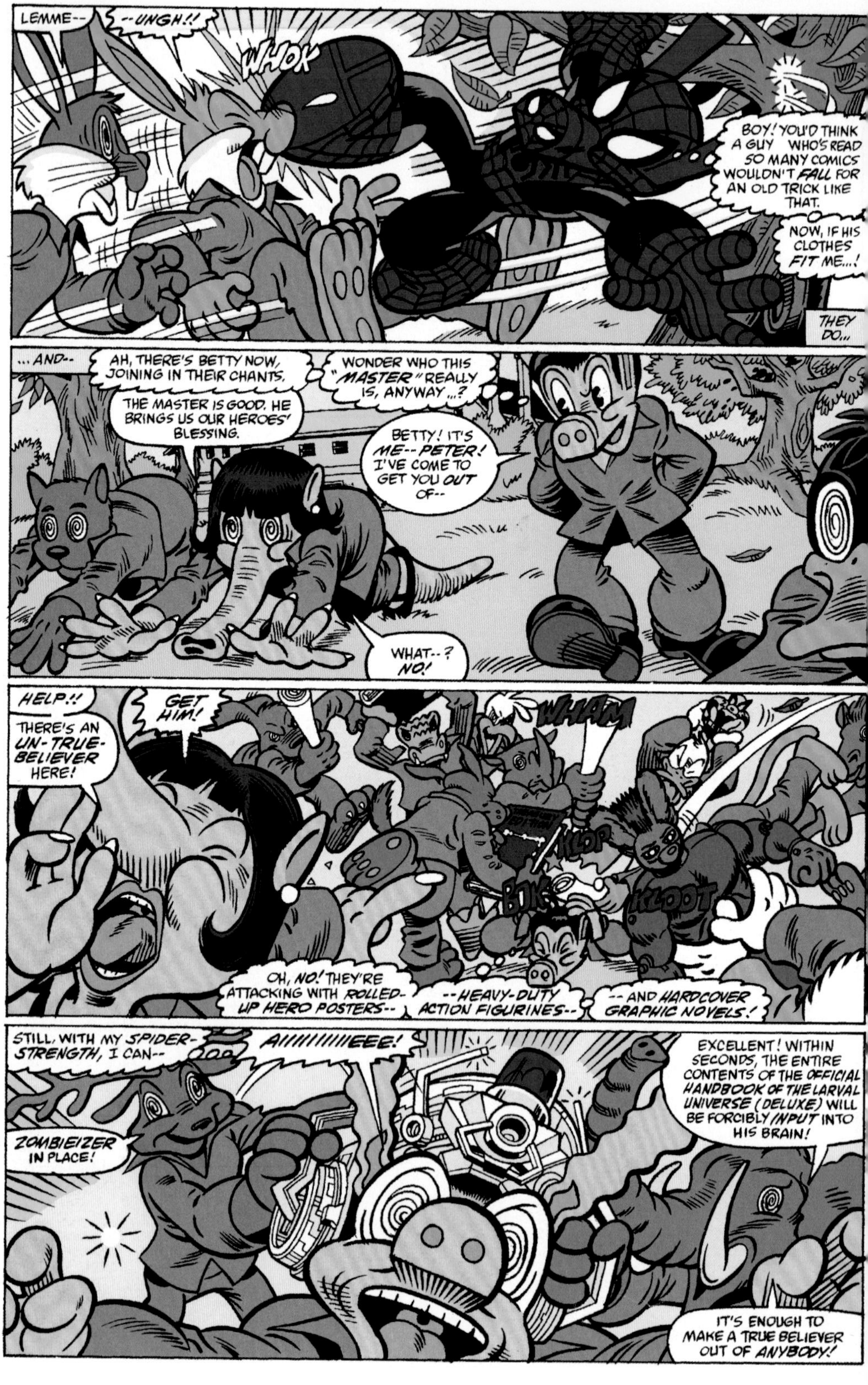
LEMME--
--UNGH!!
WHOK
BOY! YOU'D THINK A GUY WHO'S READ SO MANY COMICS WOULDN'T FALL FOR AN OLD TRICK LIKE THAT.
NOW, IF HIS CLOTHES FIT ME...!
THEY DO...
...AND--
AH, THERE'S BETTY NOW, JOINING IN THEIR CHANTS.
WONDER WHO THIS "MASTER" REALLY IS, ANYWAY...?
THE MASTER IS GOOD. HE BRINGS US OUR HEROES' BLESSING.
BETTY! IT'S ME--PETER! I'VE COME TO GET YOU OUT OF--
WHAT--? NO!
HELP!!
THERE'S AN UN-TRUE-BELIEVER HERE!
GET HIM!
WHAM
KLOP
BOK
KLOOT
OH, NO! THEY'RE ATTACKING WITH ROLLED-UP HERO POSTERS--
--HEAVY-DUTY ACTION FIGURINES--
--AND HARDCOVER GRAPHIC NOVELS!
STILL, WITH MY SPIDER-STRENGTH, I CAN--
AIIIIIIIIIEEE!
ZOMBIEIZER IN PLACE!
EXCELLENT! WITHIN SECONDS, THE ENTIRE CONTENTS OF THE OFFICIAL HANDBOOK OF THE LARVAL UNIVERSE (DELUXE) WILL BE FORCIBLY INPUT INTO HIS BRAIN!
IT'S ENOUGH TO MAKE A TRUE BELIEVER OUT OF ANYBODY!

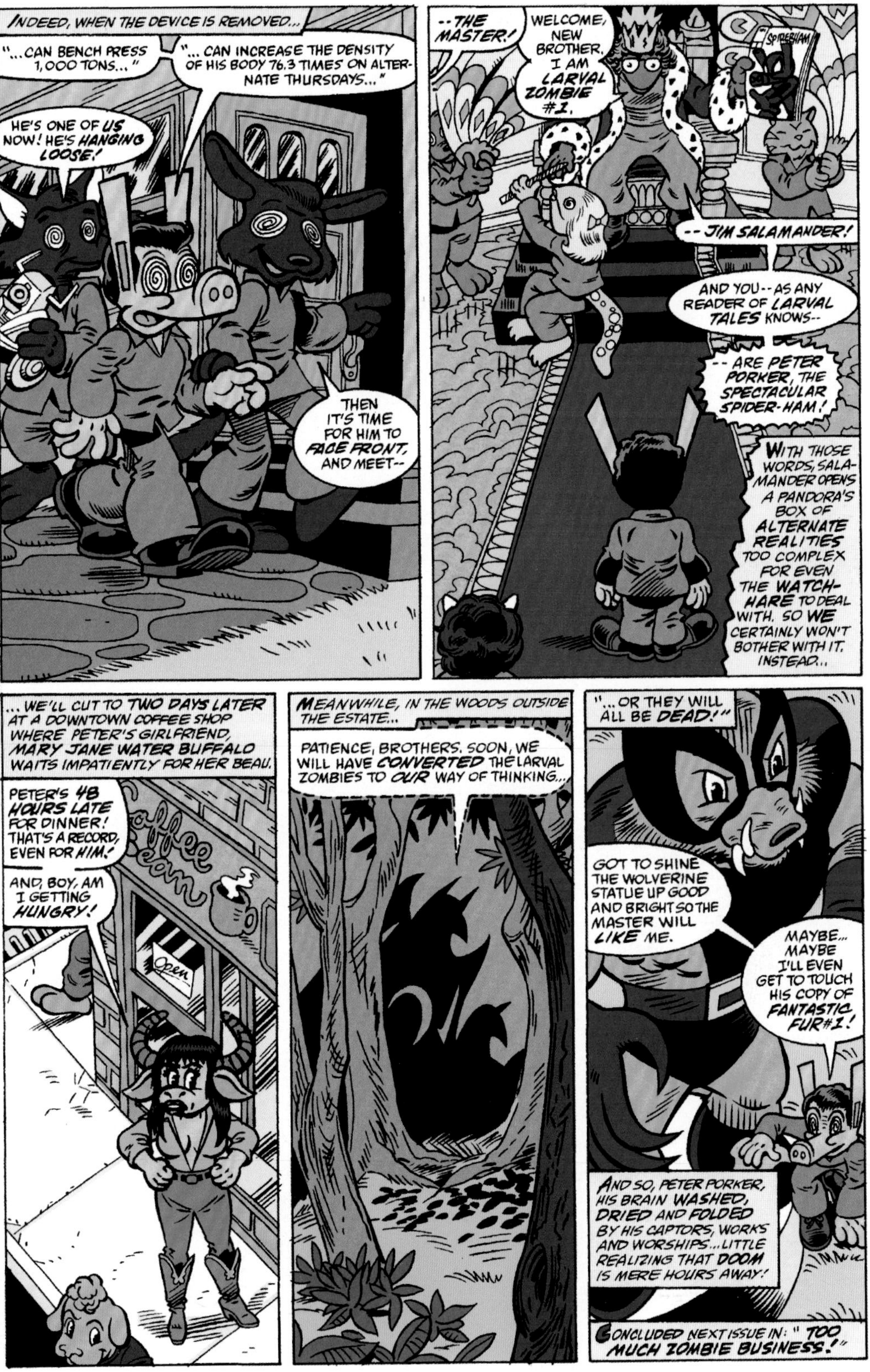
INDEED, WHEN THE DEVICE IS REMOVED...
"...CAN BENCH PRESS 1,000 TONS..."
"...CAN INCREASE THE DENSITY OF HIS BODY 76.3 TIMES ON ALTERNATE THURSDAYS..."
HE'S ONE OF US NOW! HE'S HANGING LOOSE!
THEN IT'S TIME FOR HIM TO FACE FRONT, AND MEET--
--THE MASTER!
WELCOME, NEW BROTHER. I AM LARVAL ZOMBIE #1.
SPIDERHAM
--JIM SALAMANDER!
AND YOU--AS ANY READER OF LARVAL TALES KNOWS--
--ARE PETER PORKER, THE SPECTACULAR SPIDER-HAM!
WITH THOSE WORDS, SALAMANDER OPENS A PANDORA'S BOX OF ALTERNATE REALITIES TOO COMPLEX FOR EVEN THE WATCH-HARE TO DEAL WITH. SO WE CERTAINLY WON'T BOTHER WITH IT. INSTEAD...
...WE'LL CUT TO TWO DAYS LATER AT A DOWNTOWN COFFEE SHOP WHERE PETER'S GIRLFRIEND, MARY JANE WATER BUFFALO WAITS IMPATIENTLY FOR HER BEAU.
PETER'S 48 HOURS LATE FOR DINNER! THAT'S A RECORD, EVEN FOR HIM!
AND, BOY, AM I GETTING HUNGRY!
Coffee Bean
Open
MEANWHILE, IN THE WOODS OUTSIDE THE ESTATE...
PATIENCE, BROTHERS. SOON, WE WILL HAVE CONVERTED THE LARVAL ZOMBIES TO OUR WAY OF THINKING...
"...OR THEY WILL ALL BE DEAD!"
GOT TO SHINE THE WOLVERINE STATUE UP GOOD AND BRIGHT SO THE MASTER WILL LIKE ME.
MAYBE... MAYBE I'LL EVEN GET TO TOUCH HIS COPY OF FANTASTIC FUR #1!
AND SO, PETER PORKER, HIS BRAIN WASHED, DRIED AND FOLDED BY HIS CAPTORS, WORKS AND WORSHIPS... LITTLE REALIZING THAT DOOM IS MERE HOURS AWAY!
CONCLUDED NEXT ISSUE IN: "TOO MUCH ZOMBIE BUSINESS!"

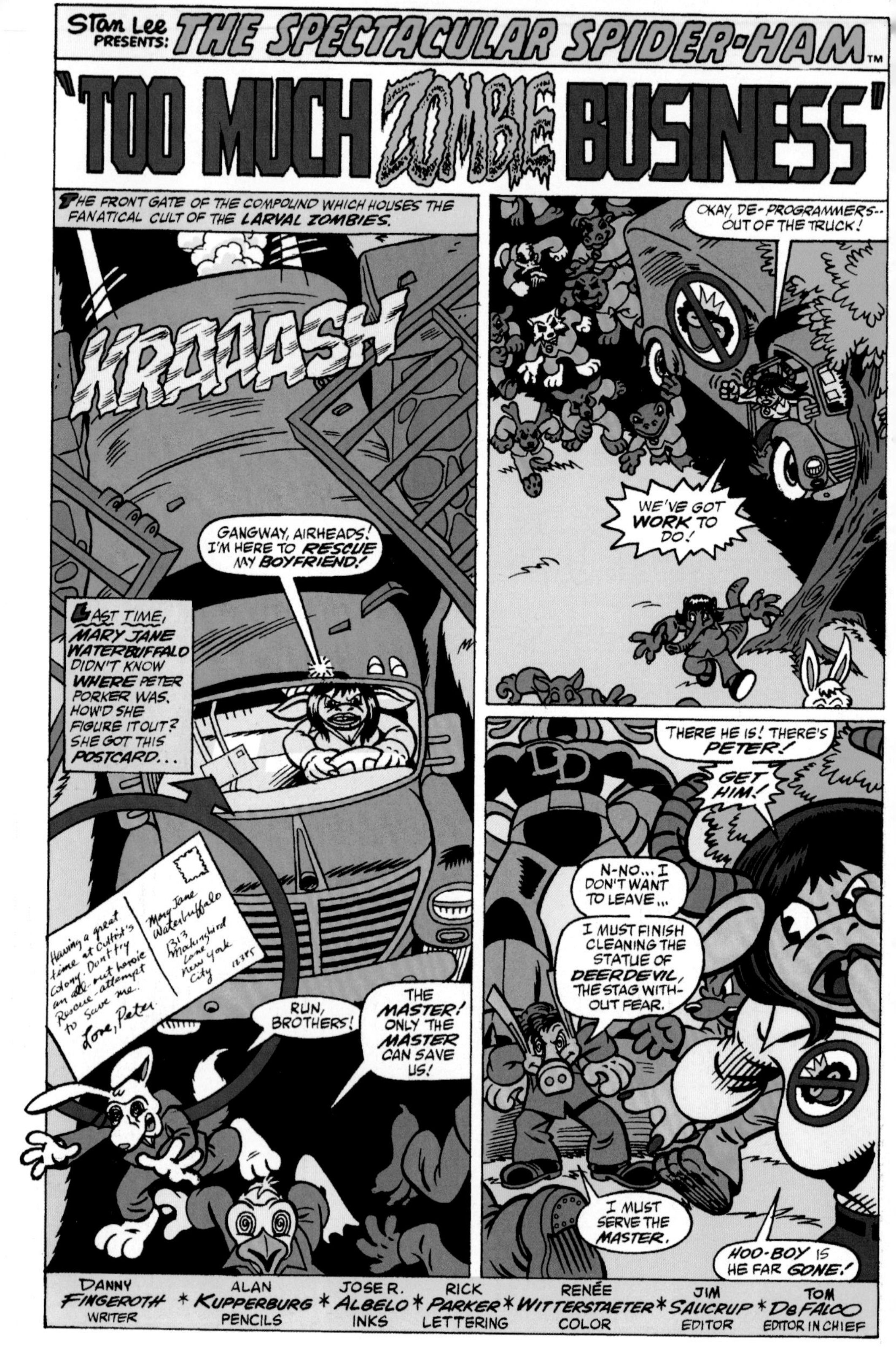
STAN LEE PRESENTS: THE SPECTACULAR SPIDER-HAM™
"TOO MUCH ZOMBIE BUSINESS"
THE FRONT GATE OF THE COMPOUND WHICH HOUSES THE FANATICAL CULT OF THE LARVAL ZOMBIES.
KRAAASH
GANGWAY, AIRHEADS! I'M HERE TO RESCUE MY BOYFRIEND!
LAST TIME, MARY JANE WATERBUFFALO DIDN'T KNOW WHERE PETER PORKER WAS. HOW'D SHE FIGURE IT OUT? SHE GOT THIS POSTCARD...
Having a great time at Cultist's Colony. Don't try an all-out heroic Rescue-attempt to save me. Love, Peter
Mary Jane Waterbuffalo 313 Mockingbird Lane New York City 12385
RUN, BROTHERS!
THE MASTER! ONLY THE MASTER CAN SAVE US!
OKAY, DE-PROGRAMMERS-- OUT OF THE TRUCK!
WE'VE GOT WORK TO DO!
THERE HE IS! THERE'S PETER!
GET HIM!
N-NO... I DON'T WANT TO LEAVE...
I MUST FINISH CLEANING THE STATUE OF DEERDEVIL, THE STAG WITH-OUT FEAR.
I MUST SERVE THE MASTER.
HOO-BOY IS HE FAR GONE!
DANNY FINGEROTH WRITER * ALAN KUPPERBURG PENCILS * JOSE R. ALBELO INKS * RICK PARKER LETTERING * RENÉE WITTERSTAETER COLOR * JIM SALICRUP EDITOR * TOM DEFALCO EDITOR IN CHIEF

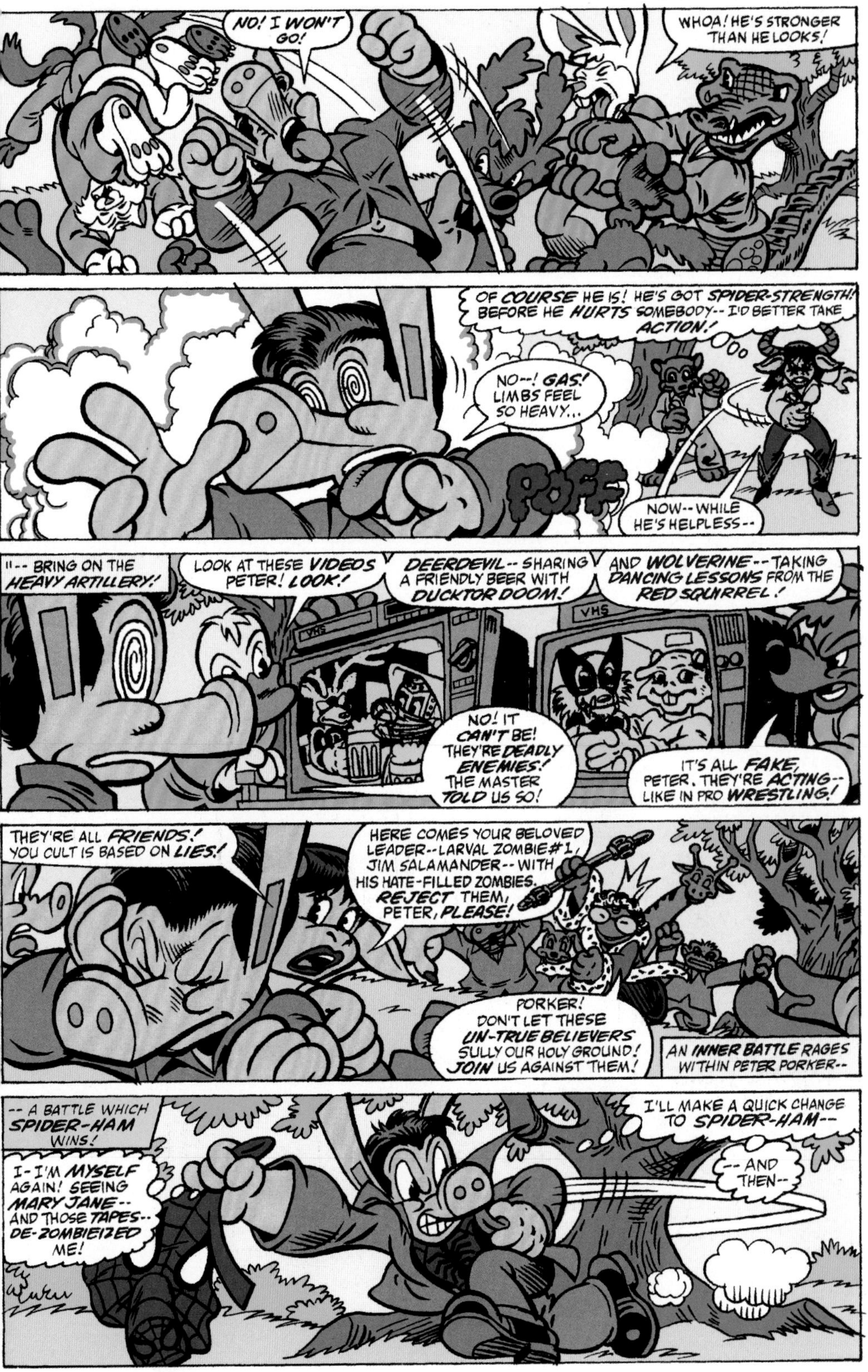
NO! I WON'T GO!
WHOA! HE'S STRONGER THAN HE LOOKS!
OF COURSE HE IS! HE'S GOT SPIDER-STRENGTH! BEFORE HE HURTS SOMEBODY-- I'D BETTER TAKE ACTION!
NO--! GAS! LIMBS FEEL SO HEAVY...
POFF
NOW-- WHILE HE'S HELPLESS--
"-- BRING ON THE HEAVY ARTILLERY!
LOOK AT THESE VIDEOS PETER! LOOK!
DEERDEVIL-- SHARING A FRIENDLY BEER WITH DUCKTOR DOOM!
AND WOLVERINE--TAKING DANCING LESSONS FROM THE RED SQUIRREL!
VHS
VHS
NO! IT CAN'T BE! THEY'RE DEADLY ENEMIES! THE MASTER TOLD US SO!
IT'S ALL FAKE, PETER. THEY'RE ACTING-- LIKE IN PRO WRESTLING!
THEY'RE ALL FRIENDS! YOU CULT IS BASED ON LIES!
HERE COMES YOUR BELOVED LEADER--LARVAL ZOMBIE #1, JIM SALAMANDER-- WITH HIS HATE-FILLED ZOMBIES. REJECT THEM, PETER, PLEASE!
PORKER! DON'T LET THESE UN-TRUE BELIEVERS SULLY OUR HOLY GROUND! JOIN US AGAINST THEM!
AN INNER BATTLE RAGES WITHIN PETER PORKER--
-- A BATTLE WHICH SPIDER-HAM WINS!
I'LL MAKE A QUICK CHANGE TO SPIDER-HAM--
I-I'M MYSELF AGAIN! SEEING MARY JANE-- AND THOSE TAPES-- DE-ZOMBIEIZED ME!
-- AND THEN--

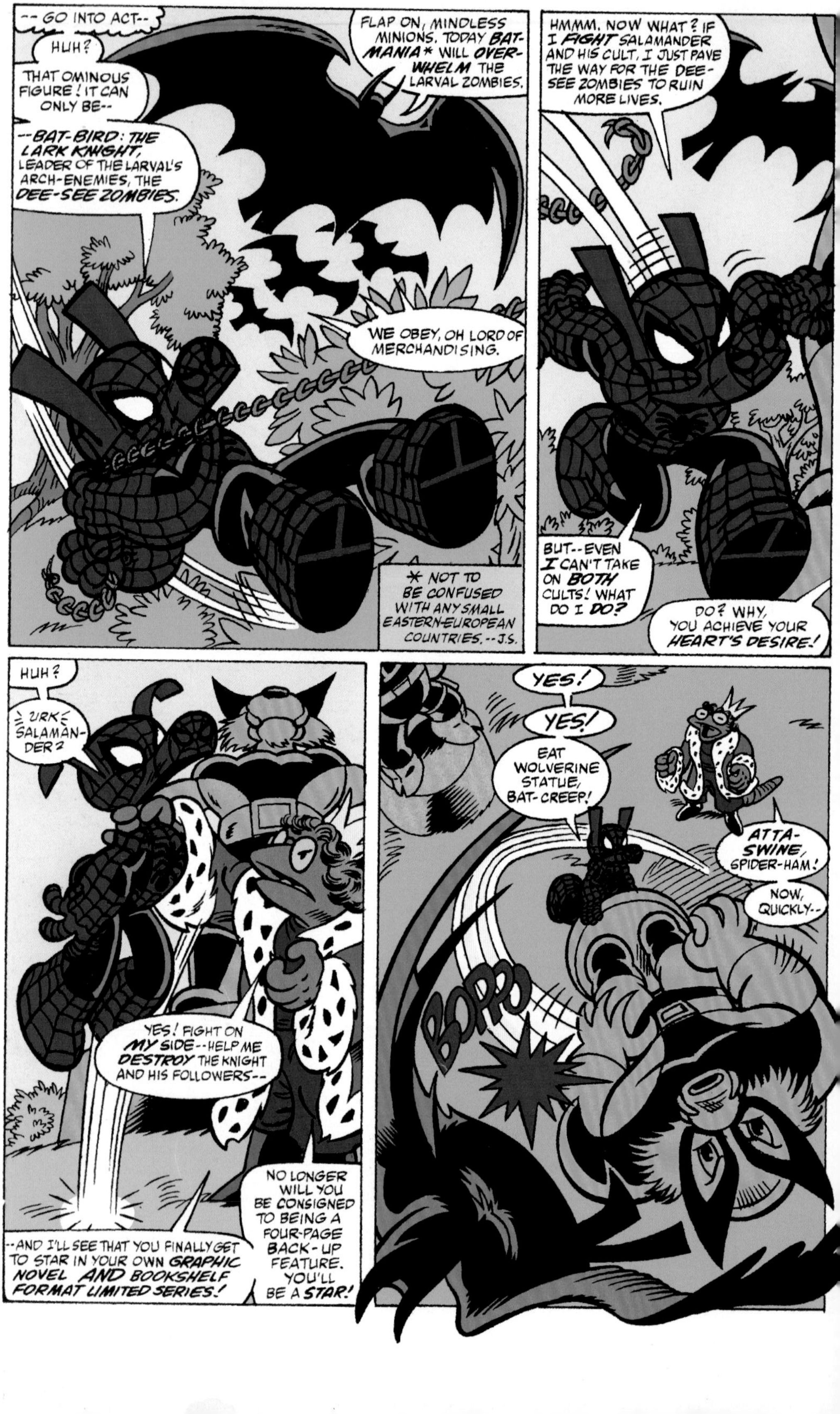

-- GO INTO ACT--
HUH?
THAT OMINOUS FIGURE! IT CAN ONLY BE--
--BAT-BIRD: THE LARK KNIGHT, LEADER OF THE LARVAL'S ARCH-ENEMIES, THE DEE-SEE ZOMBIES.
FLAP ON, MINDLESS MINIONS. TODAY BAT-MANIA* WILL OVER-WHELM THE LARVAL ZOMBIES.
WE OBEY, OH LORD OF MERCHANDISING.
* NOT TO BE CONFUSED WITH ANY SMALL EASTERN-EUROPEAN COUNTRIES. --J.S.
HMMM. NOW WHAT? IF I FIGHT SALAMANDER AND HIS CULT, I JUST PAVE THE WAY FOR THE DEE-SEE ZOMBIES TO RUIN MORE LIVES.
BUT--EVEN I CAN'T TAKE ON BOTH CULTS! WHAT DO I DO?
DO? WHY, YOU ACHIEVE YOUR HEART'S DESIRE!
HUH?
URK SALAMANDER?
YES! FIGHT ON MY SIDE--HELP ME DESTROY THE KNIGHT AND HIS FOLLOWERS--
--AND I'LL SEE THAT YOU FINALLY GET TO STAR IN YOUR OWN GRAPHIC NOVEL AND BOOKSHELF FORMAT LIMITED SERIES!
NO LONGER WILL YOU BE CONSIGNED TO BEING A FOUR-PAGE BACK-UP FEATURE. YOU'LL BE A STAR!
YES!
YES!
EAT WOLVERINE STATUE, BAT-CREEP!
ATTA-SWINE, SPIDER-HAM!
NOW, QUICKLY--
BOPP

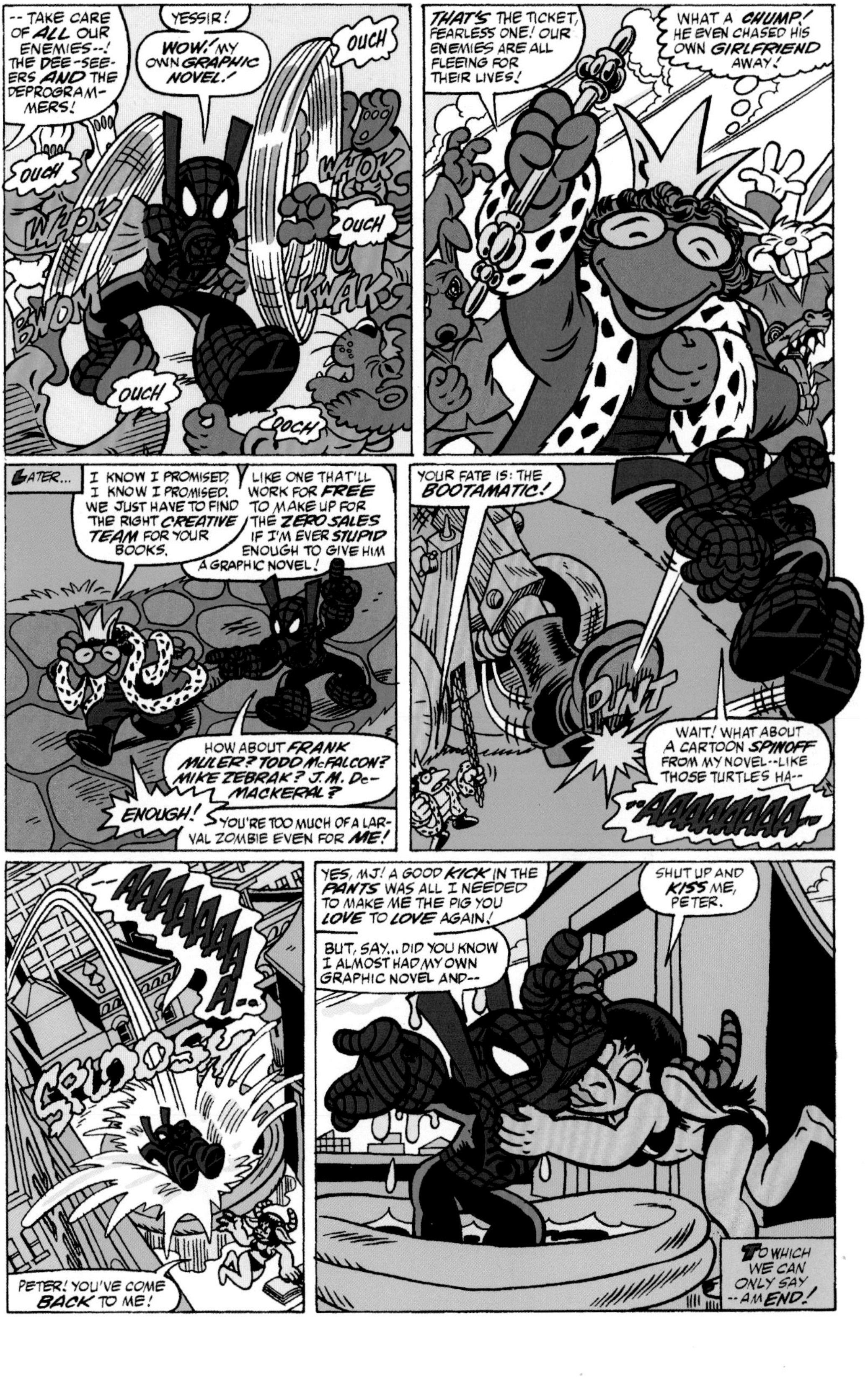
-- TAKE CARE OF ALL OUR ENEMIES--! THE DEE-SEE-ERS AND THE DEPROGRAM-MERS!
YESSIR!
WOW! MY OWN GRAPHIC NOVEL!
OUCH
OUCH
WHOK
BWOM
WHOK
OUCH
KWAK
OUCH
OOCH
THAT'S THE TICKET, FEARLESS ONE! OUR ENEMIES ARE ALL FLEEING FOR THEIR LIVES!
WHAT A CHUMP! HE EVEN CHASED HIS OWN GIRLFRIEND AWAY!
LATER...
I KNOW I PROMISED, I KNOW I PROMISED. WE JUST HAVE TO FIND THE RIGHT CREATIVE TEAM FOR YOUR BOOKS.
LIKE ONE THAT'LL WORK FOR FREE TO MAKE UP FOR THE ZERO SALES IF I'M EVER STUPID ENOUGH TO GIVE HIM A GRAPHIC NOVEL!
HOW ABOUT FRANK MULER? TODD McFALCON? MIKE ZEBRAK? J.M. De-MACKERAL?
ENOUGH!
YOU'RE TOO MUCH OF A LAR-VAL ZOMBIE EVEN FOR ME!
YOUR FATE IS: THE BOOTAMATIC!
PUNT
WAIT! WHAT ABOUT A CARTOON SPINOFF FROM MY NOVEL--LIKE THOSE TURTLES HA--
--AAAAAAAAA--
--AAAAAAAAAAA--
SPLOOSH
PETER! YOU'VE COME BACK TO ME!
YES, MJ! A GOOD KICK IN THE PANTS WAS ALL I NEEDED TO MAKE ME THE PIG YOU LOVE TO LOVE AGAIN!
BUT, SAY... DID YOU KNOW I ALMOST HAD MY OWN GRAPHIC NOVEL AND--
SHUT UP AND KISS ME, PETER.
TO WHICH WE CAN ONLY SAY --AM END!

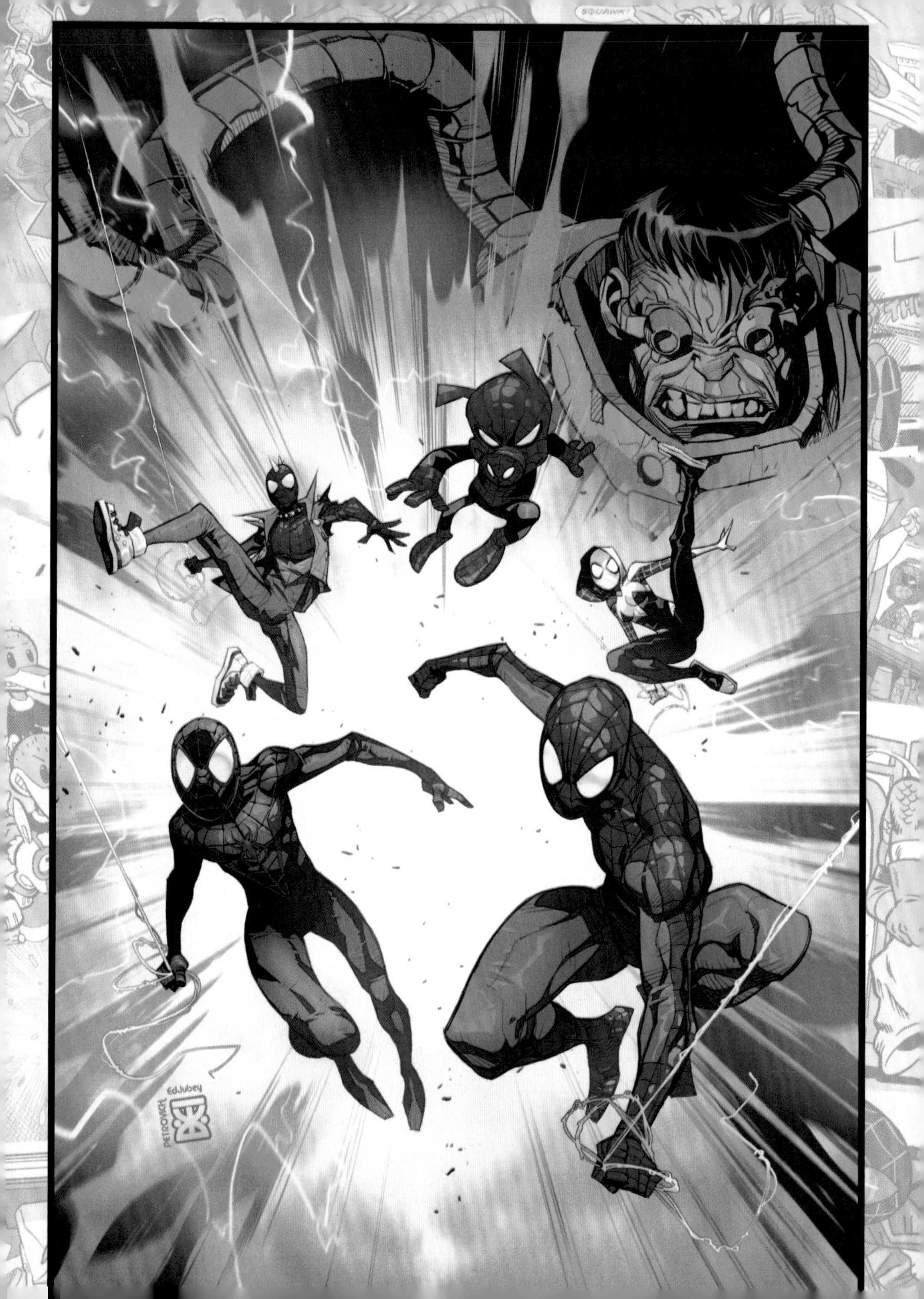
SQUAWK!
EdJubey
PETROVICH

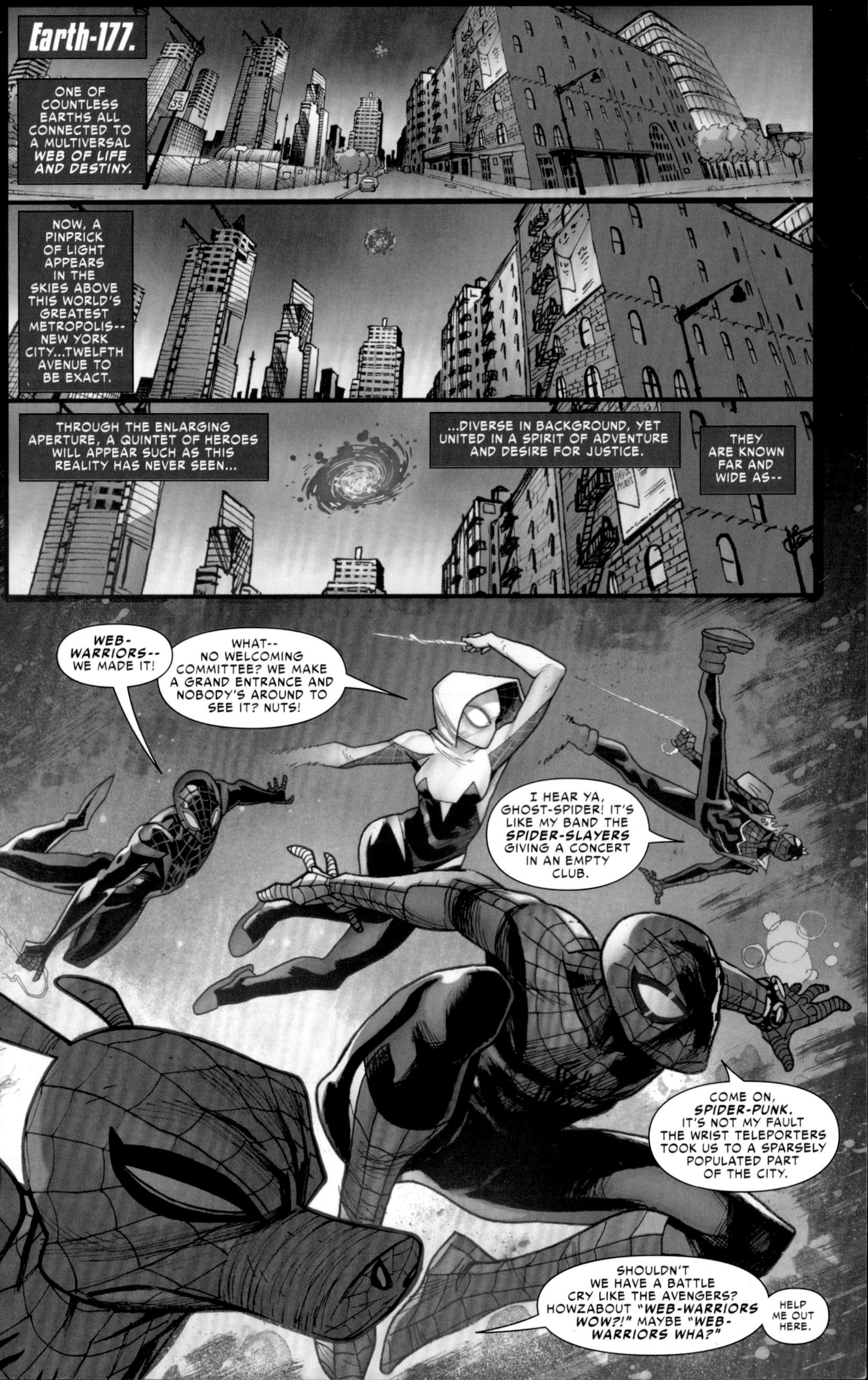
Earth-177.
ONE OF COUNTLESS EARTHS ALL CONNECTED TO A MULTIVERSAL WEB OF LIFE AND DESTINY.
NOW, A PINPRICK OF LIGHT APPEARS IN THE SKIES ABOVE THIS WORLD'S GREATEST METROPOLIS--NEW YORK CITY...TWELFTH AVENUE TO BE EXACT.
THROUGH THE ENLARGING APERTURE, A QUINTET OF HEROES WILL APPEAR SUCH AS THIS REALITY HAS NEVER SEEN...
...DIVERSE IN BACKGROUND, YET UNITED IN A SPIRIT OF ADVENTURE AND DESIRE FOR JUSTICE.
THEY ARE KNOWN FAR AND WIDE AS--
WEB-WARRIORS--WE MADE IT!
WHAT--NO WELCOMING COMMITTEE? WE MAKE A GRAND ENTRANCE AND NOBODY'S AROUND TO SEE IT? NUTS!
I HEAR YA, GHOST-SPIDER! IT'S LIKE MY BAND THE SPIDER-SLAYERS GIVING A CONCERT IN AN EMPTY CLUB.
COME ON, SPIDER-PUNK. IT'S NOT MY FAULT THE WRIST TELEPORTERS TOOK US TO A SPARSELY POPULATED PART OF THE CITY.
SHOULDN'T WE HAVE A BATTLE CRY LIKE THE AVENGERS? HOWZABOUT "WEB-WARRIORS WOW?!" MAYBE "WEB-WARRIORS WHA?"
HELP ME OUT HERE.

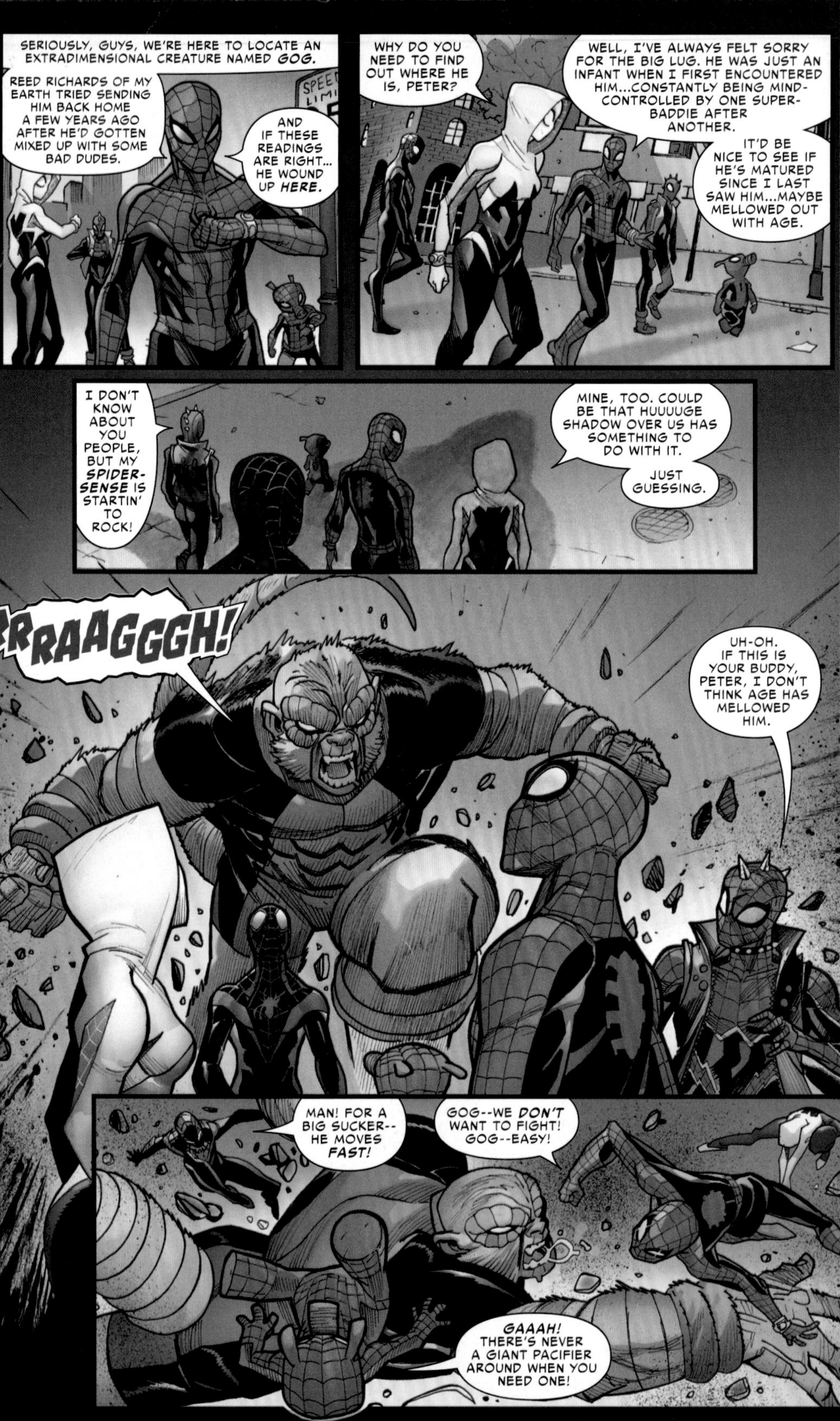
SERIOUSLY, GUYS, WE'RE HERE TO LOCATE AN EXTRADIMENSIONAL CREATURE NAMED GOG.
REED RICHARDS OF MY EARTH TRIED SENDING HIM BACK HOME A FEW YEARS AGO AFTER HE'D GOTTEN MIXED UP WITH SOME BAD DUDES.
AND IF THESE READINGS ARE RIGHT... HE WOUND UP HERE.
WHY DO YOU NEED TO FIND OUT WHERE HE IS, PETER?
WELL, I'VE ALWAYS FELT SORRY FOR THE BIG LUG. HE WAS JUST AN INFANT WHEN I FIRST ENCOUNTERED HIM...CONSTANTLY BEING MIND-CONTROLLED BY ONE SUPER-BADDIE AFTER ANOTHER.
IT'D BE NICE TO SEE IF HE'S MATURED SINCE I LAST SAW HIM...MAYBE MELLOWED OUT WITH AGE.
I DON'T KNOW ABOUT YOU PEOPLE, BUT MY SPIDER-SENSE IS STARTIN' TO ROCK!
MINE, TOO. COULD BE THAT HUUUUGE SHADOW OVER US HAS SOMETHING TO DO WITH IT.
JUST GUESSING.
RRRAAGGGH!
UH-OH. IF THIS IS YOUR BUDDY, PETER, I DON'T THINK AGE HAS MELLOWED HIM.
MAN! FOR A BIG SUCKER-- HE MOVES FAST!
GOG--WE DON'T WANT TO FIGHT! GOG--EASY!
GAAAH! THERE'S NEVER A GIANT PACIFIER AROUND WHEN YOU NEED ONE!

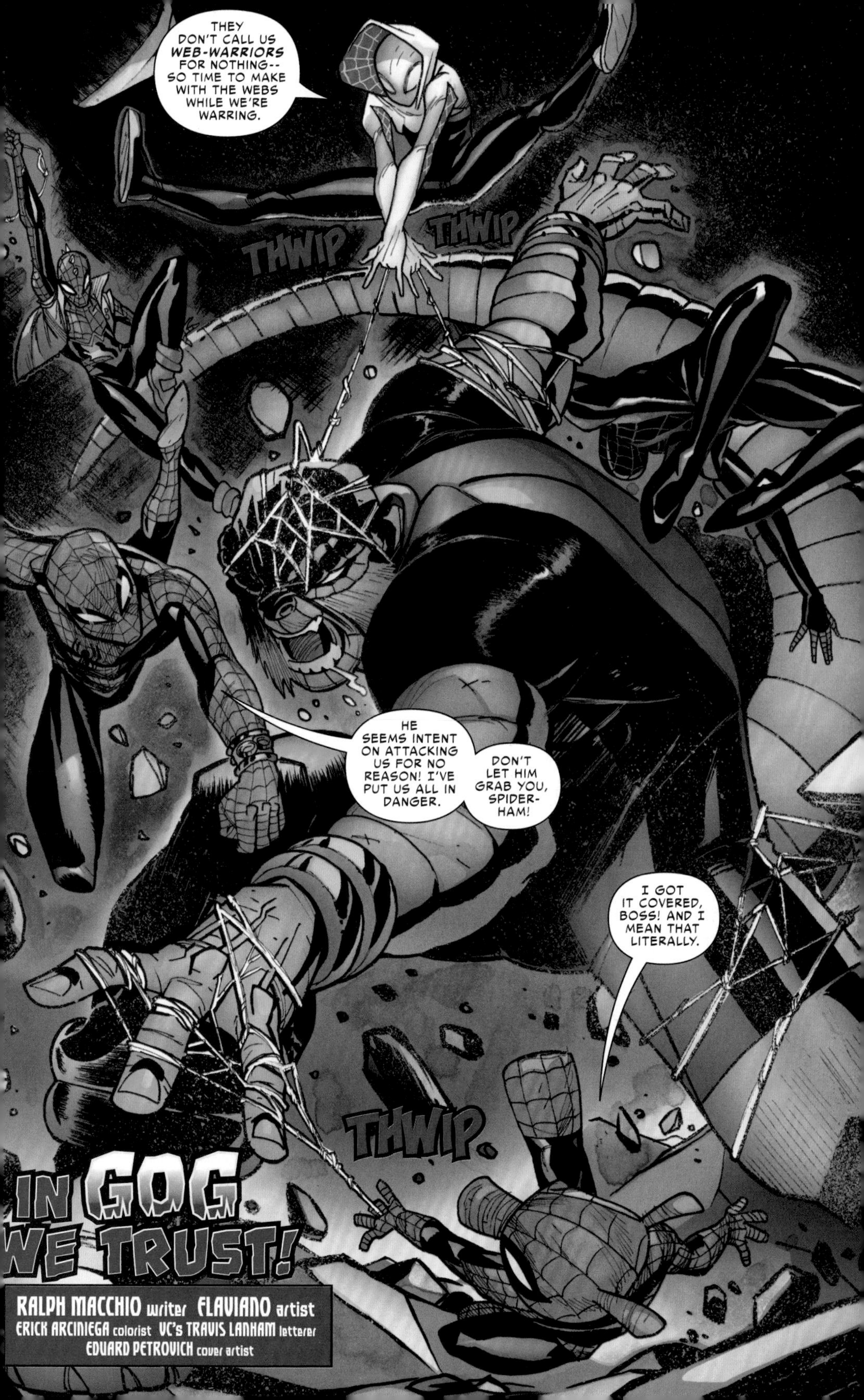
THEY DON'T CALL US WEB-WARRIORS FOR NOTHING-- SO TIME TO MAKE WITH THE WEBS WHILE WE'RE WARRING.
THWIP
THWIP
HE SEEMS INTENT ON ATTACKING US FOR NO REASON! I'VE PUT US ALL IN DANGER.
DON'T LET HIM GRAB YOU, SPIDER-HAM!
I GOT IT COVERED, BOSS! AND I MEAN THAT LITERALLY.
THWIP
IN GOG WE TRUST!
RALPH MACCHIO writer FLAVIANO artist
ERICK ARCINIEGA colorist VC's TRAVIS LANHAM letterer
EDUARD PETROVICH cover artist

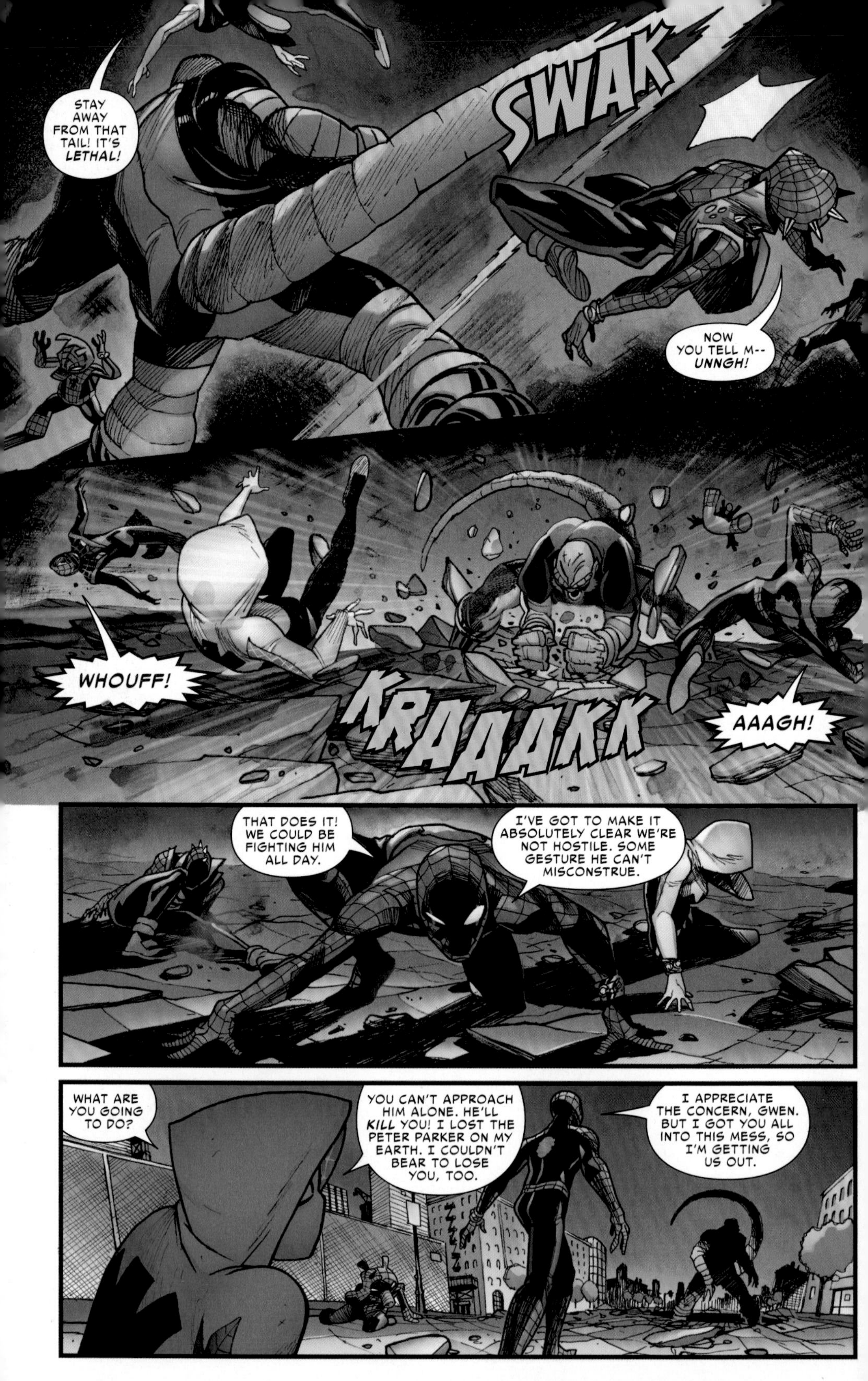
STAY AWAY FROM THAT TAIL! IT'S *LETHAL!*
SWAK
NOW YOU TELL M-- *UNNGH!*
WHOUFF!
KRAAAAKK
AAAGH!
THAT DOES IT! WE COULD BE FIGHTING HIM ALL DAY.
I'VE GOT TO MAKE IT ABSOLUTELY CLEAR WE'RE NOT HOSTILE. SOME GESTURE HE CAN'T MISCONSTRUE.
WHAT ARE YOU GOING TO DO?
YOU CAN'T APPROACH HIM ALONE. HE'LL *KILL* YOU! I LOST THE PETER PARKER ON MY EARTH. I COULDN'T BEAR TO LOSE YOU, TOO.
I APPRECIATE THE CONCERN, GWEN. BUT I GOT YOU ALL INTO THIS MESS, SO I'M GETTING US OUT.

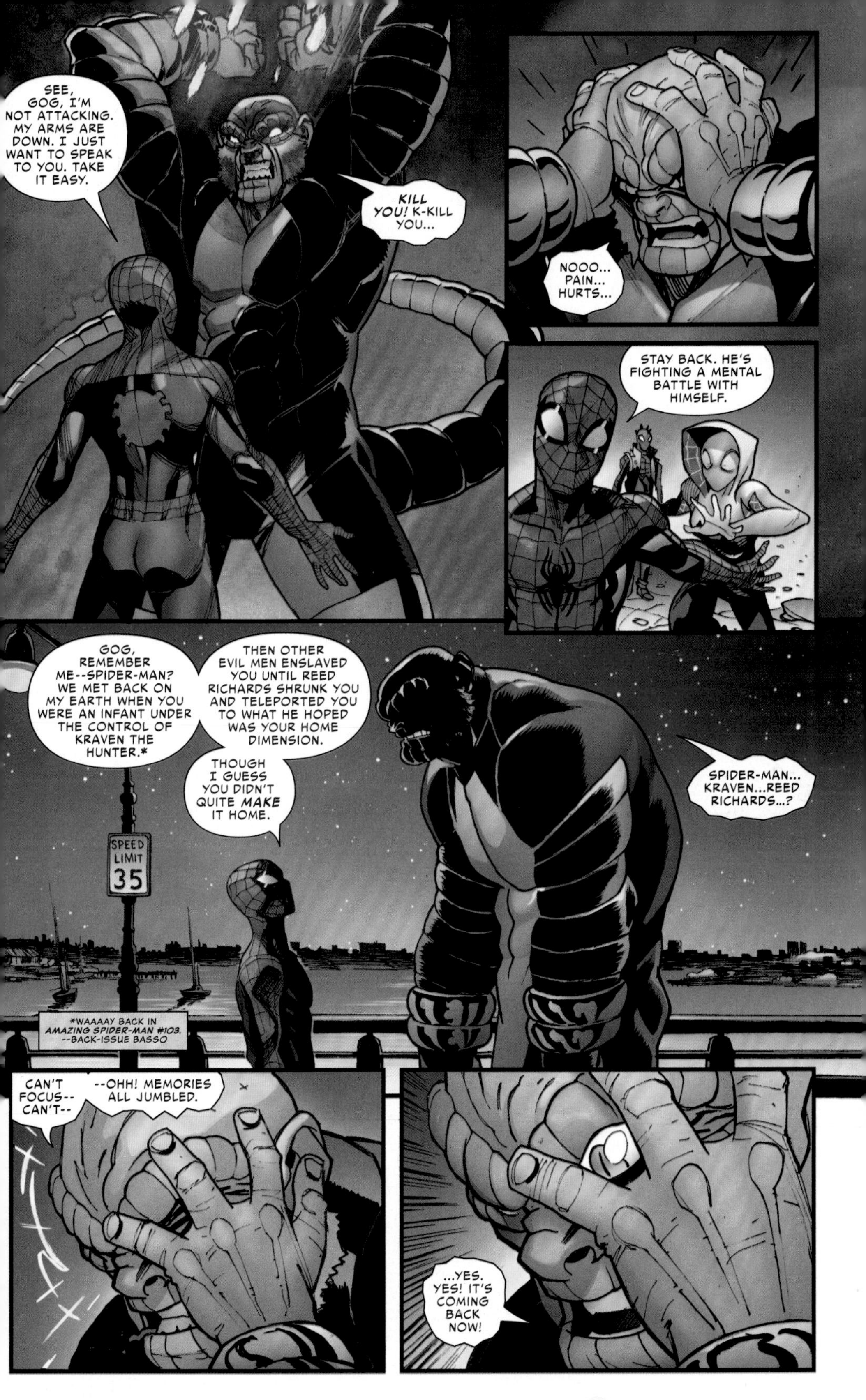

SEE, GOG, I'M NOT ATTACKING. MY ARMS ARE DOWN. I JUST WANT TO SPEAK TO YOU. TAKE IT EASY.
KILL YOU! K-KILL YOU...
NOOO... PAIN... HURTS...
STAY BACK. HE'S FIGHTING A MENTAL BATTLE WITH HIMSELF.
GOG, REMEMBER ME--SPIDER-MAN? WE MET BACK ON MY EARTH WHEN YOU WERE AN INFANT UNDER THE CONTROL OF KRAVEN THE HUNTER.*
THEN OTHER EVIL MEN ENSLAVED YOU UNTIL REED RICHARDS SHRUNK YOU AND TELEPORTED YOU TO WHAT HE HOPED WAS YOUR HOME DIMENSION.
THOUGH I GUESS YOU DIDN'T QUITE MAKE IT HOME.
SPIDER-MAN... KRAVEN...REED RICHARDS...?
SPEED LIMIT 35
*WAAAAY BACK IN AMAZING SPIDER-MAN #103. --BACK-ISSUE BASSO
CAN'T FOCUS-- CAN'T--
--OHH! MEMORIES ALL JUMBLED.
...YES. YES! IT'S COMING BACK NOW!

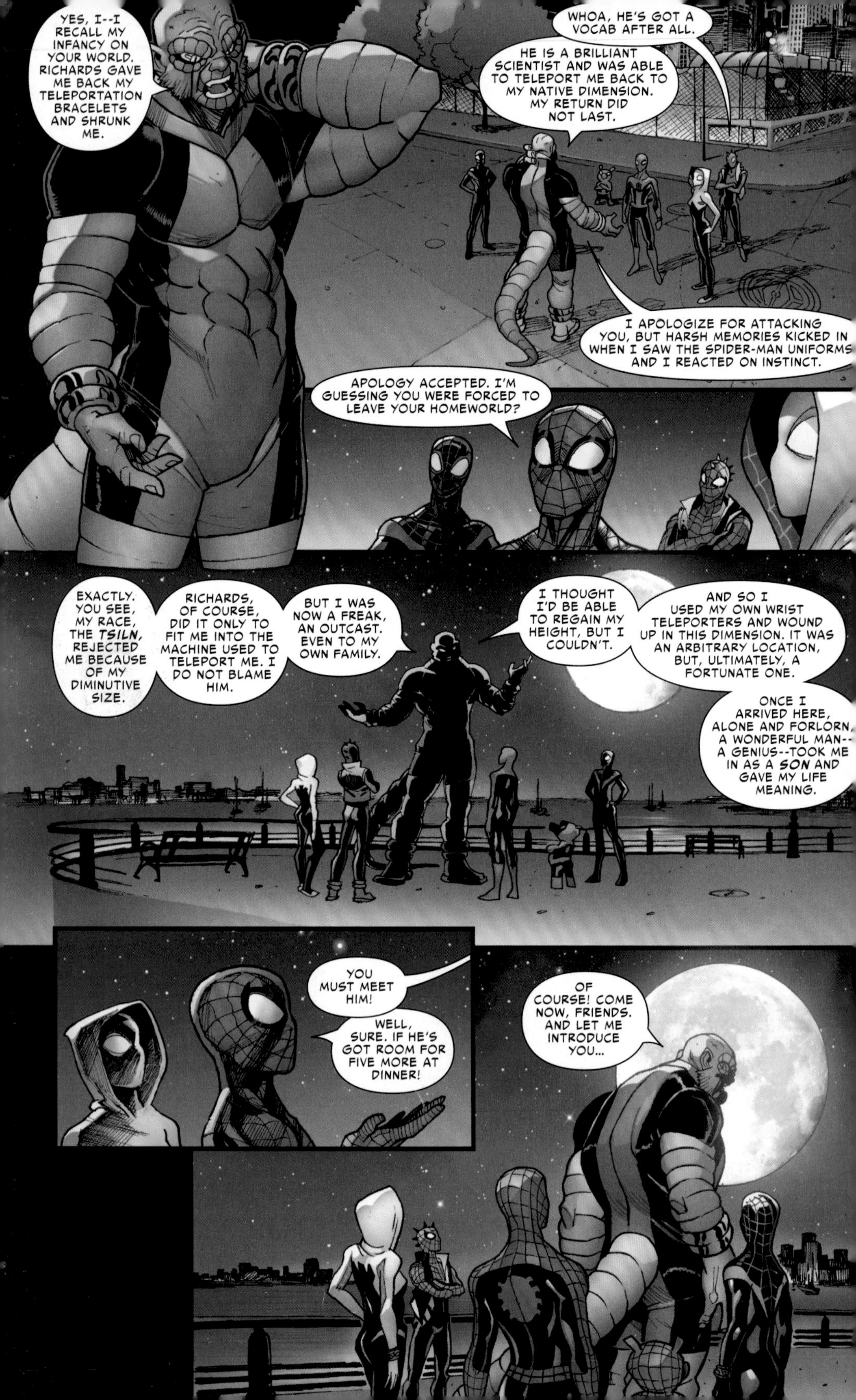

YES, I--I RECALL MY INFANCY ON YOUR WORLD. RICHARDS GAVE ME BACK MY TELEPORTATION BRACELETS AND SHRUNK ME.
WHOA, HE'S GOT A VOCAB AFTER ALL.
HE IS A BRILLIANT SCIENTIST AND WAS ABLE TO TELEPORT ME BACK TO MY NATIVE DIMENSION. MY RETURN DID NOT LAST.
I APOLOGIZE FOR ATTACKING YOU, BUT HARSH MEMORIES KICKED IN WHEN I SAW THE SPIDER-MAN UNIFORMS AND I REACTED ON INSTINCT.
APOLOGY ACCEPTED. I'M GUESSING YOU WERE FORCED TO LEAVE YOUR HOMEWORLD?
EXACTLY. YOU SEE, MY RACE, THE *TSILN*, REJECTED ME BECAUSE OF MY DIMINUTIVE SIZE.
RICHARDS, OF COURSE, DID IT ONLY TO FIT ME INTO THE MACHINE USED TO TELEPORT ME. I DO NOT BLAME HIM.
BUT I WAS NOW A FREAK, AN OUTCAST. EVEN TO MY OWN FAMILY.
I THOUGHT I'D BE ABLE TO REGAIN MY HEIGHT, BUT I COULDN'T.
AND SO I USED MY OWN WRIST TELEPORTERS AND WOUND UP IN THIS DIMENSION. IT WAS AN ARBITRARY LOCATION, BUT, ULTIMATELY, A FORTUNATE ONE.
ONCE I ARRIVED HERE, ALONE AND FORLORN, A WONDERFUL MAN--A GENIUS--TOOK ME IN AS A *SON* AND GAVE MY LIFE MEANING.
YOU MUST MEET HIM!
WELL, SURE. IF HE'S GOT ROOM FOR FIVE MORE AT DINNER!
OF COURSE! COME NOW, FRIENDS. AND LET ME INTRODUCE YOU...

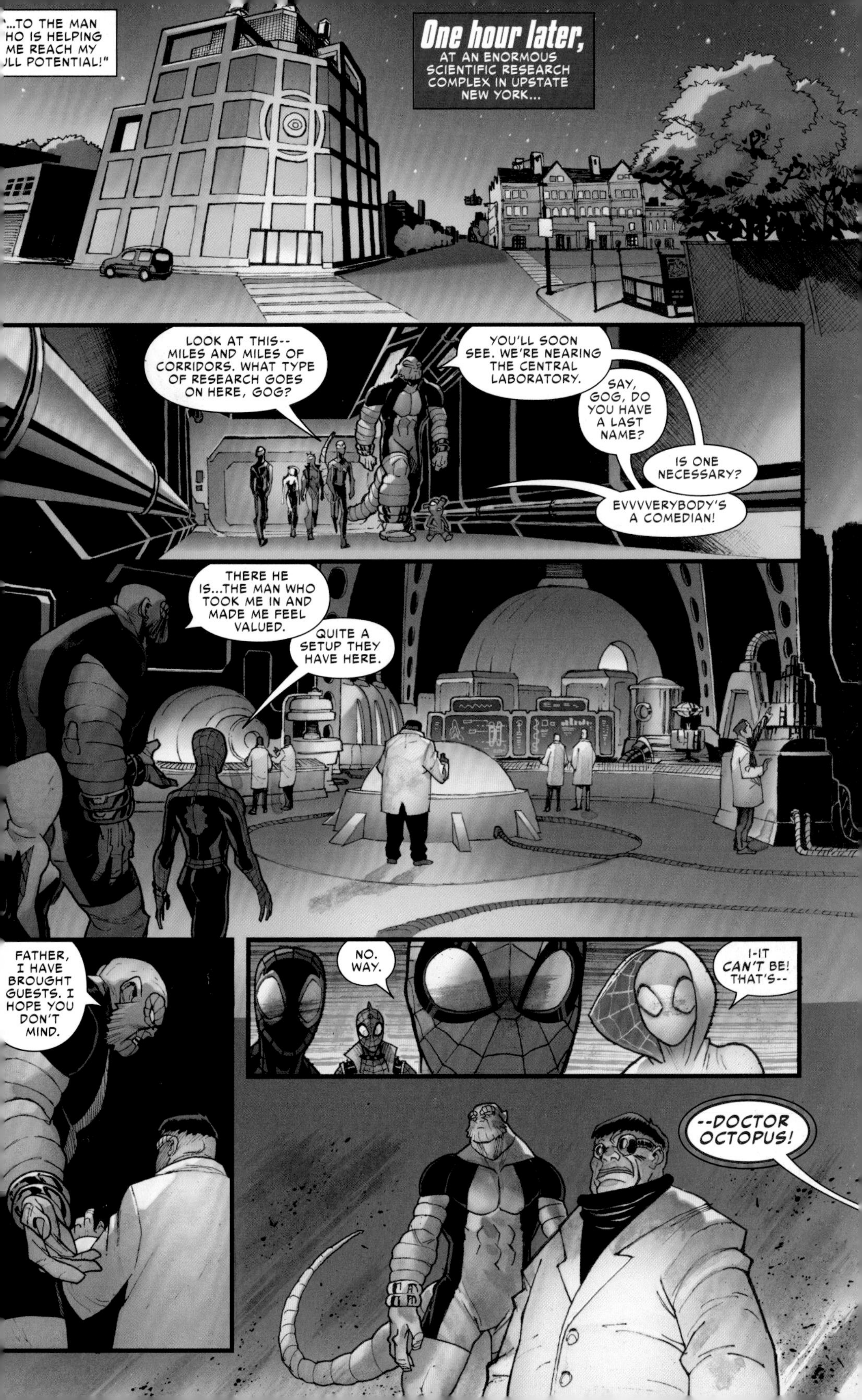
...TO THE MAN
HO IS HELPING
ME REACH MY
LL POTENTIAL!"
One hour later, AT AN ENORMOUS SCIENTIFIC RESEARCH COMPLEX IN UPSTATE NEW YORK...
LOOK AT THIS-- MILES AND MILES OF CORRIDORS. WHAT TYPE OF RESEARCH GOES ON HERE, GOG?
YOU'LL SOON SEE. WE'RE NEARING THE CENTRAL LABORATORY.
SAY, GOG, DO YOU HAVE A LAST NAME?
IS ONE NECESSARY?
EVVVVERYBODY'S A COMEDIAN!
THERE HE IS...THE MAN WHO TOOK ME IN AND MADE ME FEEL VALUED.
QUITE A SETUP THEY HAVE HERE.
FATHER, I HAVE BROUGHT GUESTS. I HOPE YOU DON'T MIND.
NO. WAY.
I-IT CAN'T BE! THAT'S--
--DOCTOR OCTOPUS!

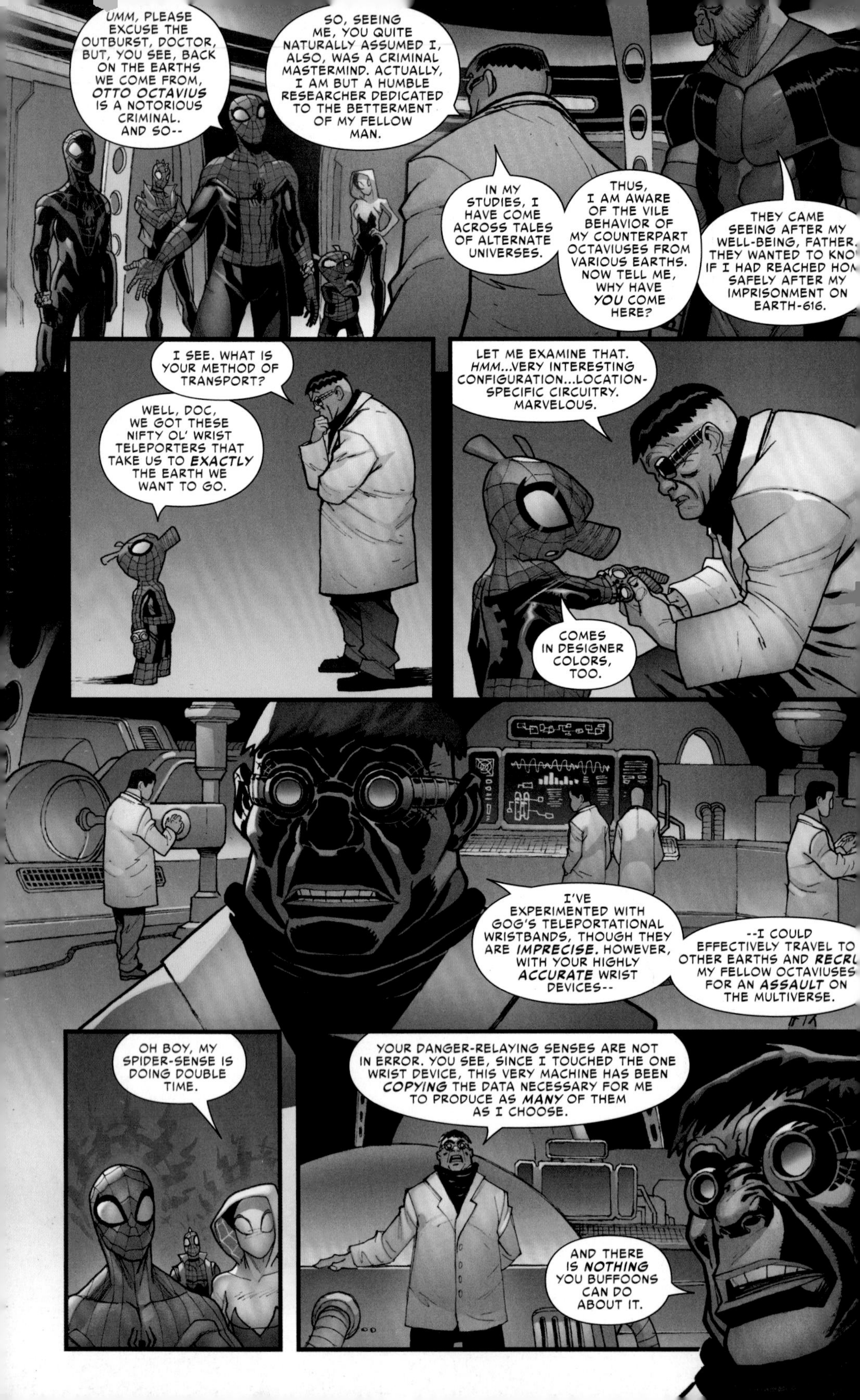
UMM, PLEASE EXCUSE THE OUTBURST, DOCTOR, BUT, YOU SEE, BACK ON THE EARTHS WE COME FROM, *OTTO OCTAVIUS* IS A NOTORIOUS CRIMINAL. AND SO--
SO, SEEING ME, YOU QUITE NATURALLY ASSUMED I, ALSO, WAS A CRIMINAL MASTERMIND. ACTUALLY, I AM BUT A HUMBLE RESEARCHER DEDICATED TO THE BETTERMENT OF MY FELLOW MAN.
IN MY STUDIES, I HAVE COME ACROSS TALES OF ALTERNATE UNIVERSES.
THUS, I AM AWARE OF THE VILE BEHAVIOR OF MY COUNTERPART OCTAVIUSES FROM VARIOUS EARTHS. NOW TELL ME, WHY HAVE *YOU* COME HERE?
THEY CAME SEEING AFTER MY WELL-BEING, FATHER. THEY WANTED TO KNO IF I HAD REACHED HOM SAFELY AFTER MY IMPRISONMENT ON EARTH-616.
I SEE. WHAT IS YOUR METHOD OF TRANSPORT?
WELL, DOC, WE GOT THESE NIFTY OL' WRIST TELEPORTERS THAT TAKE US TO *EXACTLY* THE EARTH WE WANT TO GO.
LET ME EXAMINE THAT. *HMM*...VERY INTERESTING CONFIGURATION...LOCATION-SPECIFIC CIRCUITRY. MARVELOUS.
COMES IN DESIGNER COLORS, TOO.
I'VE EXPERIMENTED WITH GOG'S TELEPORTATIONAL WRISTBANDS, THOUGH THEY ARE *IMPRECISE*. HOWEVER, WITH YOUR HIGHLY *ACCURATE* WRIST DEVICES--
--I COULD EFFECTIVELY TRAVEL TO OTHER EARTHS AND *RECRU* MY FELLOW OCTAVIUSES FOR AN *ASSAULT* ON THE MULTIVERSE.
OH BOY, MY SPIDER-SENSE IS DOING DOUBLE TIME.
YOUR DANGER-RELAYING SENSES ARE NOT IN ERROR. YOU SEE, SINCE I TOUCHED THE ONE WRIST DEVICE, THIS VERY MACHINE HAS BEEN *COPYING* THE DATA NECESSARY FOR ME TO PRODUCE AS *MANY* OF THEM AS I CHOOSE.
AND THERE IS *NOTHING* YOU BUFFOONS CAN DO ABOUT IT.

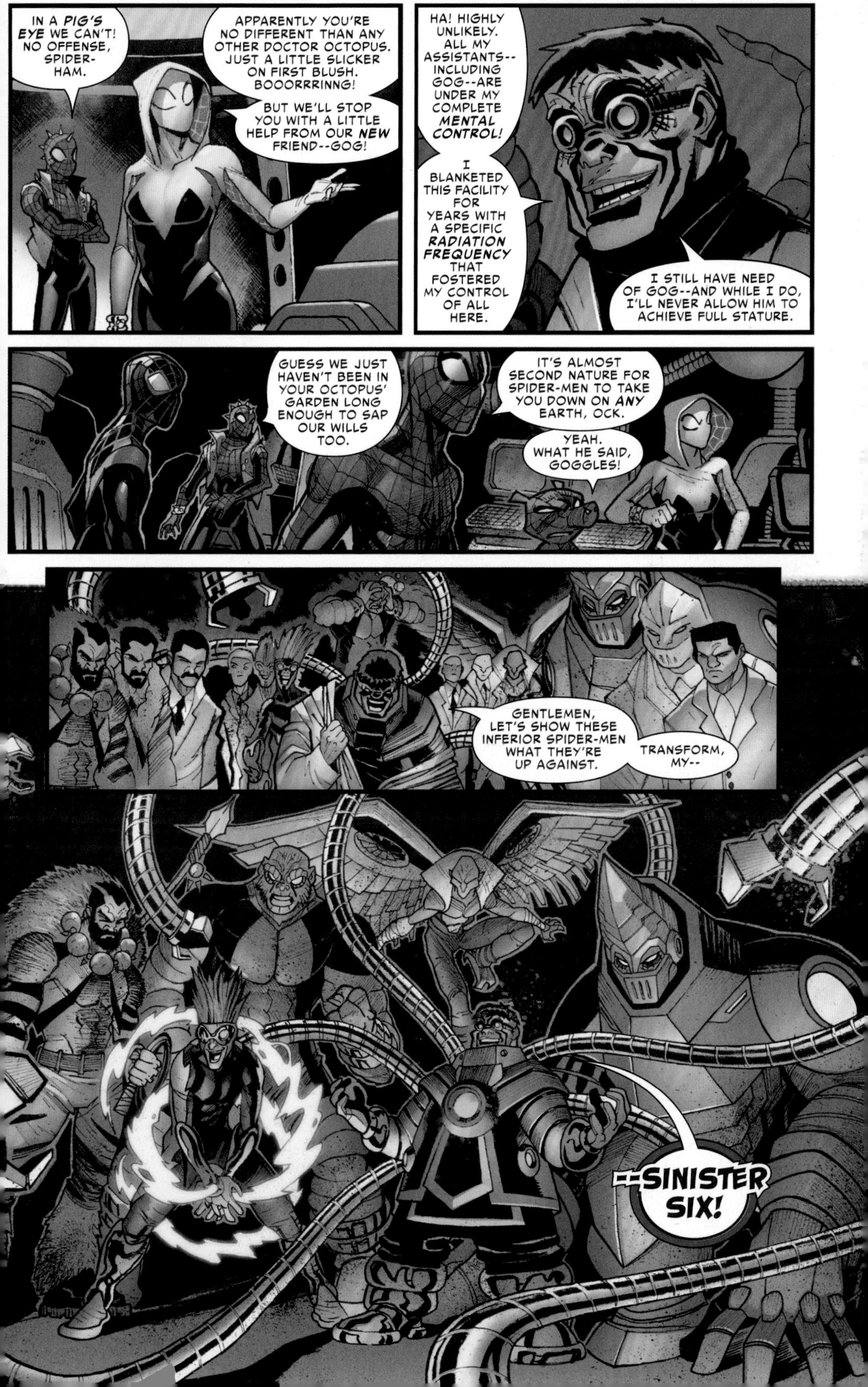
IN A PIG'S EYE WE CAN'T! NO OFFENSE, SPIDER-HAM.
APPARENTLY YOU'RE NO DIFFERENT THAN ANY OTHER DOCTOR OCTOPUS. JUST A LITTLE SLICKER ON FIRST BLUSH. BOOORRRINNG!
BUT WE'LL STOP YOU WITH A LITTLE HELP FROM OUR NEW FRIEND--GOG!
HA! HIGHLY UNLIKELY. ALL MY ASSISTANTS--INCLUDING GOG--ARE UNDER MY COMPLETE MENTAL CONTROL!
I BLANKETED THIS FACILITY FOR YEARS WITH A SPECIFIC RADIATION FREQUENCY THAT FOSTERED MY CONTROL OF ALL HERE.
I STILL HAVE NEED OF GOG--AND WHILE I DO, I'LL NEVER ALLOW HIM TO ACHIEVE FULL STATURE.
GUESS WE JUST HAVEN'T BEEN IN YOUR OCTOPUS' GARDEN LONG ENOUGH TO SAP OUR WILLS TOO.
IT'S ALMOST SECOND NATURE FOR SPIDER-MEN TO TAKE YOU DOWN ON ANY EARTH, OCK.
YEAH. WHAT HE SAID, GOGGLES!
GENTLEMEN, LET'S SHOW THESE INFERIOR SPIDER-MEN WHAT THEY'RE UP AGAINST.
TRANSFORM, MY--
--SINISTER SIX!

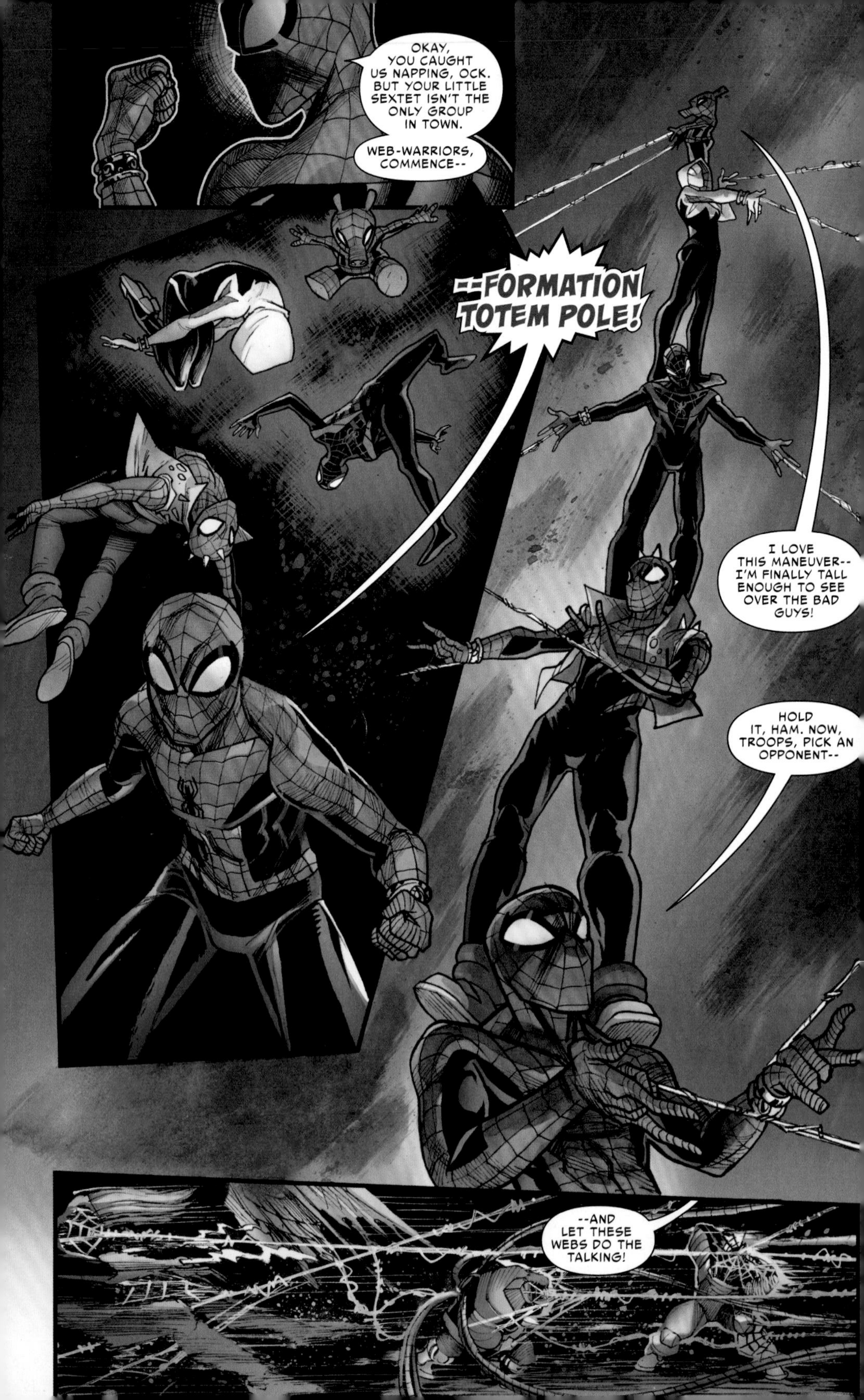
OKAY, YOU CAUGHT US NAPPING, OCK. BUT YOUR LITTLE SEXTET ISN'T THE ONLY GROUP IN TOWN.
WEB-WARRIORS, COMMENCE--
--FORMATION TOTEM POLE!
I LOVE THIS MANEUVER-- I'M FINALLY TALL ENOUGH TO SEE OVER THE BAD GUYS!
HOLD IT, HAM. NOW, TROOPS, PICK AN OPPONENT--
--AND LET THESE WEBS DO THE TALKING!

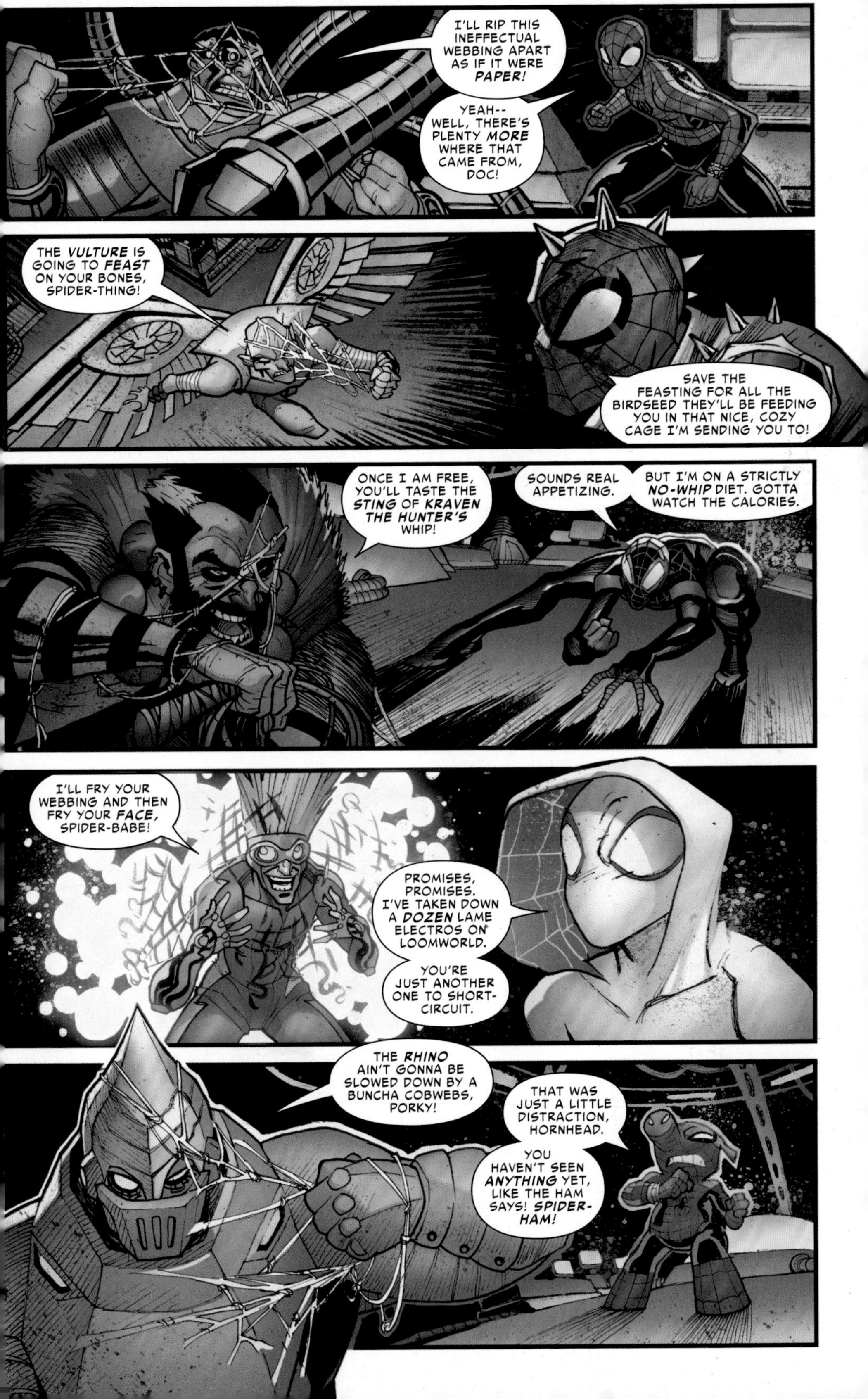
I'LL RIP THIS INEFFECTUAL WEBBING APART AS IF IT WERE *PAPER!*
YEAH-- WELL, THERE'S PLENTY *MORE* WHERE THAT CAME FROM, DOC!
THE *VULTURE* IS GOING TO *FEAST* ON YOUR BONES, SPIDER-THING!
SAVE THE FEASTING FOR ALL THE BIRDSEED THEY'LL BE FEEDING YOU IN THAT NICE, COZY CAGE I'M SENDING YOU TO!
ONCE I AM FREE, YOU'LL TASTE THE *STING* OF *KRAVEN THE HUNTER'S* WHIP!
SOUNDS REAL APPETIZING.
BUT I'M ON A STRICTLY *NO-WHIP* DIET. GOTTA WATCH THE CALORIES.
I'LL FRY YOUR WEBBING AND THEN FRY YOUR *FACE,* SPIDER-BABE!
PROMISES, PROMISES. I'VE TAKEN DOWN A *DOZEN* LAME ELECTROS ON LOOMWORLD.
YOU'RE JUST ANOTHER ONE TO SHORT-CIRCUIT.
THE *RHINO* AIN'T GONNA BE SLOWED DOWN BY A BUNCHA COBWEBS, PORKY!
THAT WAS JUST A LITTLE DISTRACTION, HORNHEAD.
YOU HAVEN'T SEEN *ANYTHING* YET, LIKE THE HAM SAYS! *SPIDER-HAM!*

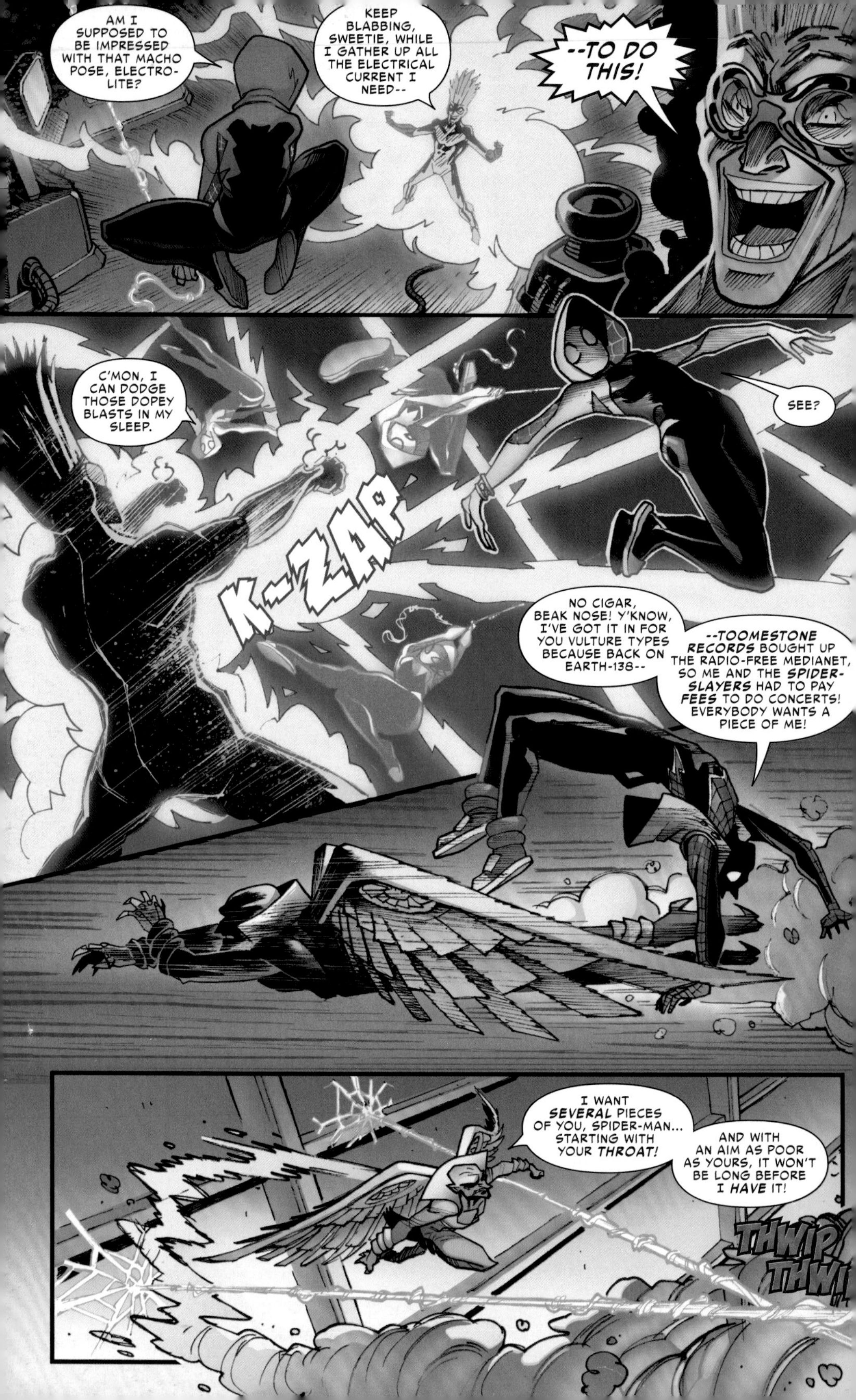
AM I SUPPOSED TO BE IMPRESSED WITH THAT MACHO POSE, ELECTRO-LITE?
KEEP BLABBING, SWEETIE, WHILE I GATHER UP ALL THE ELECTRICAL CURRENT I NEED--
--TO DO THIS!
C'MON, I CAN DODGE THOSE DOPEY BLASTS IN MY SLEEP.
SEE?
K-ZAP
NO CIGAR, BEAK NOSE! Y'KNOW, I'VE GOT IT IN FOR YOU VULTURE TYPES BECAUSE BACK ON EARTH-138--
--TOOMESTONE RECORDS BOUGHT UP THE RADIO-FREE MEDIANET, SO ME AND THE SPIDER-SLAYERS HAD TO PAY FEES TO DO CONCERTS! EVERYBODY WANTS A PIECE OF ME!
I WANT SEVERAL PIECES OF YOU, SPIDER-MAN... STARTING WITH YOUR THROAT!
AND WITH AN AIM AS POOR AS YOURS, IT WON'T BE LONG BEFORE I HAVE IT!
THWIP

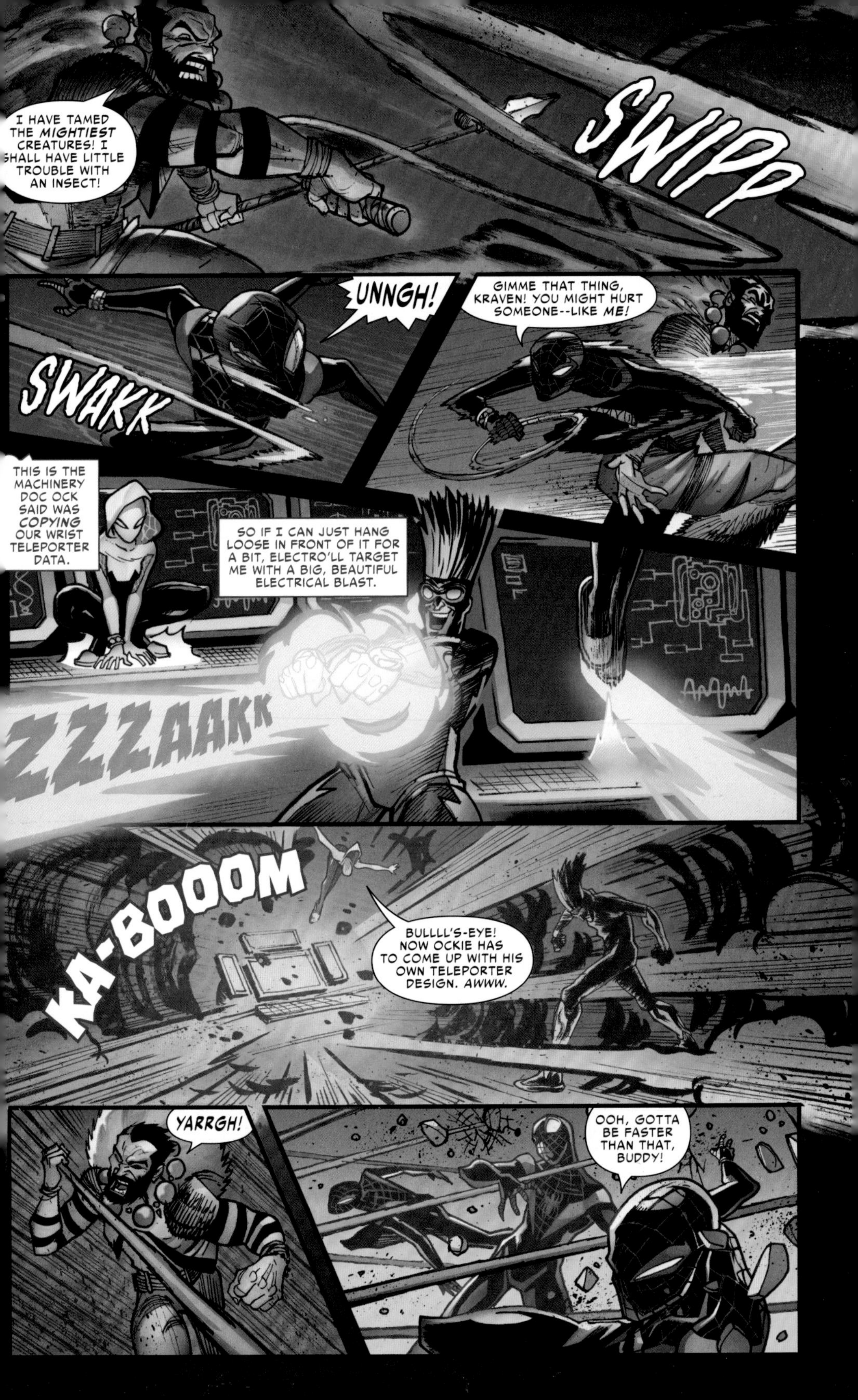
I HAVE TAMED THE *MIGHTIEST* CREATURES! I SHALL HAVE LITTLE TROUBLE WITH AN INSECT!
SWIPP
UNNGH!
SWAKK
GIMME THAT THING, KRAVEN! YOU MIGHT HURT SOMEONE--LIKE *ME!*
THIS IS THE MACHINERY DOC OCK SAID WAS *COPYING* OUR WRIST TELEPORTER DATA.
SO IF I CAN JUST HANG LOOSE IN FRONT OF IT FOR A BIT, ELECTRO'LL TARGET ME WITH A BIG, BEAUTIFUL ELECTRICAL BLAST.
ZZZAAKK
KA-BOOOM
BULLLL'S-EYE! NOW OCKIE HAS TO COME UP WITH HIS OWN TELEPORTER DESIGN. *AWWW.*
YARRGH!
OOH, GOTTA BE FASTER THAN THAT, BUDDY!

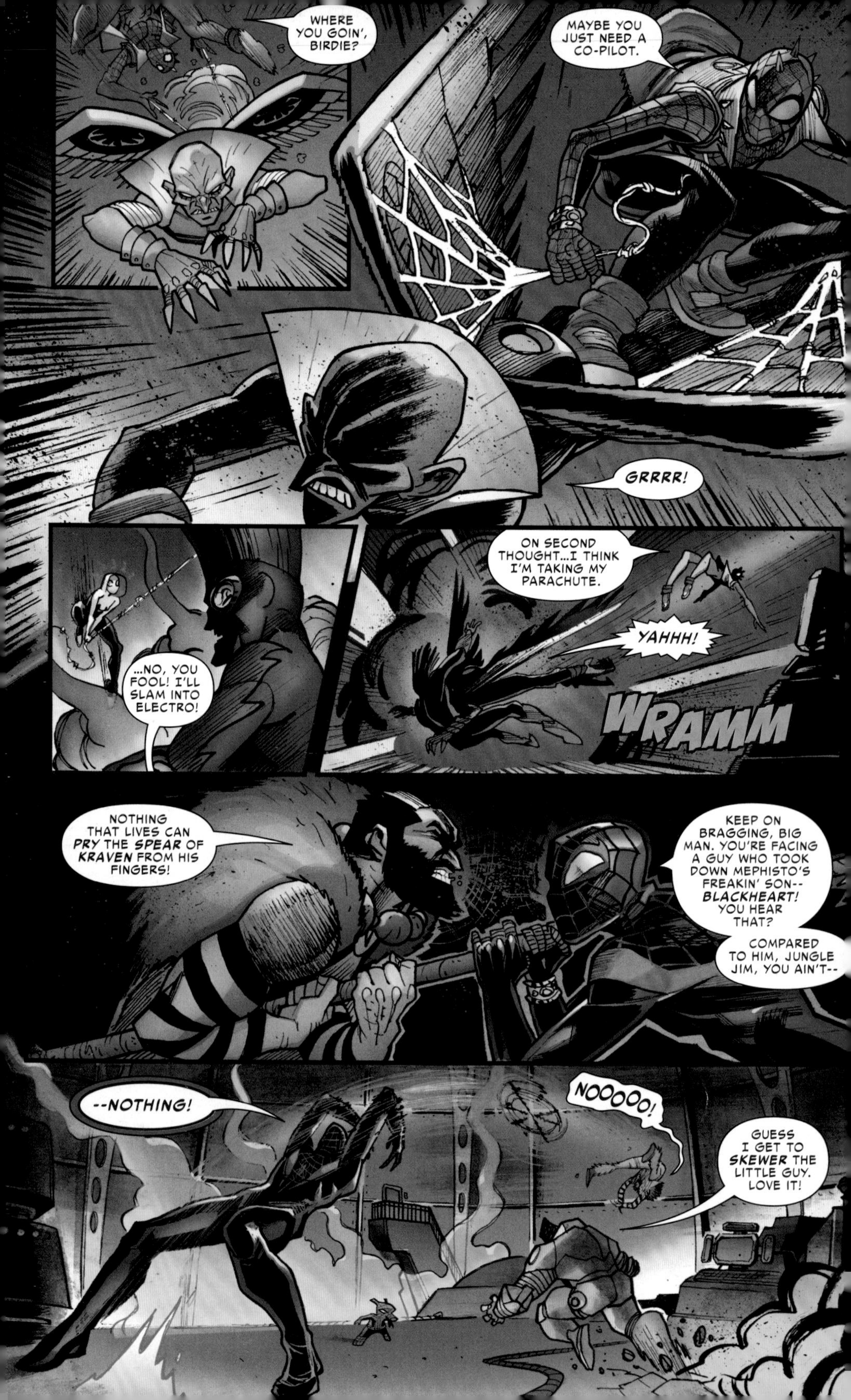
WHERE YOU GOIN', BIRDIE?
MAYBE YOU JUST NEED A CO-PILOT.
GRRRR!
...NO, YOU FOOL! I'LL SLAM INTO ELECTRO!
ON SECOND THOUGHT...I THINK I'M TAKING MY PARACHUTE.
YAHHH!
WRAMM
NOTHING THAT LIVES CAN PRY THE SPEAR OF KRAVEN FROM HIS FINGERS!
KEEP ON BRAGGING, BIG MAN. YOU'RE FACING A GUY WHO TOOK DOWN MEPHISTO'S FREAKIN' SON-- BLACKHEART! YOU HEAR THAT?
COMPARED TO HIM, JUNGLE JIM, YOU AIN'T--
--NOTHING!
NOOOOO!
GUESS I GET TO SKEWER THE LITTLE GUY. LOVE IT!

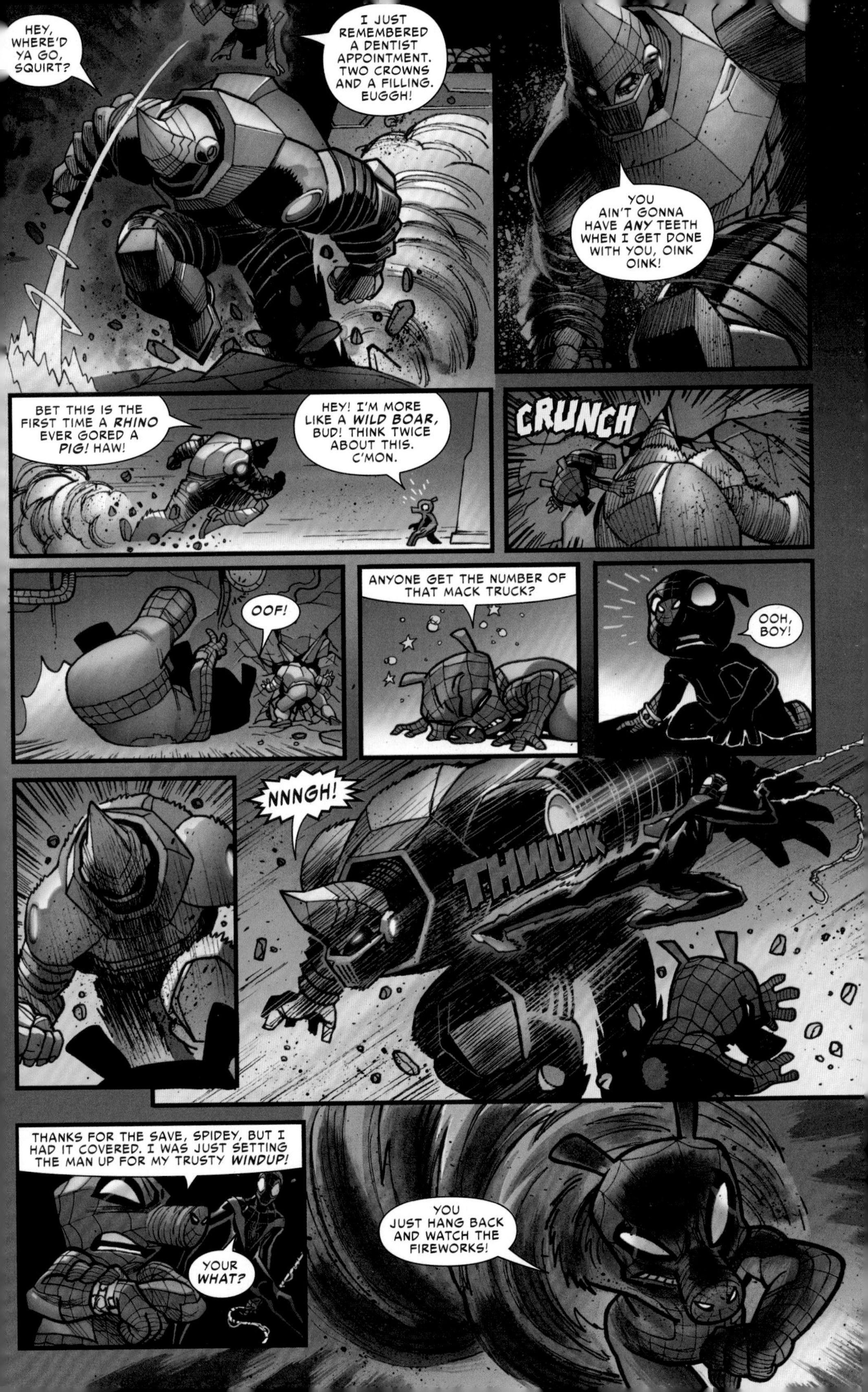
HEY, WHERE'D YA GO, SQUIRT?
I JUST REMEMBERED A DENTIST APPOINTMENT. TWO CROWNS AND A FILLING. EUGGH!
YOU AIN'T GONNA HAVE ANY TEETH WHEN I GET DONE WITH YOU, OINK OINK!
BET THIS IS THE FIRST TIME A RHINO EVER GORED A PIG! HAW!
HEY! I'M MORE LIKE A WILD BOAR, BUD! THINK TWICE ABOUT THIS. C'MON.
CRUNCH
OOF!
ANYONE GET THE NUMBER OF THAT MACK TRUCK?
OOH, BOY!
NNNGH!
THWUNK
THANKS FOR THE SAVE, SPIDEY, BUT I HAD IT COVERED. I WAS JUST SETTING THE MAN UP FOR MY TRUSTY WINDUP!
YOUR WHAT?
YOU JUST HANG BACK AND WATCH THE FIREWORKS!

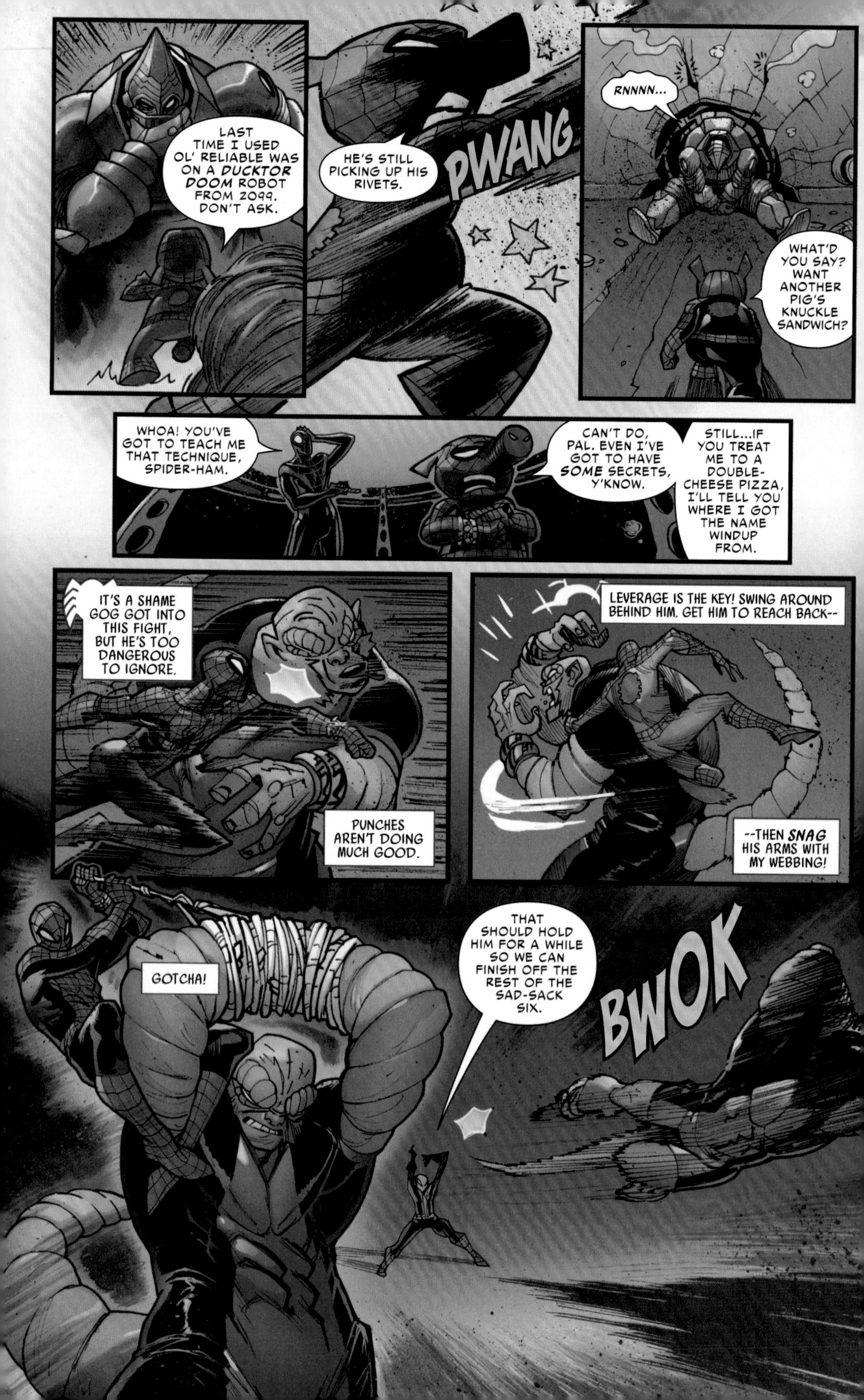
LAST TIME I USED OL' RELIABLE WAS ON A DUCKTOR DOOM ROBOT FROM 2099. DON'T ASK.
HE'S STILL PICKING UP HIS RIVETS.
PWANG
RNNNN...
WHAT'D YOU SAY? WANT ANOTHER PIG'S KNUCKLE SANDWICH?
WHOA! YOU'VE GOT TO TEACH ME THAT TECHNIQUE, SPIDER-HAM.
CAN'T DO, PAL. EVEN I'VE GOT TO HAVE SOME SECRETS, Y'KNOW.
STILL...IF YOU TREAT ME TO A DOUBLE-CHEESE PIZZA, I'LL TELL YOU WHERE I GOT THE NAME WINDUP FROM.
IT'S A SHAME GOG GOT INTO THIS FIGHT, BUT HE'S TOO DANGEROUS TO IGNORE.
PUNCHES AREN'T DOING MUCH GOOD.
LEVERAGE IS THE KEY! SWING AROUND BEHIND HIM. GET HIM TO REACH BACK--
--THEN SNAG HIS ARMS WITH MY WEBBING!
GOTCHA!
THAT SHOULD HOLD HIM FOR A WHILE SO WE CAN FINISH OFF THE REST OF THE SAD-SACK SIX.
BWOK

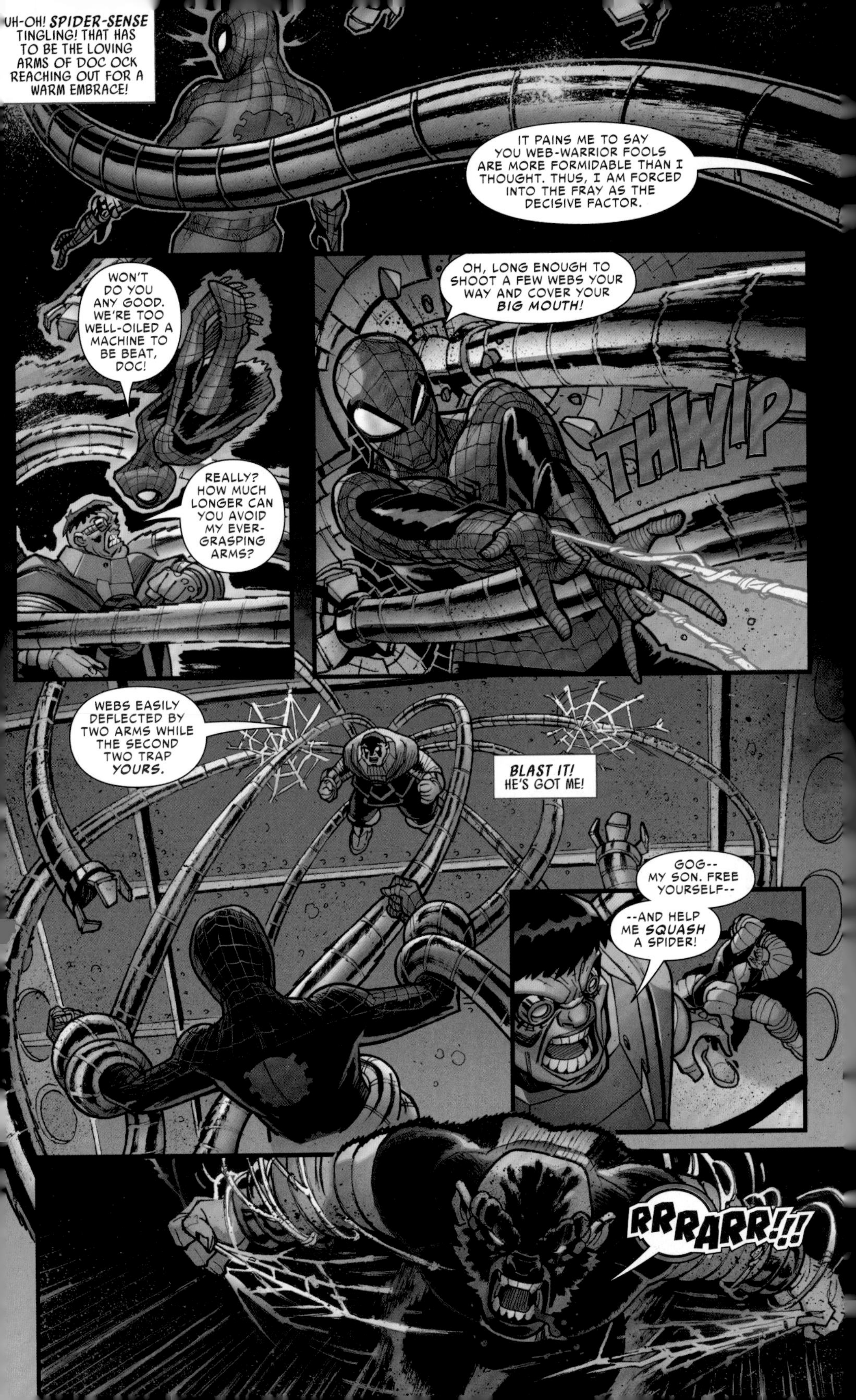
UH-OH! SPIDER-SENSE TINGLING! THAT HAS TO BE THE LOVING ARMS OF DOC OCK REACHING OUT FOR A WARM EMBRACE!
IT PAINS ME TO SAY YOU WEB-WARRIOR FOOLS ARE MORE FORMIDABLE THAN I THOUGHT. THUS, I AM FORCED INTO THE FRAY AS THE DECISIVE FACTOR.
WON'T DO YOU ANY GOOD. WE'RE TOO WELL-OILED A MACHINE TO BE BEAT, DOC!
REALLY? HOW MUCH LONGER CAN YOU AVOID MY EVER-GRASPING ARMS?
OH, LONG ENOUGH TO SHOOT A FEW WEBS YOUR WAY AND COVER YOUR BIG MOUTH!
THWIP
WEBS EASILY DEFLECTED BY TWO ARMS WHILE THE SECOND TWO TRAP YOURS.
BLAST IT! HE'S GOT ME!
GOG-- MY SON. FREE YOURSELF--
--AND HELP ME SQUASH A SPIDER!
RRRARR!!!

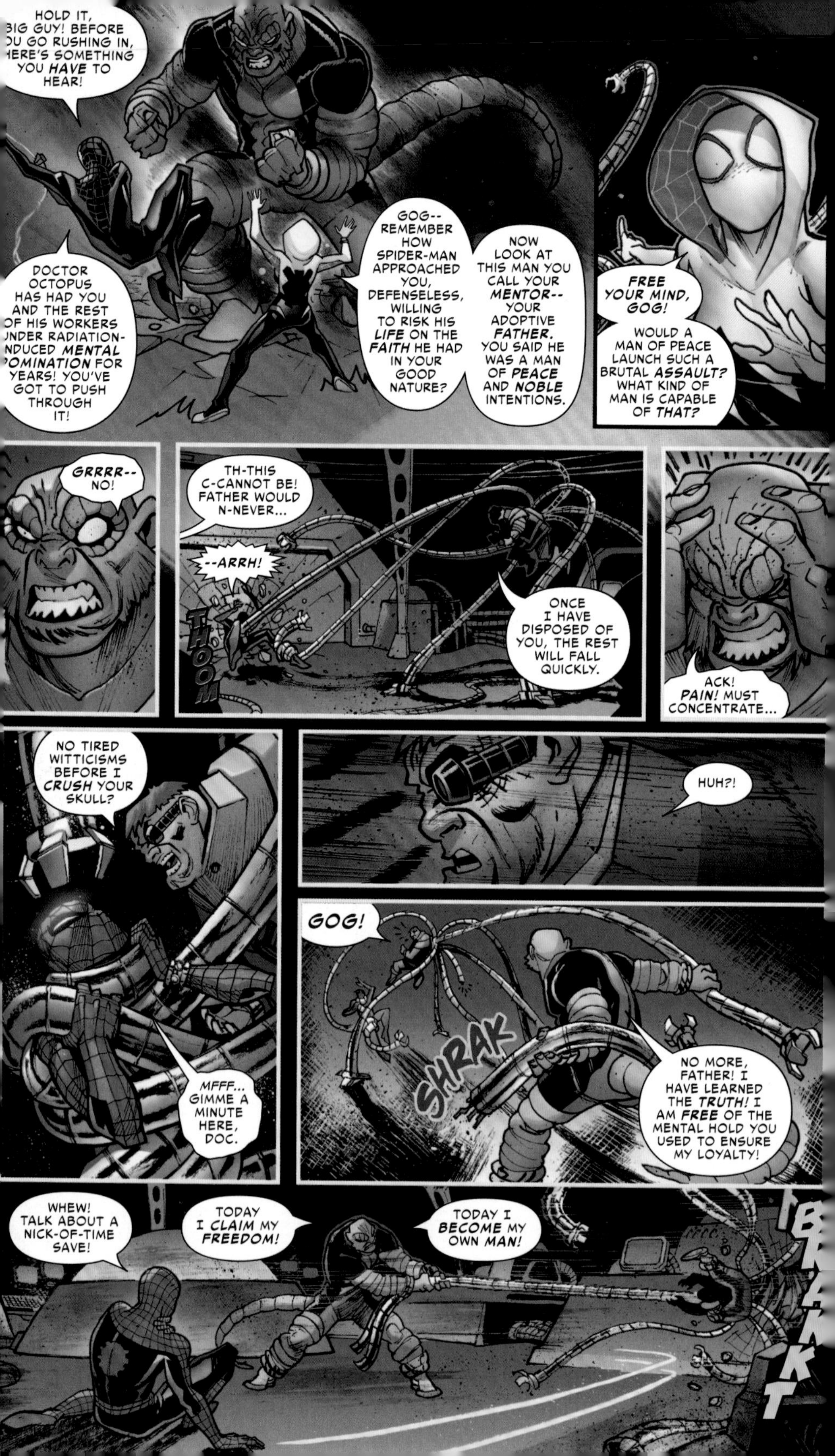

HOLD IT, BIG GUY! BEFORE OU GO RUSHING IN, HERE'S SOMETHING YOU HAVE TO HEAR!
DOCTOR OCTOPUS HAS HAD YOU AND THE REST OF HIS WORKERS NDER RADIATION-NDUCED MENTAL OMINATION FOR YEARS! YOU'VE GOT TO PUSH THROUGH IT!
GOG-- REMEMBER HOW SPIDER-MAN APPROACHED YOU, DEFENSELESS, WILLING TO RISK HIS LIFE ON THE FAITH HE HAD IN YOUR GOOD NATURE?
NOW LOOK AT THIS MAN YOU CALL YOUR MENTOR-- YOUR ADOPTIVE FATHER. YOU SAID HE WAS A MAN OF PEACE AND NOBLE INTENTIONS.
FREE YOUR MIND, GOG!
WOULD A MAN OF PEACE LAUNCH SUCH A BRUTAL ASSAULT? WHAT KIND OF MAN IS CAPABLE OF THAT?
GRRRR-- NO!
TH-THIS C-CANNOT BE! FATHER WOULD N-NEVER...
--ARRH!
THOOM
ONCE I HAVE DISPOSED OF YOU, THE REST WILL FALL QUICKLY.
ACK! PAIN! MUST CONCENTRATE...
NO TIRED WITTICISMS BEFORE I CRUSH YOUR SKULL?
MFFF... GIMME A MINUTE HERE, DOC.
HUH?!
GOG!
SHRAK
NO MORE, FATHER! I HAVE LEARNED THE TRUTH! I AM FREE OF THE MENTAL HOLD YOU USED TO ENSURE MY LOYALTY!
WHEW! TALK ABOUT A NICK-OF-TIME SAVE!
TODAY I CLAIM MY FREEDOM!
TODAY I BECOME MY OWN MAN!
BRAKT

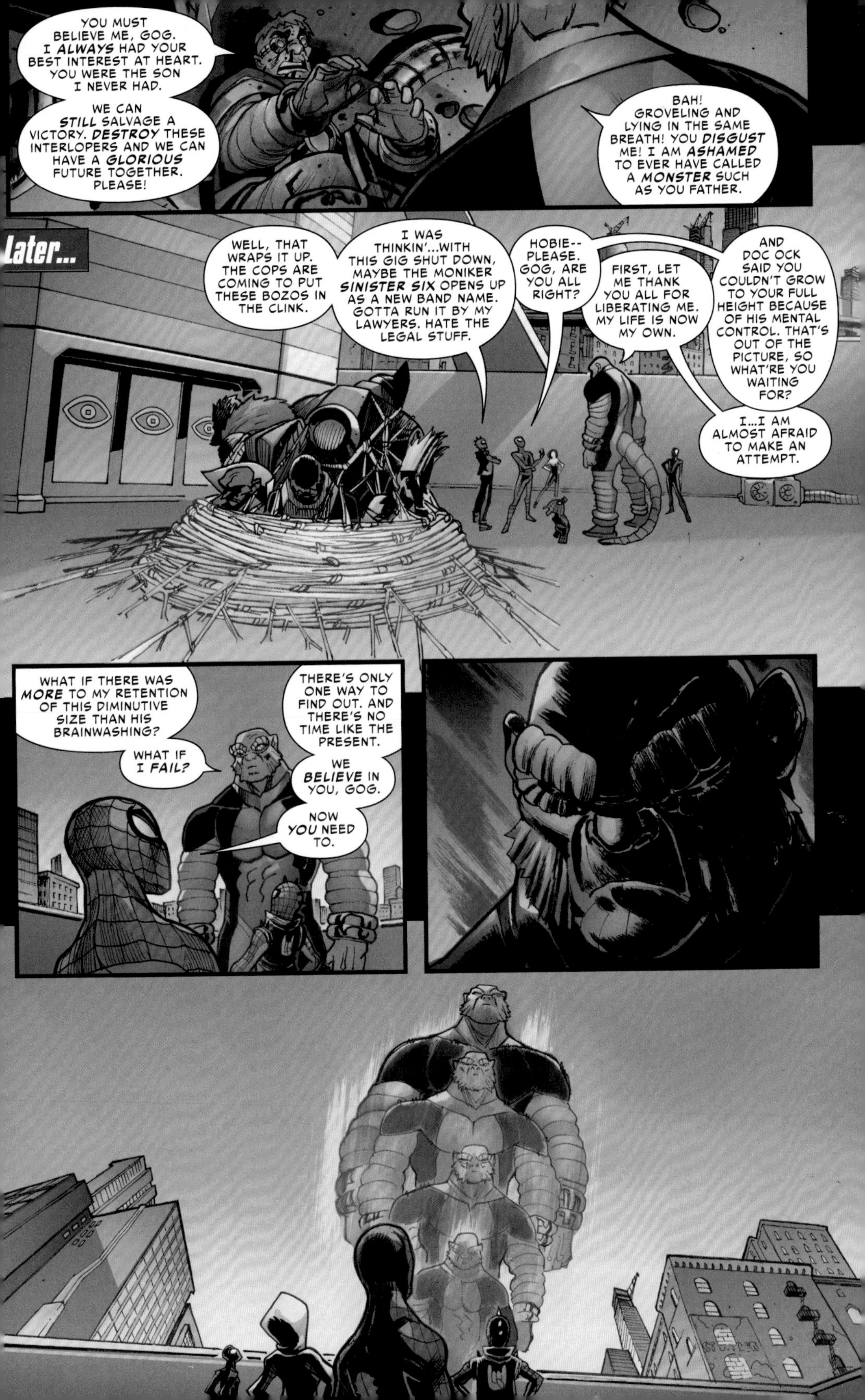
YOU MUST BELIEVE ME, GOG. I ALWAYS HAD YOUR BEST INTEREST AT HEART. YOU WERE THE SON I NEVER HAD.
WE CAN STILL SALVAGE A VICTORY. DESTROY THESE INTERLOPERS AND WE CAN HAVE A GLORIOUS FUTURE TOGETHER. PLEASE!
BAH! GROVELING AND LYING IN THE SAME BREATH! YOU DISGUST ME! I AM ASHAMED TO EVER HAVE CALLED A MONSTER SUCH AS YOU FATHER.
Later...
WELL, THAT WRAPS IT UP. THE COPS ARE COMING TO PUT THESE BOZOS IN THE CLINK.
I WAS THINKIN'...WITH THIS GIG SHUT DOWN, MAYBE THE MONIKER SINISTER SIX OPENS UP AS A NEW BAND NAME. GOTTA RUN IT BY MY LAWYERS. HATE THE LEGAL STUFF.
HOBIE-- PLEASE. GOG, ARE YOU ALL RIGHT?
FIRST, LET ME THANK YOU ALL FOR LIBERATING ME. MY LIFE IS NOW MY OWN.
AND DOC OCK SAID YOU COULDN'T GROW TO YOUR FULL HEIGHT BECAUSE OF HIS MENTAL CONTROL. THAT'S OUT OF THE PICTURE, SO WHAT'RE YOU WAITING FOR?
I...I AM ALMOST AFRAID TO MAKE AN ATTEMPT.
WHAT IF THERE WAS MORE TO MY RETENTION OF THIS DIMINUTIVE SIZE THAN HIS BRAINWASHING?
WHAT IF I FAIL?
THERE'S ONLY ONE WAY TO FIND OUT. AND THERE'S NO TIME LIKE THE PRESENT.
WE BELIEVE IN YOU, GOG.
NOW YOU NEED TO.

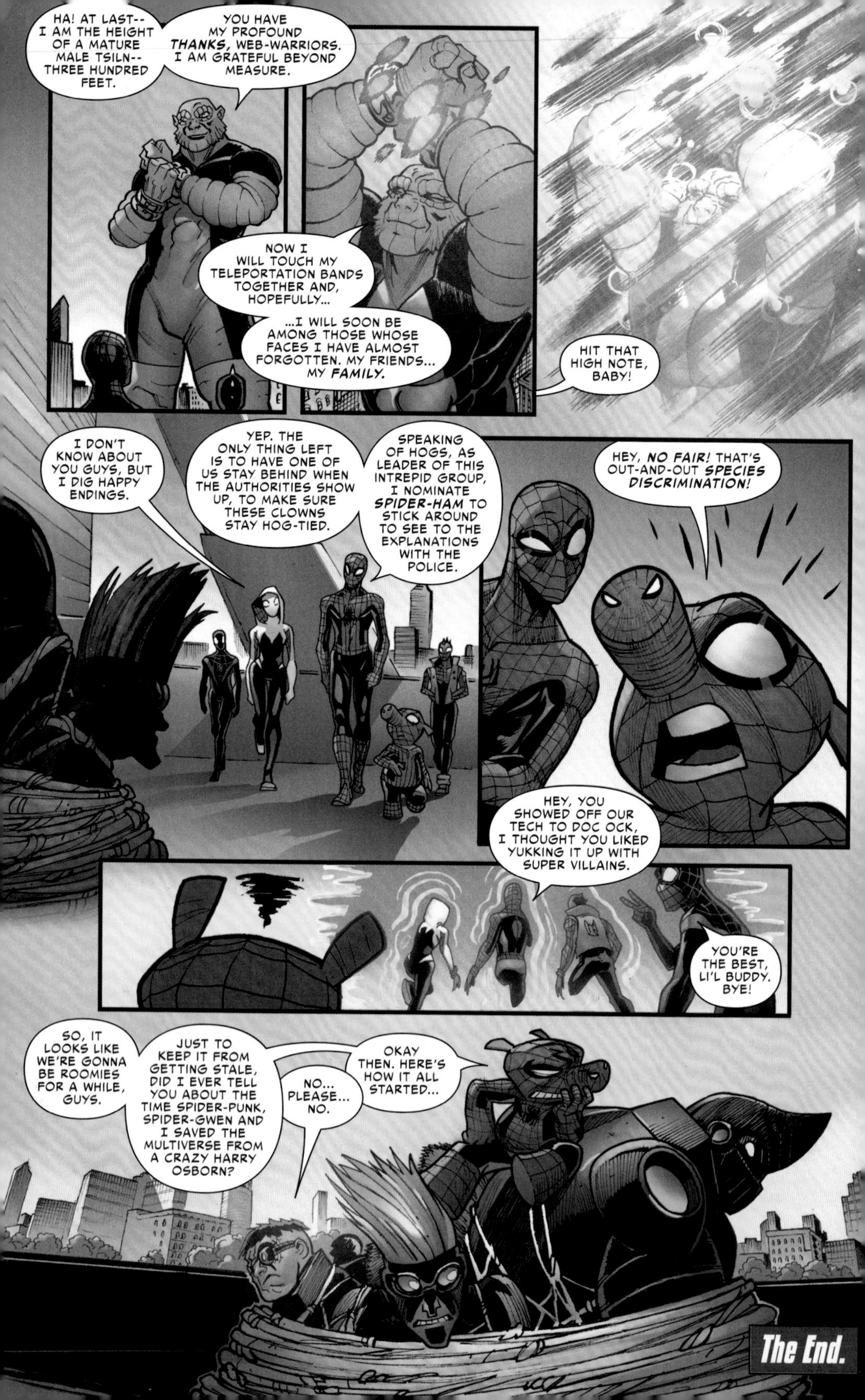
HA! AT LAST-- I AM THE HEIGHT OF A MATURE MALE TSILN-- THREE HUNDRED FEET.
YOU HAVE MY PROFOUND THANKS, WEB-WARRIORS. I AM GRATEFUL BEYOND MEASURE.
NOW I WILL TOUCH MY TELEPORTATION BANDS TOGETHER AND, HOPEFULLY...
...I WILL SOON BE AMONG THOSE WHOSE FACES I HAVE ALMOST FORGOTTEN. MY FRIENDS... MY FAMILY.
HIT THAT HIGH NOTE, BABY!
I DON'T KNOW ABOUT YOU GUYS, BUT I DIG HAPPY ENDINGS.
YEP. THE ONLY THING LEFT IS TO HAVE ONE OF US STAY BEHIND WHEN THE AUTHORITIES SHOW UP, TO MAKE SURE THESE CLOWNS STAY HOG-TIED.
SPEAKING OF HOGS, AS LEADER OF THIS INTREPID GROUP, I NOMINATE SPIDER-HAM TO STICK AROUND TO SEE TO THE EXPLANATIONS WITH THE POLICE.
HEY, NO FAIR! THAT'S OUT-AND-OUT SPECIES DISCRIMINATION!
HEY, YOU SHOWED OFF OUR TECH TO DOC OCK, I THOUGHT YOU LIKED YUKKING IT UP WITH SUPER VILLAINS.
YOU'RE THE BEST, LI'L BUDDY. BYE!
SO, IT LOOKS LIKE WE'RE GONNA BE ROOMIES FOR A WHILE, GUYS.
JUST TO KEEP IT FROM GETTING STALE, DID I EVER TELL YOU ABOUT THE TIME SPIDER-PUNK, SPIDER-GWEN AND I SAVED THE MULTIVERSE FROM A CRAZY HARRY OSBORN?
NO... PLEASE... NO.
OKAY THEN. HERE'S HOW IT ALL STARTED...
The End.

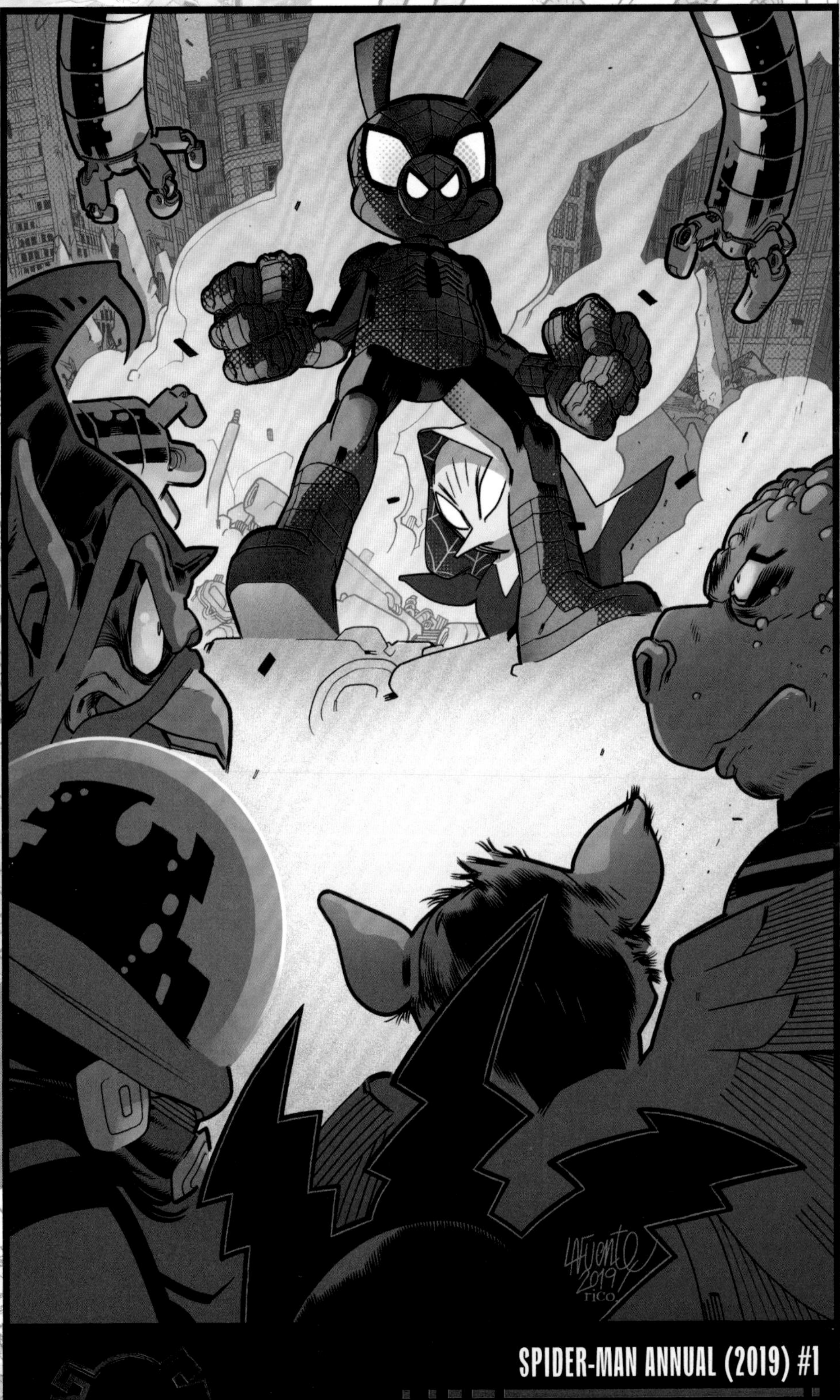

SPIDER-MAN ANNUAL (2019) #1

SPIDER-GWEN'S DIMENSION-HOPPING WEB-WATCH HAS FALLEN INTO THE HANDS OF THE CIRCUS OF CRIME! NOW IT'S UP TO SPIDER-HAM TO PUNCH THEIR CLOCKS.

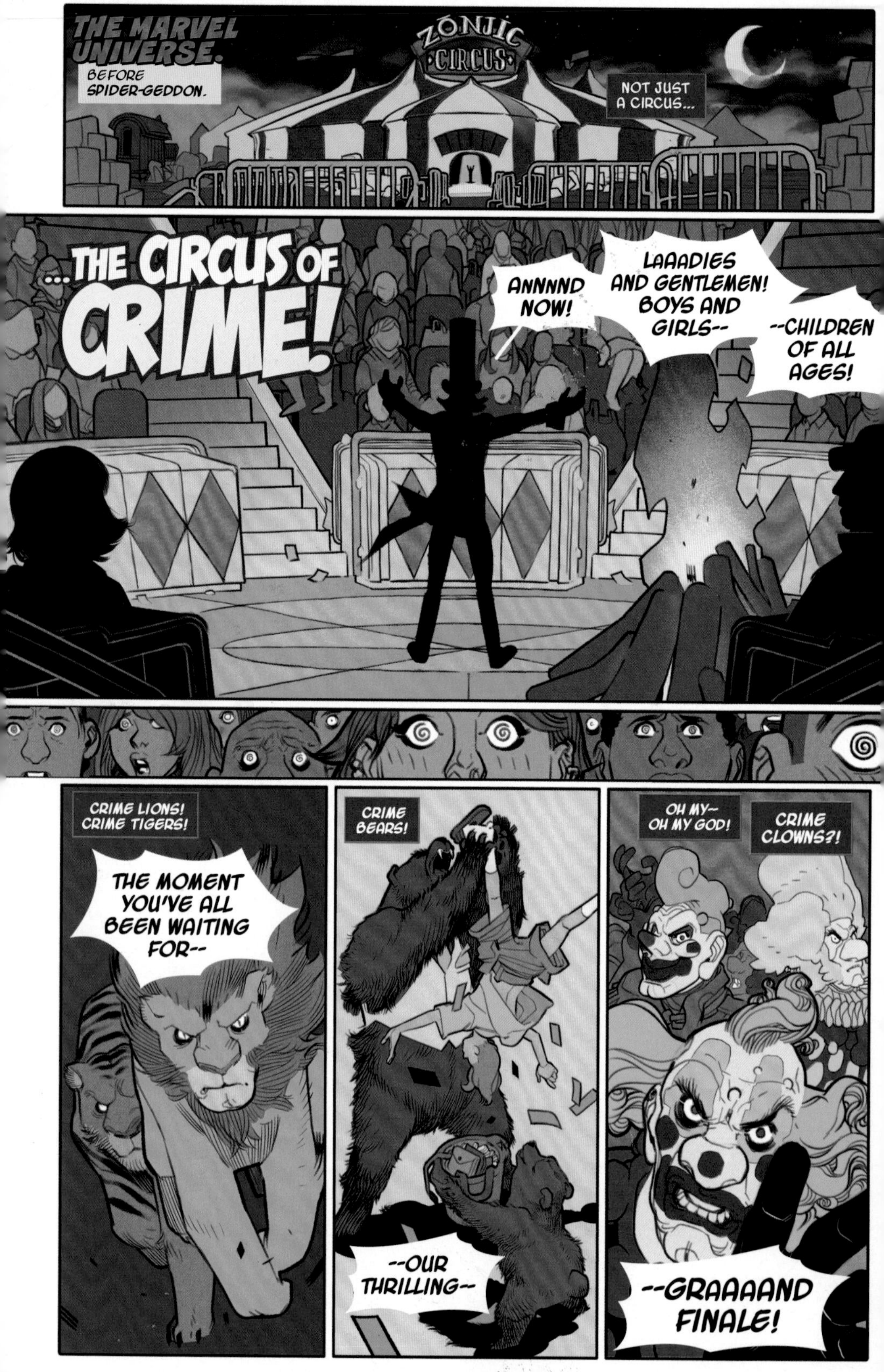
THE MARVEL UNIVERSE.
BEFORE SPIDER-GEDDON.
ZONJIC CIRCUS
NOT JUST A CIRCUS...
...THE CIRCUS OF CRIME!
ANNNND NOW!
LAAADIES AND GENTLEMEN! BOYS AND GIRLS--
--CHILDREN OF ALL AGES!
CRIME LIONS! CRIME TIGERS!
THE MOMENT YOU'VE ALL BEEN WAITING FOR--
CRIME BEARS!
--OUR THRILLING--
OH MY-- OH MY GOD!
CRIME CLOWNS?!
--GRAAAAND FINALE!

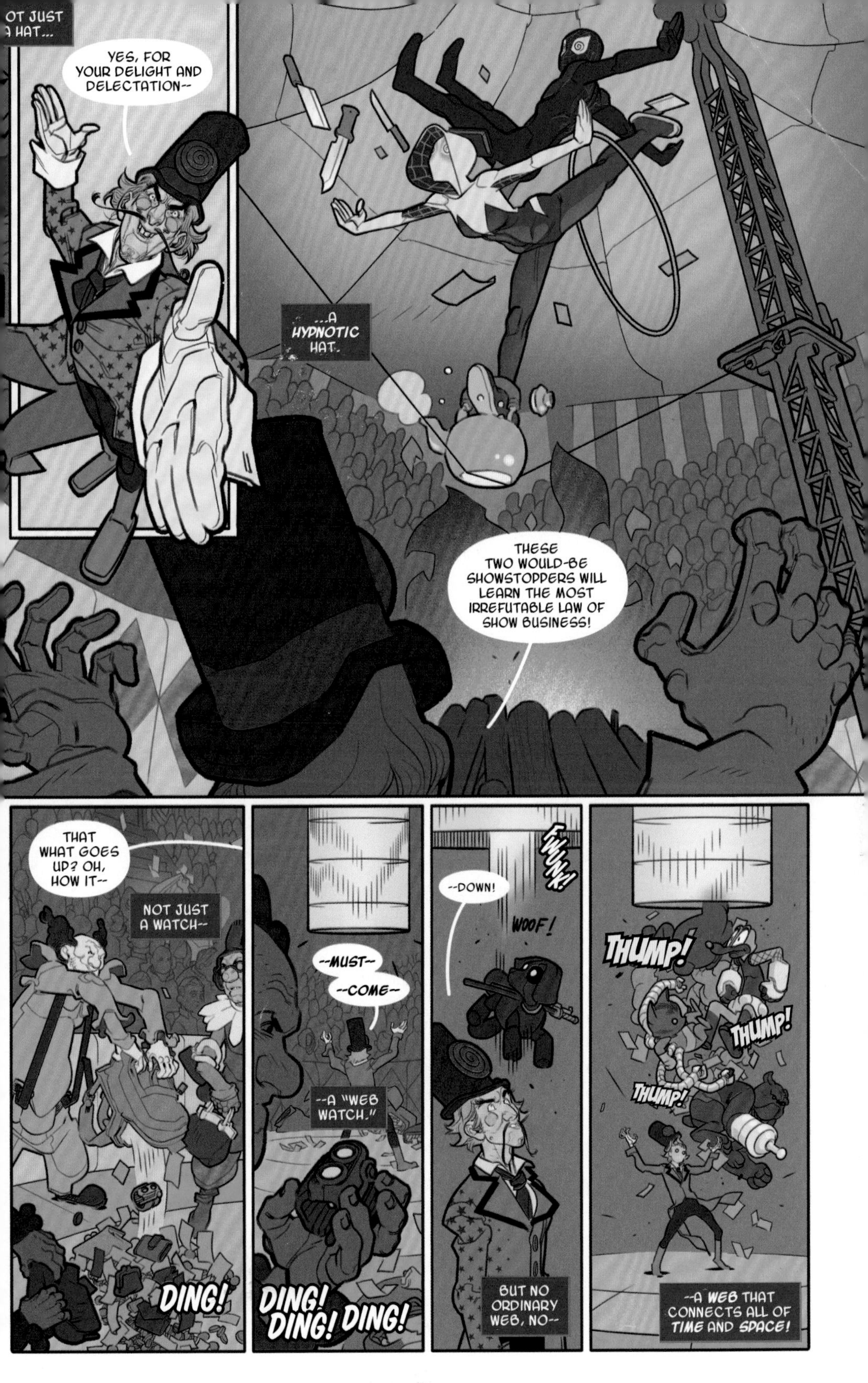
OT JUST
A HAT...
YES, FOR YOUR DELIGHT AND DELECTATION--
...A HYPNOTIC HAT.
THESE TWO WOULD-BE SHOWSTOPPERS WILL LEARN THE MOST IRREFUTABLE LAW OF SHOW BUSINESS!
THAT WHAT GOES UP? OH, HOW IT--
NOT JUST A WATCH--
DING!
--MUST--
--COME--
--A "WEB WATCH."
DING! DING! DING!
FWUNK!
--DOWN!
WOOF!
BUT NO ORDINARY WEB, NO--
THUMP!
THUMP!
THUMP!
--A WEB THAT CONNECTS ALL OF TIME AND SPACE!

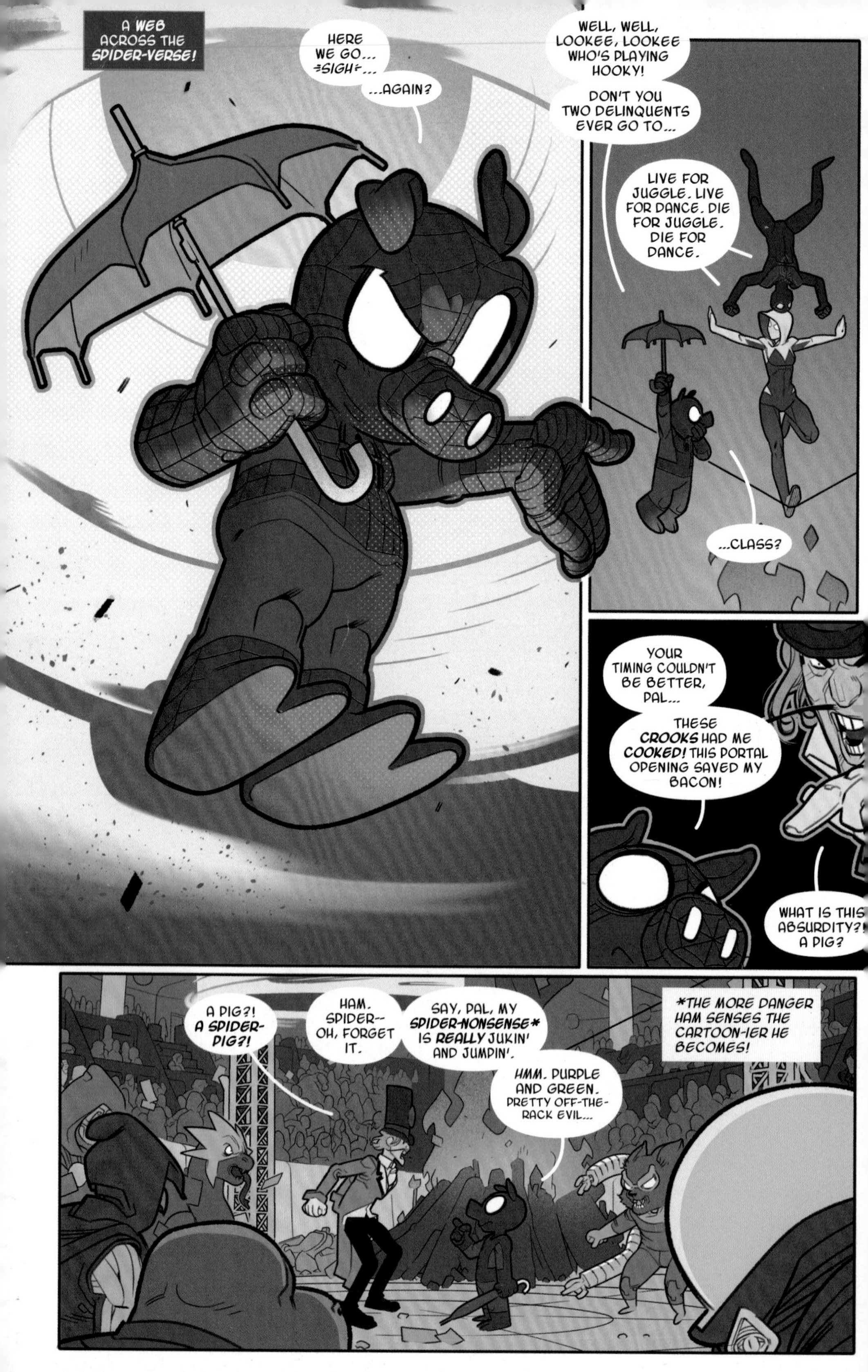
A WEB ACROSS THE SPIDER-VERSE!
HERE WE GO... =SIGH=...
...AGAIN?
WELL, WELL, LOOKEE, LOOKEE WHO'S PLAYING HOOKY!
DON'T YOU TWO DELINQUENTS EVER GO TO...
LIVE FOR JUGGLE. LIVE FOR DANCE. DIE FOR JUGGLE. DIE FOR DANCE.
...CLASS?
YOUR TIMING COULDN'T BE BETTER, PAL...
THESE CROOKS HAD ME COOKED! THIS PORTAL OPENING SAVED MY BACON!
WHAT IS THIS ABSURDITY?! A PIG?
A PIG?! A SPIDER-PIG?!
HAM. SPIDER-- OH, FORGET IT.
SAY, PAL, MY SPIDER-NONSENSE* IS REALLY JUKIN' AND JUMPIN'.
*THE MORE DANGER HAM SENSES THE CARTOON-IER HE BECOMES!
HMM. PURPLE AND GREEN. PRETTY OFF-THE-RACK EVIL...

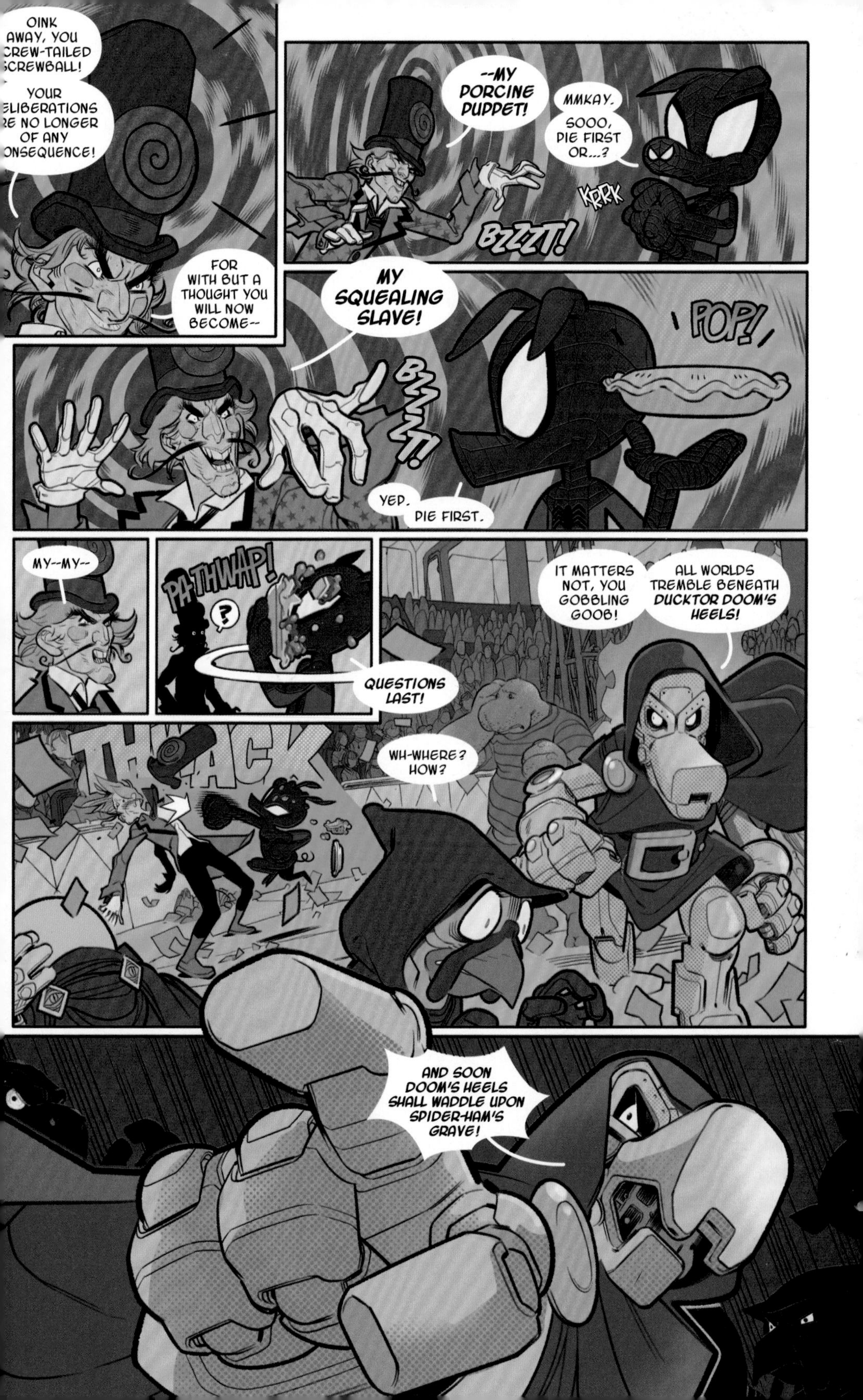

OINK AWAY, YOU CREW-TAILED SCREWBALL!
YOUR ELIBERATIONS RE NO LONGER OF ANY ONSEQUENCE!
FOR WITH BUT A THOUGHT YOU WILL NOW BECOME--
--MY PORCINE PUPPET!
MMKAY.
SOOO, PIE FIRST OR...?
KRRK
BZZZT!
MY SQUEALING SLAVE!
POP!
BZZZT!
YEP.
PIE FIRST.
MY--MY--
PATHWAP!
?
QUESTIONS LAST!
IT MATTERS NOT, YOU GOBBLING GOOB!
ALL WORLDS TREMBLE BENEATH DUCKTOR DOOM'S HEELS!
THWACK
WH-WHERE? HOW?
AND SOON DOOM'S HEELS SHALL WADDLE UPON SPIDER-HAM'S GRAVE!

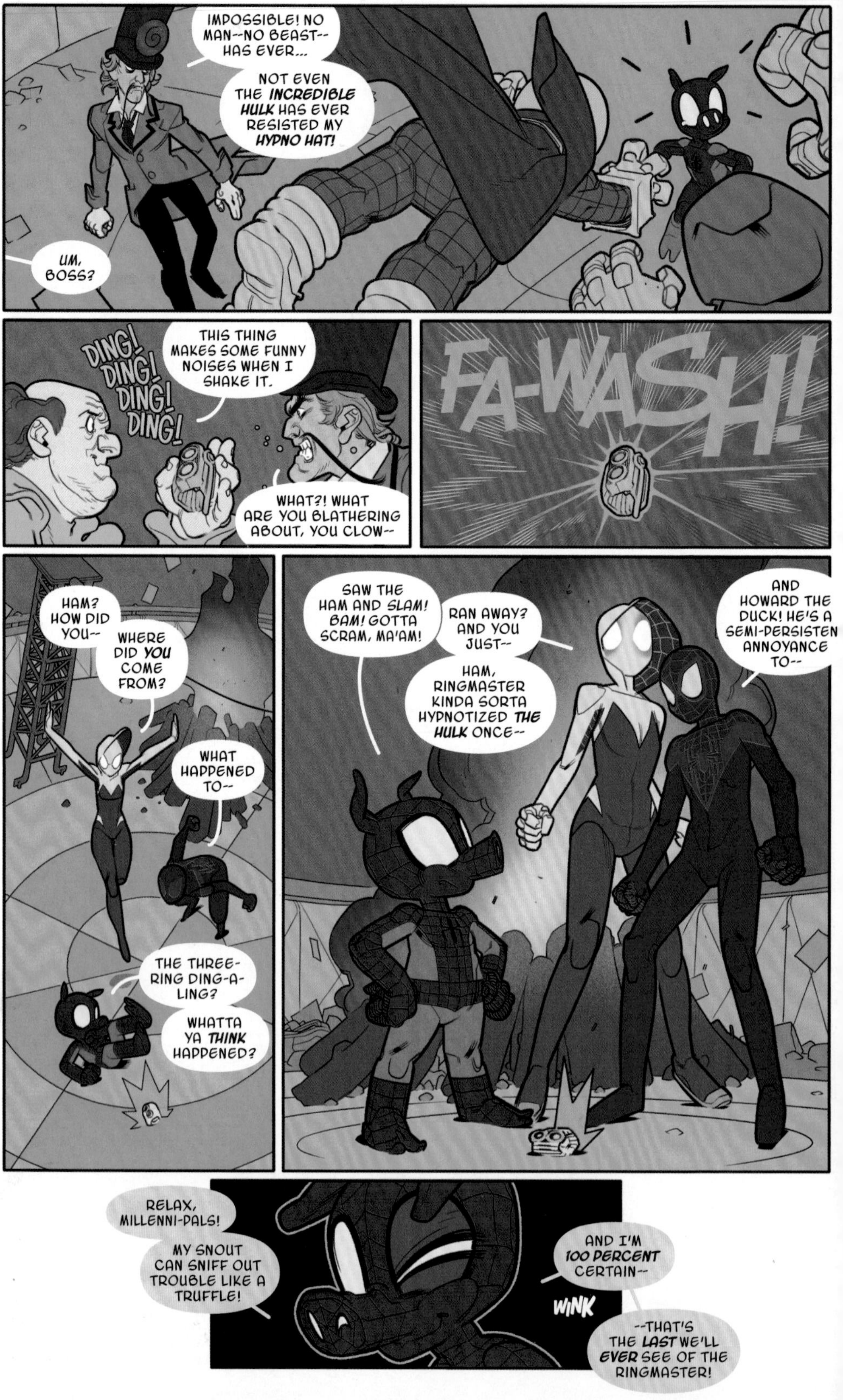

IMPOSSIBLE! NO MAN--NO BEAST--HAS EVER...
NOT EVEN THE INCREDIBLE HULK HAS EVER RESISTED MY HYPNO HAT!
UM, BOSS?
DING! DING! DING! DING!
THIS THING MAKES SOME FUNNY NOISES WHEN I SHAKE IT.
WHAT?! WHAT ARE YOU BLATHERING ABOUT, YOU CLOW--
FA-WASH!
HAM? HOW DID YOU--
WHERE DID YOU COME FROM?
WHAT HAPPENED TO--
THE THREE-RING DING-A-LING?
WHATTA YA THINK HAPPENED?
SAW THE HAM AND SLAM! BAM! GOTTA SCRAM, MA'AM!
RAN AWAY? AND YOU JUST--
HAM, RINGMASTER KINDA SORTA HYPNOTIZED THE HULK ONCE--
AND HOWARD THE DUCK! HE'S A SEMI-PERSISTEN ANNOYANCE TO--
RELAX, MILLENNI-PALS!
MY SNOUT CAN SNIFF OUT TROUBLE LIKE A TRUFFLE!
AND I'M 100 PERCENT CERTAIN--
WINK
--THAT'S THE LAST WE'LL EVER SEE OF THE RINGMASTER!

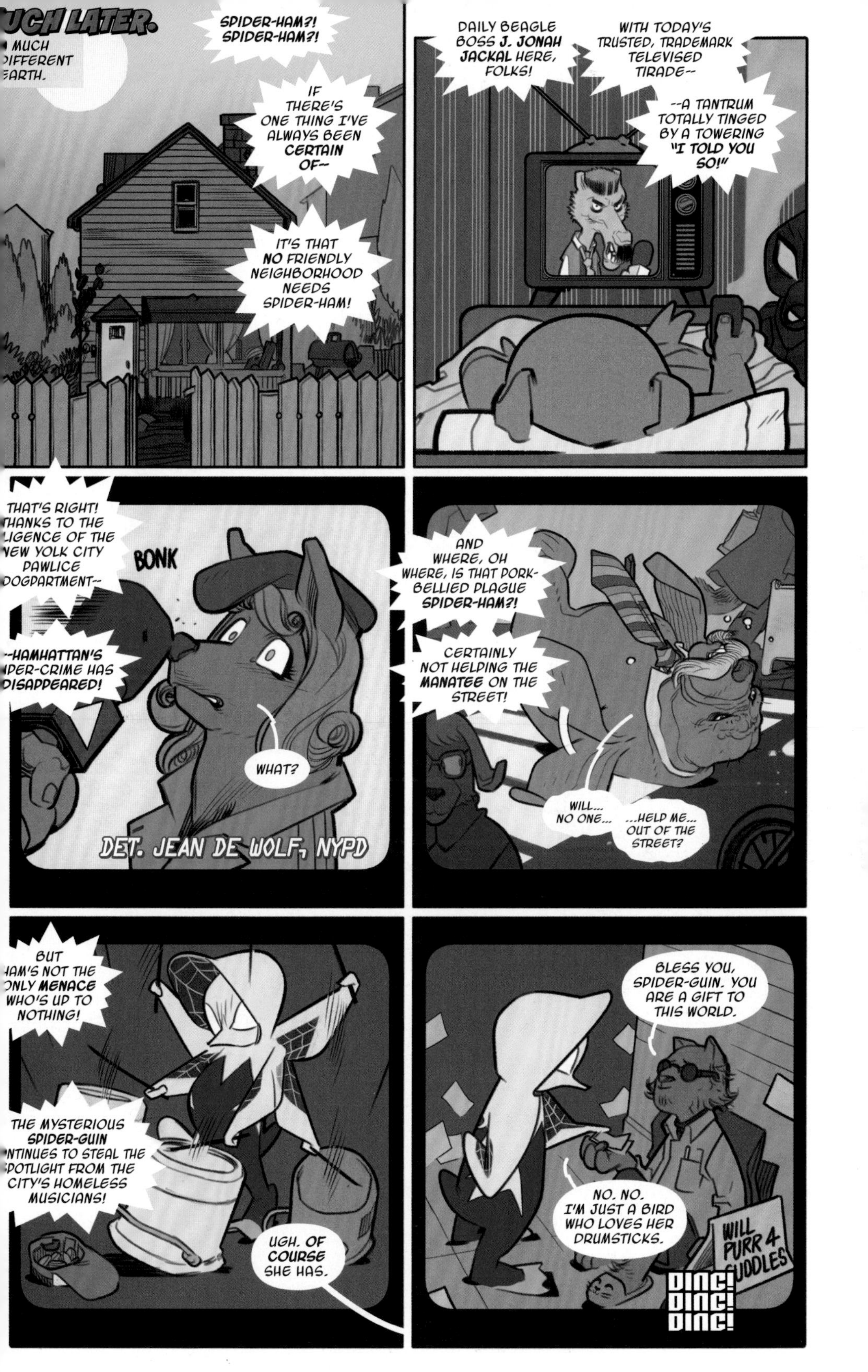
UCH LATER.
MUCH DIFFERENT EARTH.
SPIDER-HAM?! SPIDER-HAM?!
IF THERE'S ONE THING I'VE ALWAYS BEEN CERTAIN OF--
IT'S THAT NO FRIENDLY NEIGHBORHOOD NEEDS SPIDER-HAM!
DAILY BEAGLE BOSS J. JONAH JACKAL HERE, FOLKS!
WITH TODAY'S TRUSTED, TRADEMARK TELEVISED TIRADE--
--A TANTRUM TOTALLY TINGED BY A TOWERING "I TOLD YOU SO!"
THAT'S RIGHT! THANKS TO THE LIGENCE OF THE NEW YOLK CITY PAWLICE DOGPARTMENT--
BONK
--HAMHATTAN'S PER-CRIME HAS DISAPPEARED!
WHAT?
DET. JEAN DE WOLF, NYPD
AND WHERE, OH WHERE, IS THAT PORK-BELLIED PLAGUE SPIDER-HAM?!
CERTAINLY NOT HELPING THE MANATEE ON THE STREET!
WILL... NO ONE...
...HELP ME... OUT OF THE STREET?
BUT HAM'S NOT THE ONLY MENACE WHO'S UP TO NOTHING!
THE MYSTERIOUS SPIDER-GUIN NTINUES TO STEAL THE POTLIGHT FROM THE CITY'S HOMELESS MUSICIANS!
UGH. OF COURSE SHE HAS.
BLESS YOU, SPIDER-GUIN. YOU ARE A GIFT TO THIS WORLD.
NO. NO. I'M JUST A BIRD WHO LOVES HER DRUMSTICKS.
WILL PURR 4 CUDDLES
DING! DING! DING!

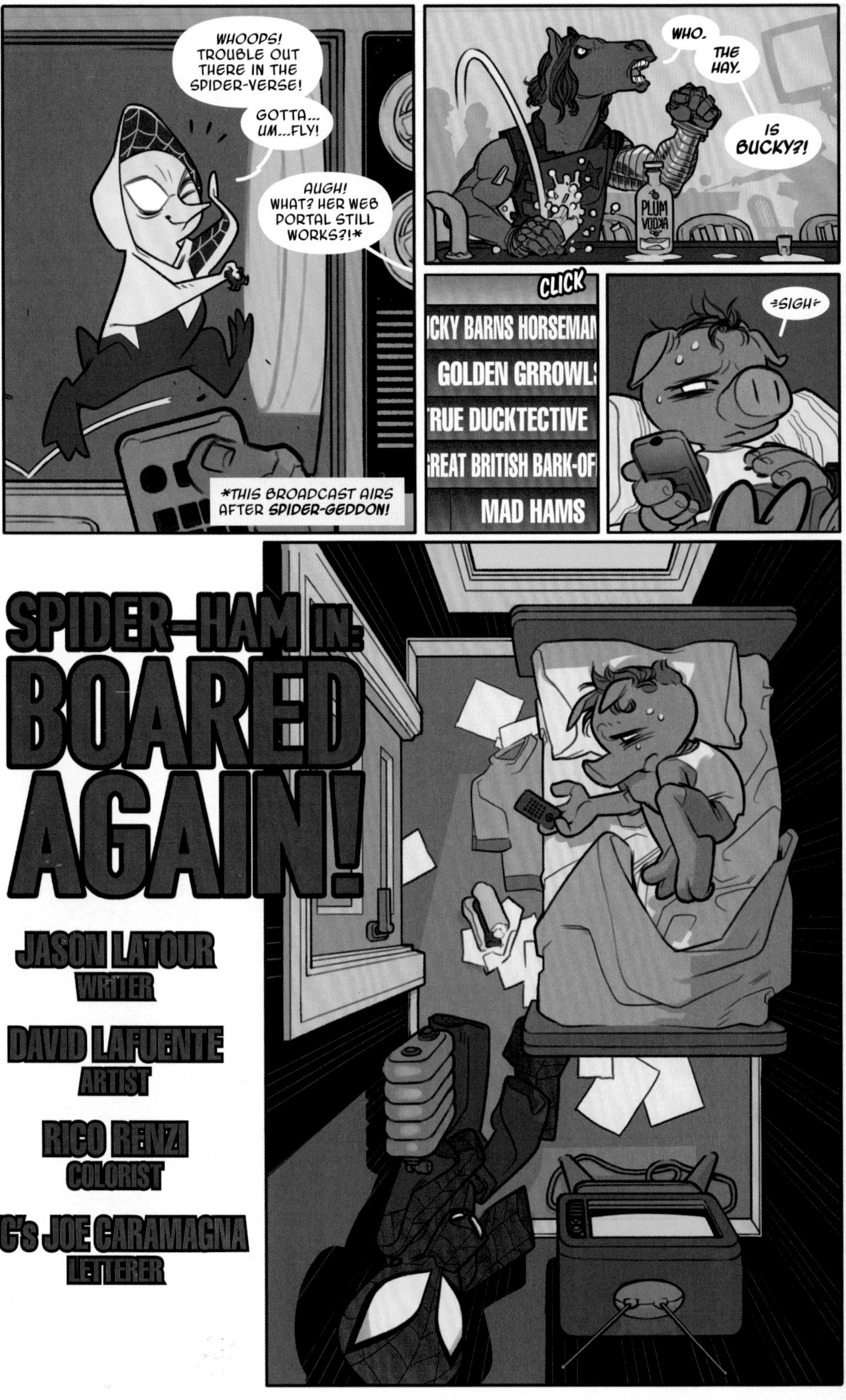
WHOOPS! TROUBLE OUT THERE IN THE SPIDER-VERSE!
GOTTA... UM...FLY!
AUGH! WHAT? HER WEB PORTAL STILL WORKS?!*
*THIS BROADCAST AIRS AFTER SPIDER-GEDDON!
WHO.
THE HAY.
IS BUCKY?!
PLUM VODKA
CLICK
UCKY BARNS HORSEMAN
GOLDEN GRROWLS
TRUE DUCKTECTIVE
GREAT BRITISH BARK-OF
MAD HAMS
=SIGH=
SPIDER-HAM IN:
BOARED AGAIN!
JASON LATOUR
WRITER
DAVID LAFUENTE
ARTIST
RICO RENZI
COLORIST
VC's JOE CARAMAGNA
LETTERER

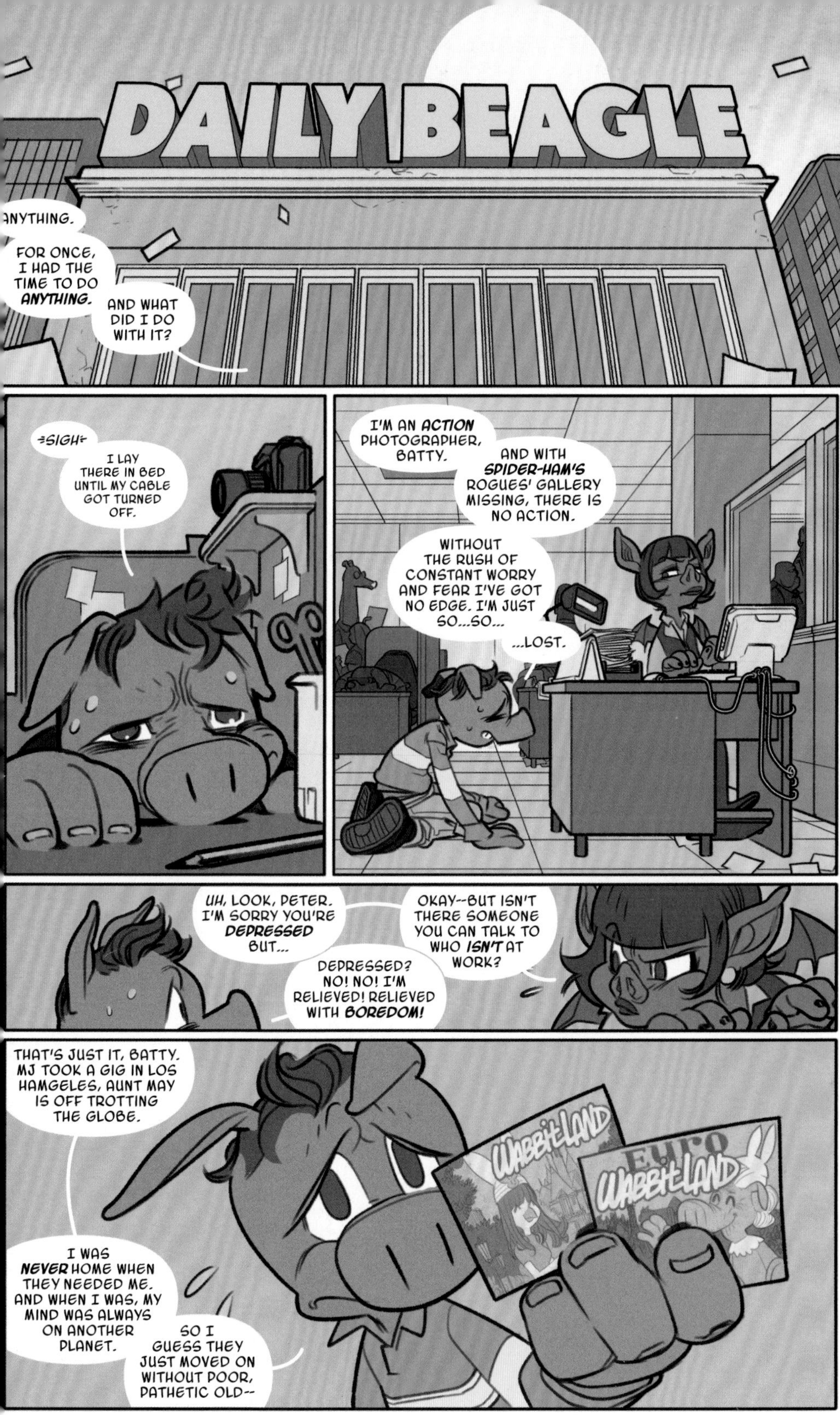
DAILY BEAGLE
ANYTHING.
FOR ONCE, I HAD THE TIME TO DO ANYTHING.
AND WHAT DID I DO WITH IT?
=SIGH=
I LAY THERE IN BED UNTIL MY CABLE GOT TURNED OFF.
I'M AN ACTION PHOTOGRAPHER, BATTY.
AND WITH SPIDER-HAM'S ROGUES' GALLERY MISSING, THERE IS NO ACTION.
WITHOUT THE RUSH OF CONSTANT WORRY AND FEAR I'VE GOT NO EDGE. I'M JUST SO...SO...
...LOST.
UH, LOOK, PETER. I'M SORRY YOU'RE DEPRESSED BUT...
DEPRESSED? NO! NO! I'M RELIEVED! RELIEVED WITH BOREDOM!
OKAY--BUT ISN'T THERE SOMEONE YOU CAN TALK TO WHO ISN'T AT WORK?
THAT'S JUST IT, BATTY. MJ TOOK A GIG IN LOS HAMGELES, AUNT MAY IS OFF TROTTING THE GLOBE.
WABBITLAND
EURO WABBITLAND
I WAS NEVER HOME WHEN THEY NEEDED ME. AND WHEN I WAS, MY MIND WAS ALWAYS ON ANOTHER PLANET.
SO I GUESS THEY JUST MOVED ON WITHOUT POOR, PATHETIC OLD--

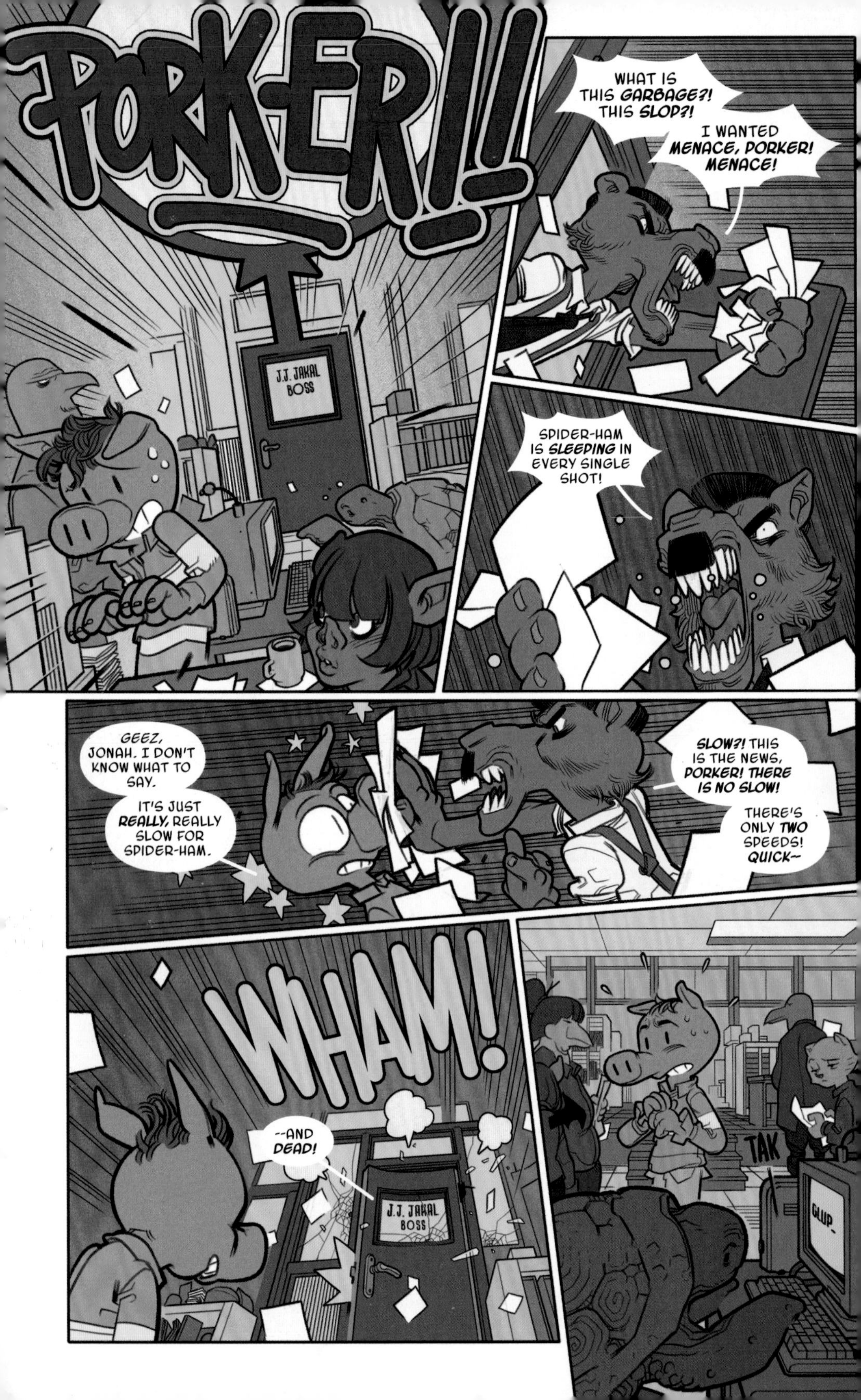
PORK-ER!!
J.J. JAKAL BOSS
WHAT IS THIS GARBAGE?! THIS SLOP?!
I WANTED MENACE, PORKER! MENACE!
SPIDER-HAM IS SLEEPING IN EVERY SINGLE SHOT!
GEEZ, JONAH. I DON'T KNOW WHAT TO SAY.
IT'S JUST REALLY, REALLY SLOW FOR SPIDER-HAM.
SLOW?! THIS IS THE NEWS, PORKER! THERE IS NO SLOW!
THERE'S ONLY TWO SPEEDS! QUICK--
WHAM!
--AND DEAD!
J.J. JAKAL BOSS
TAK
GLUP_

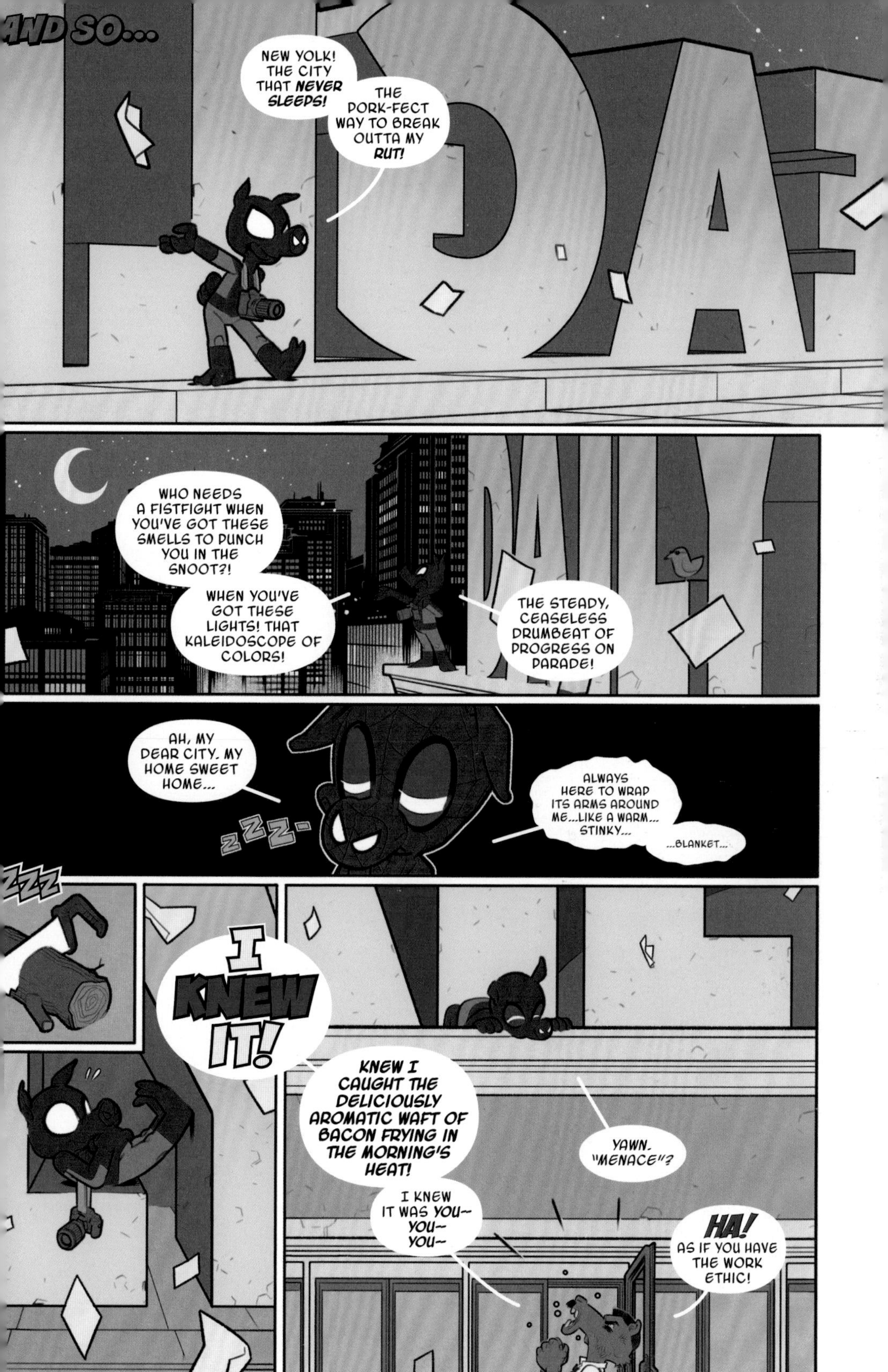

AND SO...
NEW YOLK! THE CITY THAT NEVER SLEEPS!
THE PORK-FECT WAY TO BREAK OUTTA MY RUT!
WHO NEEDS A FISTFIGHT WHEN YOU'VE GOT THESE SMELLS TO PUNCH YOU IN THE SNOOT?!
WHEN YOU'VE GOT THESE LIGHTS! THAT KALEIDOSCOPE OF COLORS!
THE STEADY, CEASELESS DRUMBEAT OF PROGRESS ON PARADE!
AH, MY DEAR CITY. MY HOME SWEET HOME...
ZZZ-
ALWAYS HERE TO WRAP ITS ARMS AROUND ME...LIKE A WARM... STINKY...
...BLANKET...
ZZZ
I KNEW IT!
KNEW I CAUGHT THE DELICIOUSLY AROMATIC WAFT OF BACON FRYING IN THE MORNING'S HEAT!
I KNEW IT WAS YOU-- YOU-- YOU--
YAWN. "MENACE"?
HA! AS IF YOU HAVE THE WORK ETHIC!

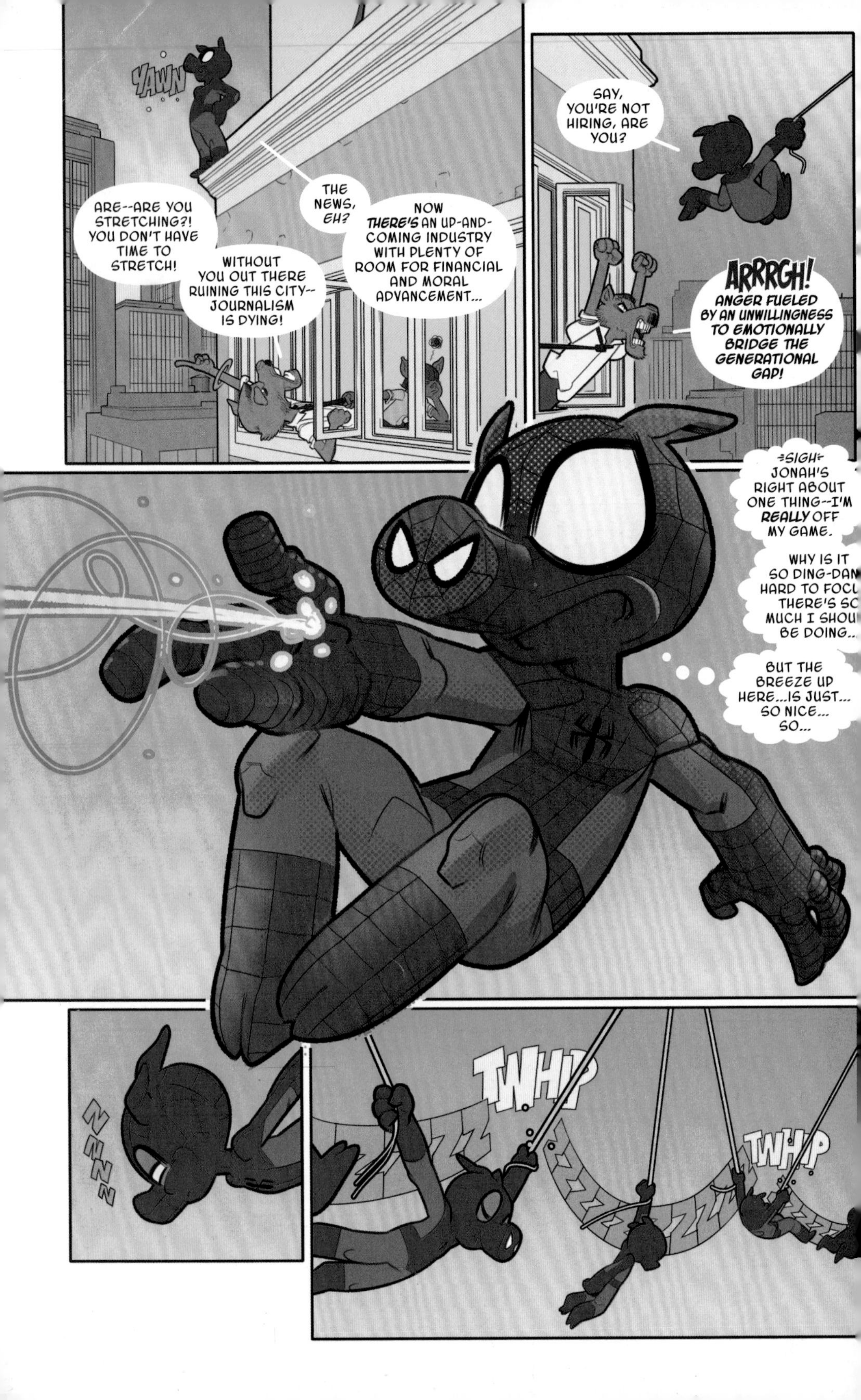
YAWN
ARE--ARE YOU STRETCHING?! YOU DON'T HAVE TIME TO STRETCH!
WITHOUT YOU OUT THERE RUINING THIS CITY-- JOURNALISM IS DYING!
THE NEWS, EH?
NOW THERE'S AN UP-AND-COMING INDUSTRY WITH PLENTY OF ROOM FOR FINANCIAL AND MORAL ADVANCEMENT...
SAY, YOU'RE NOT HIRING, ARE YOU?
ARRRGH!
ANGER FUELED BY AN UNWILLINGNESS TO EMOTIONALLY BRIDGE THE GENERATIONAL GAP!
=SIGH= JONAH'S RIGHT ABOUT ONE THING--I'M REALLY OFF MY GAME.
WHY IS IT SO DING-DAN HARD TO FOCU THERE'S SO MUCH I SHOU BE DOING...
BUT THE BREEZE UP HERE...IS JUST... SO NICE... SO...
NNNN
TWHIP
TWHIP

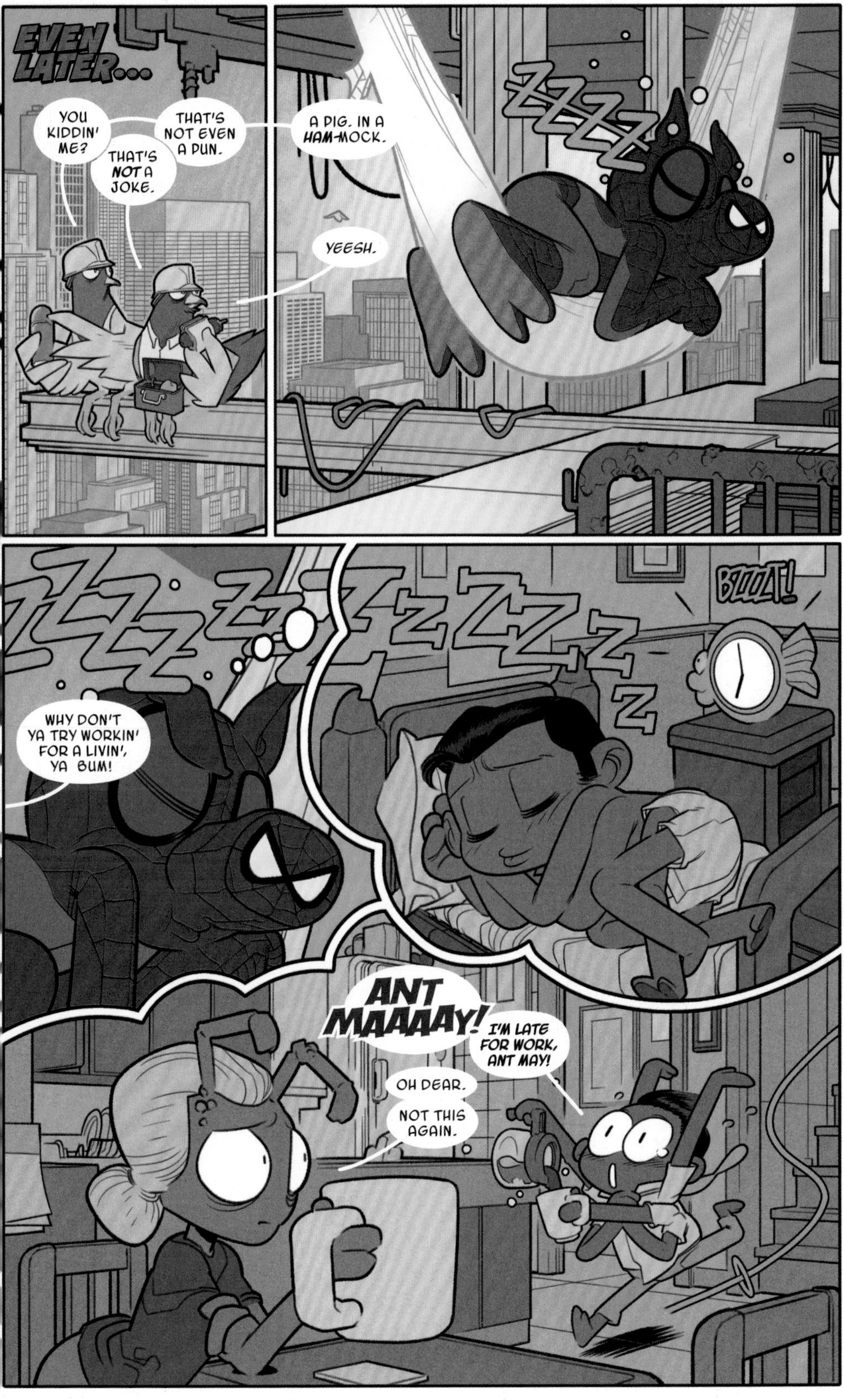
EVEN LATER...
YOU KIDDIN' ME?
THAT'S NOT A JOKE.
THAT'S NOT EVEN A PUN.
A PIG. IN A HAM-MOCK.
YEESH.
ZZZZZ
ZZZZZ
ZZZZZZ
BZZZT!
WHY DON'T YA TRY WORKIN' FOR A LIVIN', YA BUM!
ANT MAAAAY!
I'M LATE FOR WORK, ANT MAY!
OH DEAR.
NOT THIS AGAIN.

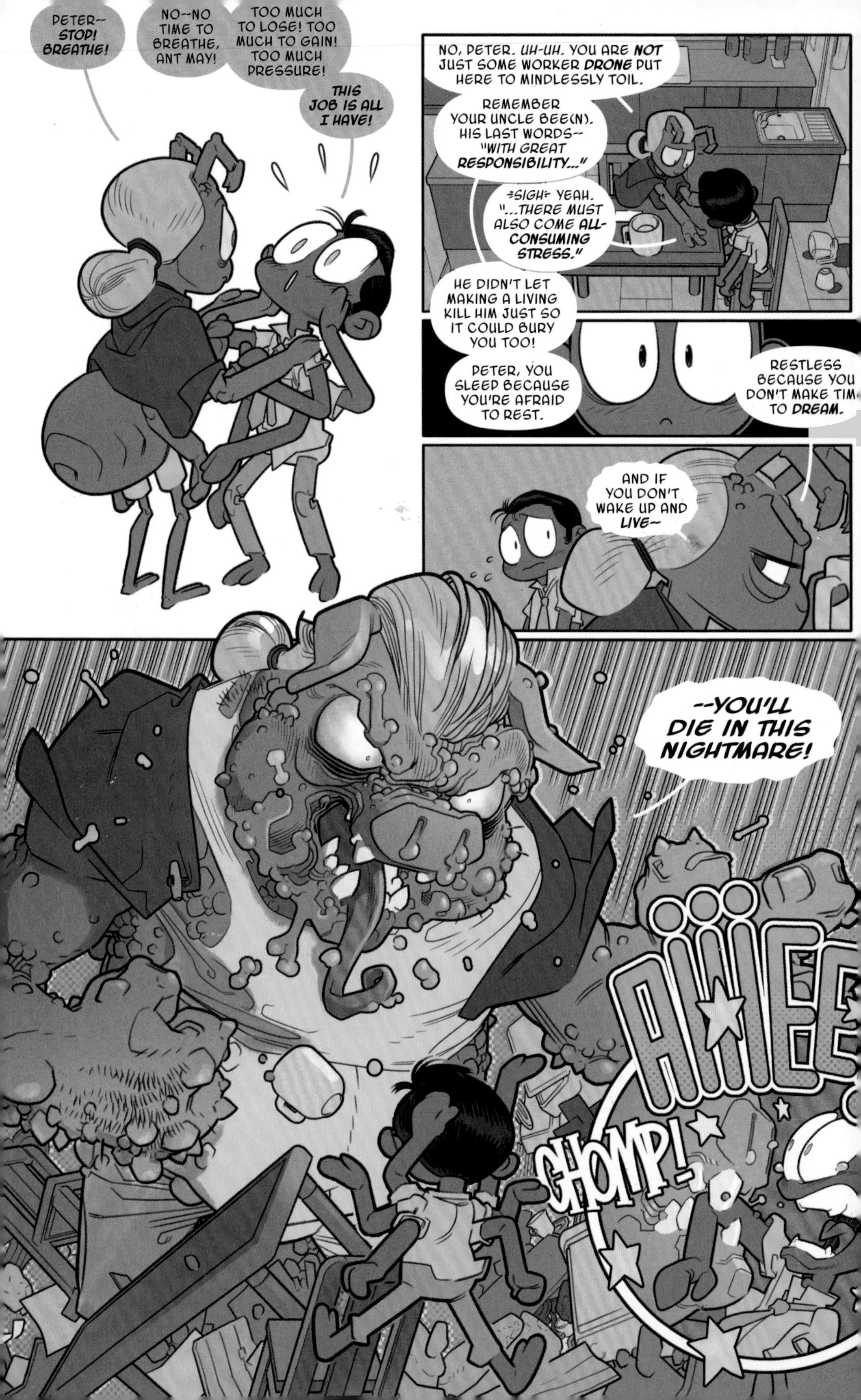
PETER-- STOP! BREATHE!
NO--NO TIME TO BREATHE, ANT MAY!
TOO MUCH TO LOSE! TOO MUCH TO GAIN! TOO MUCH PRESSURE!
THIS JOB IS ALL I HAVE!
NO, PETER. UH-UH. YOU ARE NOT JUST SOME WORKER DRONE PUT HERE TO MINDLESSLY TOIL.
REMEMBER YOUR UNCLE BEE(N). HIS LAST WORDS-- "WITH GREAT RESPONSIBILITY..."
=SIGH= YEAH. "...THERE MUST ALSO COME ALL-CONSUMING STRESS."
HE DIDN'T LET MAKING A LIVING KILL HIM JUST SO IT COULD BURY YOU TOO!
PETER, YOU SLEEP BECAUSE YOU'RE AFRAID TO REST.
RESTLESS BECAUSE YOU DON'T MAKE TIM TO DREAM.
AND IF YOU DON'T WAKE UP AND LIVE--
--YOU'LL DIE IN THIS NIGHTMARE!
CHOMP!
AIIEE

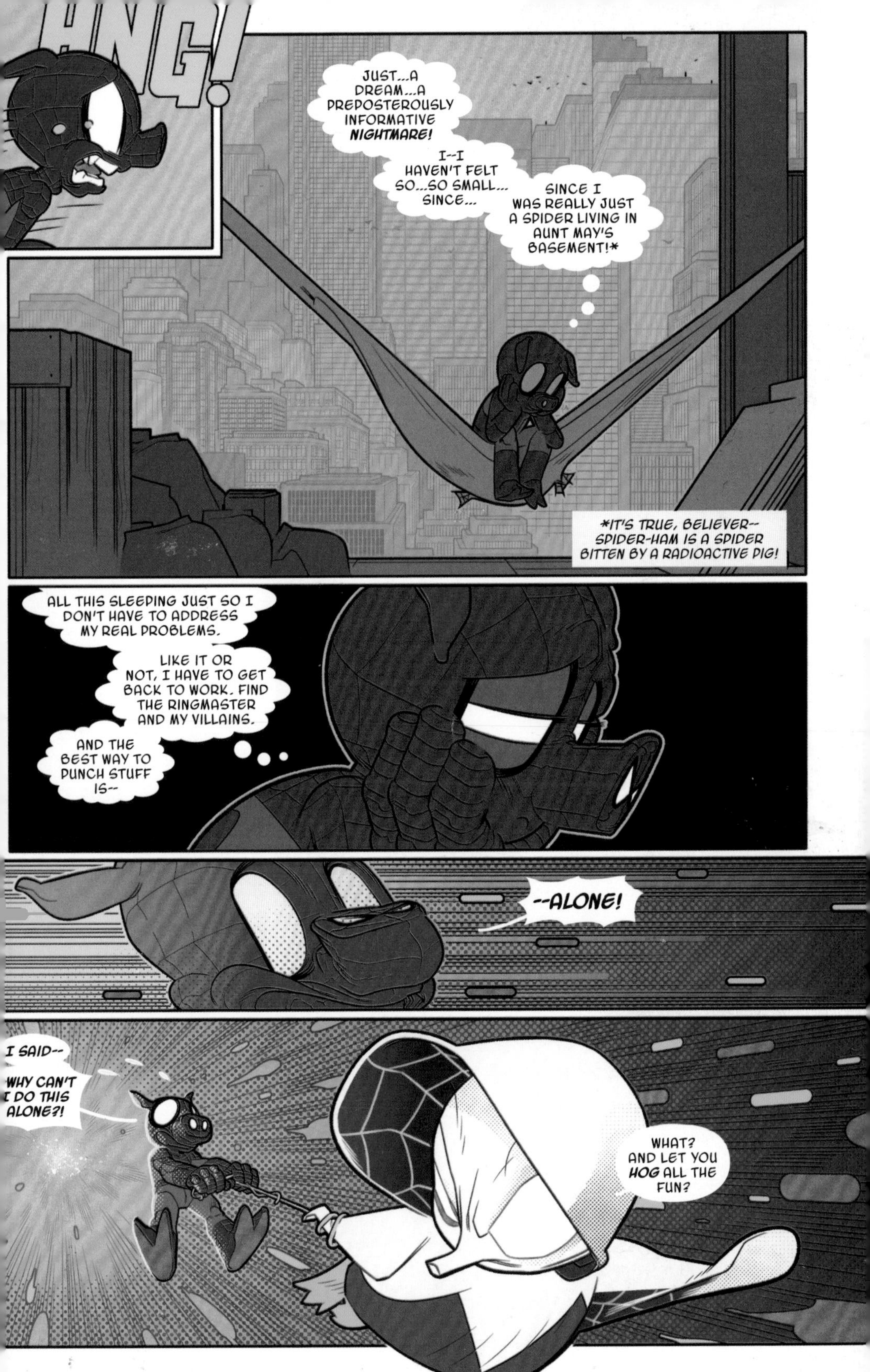
ANG!
JUST...A DREAM...A PREPOSTEROUSLY INFORMATIVE NIGHTMARE!
I--I HAVEN'T FELT SO...SO SMALL... SINCE...
SINCE I WAS REALLY JUST A SPIDER LIVING IN AUNT MAY'S BASEMENT!*
*IT'S TRUE, BELIEVER-- SPIDER-HAM IS A SPIDER BITTEN BY A RADIOACTIVE PIG!
ALL THIS SLEEPING JUST SO I DON'T HAVE TO ADDRESS MY REAL PROBLEMS.
LIKE IT OR NOT, I HAVE TO GET BACK TO WORK. FIND THE RINGMASTER AND MY VILLAINS.
AND THE BEST WAY TO PUNCH STUFF IS--
--ALONE!
I SAID--
WHY CAN'T I DO THIS ALONE?!
WHAT? AND LET YOU HOG ALL THE FUN?

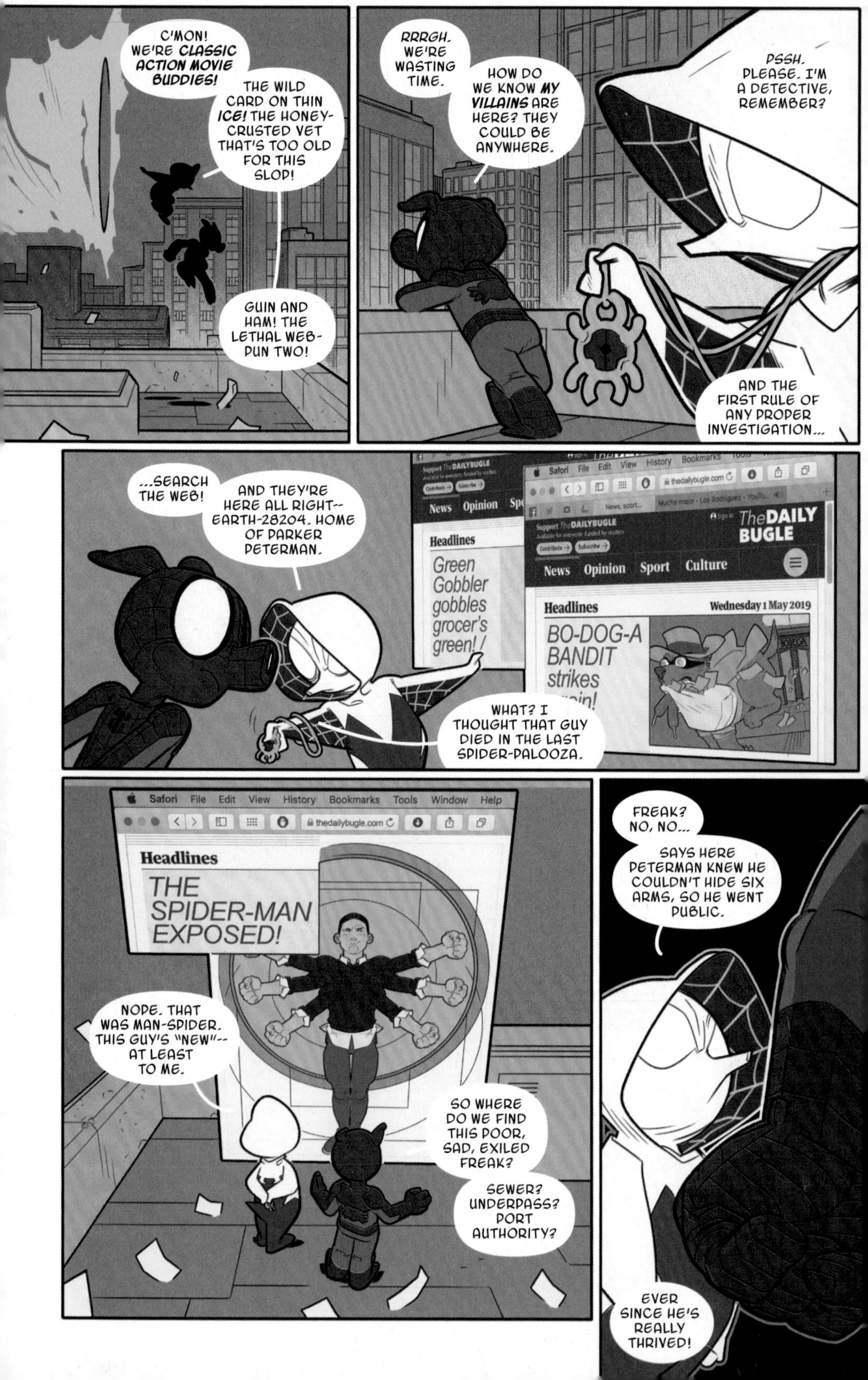
C'MON! WE'RE CLASSIC ACTION MOVIE BUDDIES!
THE WILD CARD ON THIN ICE! THE HONEY-CRUSTED VET THAT'S TOO OLD FOR THIS SLOP!
GUIN AND HAM! THE LETHAL WEB-PUN TWO!
RRRGH. WE'RE WASTING TIME.
HOW DO WE KNOW MY VILLAINS ARE HERE? THEY COULD BE ANYWHERE.
PSSH. PLEASE. I'M A DETECTIVE, REMEMBER?
AND THE FIRST RULE OF ANY PROPER INVESTIGATION...
...SEARCH THE WEB!
AND THEY'RE HERE ALL RIGHT--EARTH-28204. HOME OF PARKER PETERMAN.
Safori File Edit View History Bookmarks Tools
thedailybugle.com
The DAILY BUGLE
News Opinion Sport Culture
Headlines
Wednesday 1 May 2019
Green Gobbler gobbles grocer's green!
BO-DOG-A BANDIT strikes
WHAT? I THOUGHT THAT GUY DIED IN THE LAST SPIDER-PALOOZA.
Safori File Edit View History Bookmarks Tools Window Help
thedailybugle.com
Headlines
THE SPIDER-MAN EXPOSED!
NOPE. THAT WAS MAN-SPIDER. THIS GUY'S "NEW"--AT LEAST TO ME.
SO WHERE DO WE FIND THIS POOR, SAD, EXILED FREAK?
SEWER? UNDERPASS? PORT AUTHORITY?
FREAK? NO, NO...
SAYS HERE PETERMAN KNEW HE COULDN'T HIDE SIX ARMS, SO HE WENT PUBLIC.
EVER SINCE HE'S REALLY THRIVED!

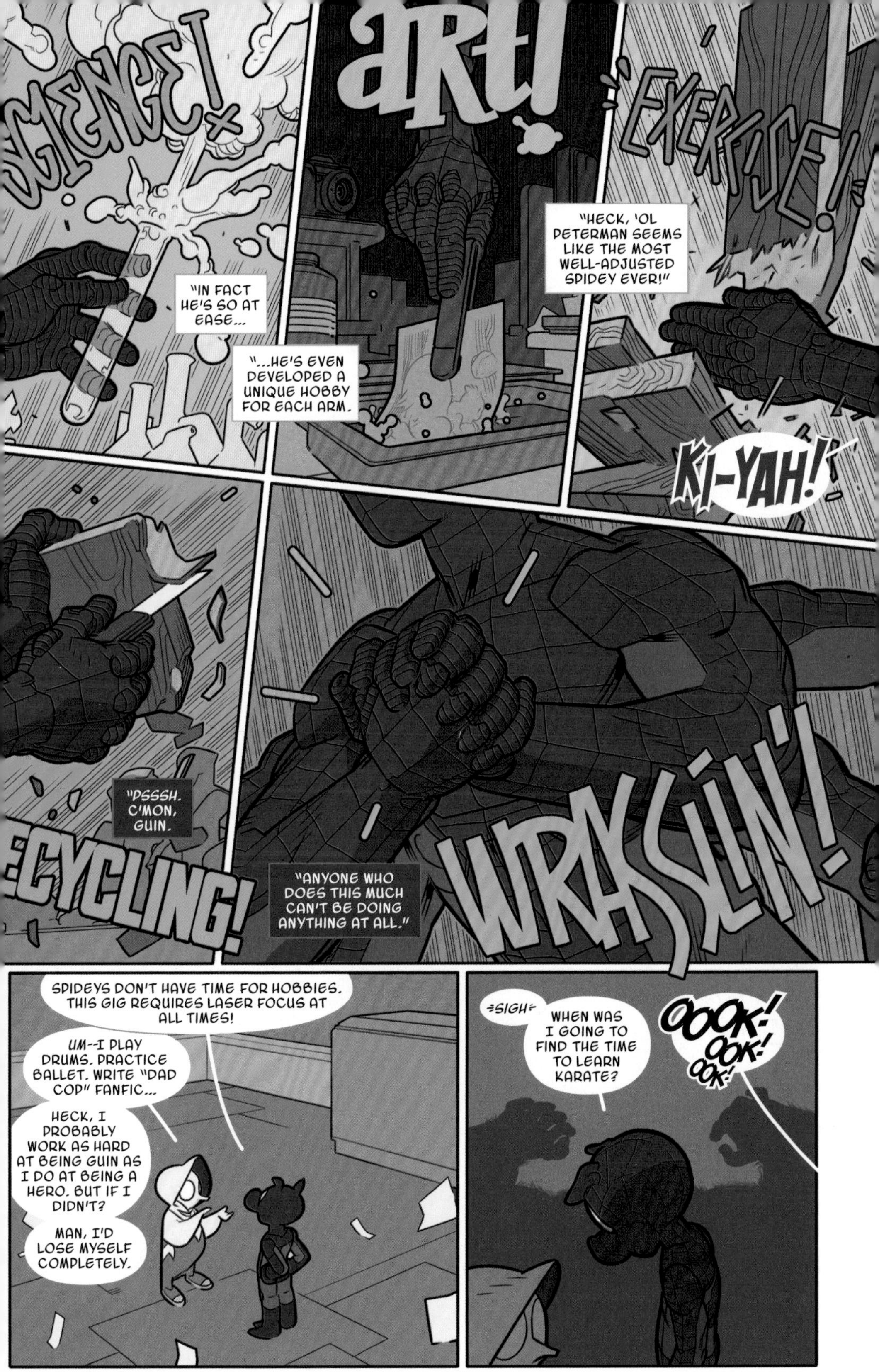
SCIENCE!
ART!
EXERCISE!
"IN FACT HE'S SO AT EASE...
"...HE'S EVEN DEVELOPED A UNIQUE HOBBY FOR EACH ARM.
"HECK, 'OL PETERMAN SEEMS LIKE THE MOST WELL-ADJUSTED SPIDEY EVER!"
KI-YAH!
"PSSSH. C'MON, GUIN.
RECYCLING!
"ANYONE WHO DOES THIS MUCH CAN'T BE DOING ANYTHING AT ALL."
WRASLIN'!
SPIDEYS DON'T HAVE TIME FOR HOBBIES. THIS GIG REQUIRES LASER FOCUS AT ALL TIMES!
UM--I PLAY DRUMS. PRACTICE BALLET. WRITE "DAD COP" FANFIC...
HECK, I PROBABLY WORK AS HARD AT BEING GUIN AS I DO AT BEING A HERO. BUT IF I DIDN'T?
MAN, I'D LOSE MYSELF COMPLETELY.
=SIGH=
WHEN WAS I GOING TO FIND THE TIME TO LEARN KARATE?
OOOK-OOK!-OOK!

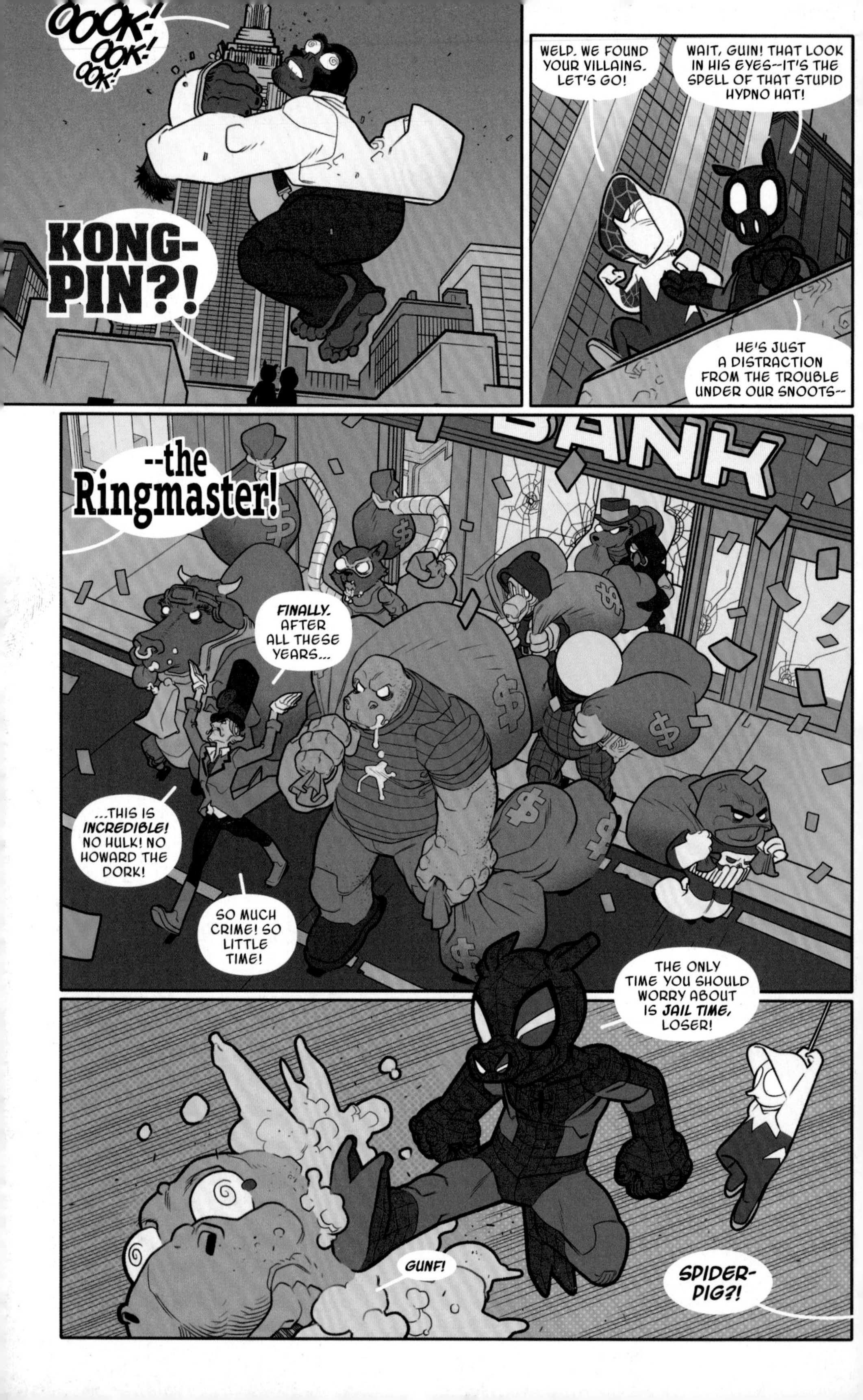
OOOK! OOK! OOK!
KONG-PIN?!
WELP. WE FOUND YOUR VILLAINS. LET'S GO!
WAIT, GUIN! THAT LOOK IN HIS EYES--IT'S THE SPELL OF THAT STUPID HYPNO HAT!
HE'S JUST A DISTRACTION FROM THE TROUBLE UNDER OUR SNOOTS--
BANK
--the Ringmaster!
FINALLY. AFTER ALL THESE YEARS...
...THIS IS INCREDIBLE! NO HULK! NO HOWARD THE DORK!
SO MUCH CRIME! SO LITTLE TIME!
THE ONLY TIME YOU SHOULD WORRY ABOUT IS JAIL TIME, LOSER!
GUNF!
SPIDER-PIG?!

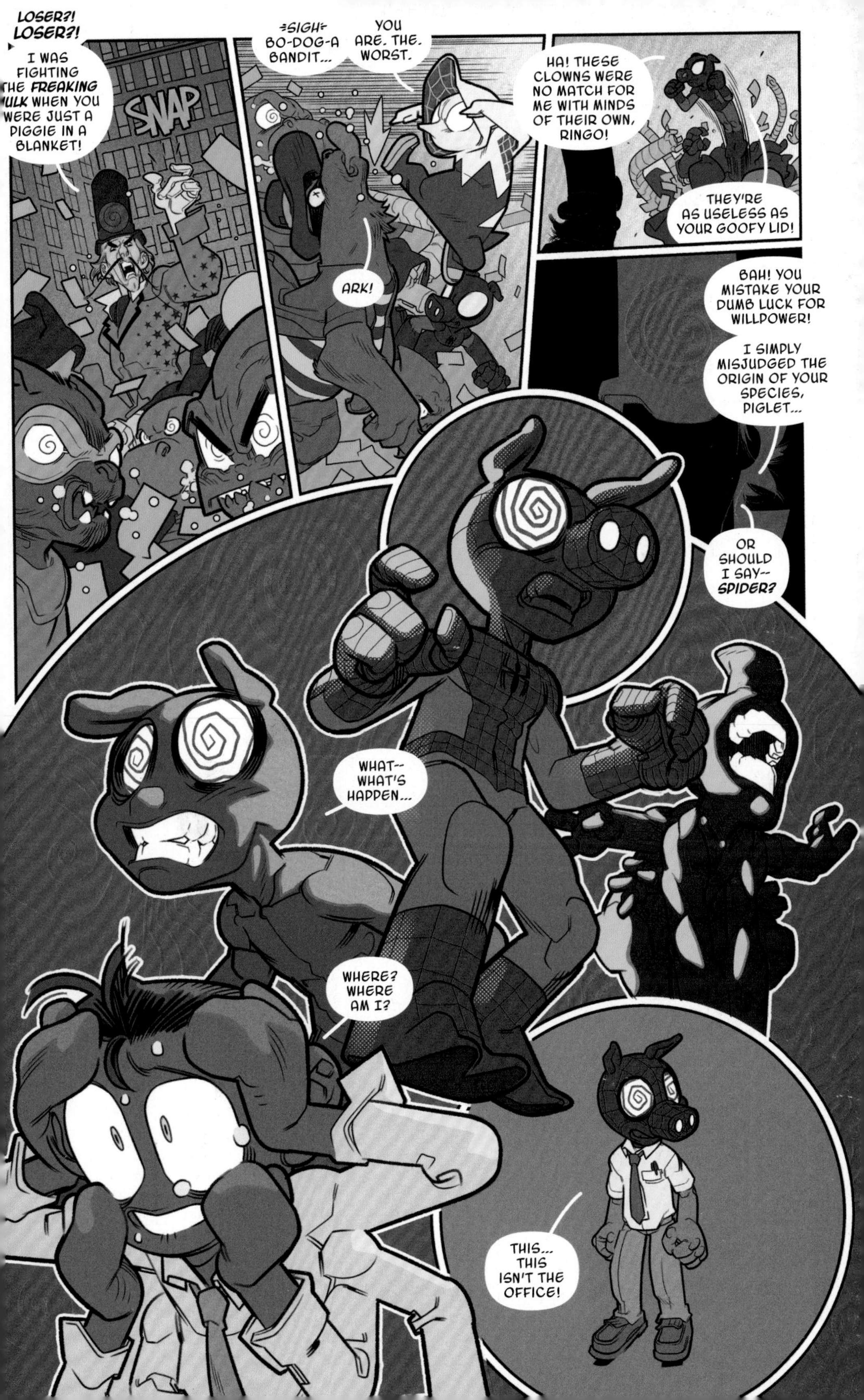
LOSER?! LOSER?!
I WAS FIGHTING THE FREAKING HULK WHEN YOU WERE JUST A PIGGIE IN A BLANKET!
SNAP
=SIGH= BO-DOG-A BANDIT...
YOU ARE. THE. WORST.
ARK!
HA! THESE CLOWNS WERE NO MATCH FOR ME WITH MINDS OF THEIR OWN, RINGO!
THEY'RE AS USELESS AS YOUR GOOFY LID!
BAH! YOU MISTAKE YOUR DUMB LUCK FOR WILLPOWER!
I SIMPLY MISJUDGED THE ORIGIN OF YOUR SPECIES, PIGLET...
OR SHOULD I SAY-- SPIDER?
WHAT-- WHAT'S HAPPEN...
WHERE? WHERE AM I?
THIS... THIS ISN'T THE OFFICE!

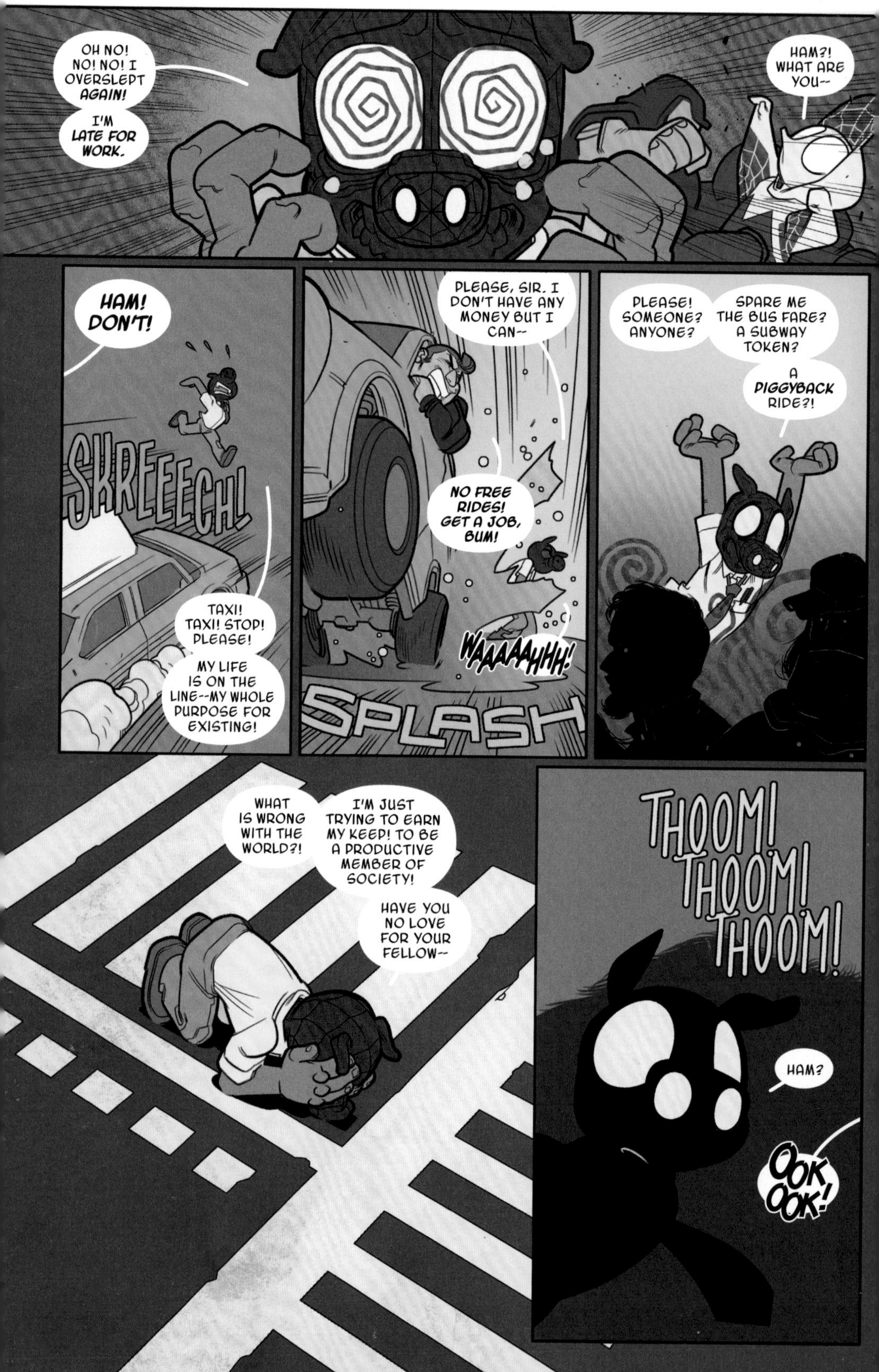
OH NO! NO! NO! I OVERSLEPT AGAIN!
I'M LATE FOR WORK.
HAM?! WHAT ARE YOU--
HAM! DON'T!
SKREEECH!
TAXI! TAXI! STOP! PLEASE!
MY LIFE IS ON THE LINE--MY WHOLE PURPOSE FOR EXISTING!
PLEASE, SIR. I DON'T HAVE ANY MONEY BUT I CAN--
NO FREE RIDES! GET A JOB, BUM!
WAAAAAHHH!
SPLASH
PLEASE! SOMEONE? ANYONE?
SPARE ME THE BUS FARE? A SUBWAY TOKEN?
A PIGGYBACK RIDE?!
WHAT IS WRONG WITH THE WORLD?!
I'M JUST TRYING TO EARN MY KEEP! TO BE A PRODUCTIVE MEMBER OF SOCIETY!
HAVE YOU NO LOVE FOR YOUR FELLOW--
THOOM! THOOM! THOOM!
HAM?
OOK OOK!

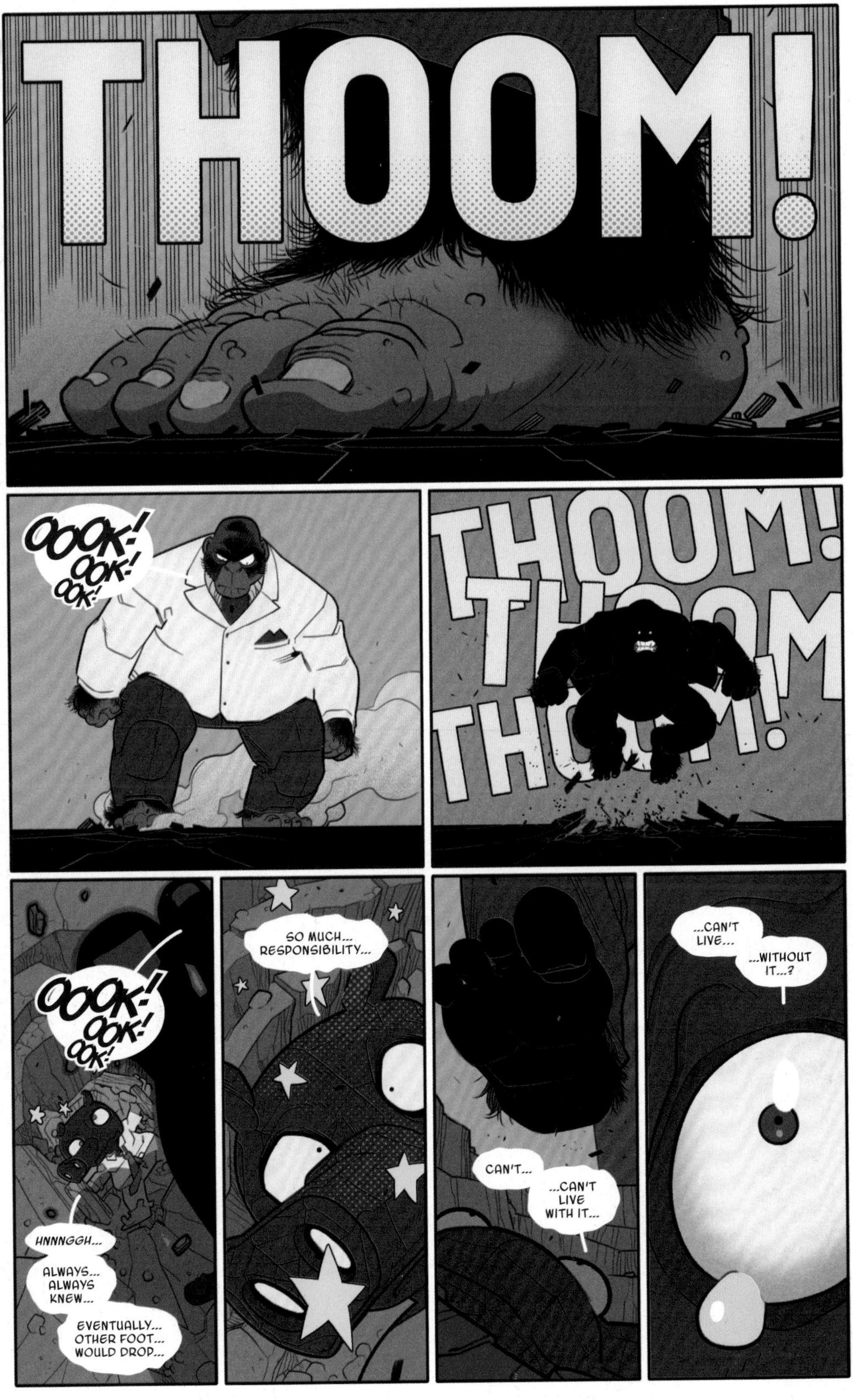
THOOM!
OOOK-! OOK-! OOK-!
THOOM! THOOM THOOM!
OOOK-! OOK-! OOK-!
HNNNGGH...
ALWAYS... ALWAYS KNEW...
EVENTUALLY... OTHER FOOT... WOULD DROP...
SO MUCH... RESPONSIBILITY...
CAN'T...
...CAN'T LIVE WITH IT...
...CAN'T LIVE...
...WITHOUT IT...?

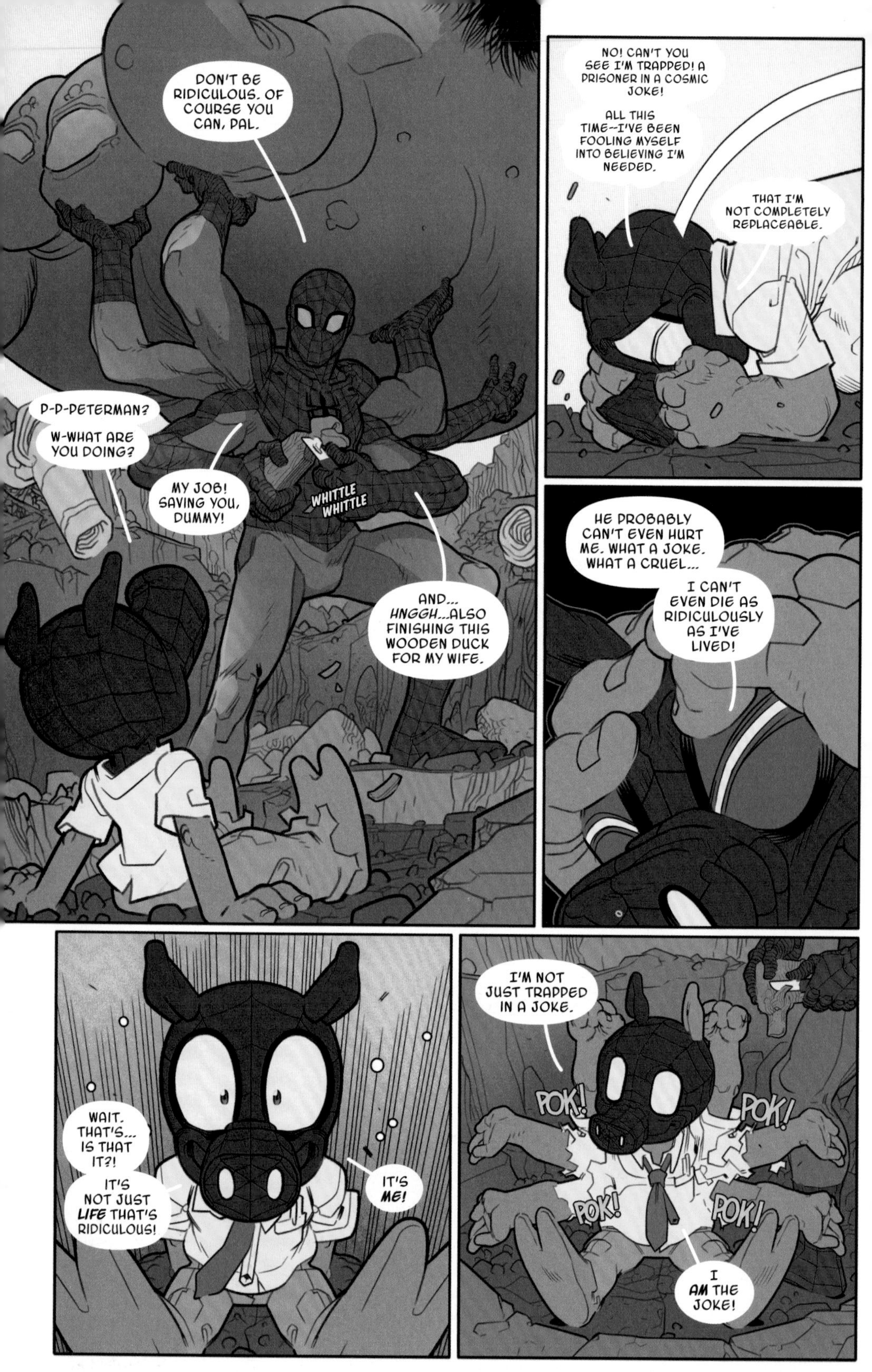
DON'T BE RIDICULOUS. OF COURSE YOU CAN, PAL.
P-P-PETERMAN?
W-WHAT ARE YOU DOING?
MY JOB! SAVING YOU, DUMMY!
WHITTLE WHITTLE
AND... HNGGH...ALSO FINISHING THIS WOODEN DUCK FOR MY WIFE.
NO! CAN'T YOU SEE I'M TRAPPED! A PRISONER IN A COSMIC JOKE!
ALL THIS TIME--I'VE BEEN FOOLING MYSELF INTO BELIEVING I'M NEEDED.
THAT I'M NOT COMPLETELY REPLACEABLE.
HE PROBABLY CAN'T EVEN HURT ME. WHAT A JOKE. WHAT A CRUEL...
I CAN'T EVEN DIE AS RIDICULOUSLY AS I'VE LIVED!
WAIT. THAT'S... IS THAT IT?!
IT'S NOT JUST LIFE THAT'S RIDICULOUS!
IT'S ME!
I'M NOT JUST TRAPPED IN A JOKE.
POK! POK! POK! POK!
I AM THE JOKE!

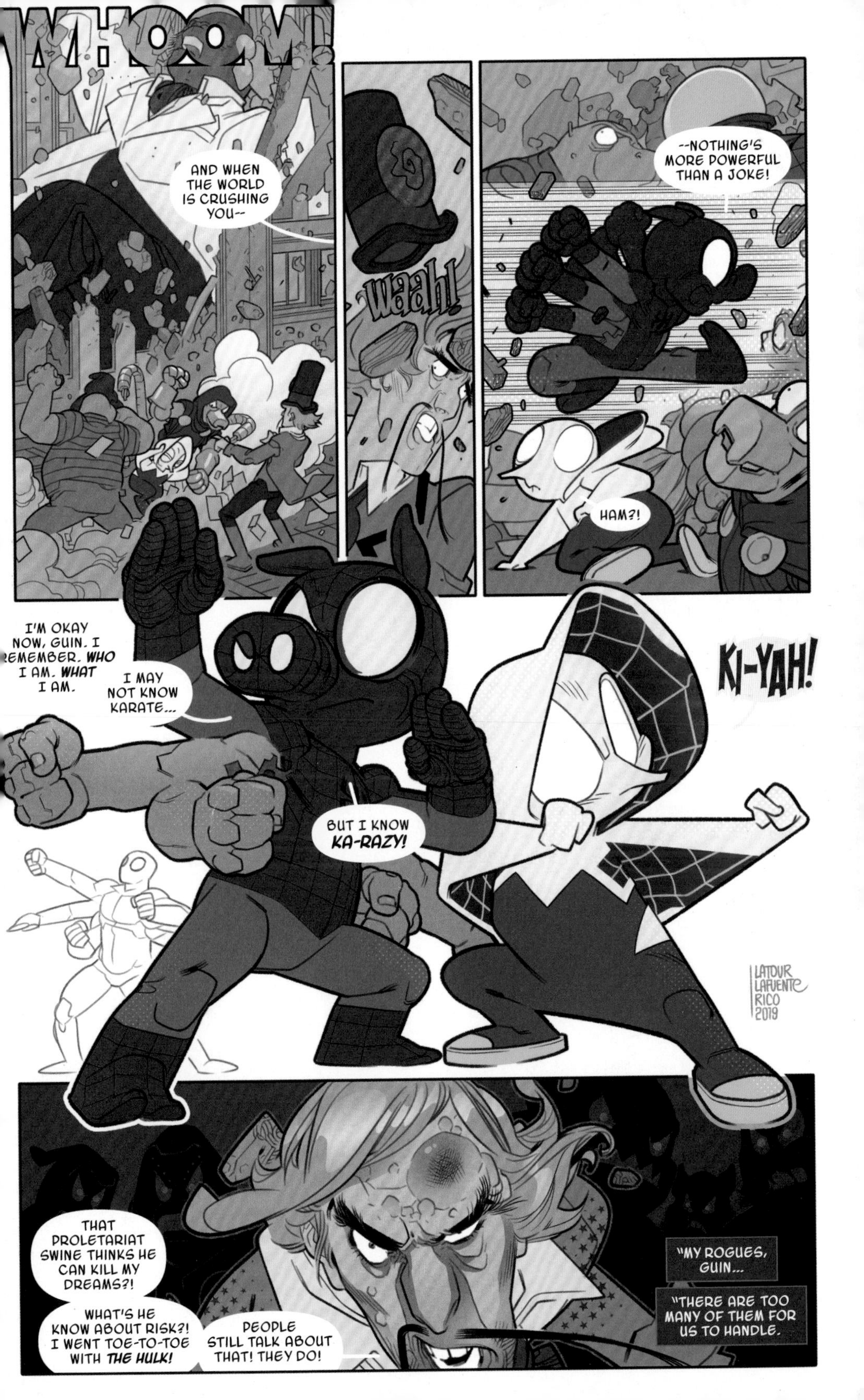
WHOOOM!
AND WHEN THE WORLD IS CRUSHING YOU--
Waaah!
--NOTHING'S MORE POWERFUL THAN A JOKE!
HAM?!
I'M OKAY NOW, GUIN. I REMEMBER. WHO I AM. WHAT I AM.
I MAY NOT KNOW KARATE...
BUT I KNOW KA-RAZY!
KI-YAH!
LATOUR LAFUENTE RICO 2019
THAT PROLETARIAT SWINE THINKS HE CAN KILL MY DREAMS?!
WHAT'S HE KNOW ABOUT RISK?! I WENT TOE-TO-TOE WITH THE HULK!
PEOPLE STILL TALK ABOUT THAT! THEY DO!
"MY ROGUES, GUIN...
"THERE ARE TOO MANY OF THEM FOR US TO HANDLE.

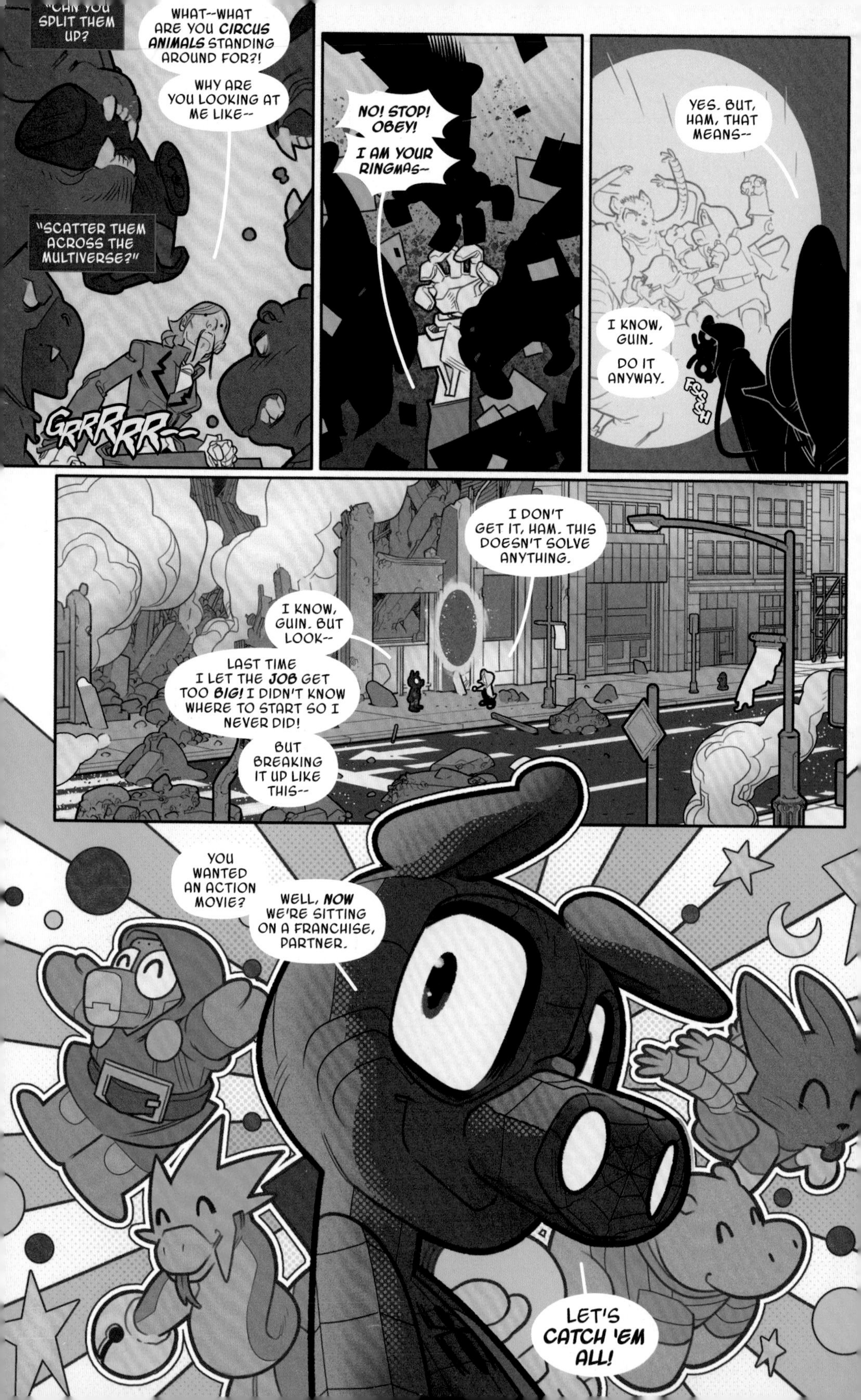
"CAN YOU SPLIT THEM UP?
WHAT--WHAT ARE YOU CIRCUS ANIMALS STANDING AROUND FOR?!
WHY ARE YOU LOOKING AT ME LIKE--
"SCATTER THEM ACROSS THE MULTIVERSE?"
GRRRRR--
NO! STOP! OBEY!
I AM YOUR RINGMAS--
YES. BUT, HAM, THAT MEANS--
I KNOW, GUIN.
DO IT ANYWAY.
FSSSH
I DON'T GET IT, HAM. THIS DOESN'T SOLVE ANYTHING.
I KNOW, GUIN. BUT LOOK--
LAST TIME I LET THE JOB GET TOO BIG! I DIDN'T KNOW WHERE TO START SO I NEVER DID!
BUT BREAKING IT UP LIKE THIS--
YOU WANTED AN ACTION MOVIE?
WELL, NOW WE'RE SITTING ON A FRANCHISE, PARTNER.
LET'S CATCH 'EM ALL!

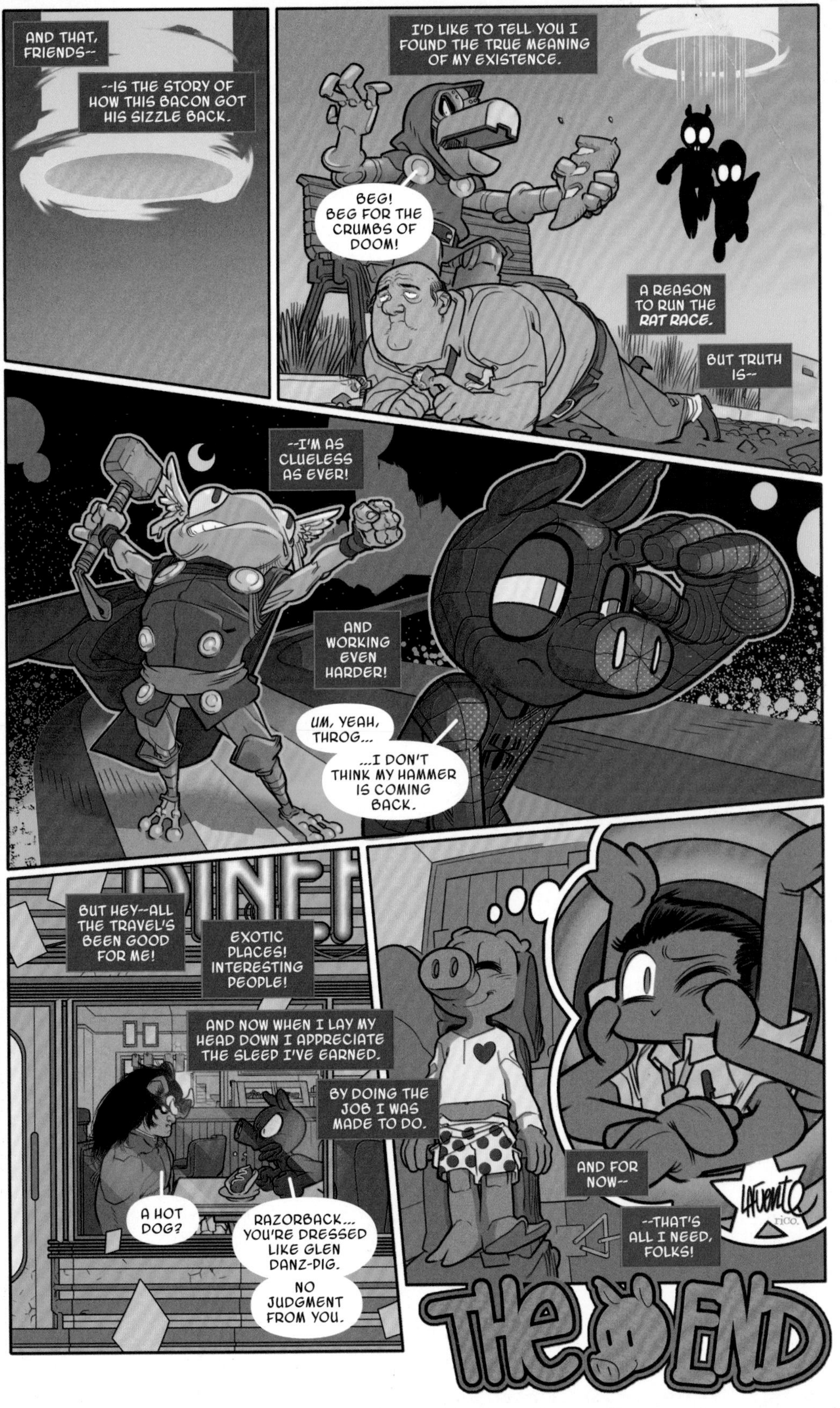
AND THAT, FRIENDS--
--IS THE STORY OF HOW THIS BACON GOT HIS SIZZLE BACK.
I'D LIKE TO TELL YOU I FOUND THE TRUE MEANING OF MY EXISTENCE.
BEG! BEG FOR THE CRUMBS OF DOOM!
A REASON TO RUN THE RAT RACE.
BUT TRUTH IS--
--I'M AS CLUELESS AS EVER!
AND WORKING EVEN HARDER!
UM, YEAH, THROG...
...I DON'T THINK MY HAMMER IS COMING BACK.
BUT HEY--ALL THE TRAVEL'S BEEN GOOD FOR ME!
EXOTIC PLACES! INTERESTING PEOPLE!
AND NOW WHEN I LAY MY HEAD DOWN I APPRECIATE THE SLEEP I'VE EARNED.
BY DOING THE JOB I WAS MADE TO DO.
A HOT DOG?
RAZORBACK... YOU'RE DRESSED LIKE GLEN DANZ-PIG.
NO JUDGMENT FROM YOU.
AND FOR NOW--
--THAT'S ALL I NEED, FOLKS!
LAFUENTE rico.
THE END

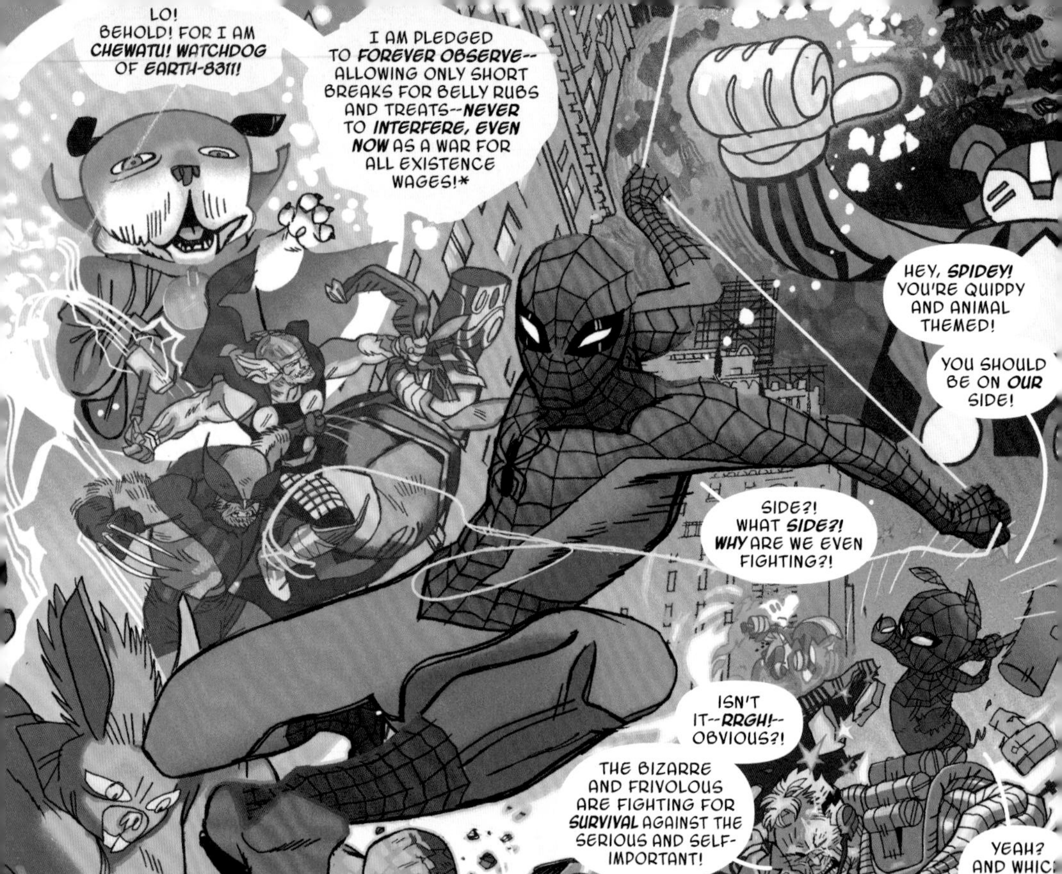
LO! BEHOLD! FOR I AM CHEWATU! WATCHDOG OF EARTH-8311!
I AM PLEDGED TO FOREVER OBSERVE-- ALLOWING ONLY SHORT BREAKS FOR BELLY RUBS AND TREATS--NEVER TO INTERFERE, EVEN NOW AS A WAR FOR ALL EXISTENCE WAGES!*
HEY, SPIDEY! YOU'RE QUIPPY AND ANIMAL THEMED!
YOU SHOULD BE ON OUR SIDE!
SIDE?! WHAT SIDE?! WHY ARE WE EVEN FIGHTING?!
ISN'T IT--RRGH!-- OBVIOUS?!
THE BIZARRE AND FRIVOLOUS ARE FIGHTING FOR SURVIVAL AGAINST THE SERIOUS AND SELF-IMPORTANT!
YEAH? AND WHIC ONE ARE YOU?!

A SECRET ROAR RAGES?

WRITTEN BY PHIL LORD, CHRISTOPHER MILLER & JASON LATOUR
ART & COLOR BY JASON LATOUR LETTERS BY VC'S JOE CARAMAGNA

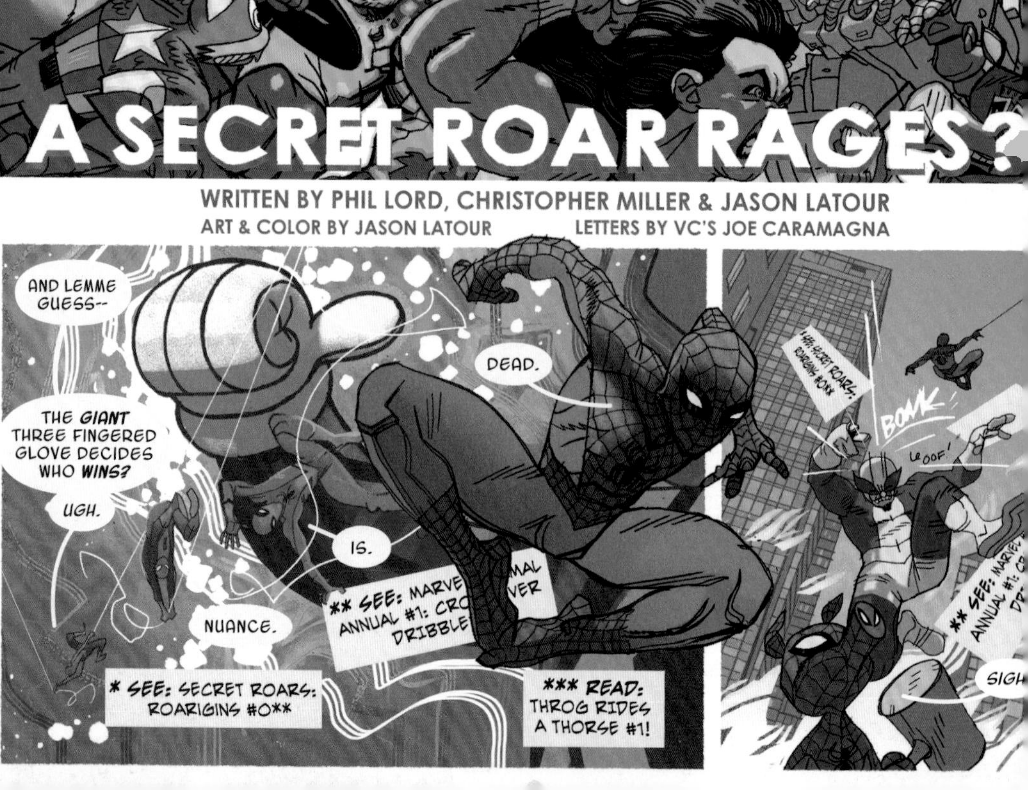
AND LEMME GUESS--
THE GIANT THREE FINGERED GLOVE DECIDES WHO WINS?
DEAD.
UGH.
IS.
NUANCE.
** SEE: MARVE
ANNUAL #1: CRO
DRIBBLE
* SEE: SECRET ROARS: ROARIGINS #0**
*** READ: THROG RIDES A THORSE #1!
BONK
UOOF!
SIGH

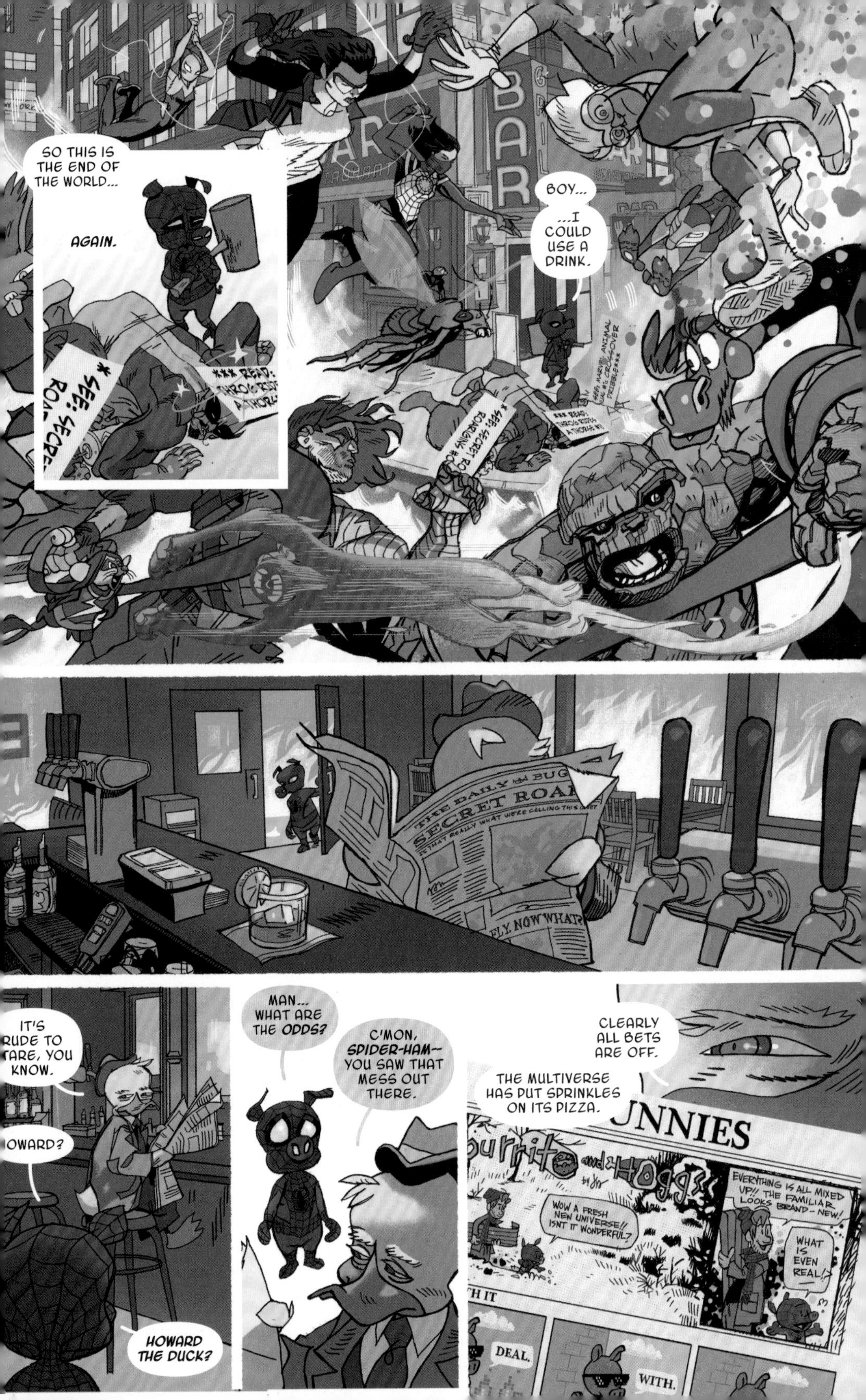
SO THIS IS THE END OF THE WORLD...
AGAIN.
BOY...
...I COULD USE A DRINK.
IT'S RUDE TO TARE, YOU KNOW.
OWARD?
HOWARD THE DUCK?
MAN... WHAT ARE THE ODDS?
C'MON, SPIDER-HAM-- YOU SAW THAT MESS OUT THERE.
CLEARLY ALL BETS ARE OFF.
THE MULTIVERSE HAS PUT SPRINKLES ON ITS PIZZA.
WOW A FRESH NEW UNIVERSE!! ISNT IT WONDERFUL?
EVERYTHING IS ALL MIXED UP!! THE FAMILIAR LOOKS BRAND-NEW!
WHAT IS EVEN REAL!?
DEAL.
WITH.

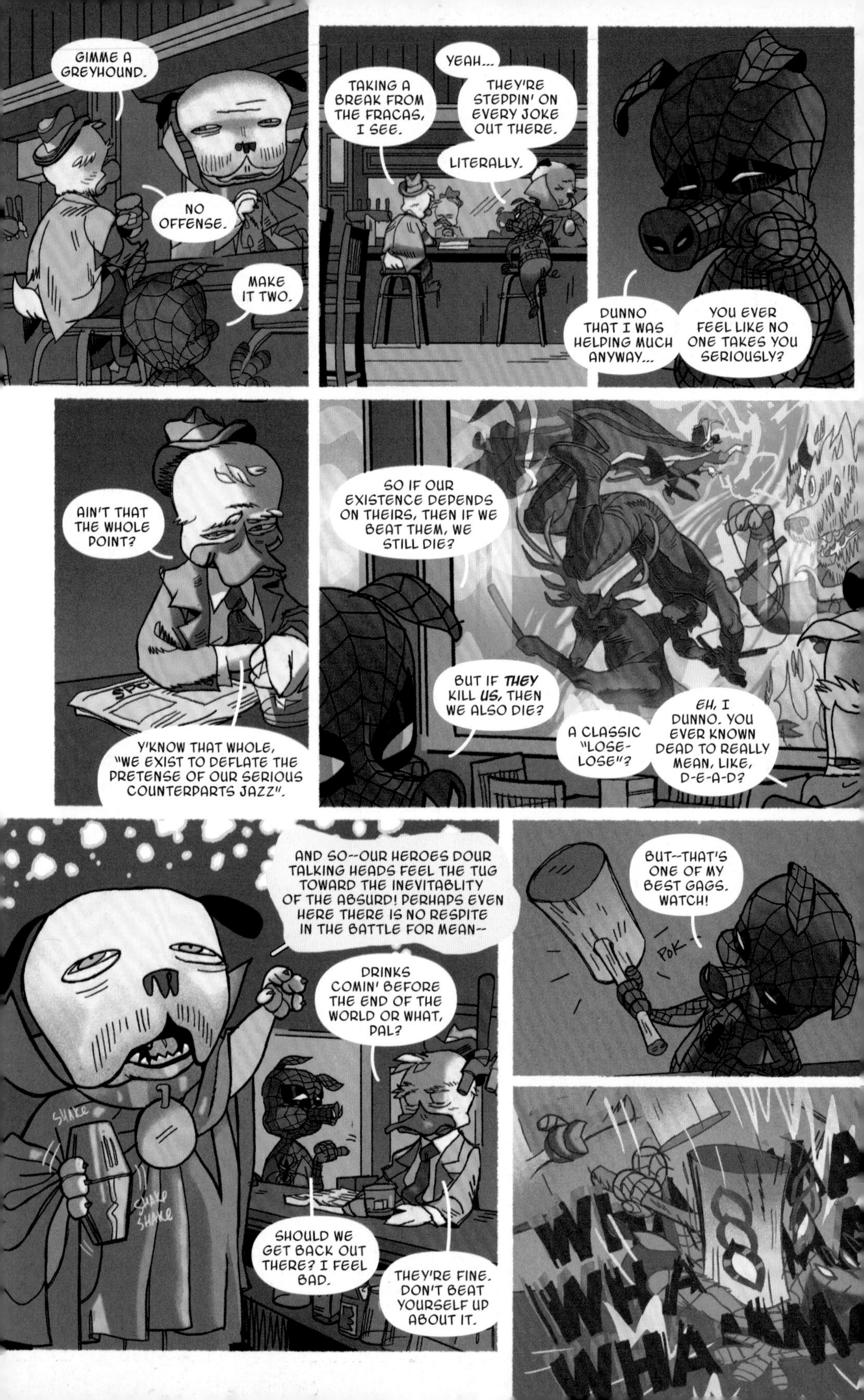
GIMME A GREYHOUND.
NO OFFENSE.
MAKE IT TWO.
TAKING A BREAK FROM THE FRACAS, I SEE.
YEAH...
THEY'RE STEPPIN' ON EVERY JOKE OUT THERE.
LITERALLY.
YOU EVER FEEL LIKE NO ONE TAKES YOU SERIOUSLY?
DUNNO THAT I WAS HELPING MUCH ANYWAY...
AIN'T THAT THE WHOLE POINT?
Y'KNOW THAT WHOLE, "WE EXIST TO DEFLATE THE PRETENSE OF OUR SERIOUS COUNTERPARTS JAZZ".
SO IF OUR EXISTENCE DEPENDS ON THEIRS, THEN IF WE BEAT THEM, WE STILL DIE?
BUT IF *THEY* KILL *US*, THEN WE ALSO DIE?
A CLASSIC "LOSE-LOSE"?
EH, I DUNNO. YOU EVER KNOWN DEAD TO REALLY MEAN, LIKE, D-E-A-D?
AND SO--OUR HEROES DOUR TALKING HEADS FEEL THE TUG TOWARD THE INEVITABLITY OF THE ABSURD! PERHAPS EVEN HERE THERE IS NO RESPITE IN THE BATTLE FOR MEAN--
DRINKS COMIN' BEFORE THE END OF THE WORLD OR WHAT, PAL?
SHAKE
SHAKE SHAKE
SHOULD WE GET BACK OUT THERE? I FEEL BAD.
THEY'RE FINE. DON'T BEAT YOURSELF UP ABOUT IT.
BUT--THAT'S ONE OF MY BEST GAGS. WATCH!
POK
WHAM
WHAM
WHAM

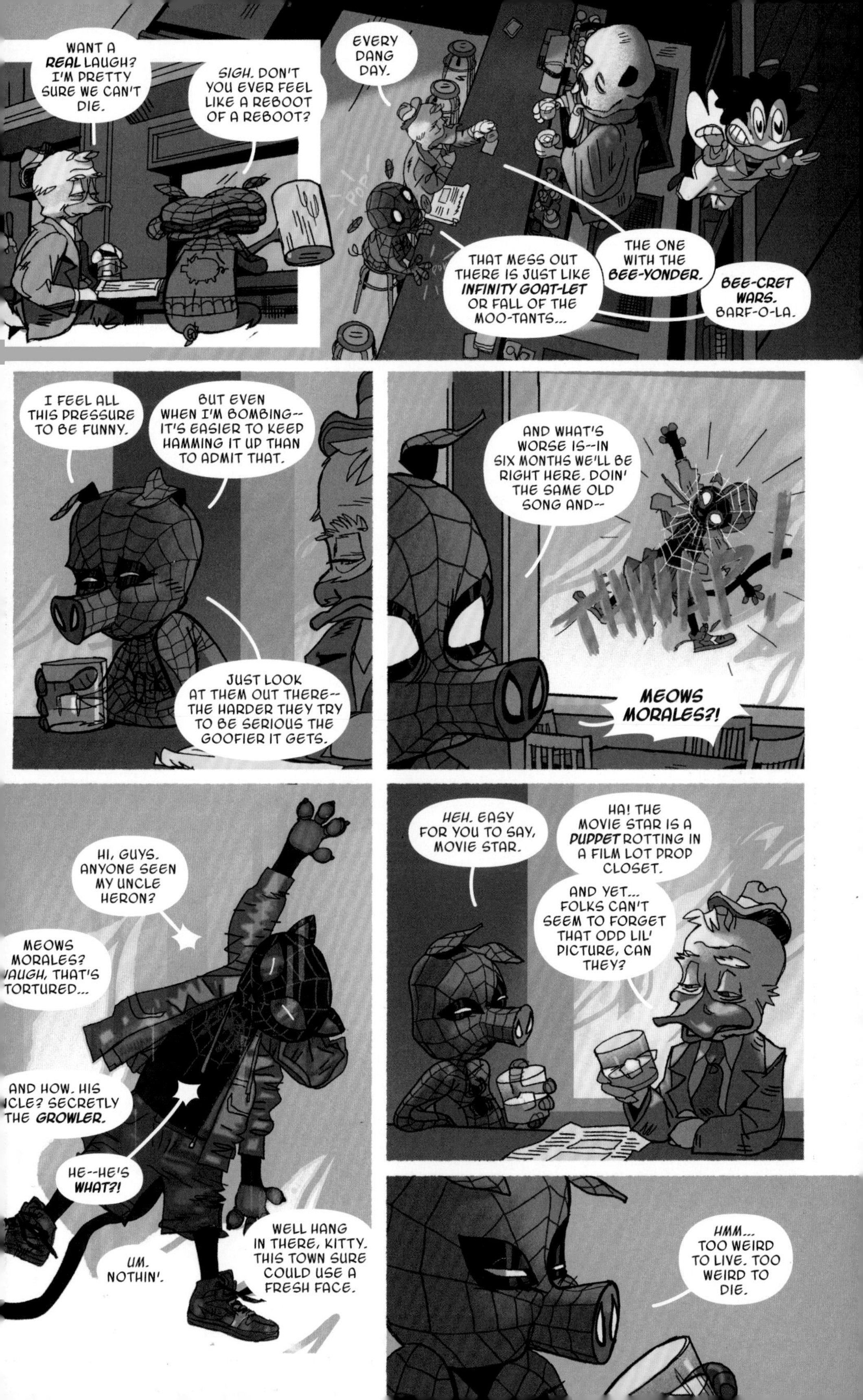
WANT A REAL LAUGH? I'M PRETTY SURE WE CAN'T DIE.
SIGH. DON'T YOU EVER FEEL LIKE A REBOOT OF A REBOOT?
EVERY DANG DAY.
POP
THAT MESS OUT THERE IS JUST LIKE INFINITY GOAT-LET OR FALL OF THE MOO-TANTS...
THE ONE WITH THE BEE-YONDER.
BEE-CRET WARS. BARF-O-LA.
I FEEL ALL THIS PRESSURE TO BE FUNNY.
BUT EVEN WHEN I'M BOMBING-- IT'S EASIER TO KEEP HAMMING IT UP THAN TO ADMIT THAT.
JUST LOOK AT THEM OUT THERE-- THE HARDER THEY TRY TO BE SERIOUS THE GOOFIER IT GETS.
AND WHAT'S WORSE IS--IN SIX MONTHS WE'LL BE RIGHT HERE. DOIN' THE SAME OLD SONG AND--
THWAP!
MEOWS MORALES?!
HI, GUYS. ANYONE SEEN MY UNCLE HERON?
MEOWS MORALES? UAUGH, THAT'S TORTURED...
AND HOW. HIS UNCLE? SECRETLY THE GROWLER.
HE--HE'S WHAT?!
UM. NOTHIN'.
WELL HANG IN THERE, KITTY. THIS TOWN SURE COULD USE A FRESH FACE.
HEH. EASY FOR YOU TO SAY, MOVIE STAR.
HA! THE MOVIE STAR IS A PUPPET ROTTING IN A FILM LOT PROP CLOSET.
AND YET... FOLKS CAN'T SEEM TO FORGET THAT ODD LIL' PICTURE, CAN THEY?
HMM... TOO WEIRD TO LIVE. TOO WEIRD TO DIE.

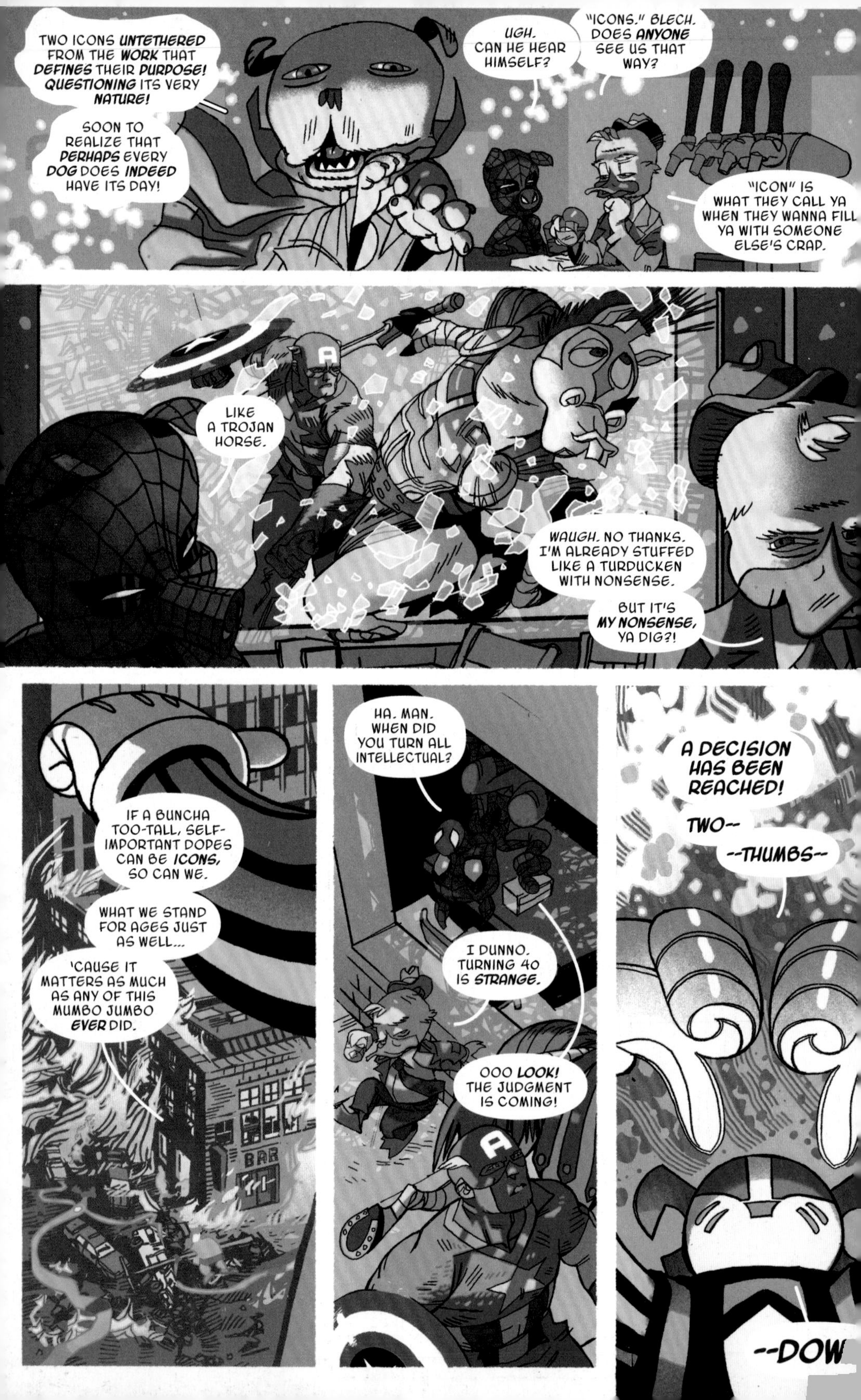
TWO ICONS **UNTETHERED** FROM THE **WORK** THAT **DEFINES** THEIR **PURPOSE**! **QUESTIONING** ITS VERY **NATURE**!
SOON TO REALIZE THAT **PERHAPS** EVERY **DOG** DOES **INDEED** HAVE ITS DAY!
UGH. CAN HE HEAR HIMSELF?
"ICONS." BLECH. DOES **ANYONE** SEE US THAT WAY?
"ICON" IS WHAT THEY CALL YA WHEN THEY WANNA FILL YA WITH SOMEONE ELSE'S CRAP.
LIKE A TROJAN HORSE.
WAUGH. NO THANKS. I'M ALREADY STUFFED LIKE A TURDUCKEN WITH NONSENSE.
BUT IT'S **MY NONSENSE**, YA DIG?!
IF A BUNCHA TOO-TALL, SELF-IMPORTANT DOPES CAN BE **ICONS**, SO CAN WE.
WHAT WE STAND FOR AGES JUST AS WELL...
'CAUSE IT MATTERS AS MUCH AS ANY OF THIS MUMBO JUMBO **EVER** DID.
BAR
HA. MAN. WHEN DID YOU TURN ALL INTELLECTUAL?
I DUNNO. TURNING 40 IS **STRANGE**.
OOO **LOOK**! THE JUDGMENT IS COMING!
A DECISION HAS BEEN REACHED!
TWO--
--THUMBS--
--DOW

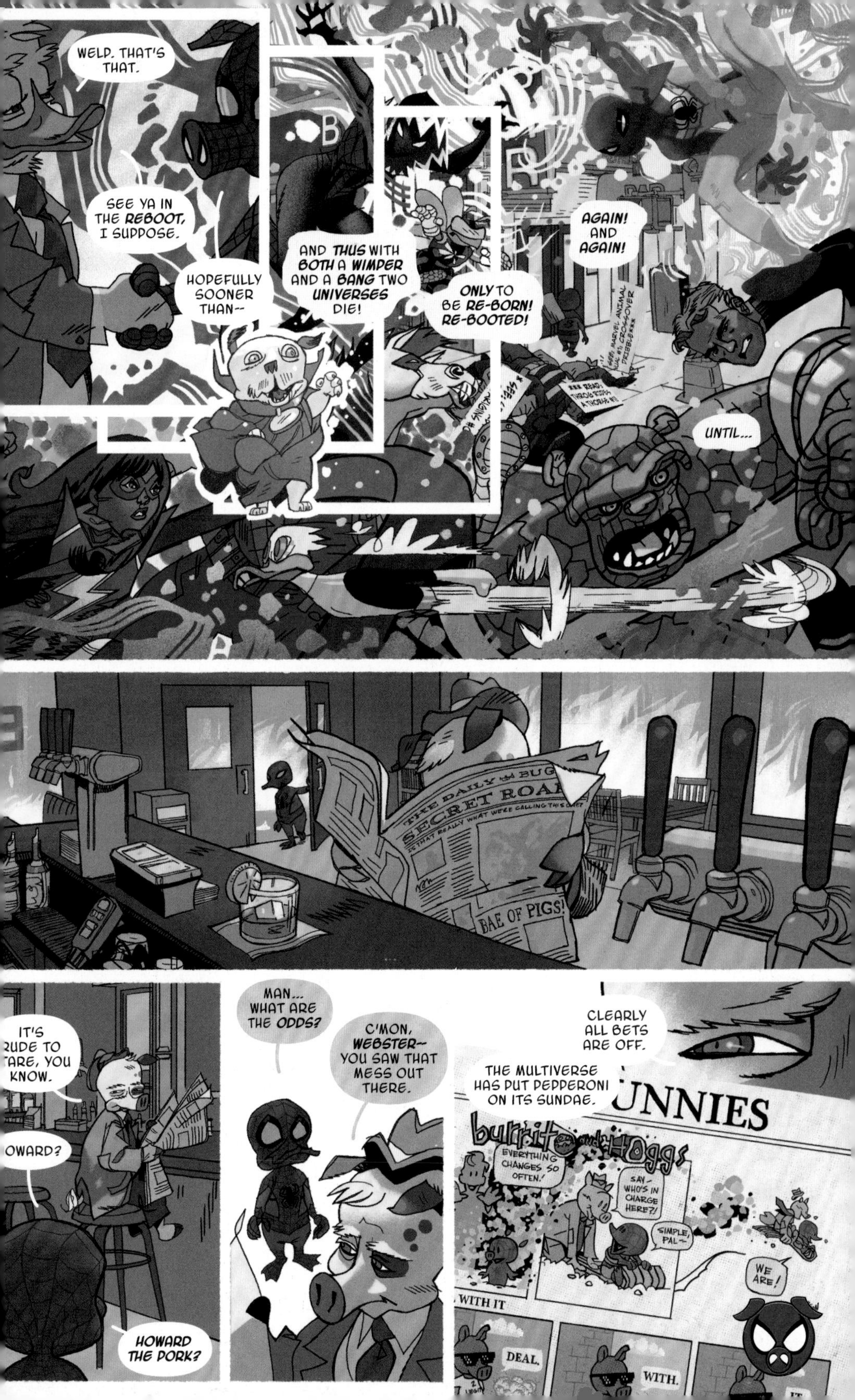

WELP. THAT'S THAT.
SEE YA IN THE REBOOT, I SUPPOSE.
HOPEFULLY SOONER THAN--
AND THUS WITH BOTH A WIMPER AND A BANG TWO UNIVERSES DIE!
ONLY TO BE RE-BORN! RE-BOOTED!
AGAIN! AND AGAIN!
UNTIL...
IS THAT REALLY WHAT WE'RE CALLING THIS ONE?
BAE OF PIGS!
IT'S RUDE TO TARE, YOU KNOW.
OWARD?
HOWARD THE PORK?
MAN... WHAT ARE THE ODDS?
C'MON, WEBSTER-- YOU SAW THAT MESS OUT THERE.
CLEARLY ALL BETS ARE OFF.
THE MULTIVERSE HAS PUT PEPPERONI ON ITS SUNDAE.
burrito and Hoggs
EVERYTHING CHANGES SO OFTEN!
SAY-- WHO'S IN CHARGE HERE?!
SIMPLE, PAL--
WE ARE!
DEAL.
WITH.

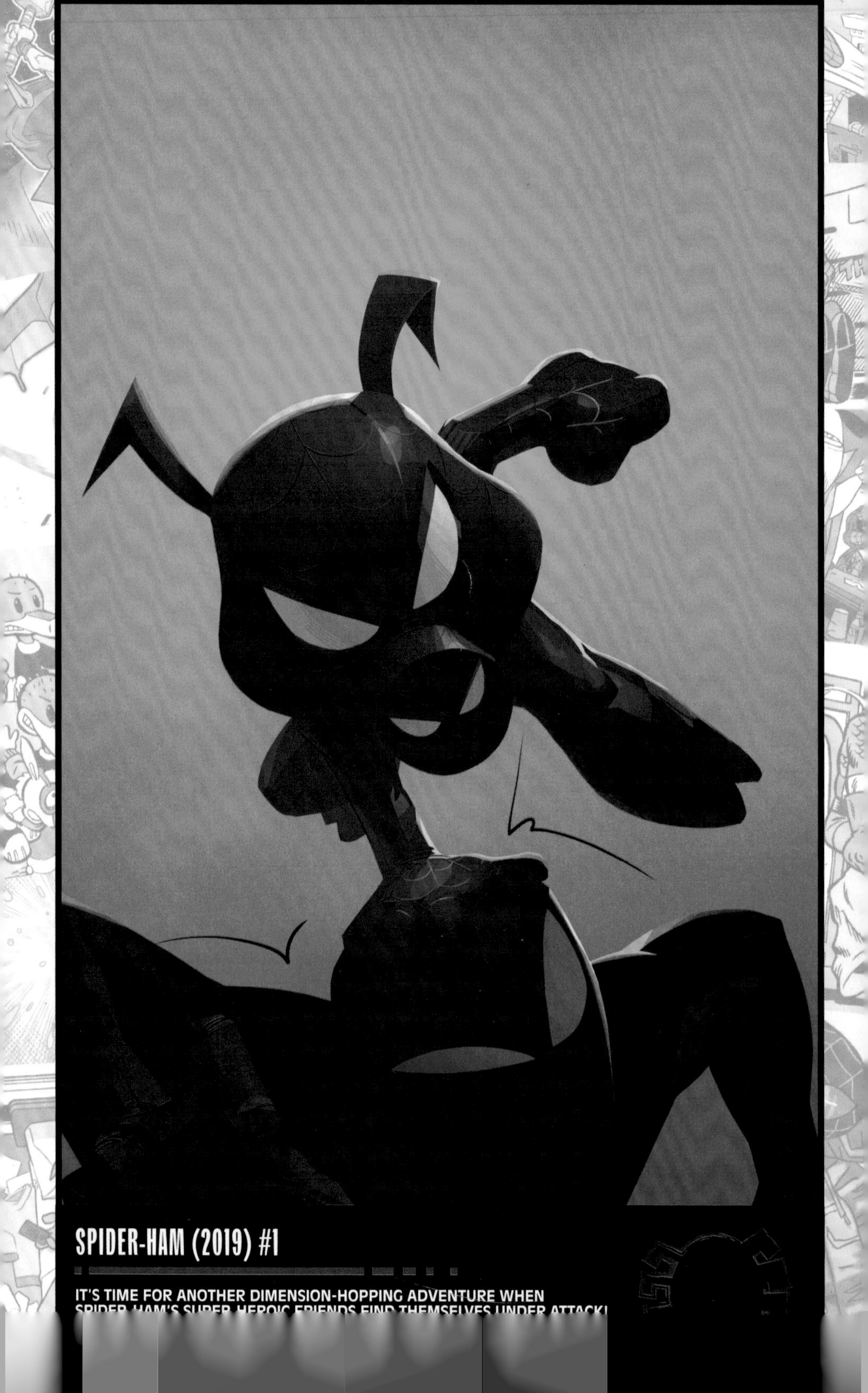

SPIDER-HAM (2019) #1

IT'S TIME FOR ANOTHER DIMENSION-HOPPING ADVENTURE WHEN SPIDER-HAM'S SUPER HEROIC FRIENDS FIND THEMSELVES UNDER ATTACK!

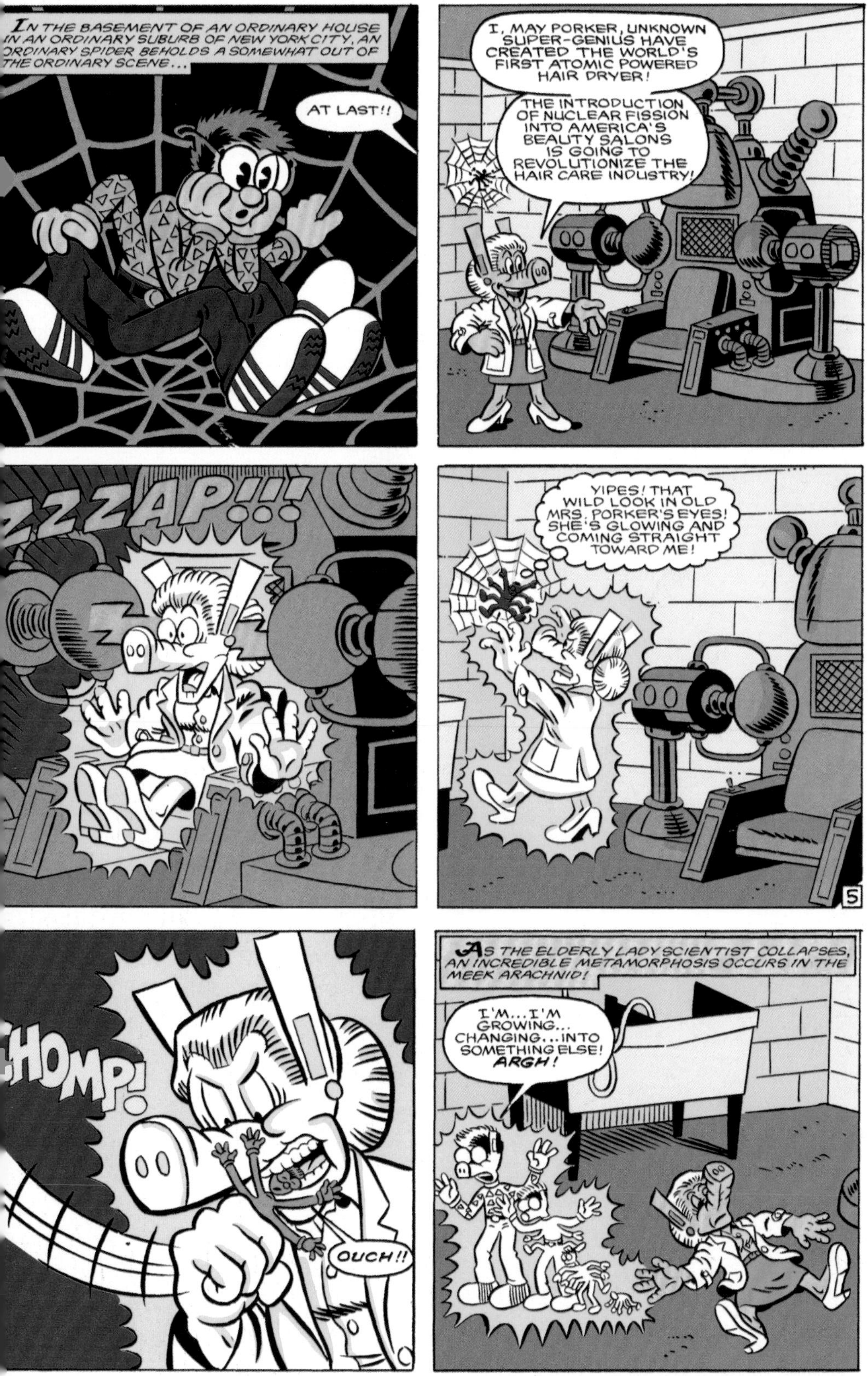
IN THE BASEMENT OF AN ORDINARY HOUSE IN AN ORDINARY SUBURB OF NEW YORK CITY, AN ORDINARY SPIDER BEHOLDS A SOMEWHAT OUT OF THE ORDINARY SCENE...
AT LAST!!
I, MAY PORKER, UNKNOWN SUPER-GENIUS HAVE CREATED THE WORLD'S FIRST ATOMIC POWERED HAIR DRYER!
THE INTRODUCTION OF NUCLEAR FISSION INTO AMERICA'S BEAUTY SALONS IS GOING TO REVOLUTIONIZE THE HAIR CARE INDUSTRY!
ZZZAP!!!
YIPES! THAT WILD LOOK IN OLD MRS. PORKER'S EYES! SHE'S GLOWING AND COMING STRAIGHT TOWARD ME!
5
CHOMP!
OUCH!!
AS THE ELDERLY LADY SCIENTIST COLLAPSES, AN INCREDIBLE METAMORPHOSIS OCCURS IN THE MEEK ARACHNID!
I'M... I'M GROWING... CHANGING... INTO SOMETHING ELSE! ARGH!

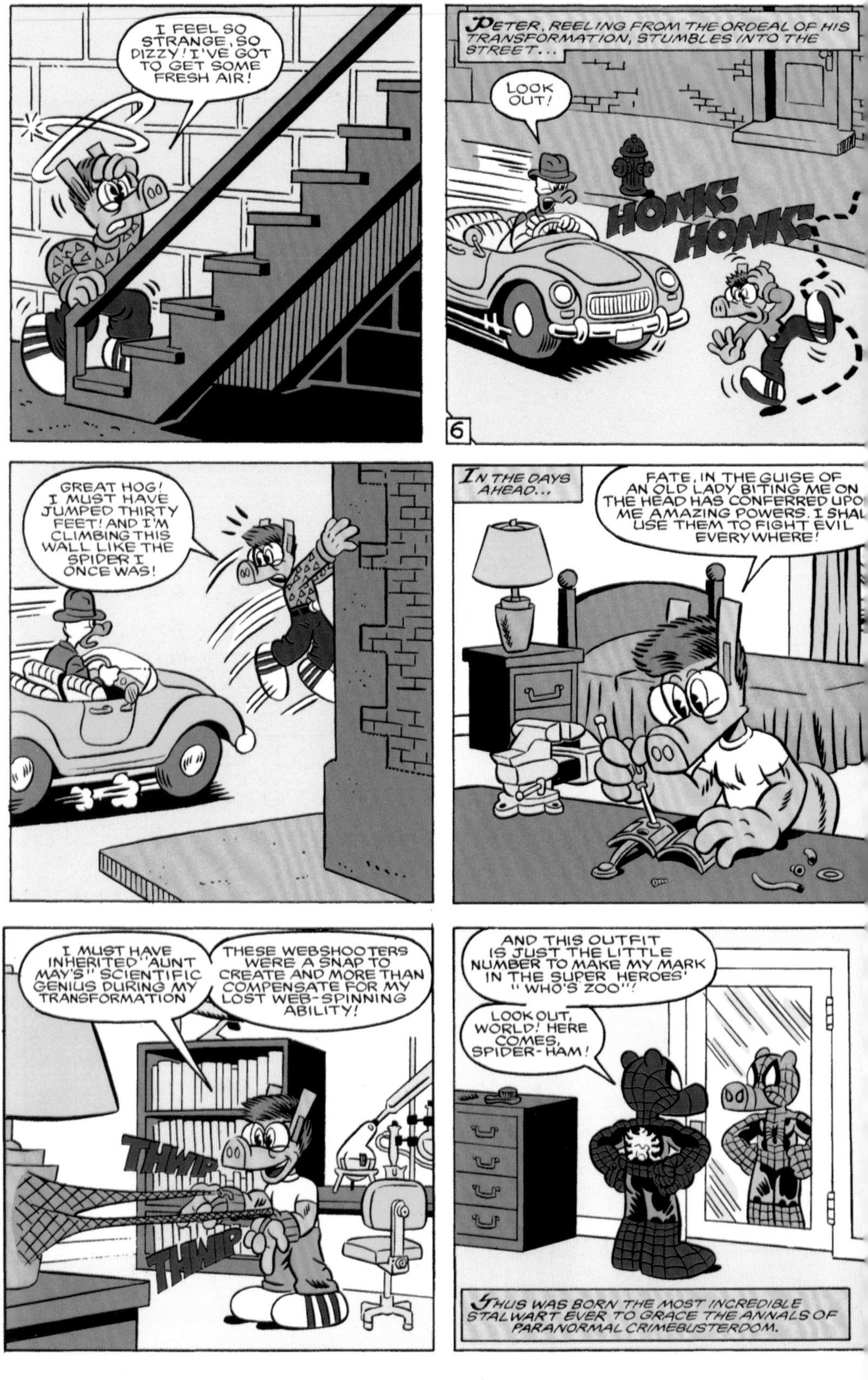
I FEEL SO STRANGE, SO DIZZY! I'VE GOT TO GET SOME FRESH AIR!
PETER, REELING FROM THE ORDEAL OF HIS TRANSFORMATION, STUMBLES INTO THE STREET...
LOOK OUT!
HONK! HONK!
6
GREAT HOG! I MUST HAVE JUMPED THIRTY FEET! AND I'M CLIMBING THIS WALL LIKE THE SPIDER I ONCE WAS!
IN THE DAYS AHEAD...
FATE, IN THE GUISE OF AN OLD LADY BITING ME ON THE HEAD HAS CONFERRED UPO ME AMAZING POWERS. I SHAL USE THEM TO FIGHT EVIL EVERYWHERE!
I MUST HAVE INHERITED "AUNT MAY'S" SCIENTIFIC GENIUS DURING MY TRANSFORMATION
THESE WEBSHOOTERS WERE A SNAP TO CREATE AND MORE THAN COMPENSATE FOR MY LOST WEB-SPINNING ABILITY!
THWIP
THWIP
AND THIS OUTFIT IS JUST THE LITTLE NUMBER TO MAKE MY MARK IN THE SUPER HEROES' "WHO'S ZOO"!
LOOK OUT, WORLD! HERE COMES, SPIDER-HAM!
THUS WAS BORN THE MOST INCREDIBLE STALWART EVER TO GRACE THE ANNALS OF PARANORMAL CRIMEBUSTERDOM.

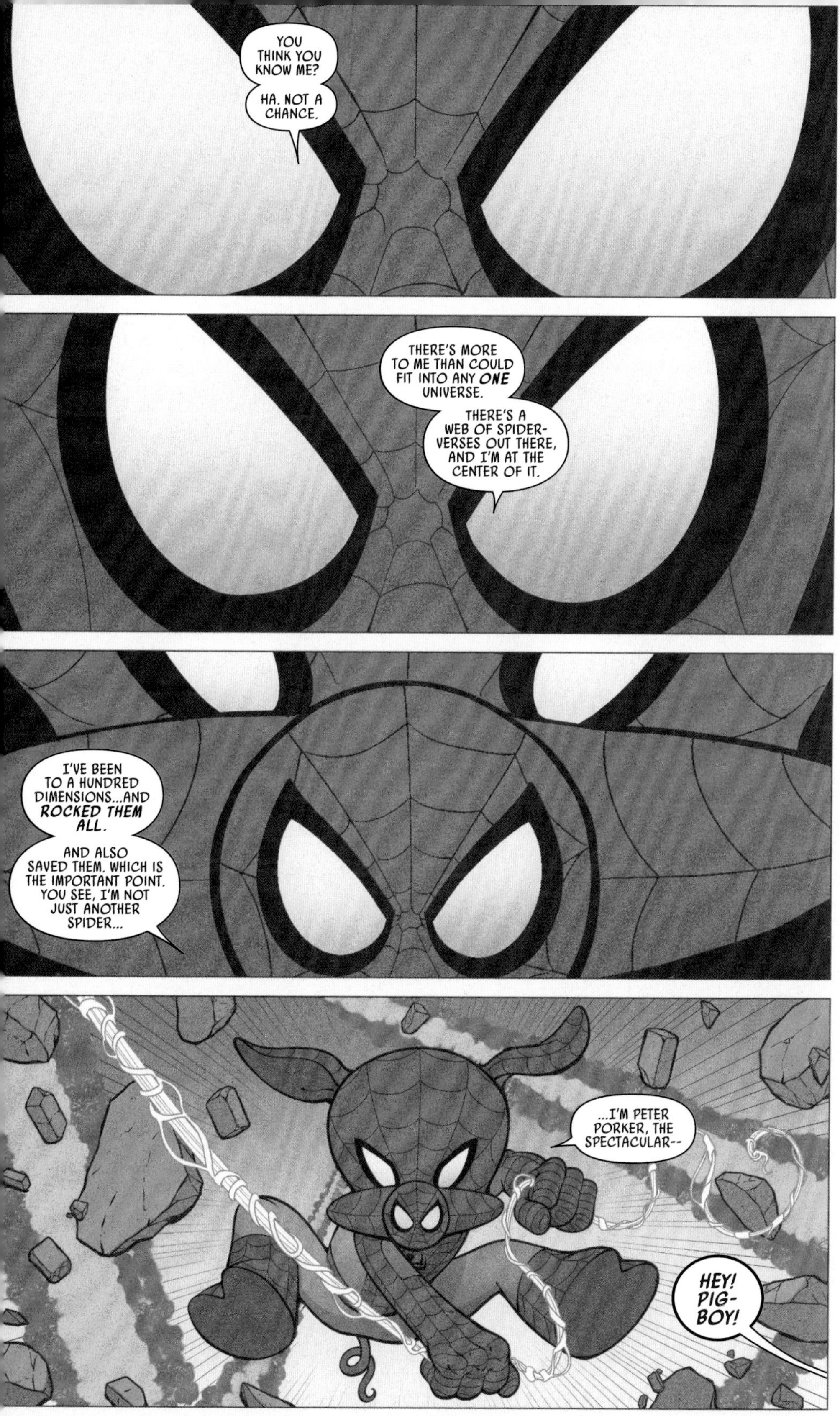
YOU THINK YOU KNOW ME?
HA. NOT A CHANCE.
THERE'S MORE TO ME THAN COULD FIT INTO ANY ONE UNIVERSE.
THERE'S A WEB OF SPIDER-VERSES OUT THERE, AND I'M AT THE CENTER OF IT.
I'VE BEEN TO A HUNDRED DIMENSIONS...AND ROCKED THEM ALL.
AND ALSO SAVED THEM. WHICH IS THE IMPORTANT POINT. YOU SEE, I'M NOT JUST ANOTHER SPIDER...
...I'M PETER PORKER, THE SPECTACULAR--
HEY! PIG-BOY!

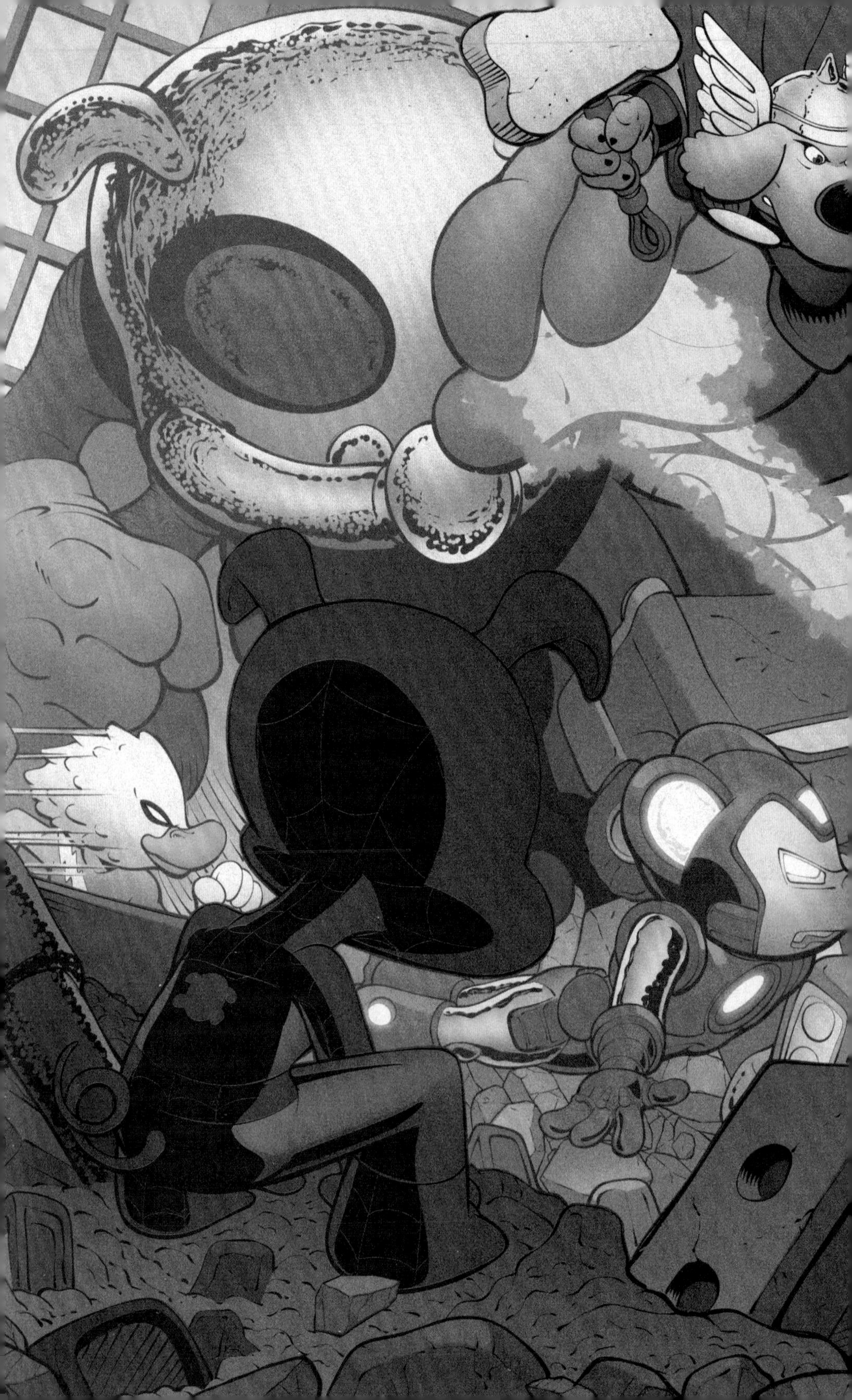

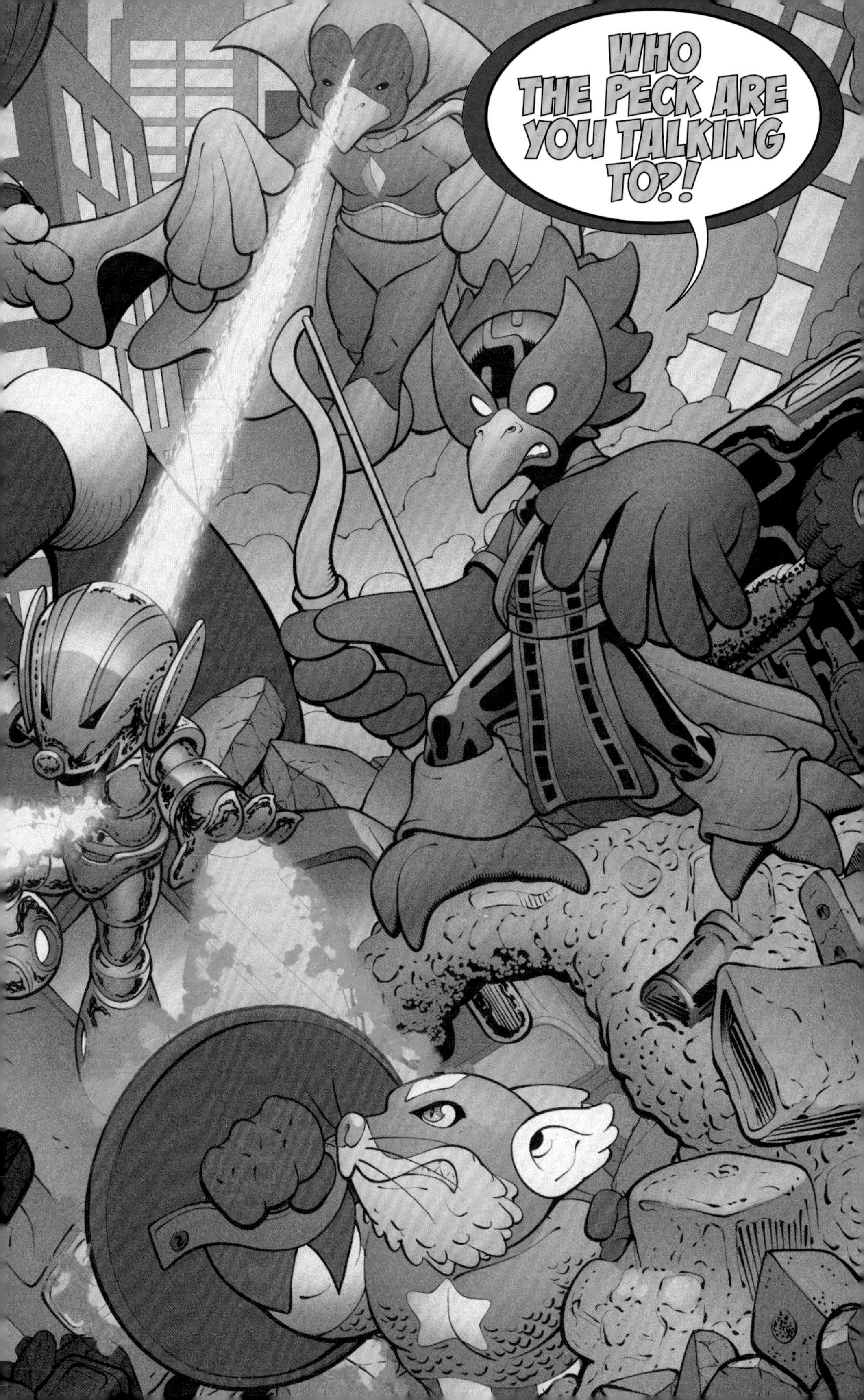
WHO THE PECK ARE YOU TALKING TO?!

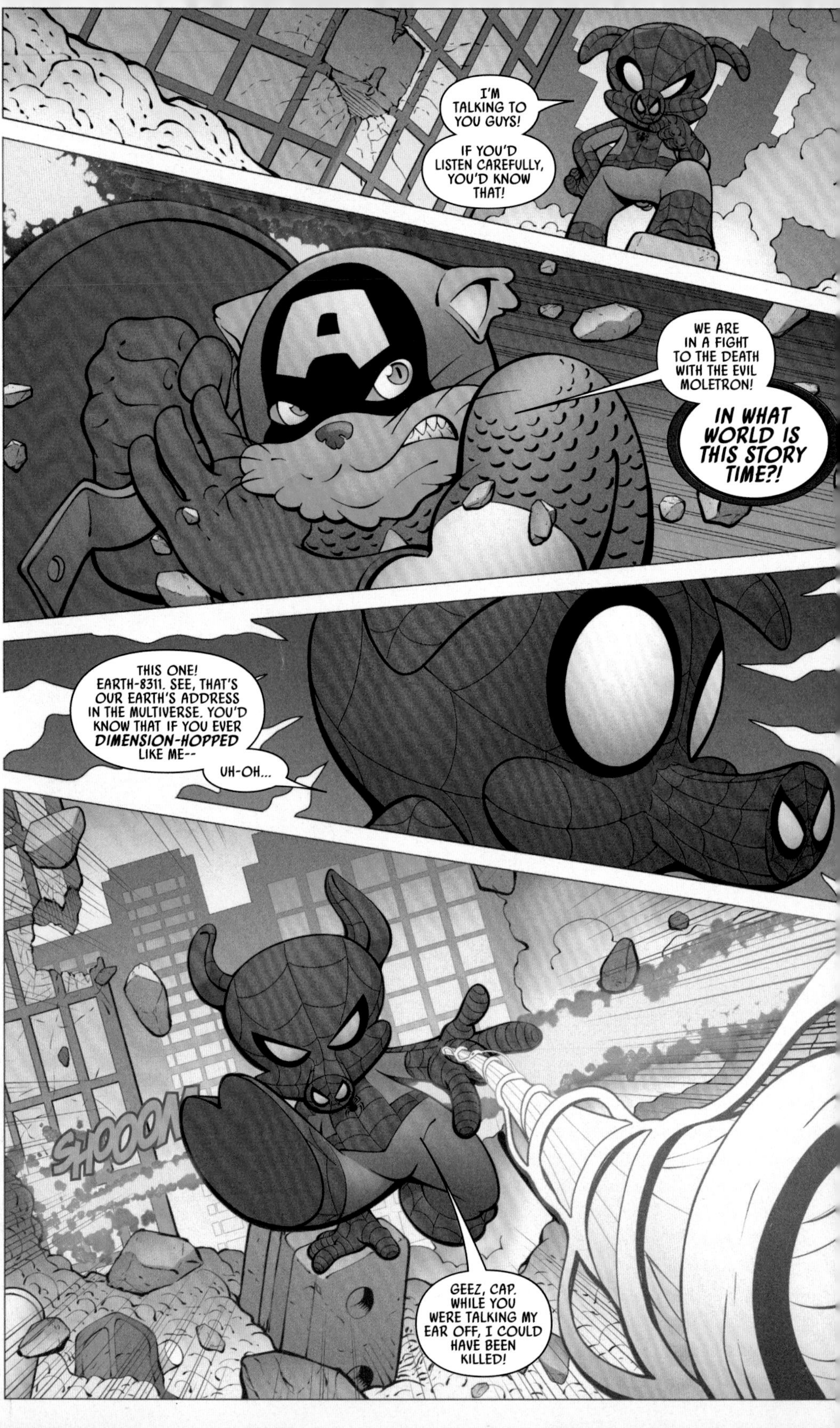
I'M TALKING TO YOU GUYS!
IF YOU'D LISTEN CAREFULLY, YOU'D KNOW THAT!
WE ARE IN A FIGHT TO THE DEATH WITH THE EVIL MOLETRON!
IN WHAT WORLD IS THIS STORY TIME?!
THIS ONE! EARTH-8311. SEE, THAT'S OUR EARTH'S ADDRESS IN THE MULTIVERSE. YOU'D KNOW THAT IF YOU EVER DIMENSION-HOPPED LIKE ME--
UH-OH...
GEEZ, CAP. WHILE YOU WERE TALKING MY EAR OFF, I COULD HAVE BEEN KILLED!

WHAT ARE YOU UP TO, IRON MOUSE?

WHAT DOES IT LOOK LIKE?! I'M TRYING TO STOP *MOLETRON* BEFORE HE REPLICATES HIMSELF!

AH, YEAH...THAT KIND OF STUFF USED TO EXCITE ME TOO. YOU KNOW, BEFORE I *SAVED THE MULTIVERSE*.

OH, SHOVE AN APPLE IN YOUR MOUTH--

BEHIND YOU!

CLANK!

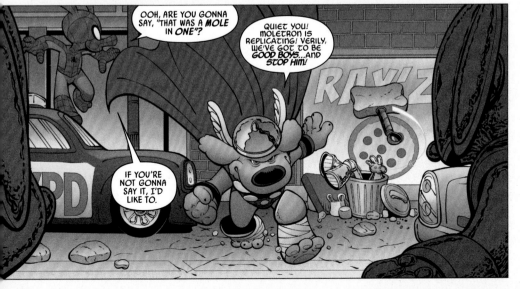

OOH, ARE YOU GONNA SAY, "THAT WAS A *MOLE* IN *ONE*"?

QUIET YOU! MOLETRON IS REPLICATING! VERILY, WE'VE GOT TO BE *GOOD BOYS*...AND *STOP HIM!*

IF YOU'RE NOT GONNA SAY IT, I'D LIKE TO.

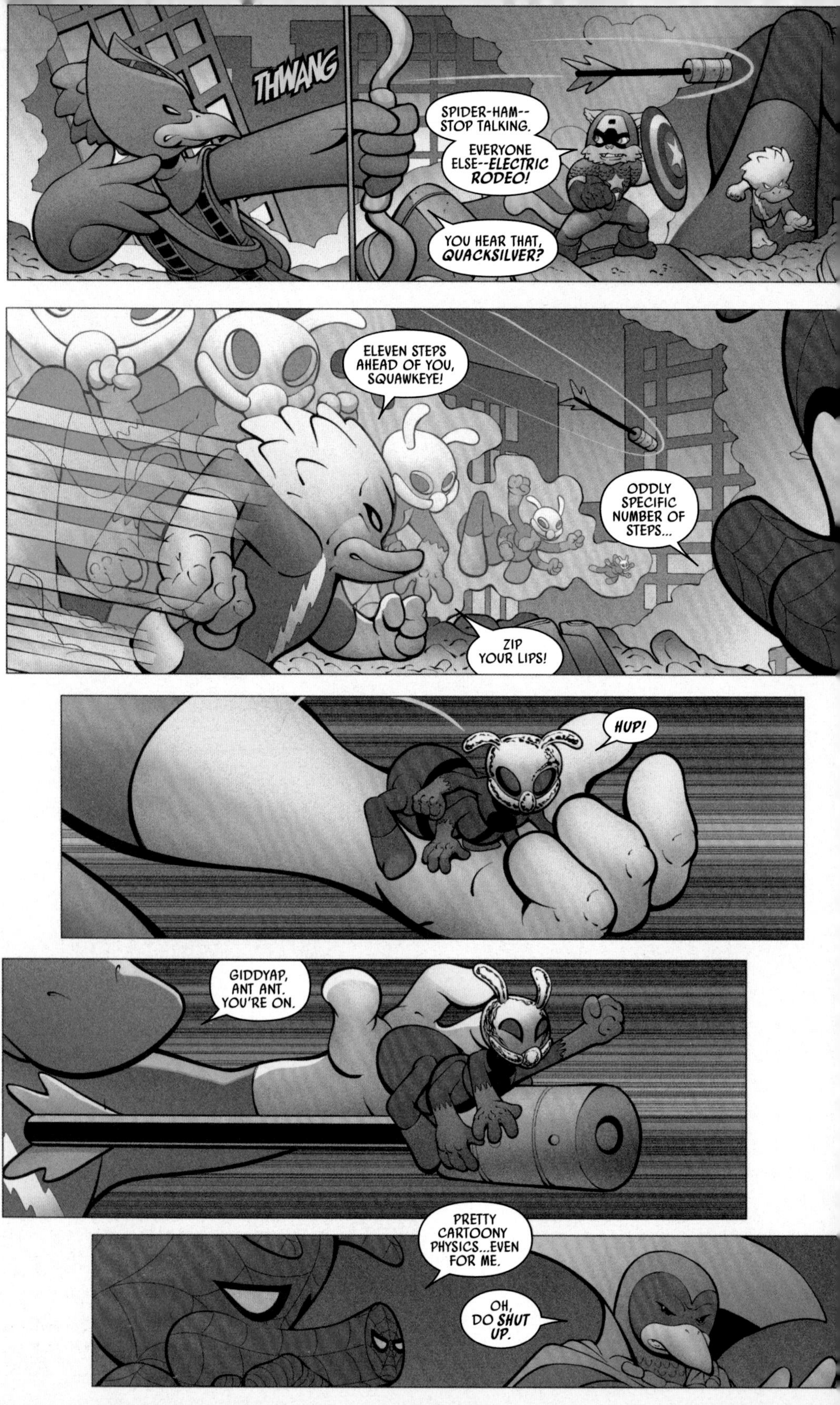
THWANG
SPIDER-HAM--STOP TALKING.
EVERYONE ELSE--ELECTRIC RODEO!
YOU HEAR THAT, QUACKSILVER?
ELEVEN STEPS AHEAD OF YOU, SQUAWKEYE!
ODDLY SPECIFIC NUMBER OF STEPS...
ZIP YOUR LIPS!
HUP!
GIDDYAP, ANT ANT. YOU'RE ON.
PRETTY CARTOONY PHYSICS...EVEN FOR ME.
OH, DO SHUT UP.

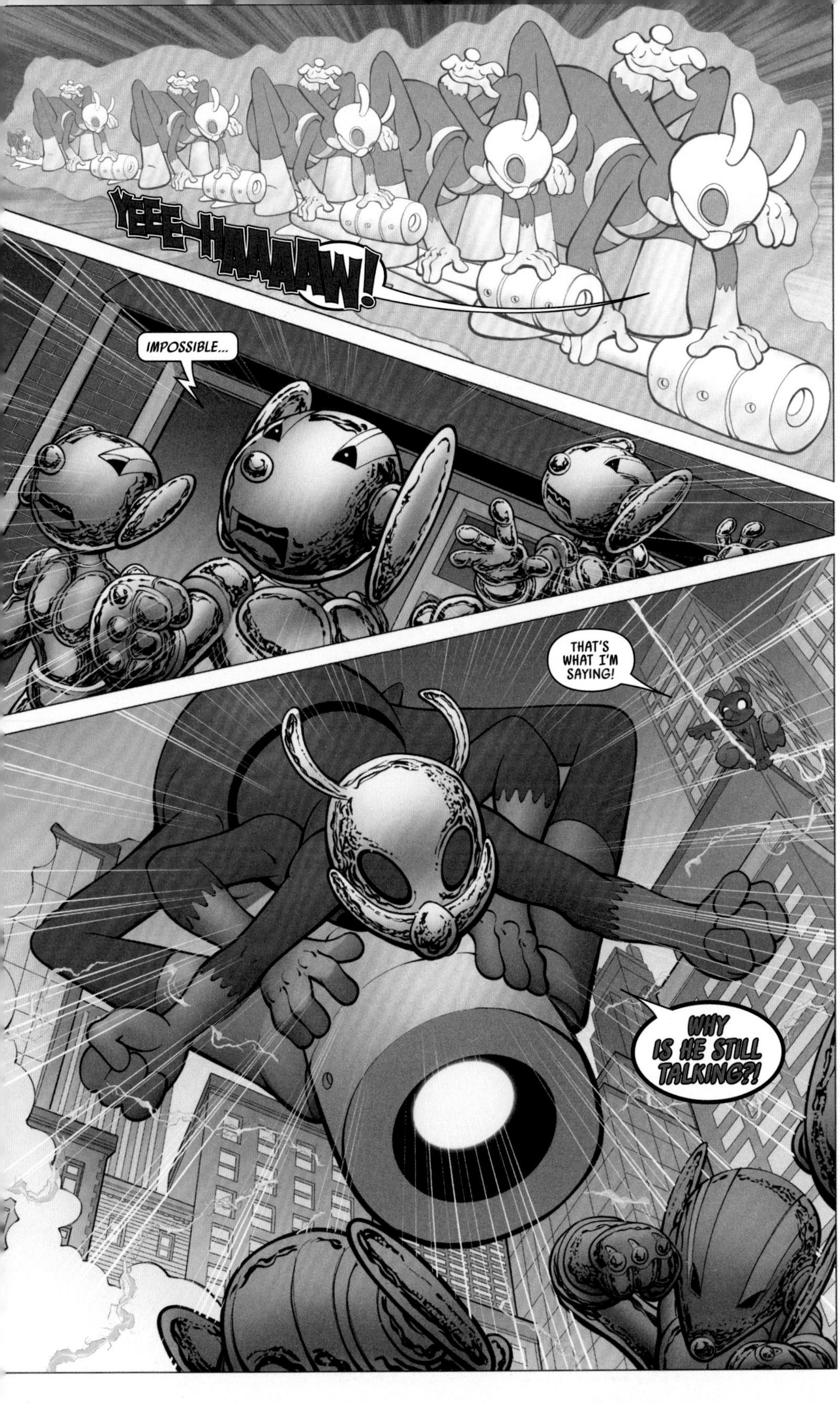
YEEE-HAAAAAW!
IMPOSSIBLE...
THAT'S WHAT I'M SAYING!
WHY IS HE STILL TALKING?!

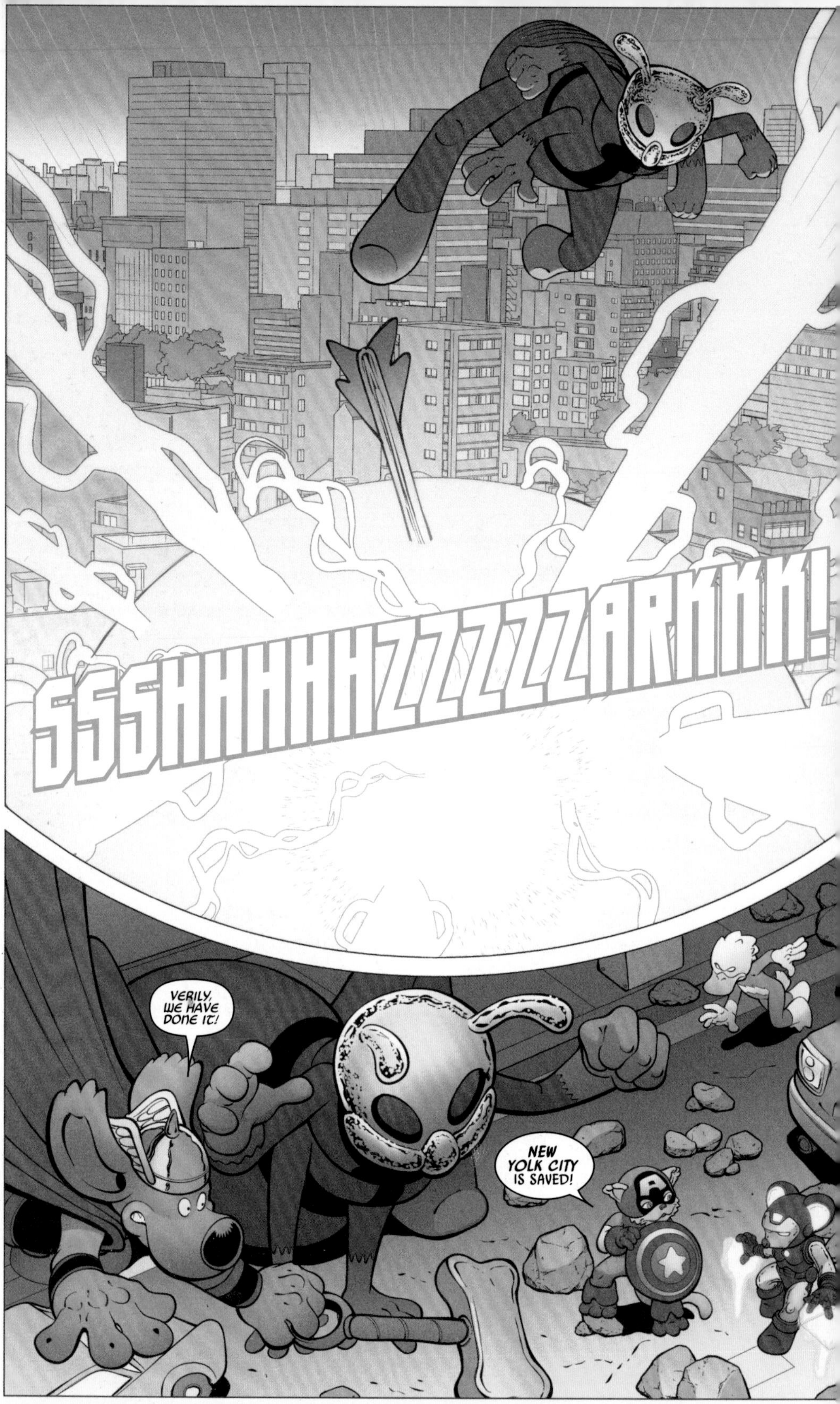
SSSHHHHHZZZZZZARKKKK!
VERILY, WE HAVE DONE IT!
NEW YOLK CITY IS SAVED!

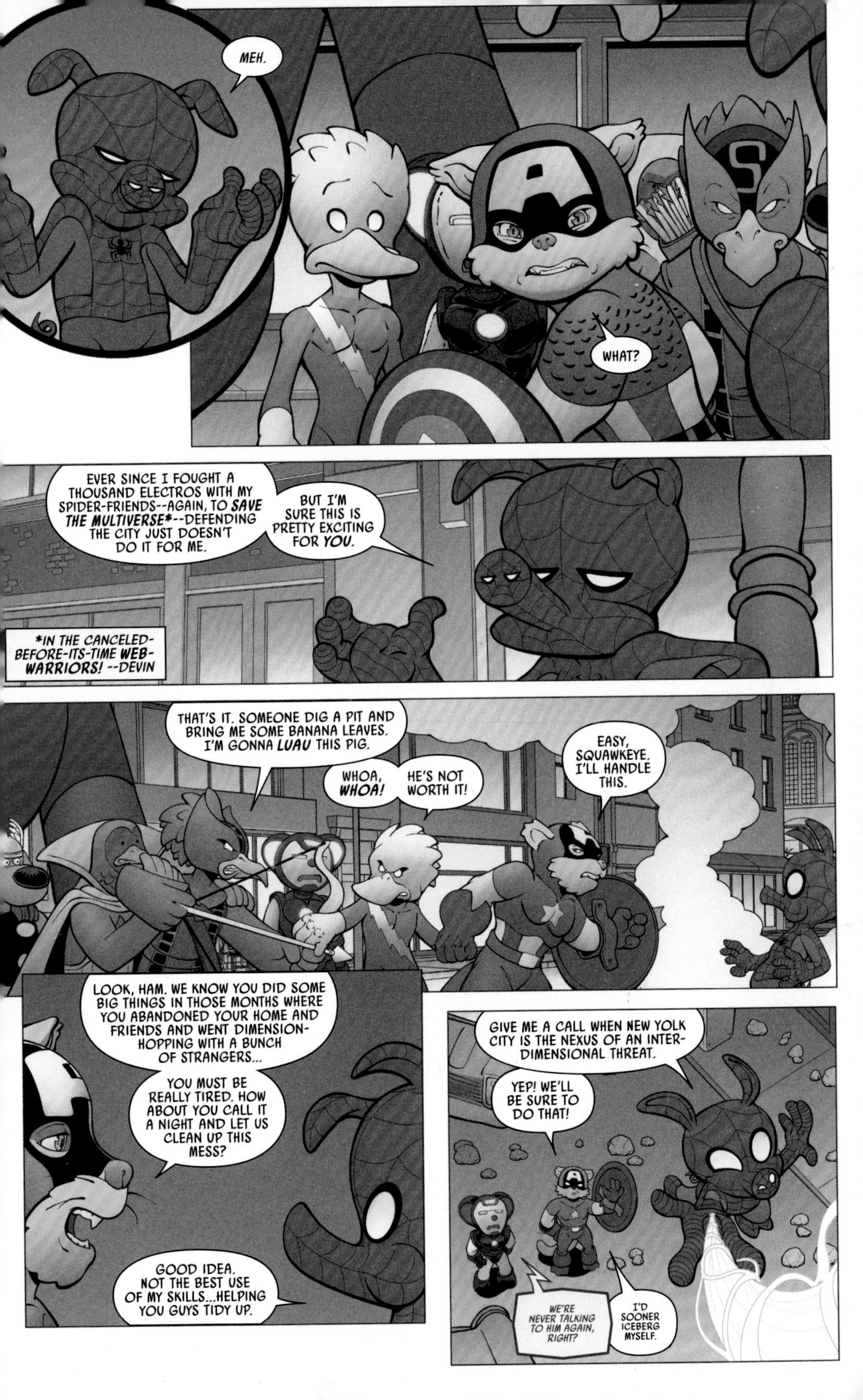
MEH.
WHAT?
EVER SINCE I FOUGHT A THOUSAND ELECTROS WITH MY SPIDER-FRIENDS--AGAIN, TO SAVE THE MULTIVERSE*--DEFENDING THE CITY JUST DOESN'T DO IT FOR ME.
BUT I'M SURE THIS IS PRETTY EXCITING FOR YOU.
*IN THE CANCELED-BEFORE-ITS-TIME WEB-WARRIORS! --DEVIN
THAT'S IT. SOMEONE DIG A PIT AND BRING ME SOME BANANA LEAVES. I'M GONNA LUAU THIS PIG.
WHOA, WHOA!
HE'S NOT WORTH IT!
EASY, SQUAWKEYE. I'LL HANDLE THIS.
LOOK, HAM. WE KNOW YOU DID SOME BIG THINGS IN THOSE MONTHS WHERE YOU ABANDONED YOUR HOME AND FRIENDS AND WENT DIMENSION-HOPPING WITH A BUNCH OF STRANGERS...
YOU MUST BE REALLY TIRED. HOW ABOUT YOU CALL IT A NIGHT AND LET US CLEAN UP THIS MESS?
GOOD IDEA. NOT THE BEST USE OF MY SKILLS...HELPING YOU GUYS TIDY UP.
GIVE ME A CALL WHEN NEW YOLK CITY IS THE NEXUS OF AN INTER-DIMENSIONAL THREAT.
YEP! WE'LL BE SURE TO DO THAT!
WE'RE NEVER TALKING TO HIM AGAIN, RIGHT?
I'D SOONER ICEBERG MYSELF.

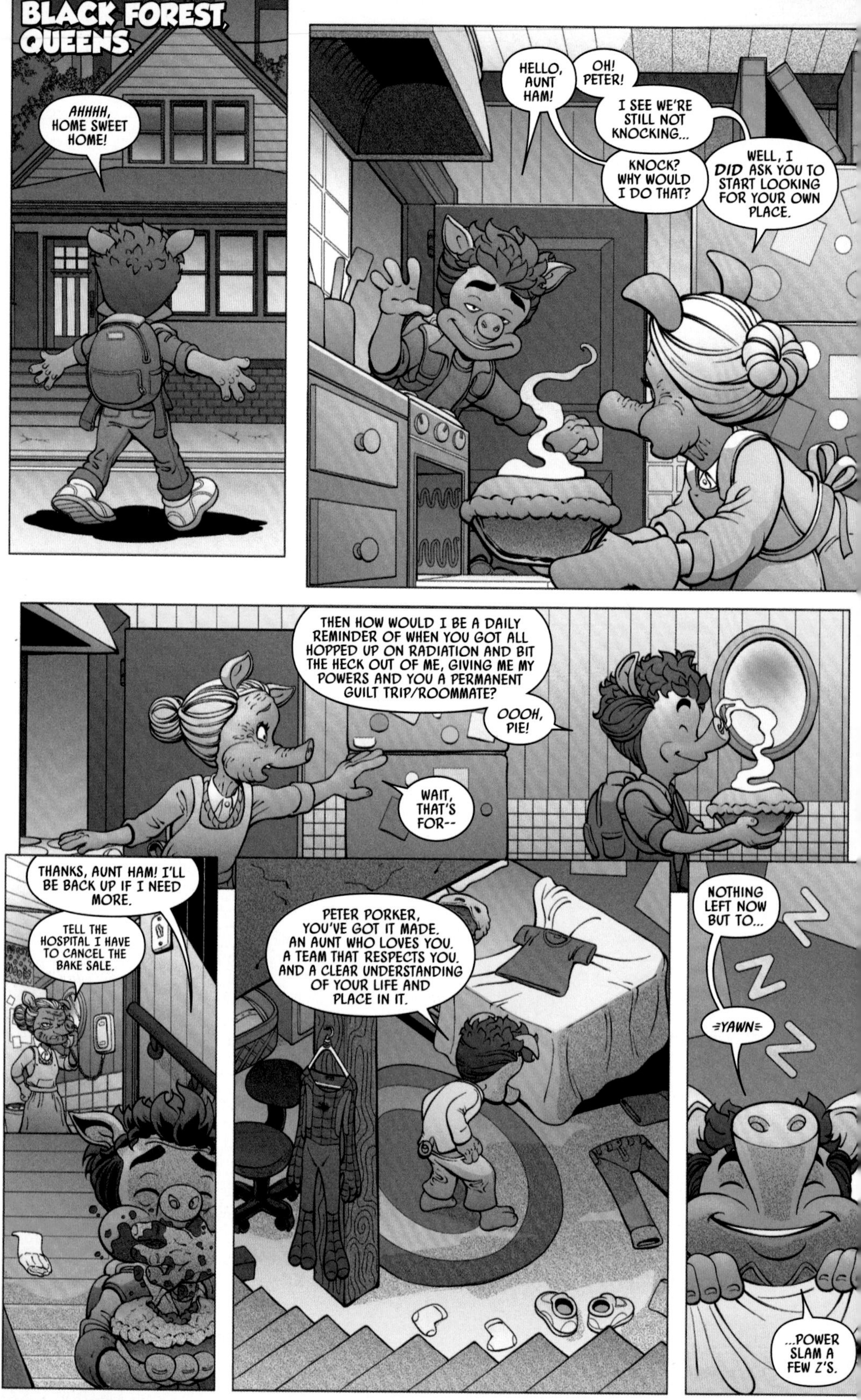
BLACK FOREST, QUEENS.
AHHHH, HOME SWEET HOME!
HELLO, AUNT HAM!
OH! PETER!
I SEE WE'RE STILL NOT KNOCKING...
KNOCK? WHY WOULD I DO THAT?
WELL, I DID ASK YOU TO START LOOKING FOR YOUR OWN PLACE.
THEN HOW WOULD I BE A DAILY REMINDER OF WHEN YOU GOT ALL HOPPED UP ON RADIATION AND BIT THE HECK OUT OF ME, GIVING ME MY POWERS AND YOU A PERMANENT GUILT TRIP/ROOMMATE?
OOOH, PIE!
WAIT, THAT'S FOR--
THANKS, AUNT HAM! I'LL BE BACK UP IF I NEED MORE.
TELL THE HOSPITAL I HAVE TO CANCEL THE BAKE SALE.
PETER PORKER, YOU'VE GOT IT MADE. AN AUNT WHO LOVES YOU. A TEAM THAT RESPECTS YOU. AND A CLEAR UNDERSTANDING OF YOUR LIFE AND PLACE IN IT.
NOTHING LEFT NOW BUT TO...
=YAWN=
...POWER SLAM A FEW Z'S.

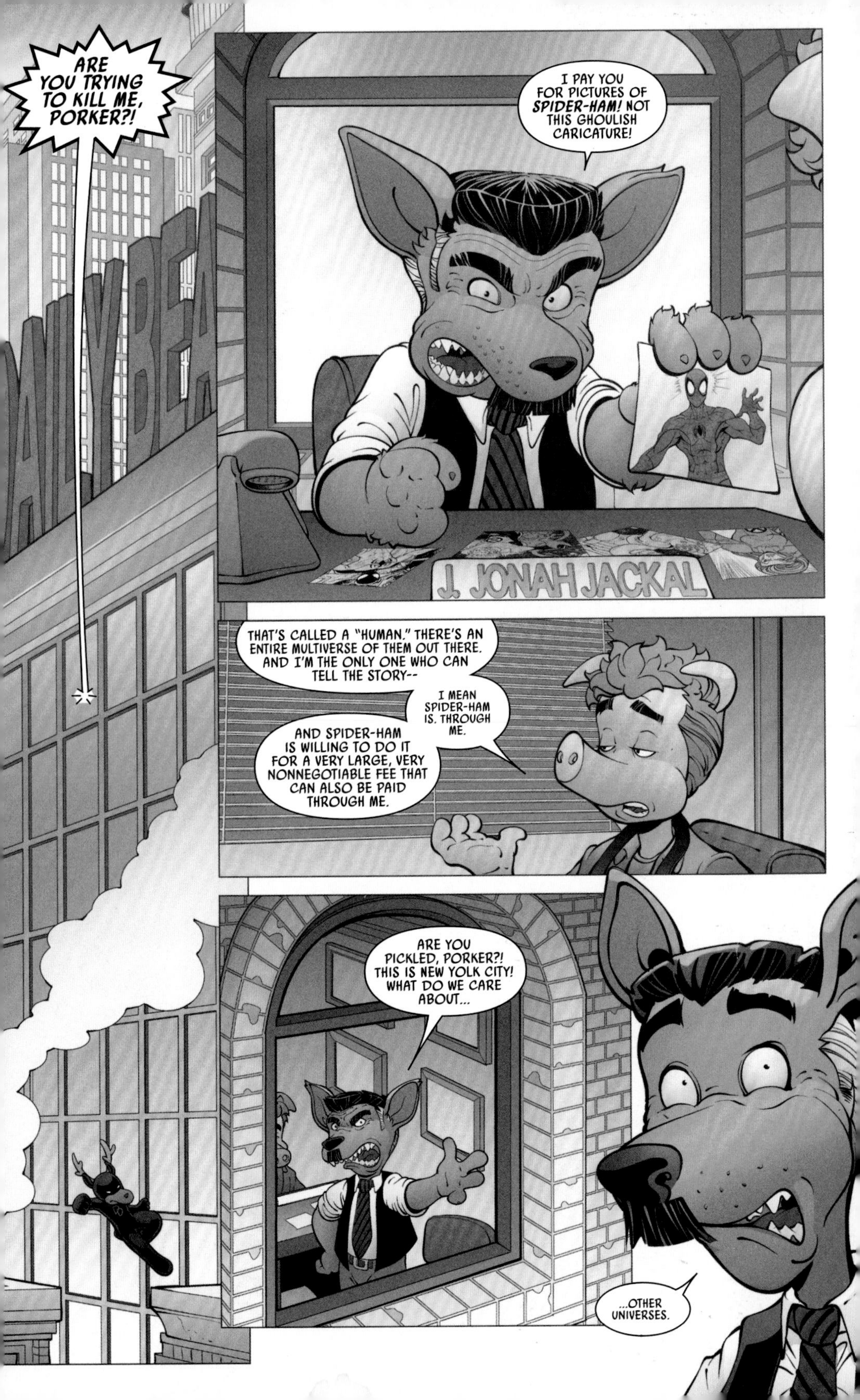

ARE YOU TRYING TO KILL ME, PORKER?!
DAILY BEA
I PAY YOU FOR PICTURES OF SPIDER-HAM! NOT THIS GHOULISH CARICATURE!
J. JONAH JACKAL
THAT'S CALLED A "HUMAN." THERE'S AN ENTIRE MULTIVERSE OF THEM OUT THERE. AND I'M THE ONLY ONE WHO CAN TELL THE STORY--
I MEAN SPIDER-HAM IS. THROUGH ME.
AND SPIDER-HAM IS WILLING TO DO IT FOR A VERY LARGE, VERY NONNEGOTIABLE FEE THAT CAN ALSO BE PAID THROUGH ME.
ARE YOU PICKLED, PORKER?! THIS IS NEW YOLK CITY! WHAT DO WE CARE ABOUT...
...OTHER UNIVERSES.

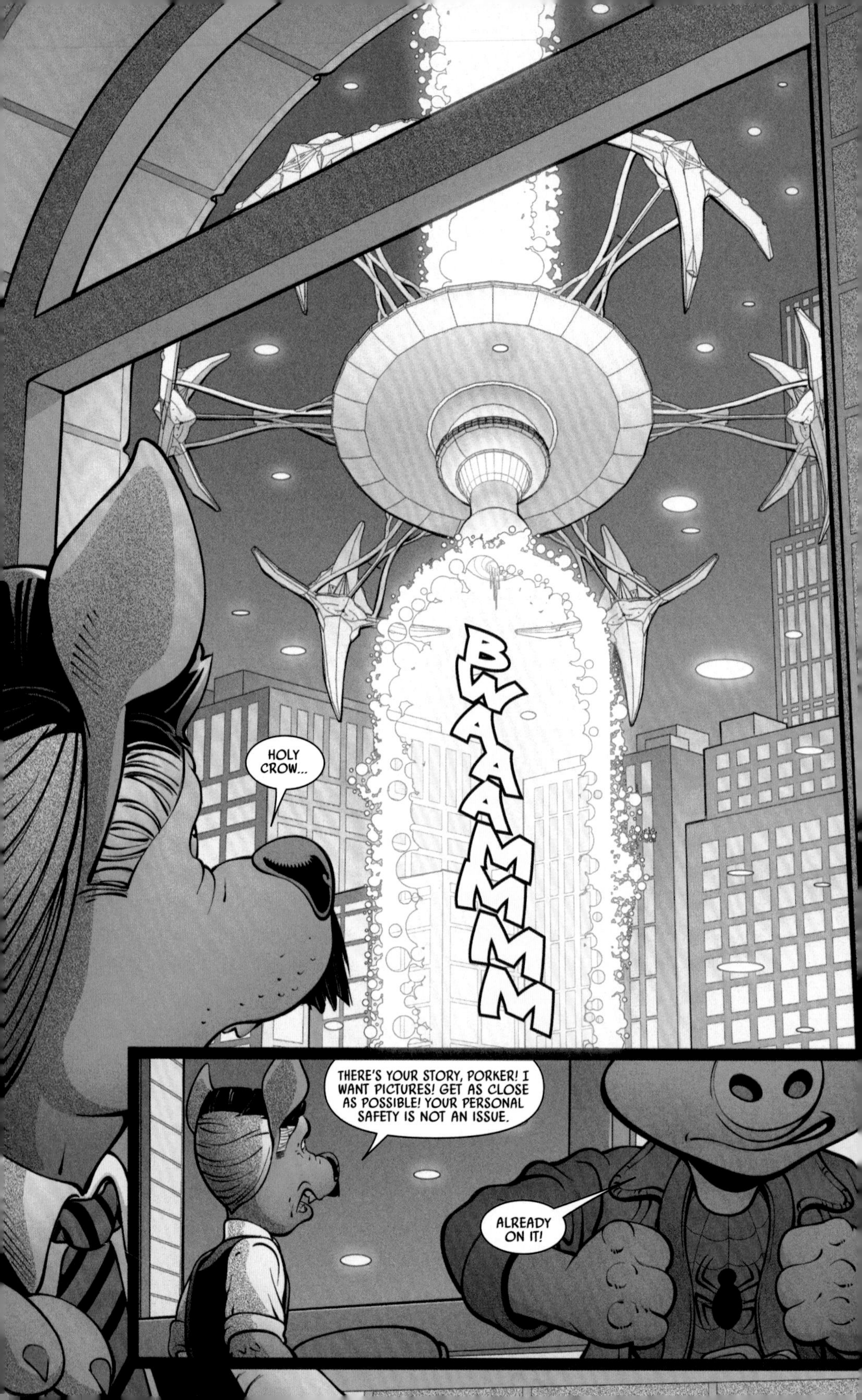
HOLY CROW...
BWAAAMMMM
THERE'S YOUR STORY, PORKER! I WANT PICTURES! GET AS CLOSE AS POSSIBLE! YOUR PERSONAL SAFETY IS NOT AN ISSUE.
ALREADY ON IT!

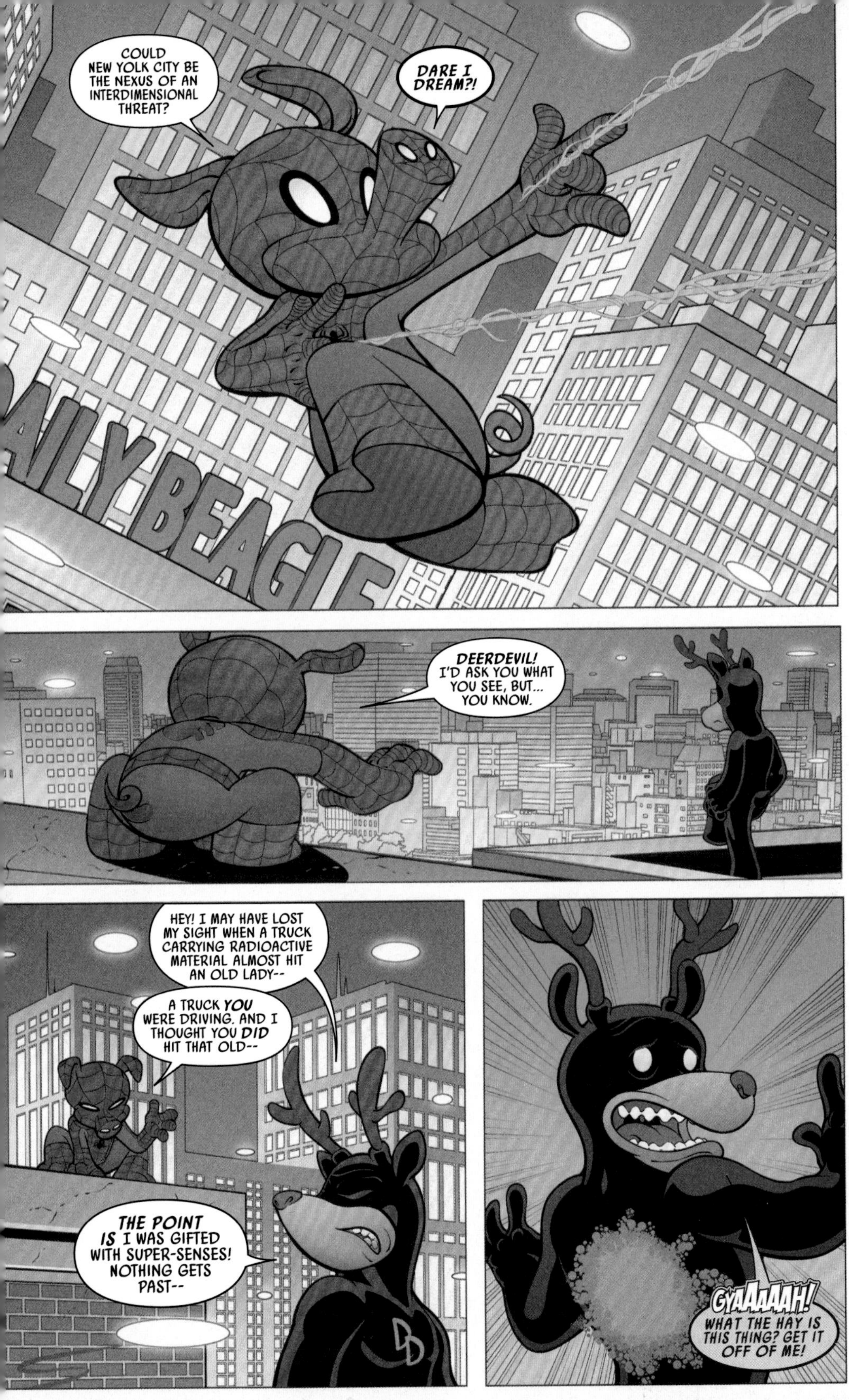
COULD NEW YOLK CITY BE THE NEXUS OF AN INTERDIMENSIONAL THREAT?
DARE I DREAM?!
DAILY BEAGLE
DEERDEVIL! I'D ASK YOU WHAT YOU SEE, BUT... YOU KNOW.
HEY! I MAY HAVE LOST MY SIGHT WHEN A TRUCK CARRYING RADIOACTIVE MATERIAL ALMOST HIT AN OLD LADY--
A TRUCK YOU WERE DRIVING. AND I THOUGHT YOU DID HIT THAT OLD--
THE POINT IS I WAS GIFTED WITH SUPER-SENSES! NOTHING GETS PAST--
GYAAAAAH!
WHAT THE HAY IS THIS THING? GET IT OFF OF ME!

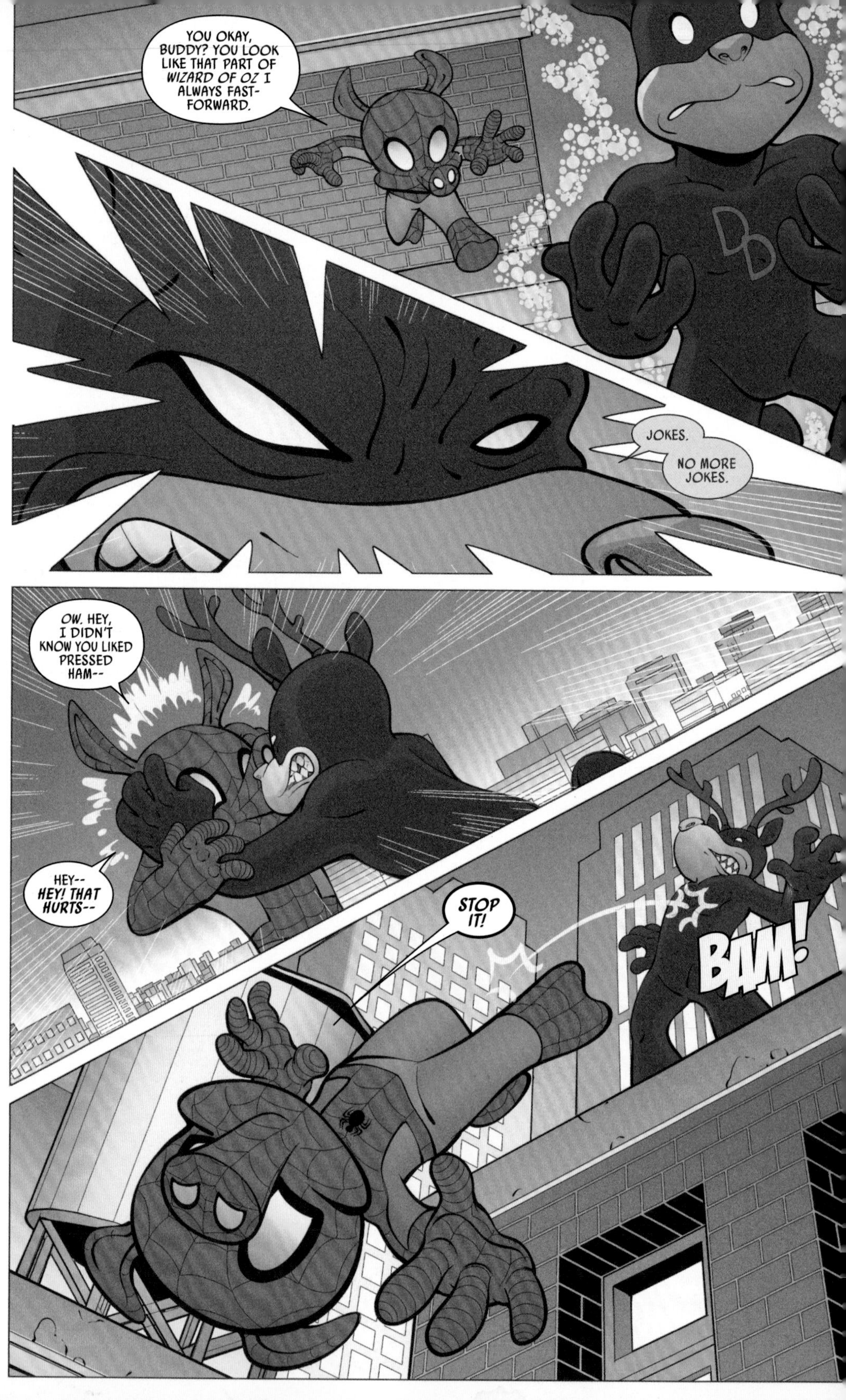
YOU OKAY, BUDDY? YOU LOOK LIKE THAT PART OF WIZARD OF OZ I ALWAYS FAST-FORWARD.
JOKES.
NO MORE JOKES.
OW. HEY, I DIDN'T KNOW YOU LIKED PRESSED HAM--
HEY-- HEY! THAT HURTS--
STOP IT!
BAM!

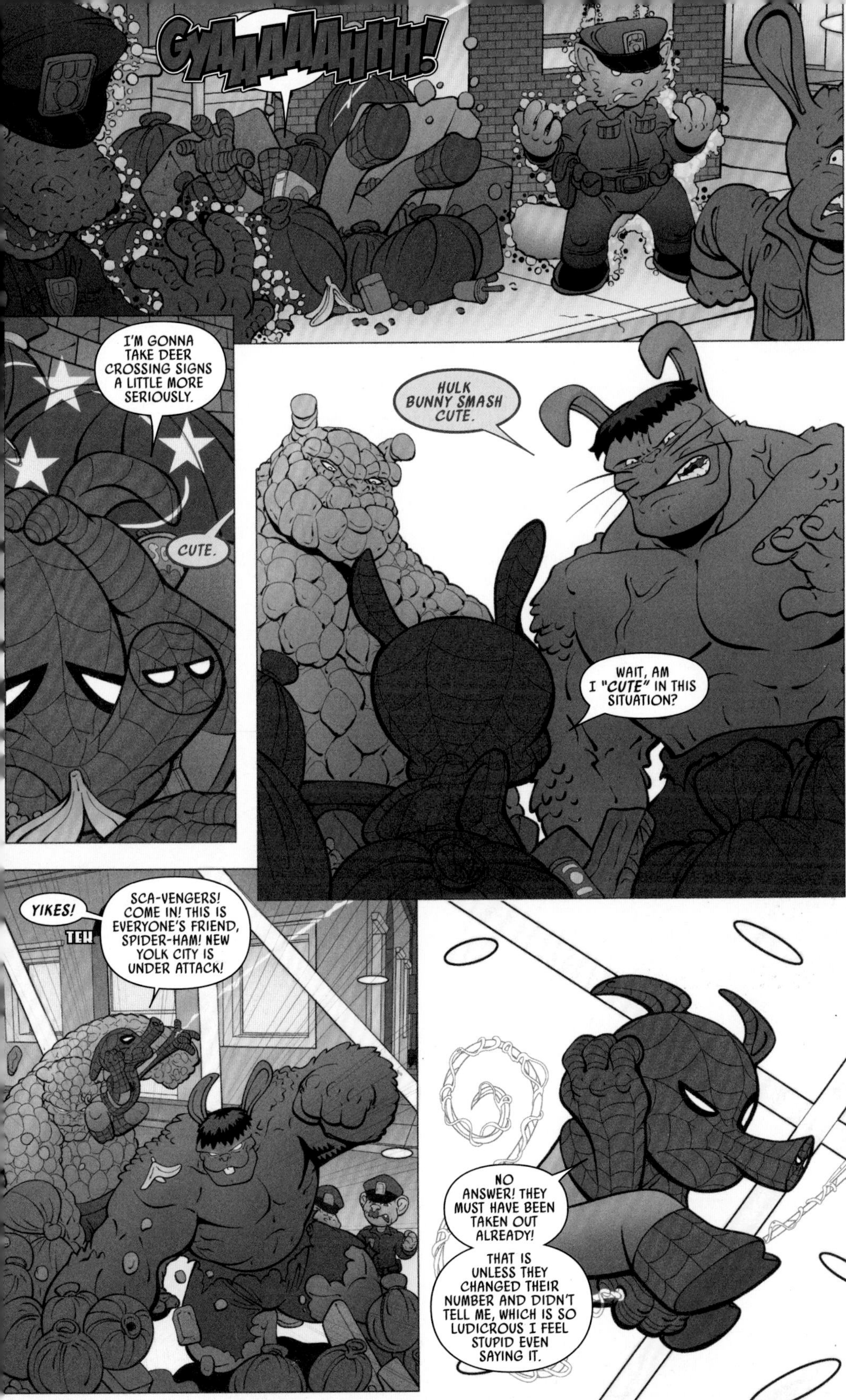
GYAAAAAHHH!
I'M GONNA TAKE DEER CROSSING SIGNS A LITTLE MORE SERIOUSLY.
CUTE.
HULK BUNNY SMASH CUTE.
WAIT, AM I "CUTE" IN THIS SITUATION?
YIKES!
TCH
SCA-VENGERS! COME IN! THIS IS EVERYONE'S FRIEND, SPIDER-HAM! NEW YOLK CITY IS UNDER ATTACK!
NO ANSWER! THEY MUST HAVE BEEN TAKEN OUT ALREADY!
THAT IS UNLESS THEY CHANGED THEIR NUMBER AND DIDN'T TELL ME, WHICH IS SO LUDICROUS I FEEL STUPID EVEN SAYING IT.

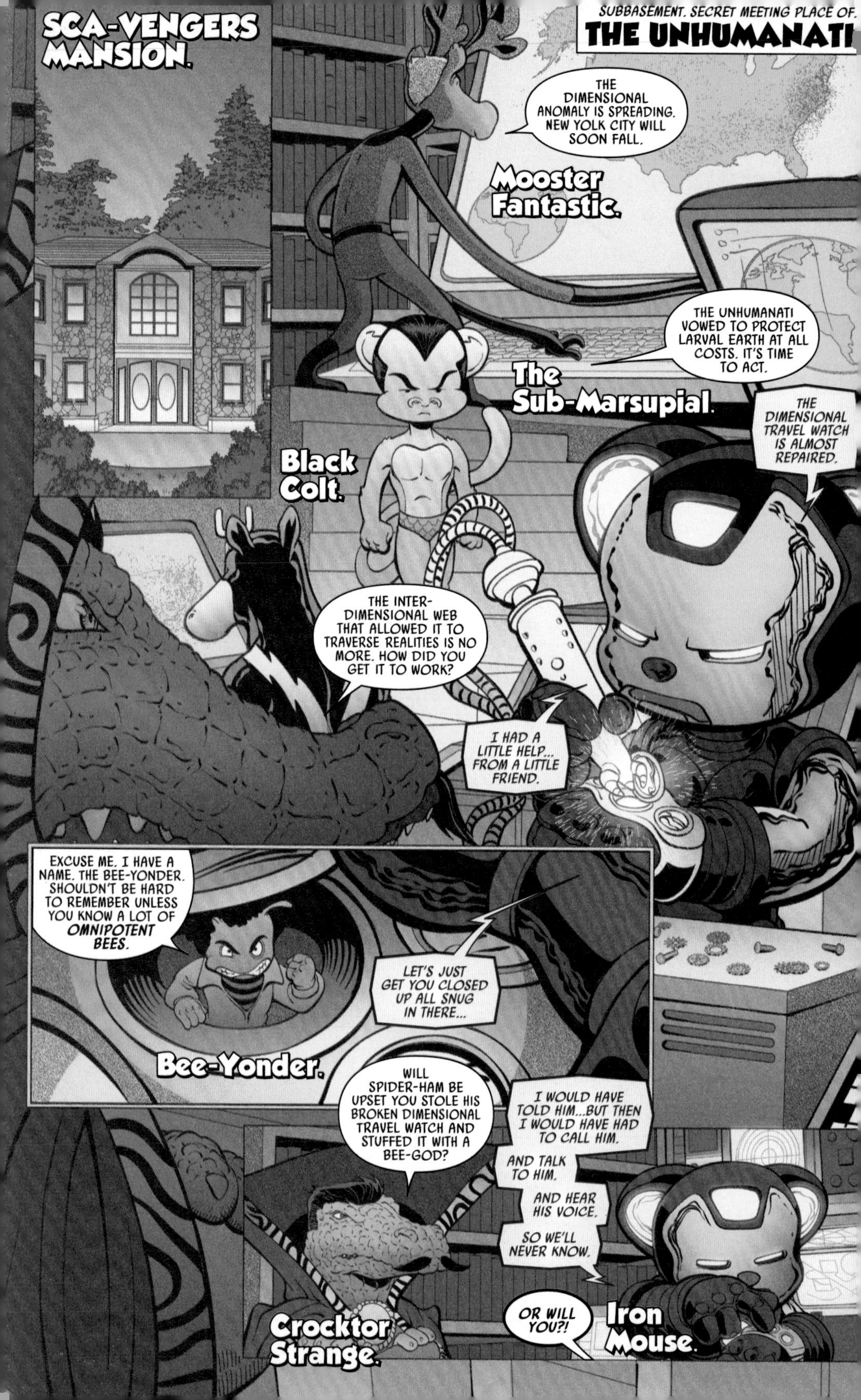
SCA-VENGERS MANSION.
SUBBASEMENT. SECRET MEETING PLACE OF:
THE UNHUMANATI
THE DIMENSIONAL ANOMALY IS SPREADING. NEW YOLK CITY WILL SOON FALL.
Mooster Fantastic.
THE UNHUMANATI VOWED TO PROTECT LARVAL EARTH AT ALL COSTS. IT'S TIME TO ACT.
The Sub-Marsupial.
THE DIMENSIONAL TRAVEL WATCH IS ALMOST REPAIRED.
Black Colt.
THE INTER-DIMENSIONAL WEB THAT ALLOWED IT TO TRAVERSE REALITIES IS NO MORE. HOW DID YOU GET IT TO WORK?
I HAD A LITTLE HELP... FROM A LITTLE FRIEND.
EXCUSE ME. I HAVE A NAME. THE BEE-YONDER. SHOULDN'T BE HARD TO REMEMBER UNLESS YOU KNOW A LOT OF OMNIPOTENT BEES.
LET'S JUST GET YOU CLOSED UP ALL SNUG IN THERE...
Bee-Yonder.
WILL SPIDER-HAM BE UPSET YOU STOLE HIS BROKEN DIMENSIONAL TRAVEL WATCH AND STUFFED IT WITH A BEE-GOD?
I WOULD HAVE TOLD HIM...BUT THEN I WOULD HAVE HAD TO CALL HIM.
AND TALK TO HIM.
AND HEAR HIS VOICE.
SO WE'LL NEVER KNOW.
OR WILL YOU?!
Crocktor Strange.
Iron Mouse.

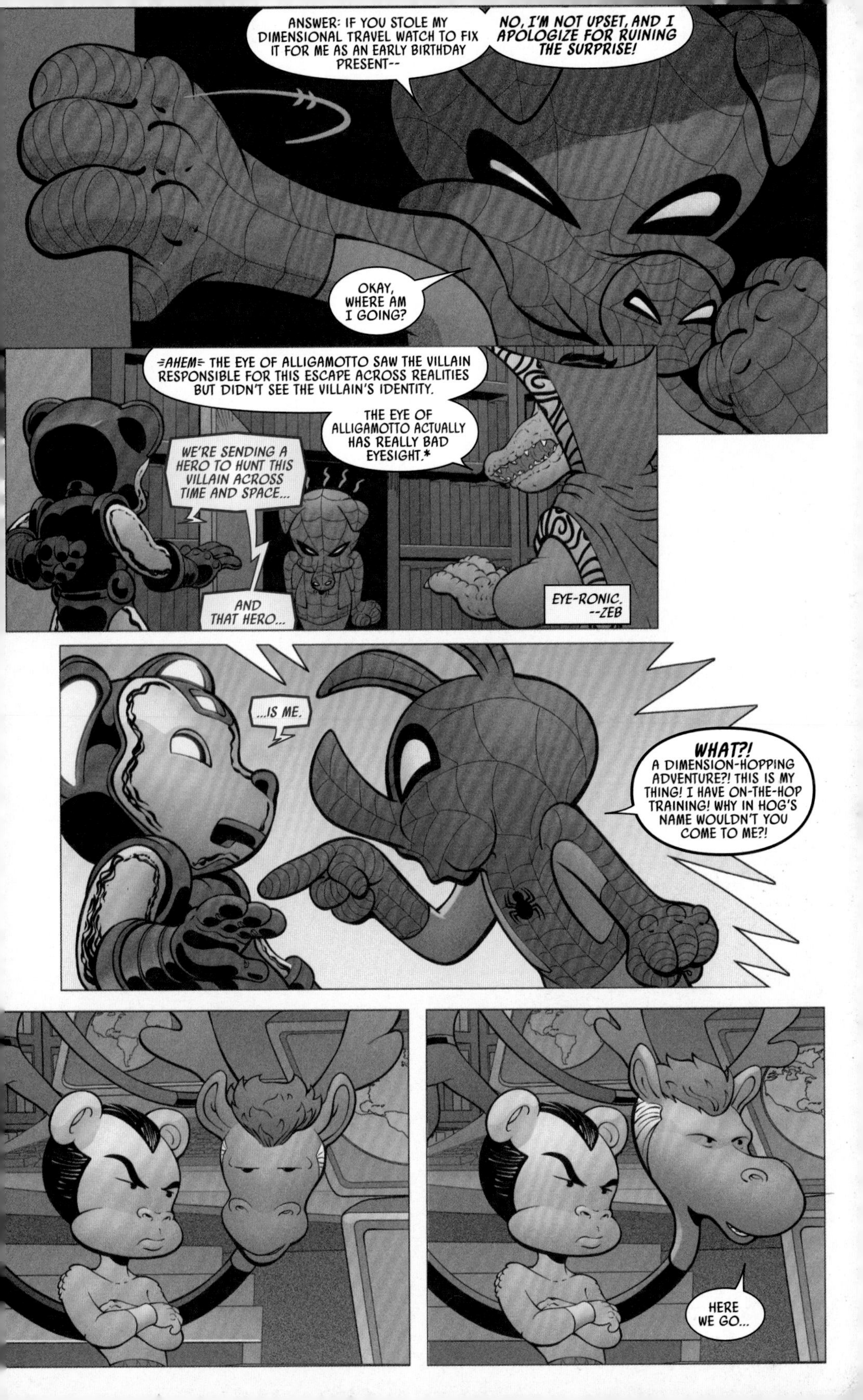

ANSWER: IF YOU STOLE MY DIMENSIONAL TRAVEL WATCH TO FIX IT FOR ME AS AN EARLY BIRTHDAY PRESENT--
NO, I'M NOT UPSET, AND I APOLOGIZE FOR RUINING THE SURPRISE!
OKAY, WHERE AM I GOING?
=AHEM= THE EYE OF ALLIGAMOTTO SAW THE VILLAIN RESPONSIBLE FOR THIS ESCAPE ACROSS REALITIES BUT DIDN'T SEE THE VILLAIN'S IDENTITY.
THE EYE OF ALLIGAMOTTO ACTUALLY HAS REALLY BAD EYESIGHT.*
WE'RE SENDING A HERO TO HUNT THIS VILLAIN ACROSS TIME AND SPACE...
AND THAT HERO...
EYE-RONIC. --ZEB
...IS ME.
WHAT?! A DIMENSION-HOPPING ADVENTURE?! THIS IS MY THING! I HAVE ON-THE-HOP TRAINING! WHY IN HOG'S NAME WOULDN'T YOU COME TO ME?!
HERE WE GO...

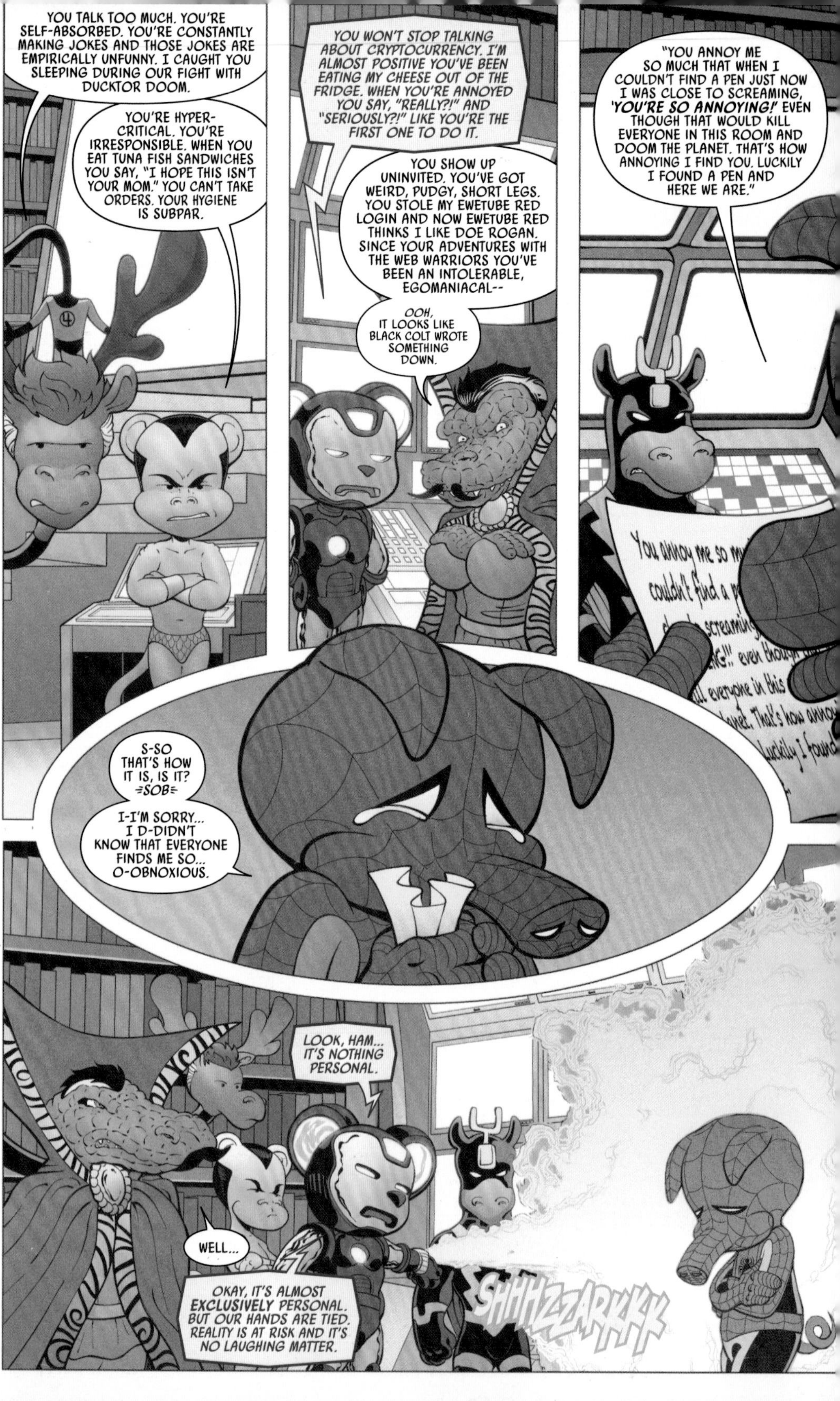
YOU TALK TOO MUCH. YOU'RE SELF-ABSORBED. YOU'RE CONSTANTLY MAKING JOKES AND THOSE JOKES ARE EMPIRICALLY UNFUNNY. I CAUGHT YOU SLEEPING DURING OUR FIGHT WITH DUCKTOR DOOM.
YOU'RE HYPER-CRITICAL. YOU'RE IRRESPONSIBLE. WHEN YOU EAT TUNA FISH SANDWICHES YOU SAY, "I HOPE THIS ISN'T YOUR MOM." YOU CAN'T TAKE ORDERS. YOUR HYGIENE IS SUBPAR.
YOU WON'T STOP TALKING ABOUT CRYPTOCURRENCY. I'M ALMOST POSITIVE YOU'VE BEEN EATING MY CHEESE OUT OF THE FRIDGE. WHEN YOU'RE ANNOYED YOU SAY, "REALLY?!" AND "SERIOUSLY?!" LIKE YOU'RE THE FIRST ONE TO DO IT.
YOU SHOW UP UNINVITED. YOU'VE GOT WEIRD, PUDGY, SHORT LEGS. YOU STOLE MY EWETUBE RED LOGIN AND NOW EWETUBE RED THINKS I LIKE DOE ROGAN. SINCE YOUR ADVENTURES WITH THE WEB WARRIORS YOU'VE BEEN AN INTOLERABLE, EGOMANIACAL--
OOH, IT LOOKS LIKE BLACK COLT WROTE SOMETHING DOWN.
"YOU ANNOY ME SO MUCH THAT WHEN I COULDN'T FIND A PEN JUST NOW I WAS CLOSE TO SCREAMING, '*YOU'RE SO ANNOYING!*' EVEN THOUGH THAT WOULD KILL EVERYONE IN THIS ROOM AND DOOM THE PLANET. THAT'S HOW ANNOYING I FIND YOU. LUCKILY I FOUND A PEN AND HERE WE ARE."
S-SO THAT'S HOW IT IS, IS IT? *SOB*
I-I'M SORRY... I D-DIDN'T KNOW THAT EVERYONE FINDS ME SO... O-OBNOXIOUS.
LOOK, HAM... IT'S NOTHING PERSONAL.
WELL...
OKAY, IT'S ALMOST **EXCLUSIVELY** PERSONAL. BUT OUR HANDS ARE TIED. REALITY IS AT RISK AND IT'S NO LAUGHING MATTER.
SHHHZZARKKK

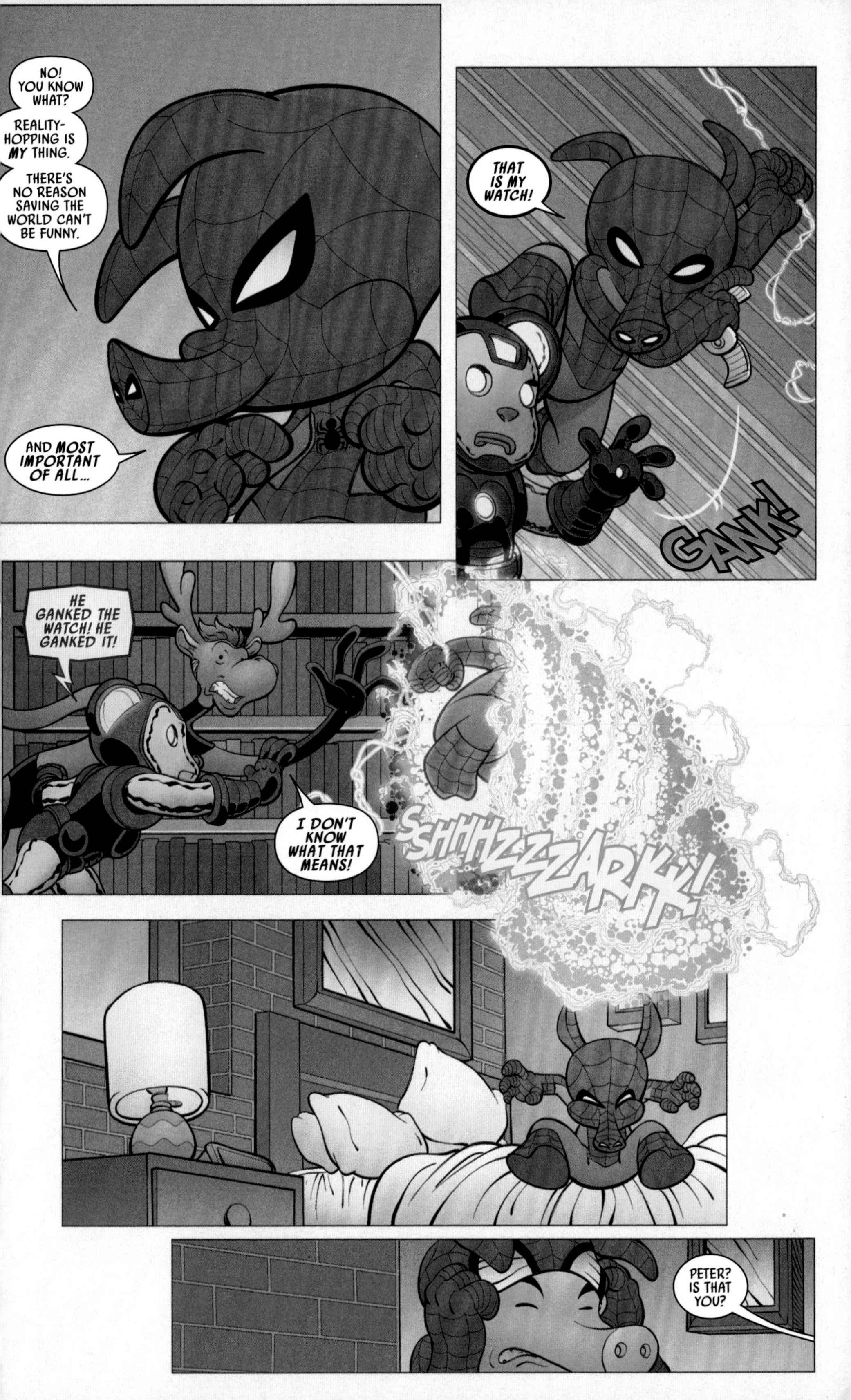
NO! YOU KNOW WHAT?
REALITY-HOPPING IS MY THING.
THERE'S NO REASON SAVING THE WORLD CAN'T BE FUNNY.
AND MOST IMPORTANT OF ALL...
THAT IS MY WATCH!
GANK!
HE GANKED THE WATCH! HE GANKED IT!
I DON'T KNOW WHAT THAT MEANS!
SHHHZZZZARK!
PETER? IS THAT YOU?

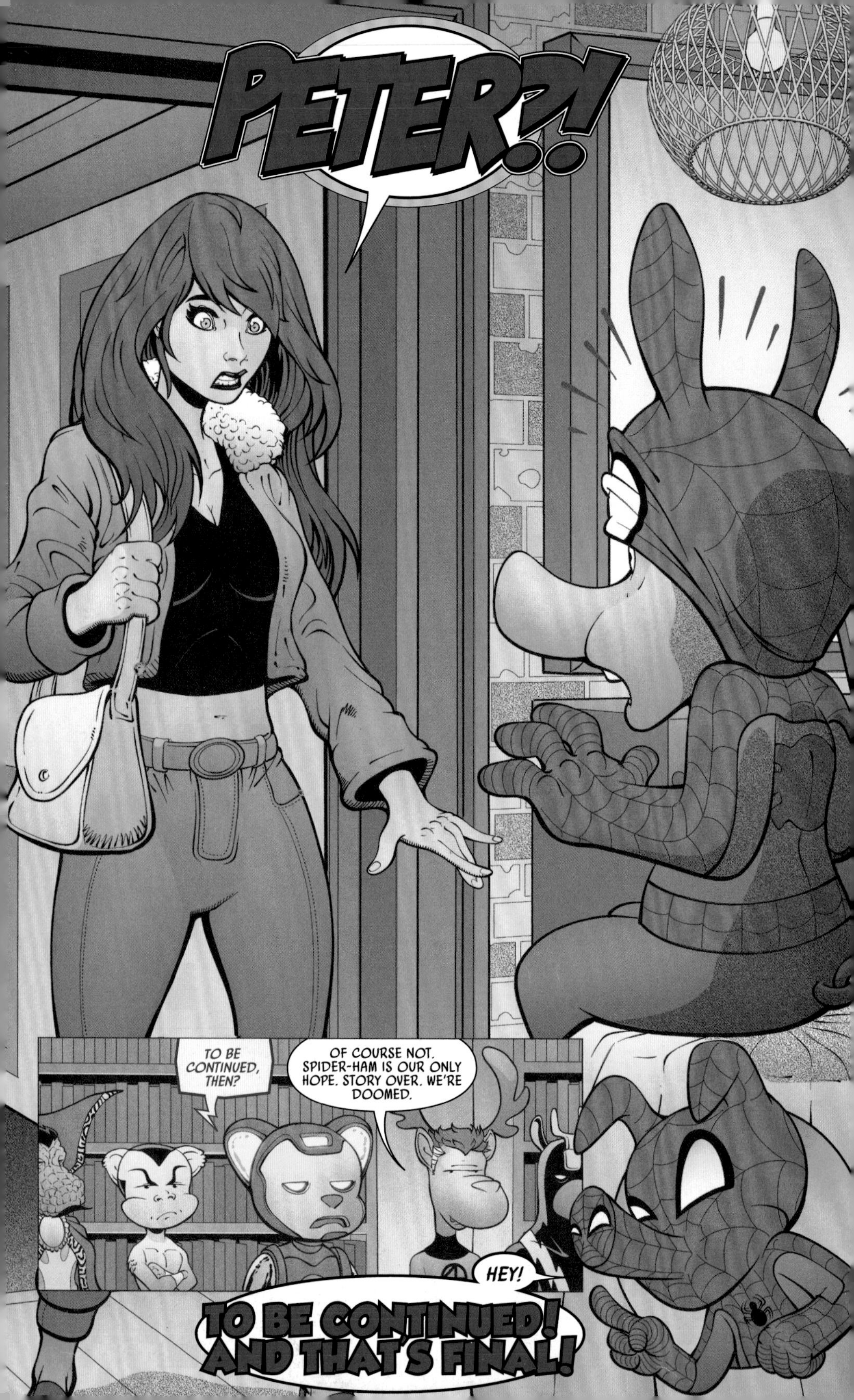
PETER?!
TO BE CONTINUED, THEN?
OF COURSE NOT. SPIDER-HAM IS OUR ONLY HOPE. STORY OVER. WE'RE DOOMED.
HEY!
TO BE CONTINUED! AND THAT'S FINAL!

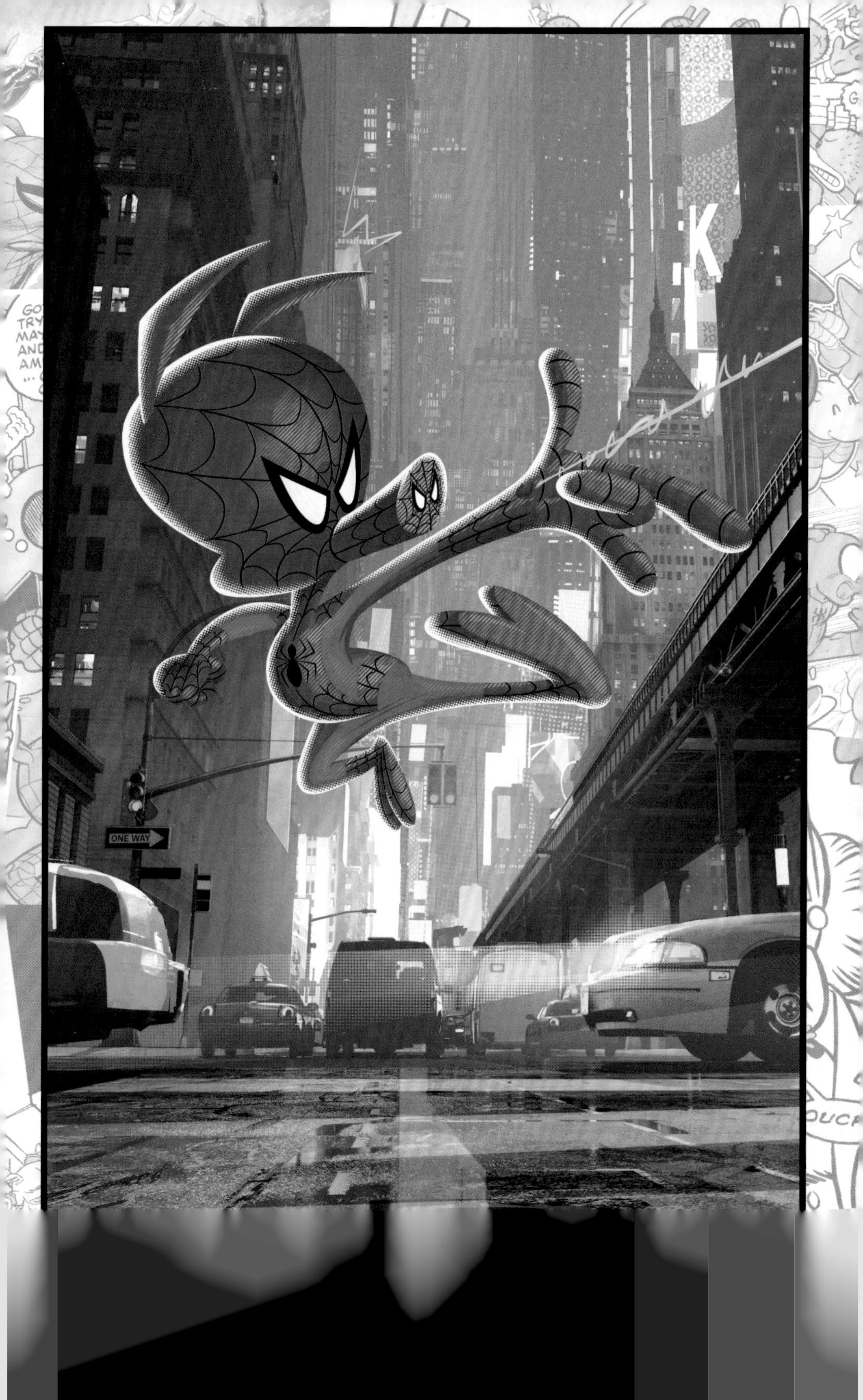
ONE WAY

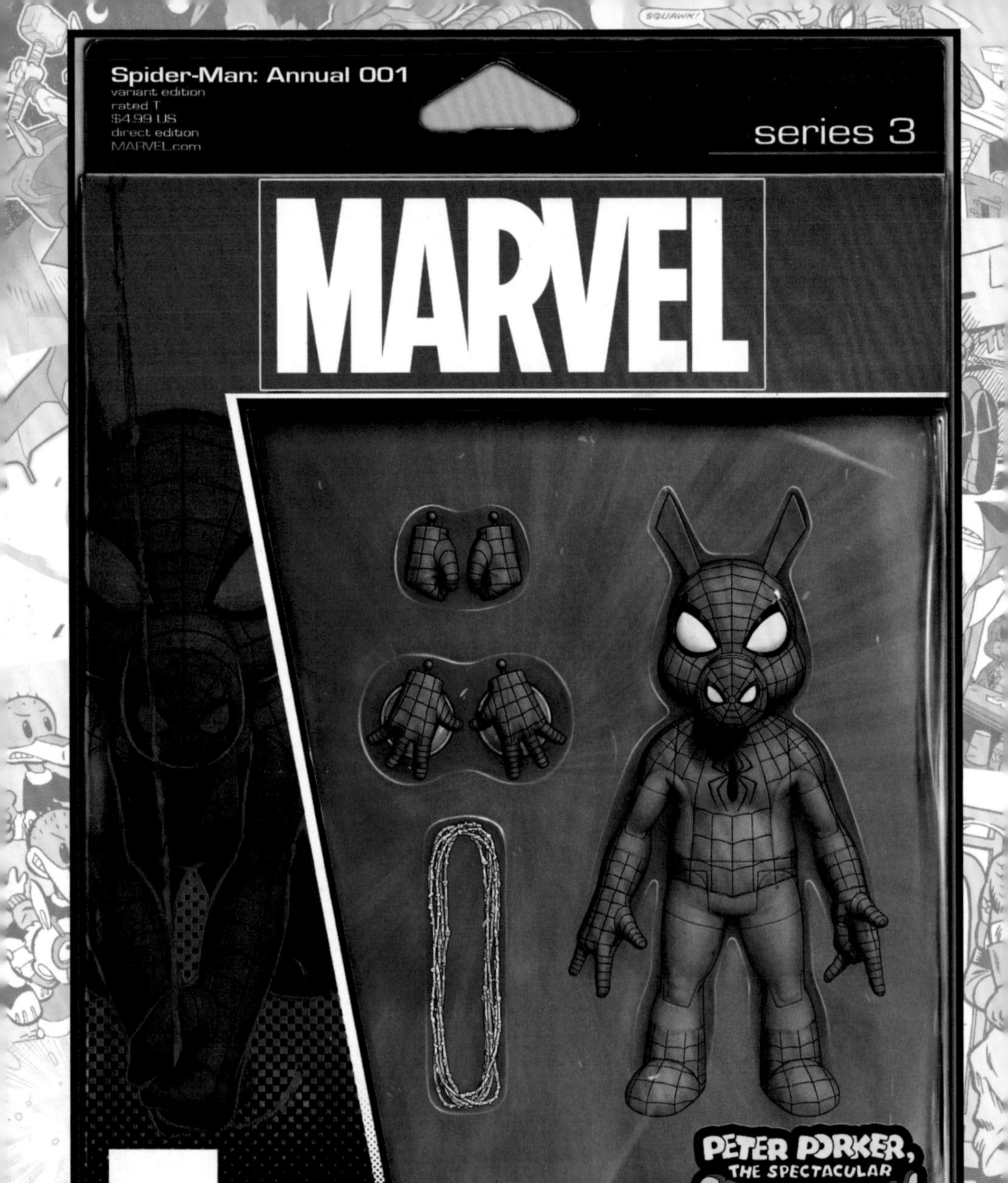
Spider-Man: Annual 001
variant edition
rated T
$4.99 US
direct edition
MARVEL.com
series 3
MARVEL
PETER PORKER, THE SPECTACULAR SPIDER-HAM
SPIDER-HAM
boariginal
SQUAWK!

SPIDER-MAN ANNUAL (2019) #1 ACTION FIGURE VARIANT

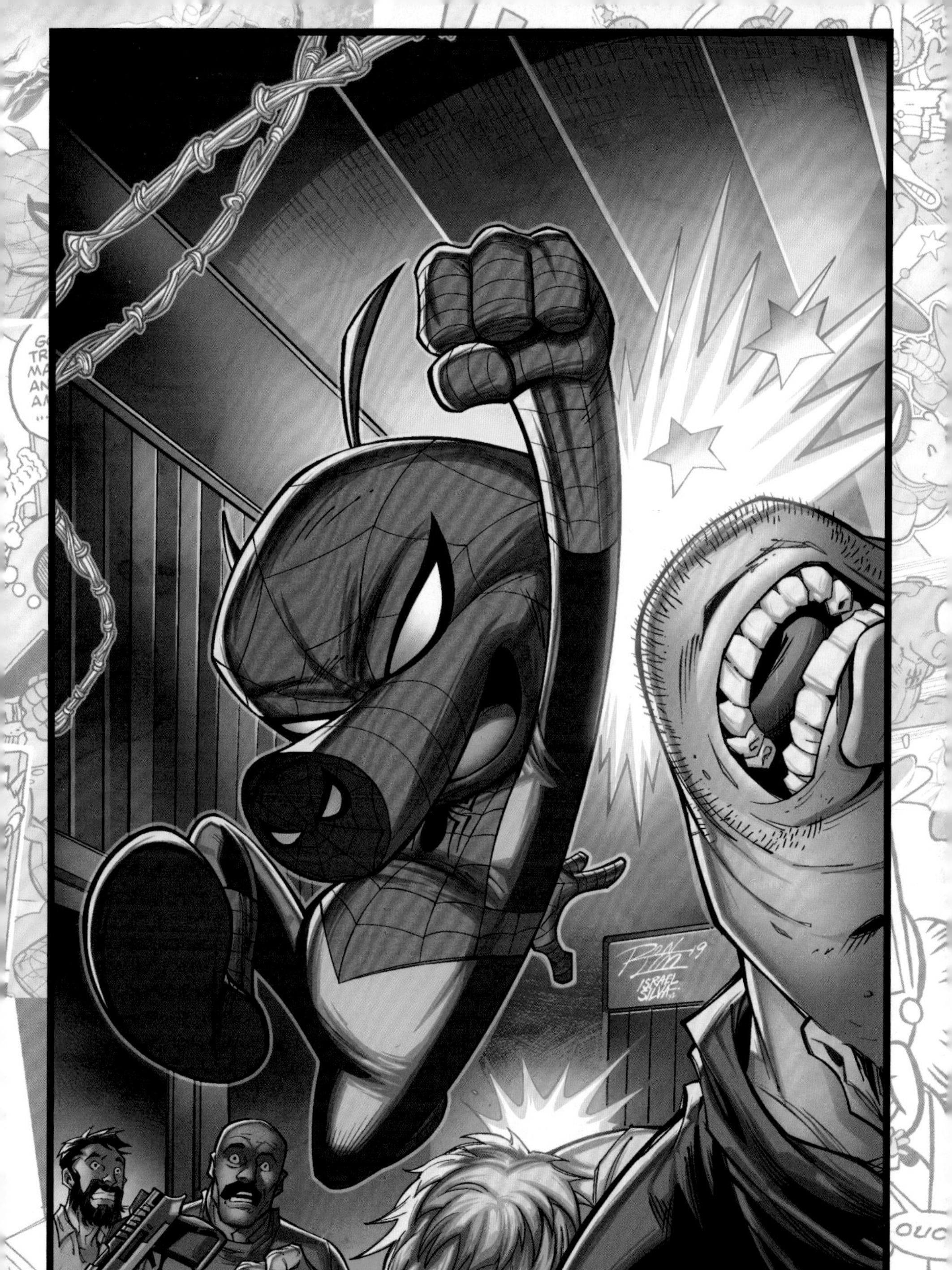
ISRAEL SILVA

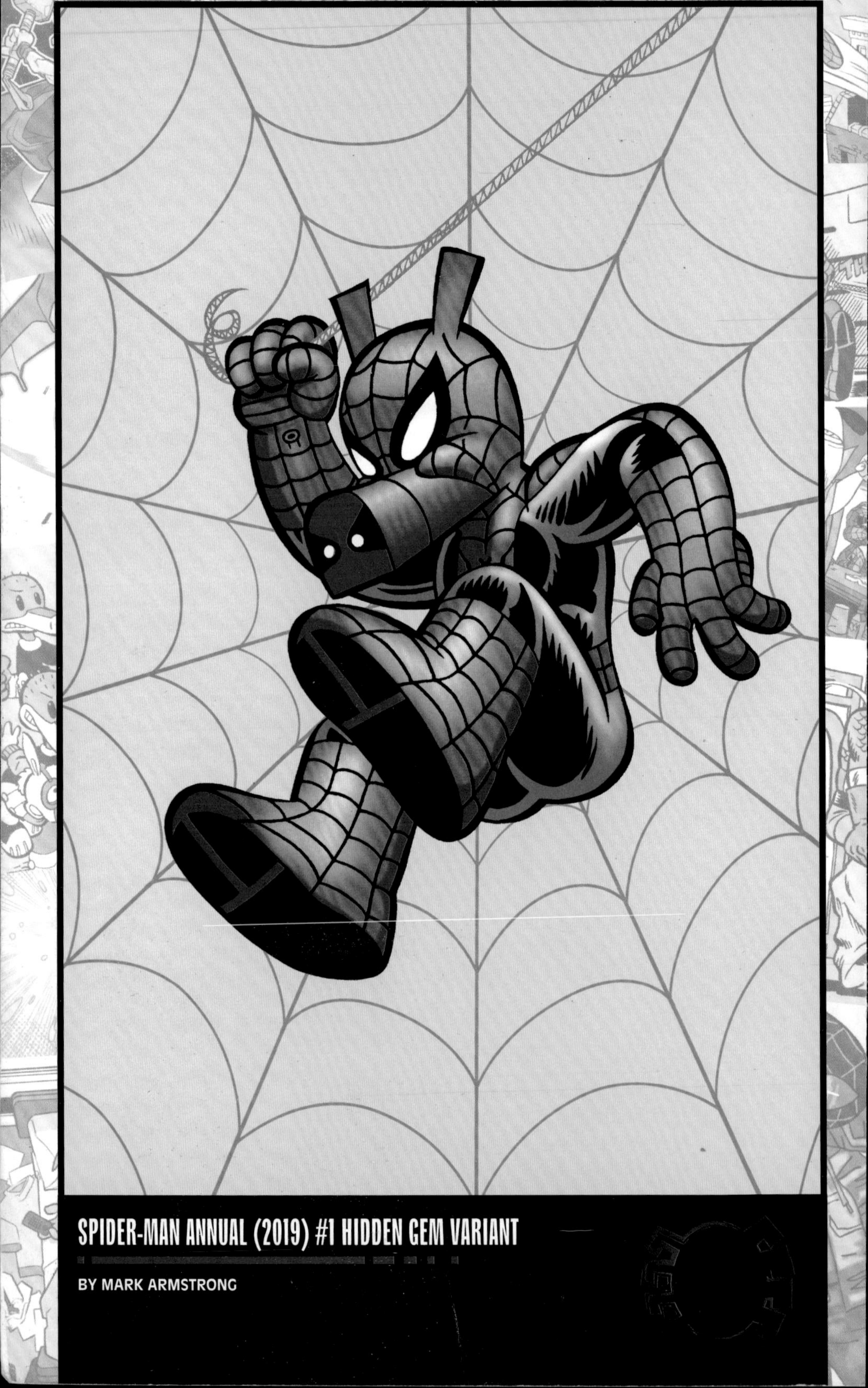

SPIDER-MAN ANNUAL (2019) #1 HIDDEN GEM VARIANT

BY MARK ARMSTRONG